TERI WOODS'

DEADLY REIGNS

THE FIRST OF A TRILOGY

TERI WOODS

For information on how individual consumers can place orders, please write to Teri Woods Publishing, P.O. Box 20069, New York, NY 10001-0005.

For orders other than individual consumers, Teri Woods Publishing grants a discount on the purchase of twenty or more copies of a single title order for special markets or premium use.

For orders purchased through the P.O. Box, Teri Woods Publishing offers a 25% discount off the sale price for orders being shipped to prisons, including, but not limited to, federal, state, and county.

Published by Teri Woods Publishing

TERI WOODS

DEADLY REIGNS

THE FIRST OF A TRILOGY

TERI WOODS

Note:
Sale of this book without a front cover may be unauthorized. If this book is purchased without a cover it may be reported to the publisher as "unsold or destroyed." Neither the author nor the publisher may receive payment for the sale of this book.

This novel is a work of fiction. Any resemblance to real people, living or dead, actual events, establishments, organizations, and/or locales are intended to give it a sense of reality and authenticity. Other names, characters, places and incidents are either products of the author's imagination or are used fictitiously, as are those fictionalized events and incidents that involve real persons and did not occur or are set in the future.

Published by:
TERI WOODS PUBLISHING
P.O. Box 20069
New York, NY 10001-0005
www.teriwoodspublishing.com

Library of Congress Catalog Card No: 2005900857
ISBN: 0-9672249-7-7
Copyright: To Be Supplied

DEADLY REIGNS CREDITS
Revised by Teri Woods
Edited by Teri Woods
Text formation by Teri Woods
Cover concept by Lucas Riggins

Printed in the USA.

Deadly Reigns, Teri Woods Publishing

TERI WOODS

DEADLY REIGNS

THE FIRST OF A TRILOGY

TERI WOODS

Chapter One

"**T**wenty million dollars," Agent Ricardo Dominguez said, lighting the fat Cuban cigar he had pulled from his pocket moments earlier. "Twenty million, all cash, and all in old bills, none of that new, easily traceable bullshit."

Dominguez exhaled, blowing large, white rings of cigar smoke into the face of his business associate. He smiled, knowing that he had made his associate uncomfortable, and that making him uncomfortable was how he got his edge. *You gotta gettem' off their balance, off their feet*, he often told himself.

Agent Ricardo Dominguez had been in the Bureau for ten years now, and he knew all of the tricks of the trade. His father, a tough, retired police detective from the mean streets of South Central Los Angeles, had taught him many of them.

Joining the Federal Bureau of Investigation Dominguez was a forgone conclusion by the time he was twelve. Movies and television shows of federal agents chasing bad guys, busting mobsters, and enforcing the laws of the land had always excited him. Besides, he liked the idea of carrying a gun. By the time Dominguez graduated from UCLA, completed two summer internships with the Bureau, used his father's connections, and the recommendation of a few federal judges, he got his feet planted in the agency he adored. Ricardo Dominguez loved the Bureau, he lived the Bureau, and tonight, he would die for the Bureau.

Dante Reigns waved his hand through the air, clearing away the rings of smoke in front of his face. He frowned and loosened a slight cough to show his displeasure at this health-deteriorating vice.

Dante despised smoking. In fact, Dante despised

1

drinking as well. To him, it showed a lack of discipline; it was a form of slothful indulgence, a weakness of willpower. Weakness was a concept which Dante found hard to understand. Life's glory came from power, and the more absolute that power, the more glorious life's rewards. Nature rewarded the strong and killed off the weak, so why people gave in to their weaknesses and made themselves even weaker by doing so, Dante could not grasp. Power was the key to life's treasures, and glory lied in power.

"Twenty million dollars means five thousand a key," Dante told Dominguez, while shaking his head ever so slightly from side to side. "No, you make it four thousand a kilo, and we shall do business."

"Four thousand a key? Are you crazy!" shouted Mickey Monciavaiz, who too was an agent of the Federal Bureau of Investigation. "Five thousand a key, just like you were paying Ramon!"

Both agents looked into the eyes of Dante Reigns to see what reaction they would get from mentioning the name of the largest drug dealer in Mexico. They wanted to know Dante's source, and were begging for his face to betray him. Dante's face remained the same and his eyes remained a dark brown. If the eyes were the windows to the soul, then clearly Dante had none. His voice remained neutral, almost mechanic in repeating his demand.

"Four thousand a key, and we shall do business," Dante repeated.

"God damn it, Dante! If you can't make the deal, or don't have the juice to negotiate, then Damian should have come!" Agent Monciavaiz shouted.

Tonight he was playing Mickey Rodriguez, a new up and coming star in the underworld, with lots of drugs to move. Tonight he was also playing the role of a pushy, take-it-or-leave-it, in-your-face drug dealer. It was a role he relished.

"Or maybe that sister of yours, Princess. Hell, I heard she has all the balls and makes all the decisions in your family anyway. Have her call me, so I can do business with a real player, and not the family flunky!"

Agent Dominguez winced. He knew Mickey had laid it on kind of thick. Agent Mickey Monciavaiz had been pulled from the Vegas field office, and briefed on the Reigns family structure, but had obviously not been briefed on each member's psychological profile. Or, if he had, he was taking Dante's lightly. Dominguez tried to restore the situation.

"Forty five hundred on this one, forty seven hundred on the next one, then five thousand on all the rest. You win a few times, we win a few times," Dominguez told him.

Dante looked to his right where his cousin Mina was standing, and waved for her to come closer.

Mina Reigns was the youngest daughter of Dante's father's older brother. Mina had always been the most precocious member of the Reigns family while growing up, and she had always been the most gullible.

When Mina stepped within arms reach of Dante, he slapped her, then pushed her back, causing her to fall over a stack of large, cardboard boxes. The noise from Mina's fall, and that of the tumbling boxes, echoed throughout the vast, corrugated steel warehouse. The warehouse's massive size combined with the extreme height of the lighting brought a dim, shadowy, surreal feeling to the entire building. Mina's moans only exacerbated the already eerie situation. Dante, not losing a step, walked calmly over to his beloved cousin, and began kicking her in the stomach and back.

"Oh my God!" mumbled Agent Dominguez.

"Jesus! Okay, okay, five thousand!" Agent Monciavaiz shouted toward the kicking Dante. "Now would ya stop it already!"

Dante continued to kick Mina brutally. The toe of his H&H brown wingtip struck her several times in the face, causing blood to fly from her nose and lips. She continued to cry out in gut wrenching pain.

"Hey! Hey!" Agent Monciavaiz shouted. He raced forward

to grab Dante and stop his brutal assault. His shaking hands reached out and gripped Dante's shoulder, and using all of his strength, he spun a smiling Dante around, bringing them face to face.

"Lay off her, man," Monciavaiz told him. "If you got personal problems, then handle them on your own time!"

Dante leaned forward, and reached down into Mina's waistband, where he pulled out a forty caliber glock, semi-automatic pistol. He balanced the gun delicately between his fingers, as he held it up into the air.

"So you care about her, huh?" Dante asked agent Monciavaiz. "You care about what happens to her, and you want to save her, huh?"

Dante's suspicions had been confirmed. Whether undercover or in uniform, the first reaction of a law enforcement officer is to save lives. These two business associates were desperate to save Mina. The thought made Dante's smile creep across his face, like a shadow across a moonlit wall.

"You know, cigar smoking is a very bad habit," Dante told Agent Dominguez. "I used to tell my former business associate, Rueben Palacios, the same thing all the time. You see, Rueben had a taste for this special brand of disgustingly putrid, Cuban cigars. They were dark brown, with a large gold and green ring around them, much like the one you're smoking. How odd... Rueben was busted by the FBI a few weeks ago, his belongings were seized and now you two turn up smoking one of his hand made, specially blended, illegally imported, yet disgustingly putrid Cuban cigars."

Dominguez was the first one to reach for his weapon, but Dante already held one inside of his hand. With the speed of an African cheetah, Dante aimed his weapon and ripped two shots into Agent Dominguez' chest.

Dante retargeted his pistol from Dominguez' chest to Monciavaiz' head before the former even hit the ground.

"Do not move, unless you wish to join your friend,"

4

Dante said to him. "Who are you anyway? Or better yet, which one are you, DEA, FBI, Customs, Treasury, or just some really stupid locals?"

Mickey Monciavaiz raised his hands slowly into the air, and began to plead. "Look, I don't know what you're talking about, man. I just came to do a deal."

"Where is the leak in my family?"

"I don't know what you're talking about."

Dante lowered his weapon from Agent Monciavaiz' head to his foot.

"Where's the leak?"

"I don't know..."

Dante's weapon popped loudly, ringing throughout the warehouse. Agent Monciavaiz fell to the floor grabbing his shattered and bloodied right foot in agonizing pain.

"Where is the leak?" Dante repeated softly.

Beads of sweat and tears of pain dripped profusely from agent Monciavaiz' face. "I don't know..."

Dante shifted his aim from Agent Monciavaiz' right foot to his left, and squeezed the trigger. The fire from the gun's muzzle streaked down to the floor and exploded on Agent Monciavaiz' left foot, along with the bullet. The agent rolled on his back grabbing his left foot as he cried out in pain.

"I don't know... I don't know what... you're..."

Dante stepped closer to the fallen agent and pointed the weapon at Monciavaiz' right shoulder. Without asking a question, he fired again.

"Help!" Agent Monciavaiz writhed in pain along the ground, while holding his newly wounded shoulder. "Help... help me... someone help..."

"What was that?" Dante asked the agent. "You want help? What you think they can hear you? What you wired up, right and now all your fellow field agents will be busting down my door to lock me up?"

Agent Monciavaiz shook his head. "I... don't know..."

Dante leaned forward and placed the barrel of the gun on Agent Monciavaiz' kneecap, and then pulled the trigger. Bits of bone fragment and soft tissue exploded into the air, along with a gush of blood.

"Aaaaaaaagh!" the agent's scream could be heard for miles, only thing was, no one was listening.

Dante laughed, and turned to his cousin Kevin, "Seems like we really struck a nerve with this guy."

Agent Monciavaiz held up his hands submissively, "I don't know who the... leak... is. I was... pulled in from... the Vegas field office... at the last... minute."

Dante turned, and looked at the dying agent in disgust.

"I didn't ask you anymore questions, did I? I was rather enjoying our little test of wills, but now... You've really brought our little fun and games to an end."

Dante raised his weapon, and pointed it toward the agent's chest. "I hate party poopers."

Dante's weapon coughed twice, causing the torso of Agent Monciavaiz to do the same. Dante then turned toward Kevin.

"Take the bodies to the cement factory, and drop them in the acid vat. Make sure there is nothing left. Remember, no bodies, no crime."

Kevin Reigns nodded, and immediately set forth to complete his assigned task. Dante turned to Mina, and grabbed her by the hair and off the floor where she fell.

"The next time you want to help the family, you better damn well make sure that the people you're hooking us up with aren't federal agents. Do you understand me?"

Mina nodded.

"Good. Now get this place cleaned up!" Dante turned and headed for the exit. "And stop all of that damn whimpering... stupid bitch."

6

Chapter Two

FBI Headquarters, Quantico, Virginia.

"**T**wo more agents, gone! Vanished from the face of the earth, just like that!" Deputy Director Henry Abrahams shouted along with a snap of his fingers, to emphasize his point. His booming voice echoed furiously throughout the large, mahogany paneled conference room, startling the other twelve occupants.

Special Agent Bob Holsten raised his hands in a calming motion. "Now Henry, let's not go and get excited here. We're conducting a very thorough search for them, as we speak."

"We're still conducting a search for the other four!" shouted Special Agent Alex Gray. "We're the FBI, and we can't even find our own people!"

Bob Holsten's shaking hand rubbed at the tension building in his temples. "Look, we're going to find them."

"They're dead!" Special Agent Gray shouted.

"They're missing!" Bob Holsten corrected.

"They're dead," Agent Gray reiterated.

This time it was Deputy Director Abrahams who waved his hands through the air to restore calm.

"Gentlemen, we're getting nowhere with this, and frankly, I'm getting tired of this whole affair. I want the Reigns brothers brought down. I want their whole operation brought to a screeching halt, and I want them to grow very old inside of a federal prison. Is that understood?"

The assistant directors and special agents around the conference table all nodded in agreement.

"Good," Deputy Director Abrahams told them. "I'm green lighting the full package. Use every means at our disposal. The United States of America has just declared all-out war on the Reigns brothers. All Texas and Mexican field offices are now under the direction of a special task force, headed by Assistant Director Tom Peoples. This task force's sole purpose is to coordinate our efforts to bring down the Reigns brothers." Deputy Director Abrahams waved his hand toward the large, burly, assistant director seated to his left, "Tom."

Assistant Director Thomas Peoples adjusted his round spectacles as he stood.

"Thank you, sir," he said nodding to the deputy director, before turning toward the other occupants of the wooded conference room.

"Gentlemen, I would like to present Operation Sunshine. It is our concerted effort to stop the Reigns."

Thomas Peoples waved his hand at a junior agent, who immediately began passing out folders to the conference members. Another junior agent brought in a large easel with a giant chart resting on it. Thomas Peoples waved at a third junior agent.

"Bring in Agents Moore and Holmes, please."

The junior agent stepped just outside the room and quickly returned, followed by two female agents. The gentlemen seated around the table rose until the ladies were seated. Assistant Director Peoples motioned to the ladies.

"Gentlemen, I would like you to meet Agent Grace Moore and Special Agent Elizabeth Holmes."

Greetings were exchanged until Deputy Director Abrahams' booming voice resonated throughout the room again.

"Liz, I see you're still at it," he told Special Agent Holmes. "I would have thought you'd retired by now."

Special Agent Elizabeth Holmes smiled and patted her small, graying afro. "Wishful thinking, Henry, I'll be here long after you're gone."

Deputy Director Abrahams smiled and chuckled. "Somehow, I believe you, Liz."

Assistant Director Peoples stroked his red beard and turned cartwheels in his mind. Bringing in Special Agent Holmes had been a stroke of genius. She had served under J. Edgar and had trained or tamed every director or deputy director that came after him. Pictures of Special Agent Holmes and President Kennedy hung in the halls of this very building. Similar pictures with her and J. Edgar, Bobby Kennedy, Ed Meese, Janet Reno, Dick Thornburgh, William Saxbe, John Ashcroft, and several other Attorney Generals, FBI Directors, and Presidents were all over Washington. It didn't hurt that her father had been a Federal Court of Appeals Judge for the DC Circuit and her husband, the United States Ambassador to Jamaica. Special Agent Holmes had great connections, seniority, and lots of pull. She would be a great asset to this mission, and they sure were going to need her.

"So, what do you have, Tom?" asked Special Agent Holmes.

"Good question," Assistant Director Peoples said smiling. He cleared his throat and looked around the conference room.

"Ladies and gentlemen, for the past three years, we have been trying to bring down a family of murdering drug dealers based in south Texas. This family is known as the Reigns family, and it controls roughly one percent of the cocaine coming into this country. That's one percent of hundreds of billions of dollars. We're talking about this family earning several billions of dollars a year in cocaine profits."

The murmurs around the room grew louder as the agents began speaking to each other. Assistant Director Peoples let the magnitude of the Reigns' empire set in for several moments and then resumed speaking.

"Now, our mistakes have been in trying to set up a deal with this family, and this has ultimately resulted in the disappearance of six federal agents. One of those agents was John Bulter, a good friend of mine, and the Godson of Senate Majority Leader, Sandra Fitzhugh. In other words, the United States Senate is pissed off. When the Senate gets pissed, the president's balls... excuse me ladies, are placed on a plate. The president then yells at the attorney general, who shouts at the director, who screams at the deputy director, who then calls me in the middle of the night and threatens to kill my firstborn. I then call the San Antonio field office, and I threaten Nathan, the director of that field office, who tells me that there is nothing more he can do. I know Nathan; he's a good man and a proud man. So when he says that he needs help, then I know that the problem is serious."

Peoples lifted his finger to his glasses and pushed them back up on his nose. He frowned and stared at the agents around the table.

"This family, the Reigns family, has too many people under its control. They control too many businesses, and way too much money. They have the local politicians and law enforcement officers inside their pockets, and they have proven to be impenetrable. Well, I don't like losing. I don't like losing friends, and I don't like losing period. We're going to bring down the Reigns family, and this is how we are going to do it. We are no longer going to set up deals; we are going to stick the extremely intelligent and extremely attractive Agent Moore on them. The leader of the Reigns family is now a young man by the name of Damian Reigns, before him, it was his sister, Princess Reigns."

Peoples waved to an agent in the corner, "Mike, could you hit the lights and turn on the slide projector? Show them their pictures as I mention their names, and also keep showing the chart on their organizational structure. Now, back to Princess, she ran the family until Damian finished

business school. In fact, she built up the drug side of the
family and ran things with an iron hand. Princess Reigns is
one ruthless young woman. In fact, we were glad when
Damian came home and took over the organization. The body
count in south Texas went down dramatically. By the way,
she's tried to kill Damian twice. She's not happy being
number two, and she wants to run things again."

Tom Peoples looked over at the agent working the
projector. "Change the slide please."

The agent pressed a button, and Princess Reigns' picture
was replaced by Damian Reigns.

"Now, this is the head of the Reigns family. Damian is
what you would call an All-American golden boy... if he
weren't in charge of a murdering criminal enterprise. Damian
is brilliant. He graduated from Harvard with honors in
ninety-four with a degree in business. Went straight into
Wharton Business School at Penn, where, again, he
graduated at the top of his class. He's never seen a B, or
even an A minus for that matter. All of his professors use
words like brilliant, genius, and gifted to describe him. He
turned down offers from all of the big investment firms on
Wall Street, in order to return home and work in the family
business. Besides drugs and murder, they have a rather
large holding corporation called Reigns Enterprises. It is
totally family owned, one hundred percent, by the Reigns'.
This corporation owns a very large chain of night clubs,
several upscale restaurants throughout Texas and Louisiana,
several tire shops and auto repair shops, numerous stereo
shops, a record label, several recording studios, a large chain
of pager and cell phone shops, and an extremely large
construction entity that not only builds housing, but large
scale commercial and industrial projects as well. They have a
large and growing internet service provider company, several
bookstores, numerous record stores, some twenty-four car
dealerships, and about four hundred fast food restaurants
throughout the states of Texas and Louisiana. Yes, the

Reigns family is a billion-dollar family. The problem is, they used their drug money to buy up legitimate enterprises. The IRS says that more than likely, they inflate their profits from their cash businesses, pay taxes on them, and stick them in the bank just like it was earned money. When you have that many clubs, restaurants, book stores, fast food places, and other cash businesses to run money through, it's rather easy to clean, and virtually untraceable. This family started out with an old nightclub, a religious book store, a couple of used car lots, and a fairly decent sized construction company. The old man built it up and expanded, then retired and left it to his kids. Princess and her drug empire took over, and the legitimate family businesses turned into nothing more than washing machines for her dirty money. The more money she washed, the more businesses they bought, and today, we see the brilliant Damian in charge. He's buying everything, investing heavily in new technology start-ups, bio-pharmaceutical companies, and on-line companies. It is estimated that in three years the Reigns family will be out of the drug business completely and will be one of the wealthiest families in the United States. Well, we don't have three years to wait. We are going to get them out of the drug business... now. Change the slide."

The young junior agent working the slide machine pressed a button, and Damian Reigns' picture was replaced by that of Dante Reigns.

"Now, this is Dante Reigns. Dante is Satan. I'll say it again, Dante, is Satan. Satan is Dante Reigns. The amount of bodies that Dante has is uncountable. He has no conscience, no emotions, no feelings and no soul. However, we do not want you to underestimate Dante's Intelligence. Dante is a product of Princeton. He has a degree in psychology and he is said to have methods and tools for torturing people that would make the Vietcong look like Tibetan Monks. Do not underestimate Dante Reigns. Intelligence has it that Princess' two assassination attempts

12

were foiled by the Colombians because they were afraid that Dante would become number two in the family organization. In other words, Dante would kill too much, Princess would kill too much, and no one would be able to reason with either of them. Damian is protected by the Colombians, the Russians, and the Mexicans. He's strictly about making money with the least amount of bloodshed possible. They all love him.

The plan is simple: Agent Grace Moore is going to become Jonel McNeal, and she is going to become Damian's girlfriend. She's going to learn as much as she can and report back to Special Agent Holmes, who will be posing as her aunt. Special Agent Nathan Hess is going to have a special team on standby at all times, waiting to raid or rescue. The search warrants are on standby, but are a definite go because of our missing agents. We have agents assigned to the courthouse just for that purpose, and we'll have a federal judge on standby to execute the warrants when we're ready. Communication intercepts are all in place. Wire taps have been placed, digital pen monitoring devices have been dispersed to everyone, and cameras have been placed in all their homes, offices, and in other buildings. We even have a low-level informant working inside one of the office buildings. He's good for small things like the brothers' itinerary. Anyway, gentlemen and ladies, Operation Sunshine is a go. We're heading to beautiful, sunny, San Antonio to bag us a family of Reigns. Good luck, God bless, and happy hunting."

Deputy Director Abrahams leaned forward and cleared his throat. "Agent Moore, you ready for this assignment?"

Grace Moore placed her small manicured hands on top of the conference table and folded them, properly enforcing a silent code. *Am I ready, really ready?* she asked herself. Was she really, truly ready?

Grace Moore knew that she had been chosen for this assignment because of her looks. She was an extremely beautiful African American woman. But she also wanted to think that she had been chosen because of her education and competence in the field. After all, she did graduate magna cum laude from Sarah Lawrence, and she did help break up three counterfeiting rings, solve four bank robberies, and return two kidnapped children to their respective families. She had busted her share of drug dealers and had done excellent fieldwork. If Damian Reigns thought that he was so smart and was going to take her for just another pretty face, then that would be his greatest mistake. She was smart, quite possibly the smartest person in this room. Smarter even than this superboy Damian, who they all feared. She would show them. She would bust Damian Reigns, bring down his whole organization, and show everyone how brilliant she truly was. There would also probably be a big promotion for this one too. She would become Special Agent Grace Moore. *Special Agent... hmmm...* it certainly had a nice ring to it. Yes, she was ready for this mission. She would kill for this mission. *Bring on the promotion. Bring on Mr. Damian Reigns.*

A smile slowly crept across her face as she nodded her head. "Yes sir, I'm ready. I'm ready."

"Good then."

Abrahams surveyed the crowd of agents inside the room. "I want to tell you all that you are about to undertake a very important mission, a mission that has a very direct correlation to how much cocaine will enter the streets of Texas this year. The downfall of the Reigns organization will leave a giant vacuum for many years to come. I can now look into the faces of the widows and children of our fallen agents, and tell them confidently that something is being done, that we are going to bring the culprits who murdered our agents to justice. I want to tell you all that I'm proud of you and proud to have served our country with you. I wanted to tell you this now, because that's something I never said to those who didn't make it back. Just make sure that you get

14

Dante Reigns and the Reigns family. God bless. This meeting is over. Good luck."

Chapter Three

The bass from the club's multi million dollar sound system resonated loudly throughout the establishment. It was this sound system that made G-Wiz the premiere nightclub for the city's urban rich, year in and year out. The fact that the club was filled with crystal chandeliers, contained five Italian travertine marble dance floors, three hand carved, ebony bars imported from southern Africa, and was perched on the 41st, 42nd, and 43rd floors of the Reigns Executive Building overlooking a majestic view of the city didn't exactly hurt business either.

This was a club for the rich and famous, the young, black, rich, and famous. The Brioni, Armani, and Brooks Brothers suited patrons were all the best, the brightest, and the hottest within their respective professions. Young up-and-coming lawyers, bankers, doctors, accountants, business executives, business owners, professional athletes, drug underlords, and legions of others all schmoozed, drank, lied, cheated, and exaggerated their wealth and importance to one another. You had to *be* someone to get in.

"Hello, my name is Dante," he smiled and extended his hand, and the young lady shook it. Dante waved his other hand toward the barstool next to hers. "May I?"

Agent Grace Moore nodded at the bar seat to her right. It wasn't until several moments had passed that she realized that this gentleman seated next to her was none other than the infamous Dante Reigns. She had made contact.

"I'm sorry, but I don't believe I've seen you in here

before," Dante said looking at her, wondering where she suddenly came from.

"Are you new in town or did you just finally decide to step out of the house and have a little fun?"

"Both, actually," Grace insinuated, admiring Dante's line of questioning.

"Oh, well, please allow me to introduce myself properly. My name is Dante Reigns. Welcome to our fair city," he said as he stood and extended his hand for a more proper introduction.

"Thank you. My name is Jonel. Jonel McNeal," Grace said taking his hand into hers and shaking ever so slightly.

"Well, it's a pleasure to meet you Mrs. McNeal."

"Oh, no, Ms. McNeal, I'm not married. Not yet anyway, but that's another story," said Grace before she let out a guarded laugh.

"Please, call me Jonel."

"Well, Jonel, what brings you to our wonderful neck of the woods?" Dante inquired.

"Job change, life change, lifestyle change, attitude change, the works."

Dante smiled, and leaned into Grace, nudging her shoulder, "he was that bad, huh?"

Grace let out an unbridled laugh, "Actually, yes."

"Loved him that much?"

Grace nodded slowly, and stared down into her glass of Jack Daniels.

"Very much..." she answered with a whisper.

Dante had guessed right, just the wrong city, wrong time. She had run away from a broken relationship and carried with her a broken heart. It was what had brought her to Baltimore, and then ultimately, to Washington DC.

Using her thumb and forefinger she caressed the rim of her glass as her thoughts carried her briefly back to another time, another place. She had loved him. In fact, she often felt that she had loved him too much. That night, in the emergency room at the Mayo Clinic, surrounded by doctors and nurses and stomach pumps could testify to that. But that was another time, another place, and now she was here. Here...on assignment, acting her ass off.

"I said, time heals all," Dante told her.

"I'm...I'm sorry?" Grace said, startled from her reverie by the rise in Dante's voice.

"I said, time," Dante repeated. "It just takes time."

"Yes, yes," she agreed, with a slight nod of her head, "time has made things a lot easier."

"Well, Jonel. It has been a great pleasure, making your acquaintance. I hope that all goes well for you in your new city, your new job, and your new life. I'm usually here on Friday nights, so if you run into difficulties or need a little help with anything, I'm here for you. If you need help getting around, getting settled in, or just a friendly ear to listen, again... I'll be here for you," said Dante, satisfied this woman sitting at his bar was nothing more than a mere acquaintance.

Dante leaned forward, and took Agent Moore's hand into his. He kissed it gently. "Enjoy your evening."

Agent Moore watched Dante Reigns glide smoothly away from the bar, leaving her wafting in the scent of his Angel cologne. His Armani suit was tailored to fit him like he had been born wearing it. Impeccably groomed, trimmed, manicured, and mannered, Grace could not imagine him to be the demon that the Bureau's psychiatrist made him out to be. But then again, Gotti had also been well dressed and well mannered too.

"Why hello there!" Agent Moore turned to find another gentleman seated next to her. His breath, and clothing, reeked of alcohol. And his face was prohibitively close to hers.

"My name is Tyrone, what's yours, baby?" he asked.

"Jonel."

"Well, Jonel, I noticed that you came here alone, and

18

well... I was wondering if you would like some company?"

Agent Moore shook her head in the negative. "Thank you, but I'm fine. I just came here to have a drink and do some thinking."

"Well, at least dance with me one time."

Grace shook her head in the negative again. *I know that psychopath, Dante, did not send this fool over here to talk to me.* "Thank you really, but no, I'm fine. Maybe another time."

"Oh, I get it, you're one of those stuck up bitches!"

"Because I don't want to dance with you?" Grace questioned, wondering why he had to turn so vile, just because she didn't want to dance.

"You know what I do to hos like you?" a clearly drunk and now upset Tyrone asked. "I send you hos home all wet."

Tyrone wrapped his hand around Grace's drink and lifted it. Just as quickly as he grabbed it, another hand wrapped itself around his, and forcefully placed the glass back down onto the bar.

Agent Moore's eyes slowly walked up the well-manicured, diamond bedecked hand, past the platinum and diamond cuff links, past the shapely tailored, charcoal colored coat sleeve to the well groomed face of the gentleman standing behind Tyrone. It was a face she had seen many times in the past few weeks, it was a face she had studied in detail, and it was the face of Damian Reigns.

"Tyrone, you've had too many drinks," Damian said in his deep, melodic, baritone voice. "Say good night to the lady, Tyrone."

"Damian!" Tyrone Washington's eyes flew wide with fear. "I was... I was..."

"You were about to buy the lady a drink, and then say good night. Don't worry about the bill. I'll buy the drink, you just say goodnight."

Damian released Tyrone's hand, and Tyrone quickly released the glass and began to walk away. "Good night," Tyrone said, as he hauled himself quickly and made his escape toward the club's exit doors.

Agent Grace Moore turned to Damian, "Thank you."

Damian seated himself next to her. "Don't mention it." He looked down toward the seat beneath him.

"May I?" he asked, though already seated.

"Of course," Agent Moore said as she stared at the exit door. "You just saved me from a potentially embarrassing situation."

"My sincere apologies for that," Damian told her. "Sometimes we guys can be a bit over-zealous."

Although she had studied every crease, every pore, every lash on his face, Grace was still taken aback by the appearance of Damian Reigns. Not only was he a brainiac, he was a drop-dead handsome brainiac.

"Are you okay?" Damian asked, leaning forward.

Grace covered the lower half of her face and giggled. She had been caught staring.

"I'm fine," she told him, "I'm sorry, I'm still a little taken aback by that guy."

"Oh, yes, that's understandable," Damian extended his hand. "I'm sorry, my name is Damian."

Agent Moore clasped his hand firmly and smiled.

"Jonel."

"Well, it's a pleasure to meet you, Jonel."

"Oh, no, the pleasure is all mine."

"So, are you from San Antonio?"

Agent Grace Moore shook her head. "No, I'm from Virginia. I just moved here recently." This is where training and skill could land the best of field agents an Oscar nomination.

"Oh, I see, husband's moved up the corporate ladder, and took a management position out here, am I right?"

Grace laughed. "You're wrong. I'm single, and I got the big promotion and relocated! Don't tell me you're a male chauvinist."

Damian shook his head. "No, no, of course not, I'm the

20

most liberal, equal minded man you'll ever meet."

He raised his hands into the air, signaling his unwillingness to quarrel.

"I haven't opened the door for a lady in quite some time. I do my own laundry, I wash dishes, and I even cook my own meals. And just between us," he leaned in and whispered. "I can even sew."

Grace threw her head back in laughter. "Oh, so you're a reformed chauvinist."

"How dare you! I can't believe you just said that! You know what, the next time I'm out in public, I'm going to open the door for a hundred women, I'm going to help a bunch of old ladies cross the street, and I'm going to lay my coat down over a puddle of water so that young damsels can step across it! That'll show you!"

Grace Moore slapped Damian across the right shoulder. "Oh please, you probably do all of those things all day, everyday. Face it, you still live in the Stone Age. You're a male chauvinist."

"How can I prove to you that I'm not a caveman?"

"I don't know, what do you have in mind?"

"Dinner. I'm cooking."

Grace Moore shook her head from side to side. "I don't eat hot dogs."

"Hot dogs! *Hot dogs?!* I don't believe you! I'll have you know I'm a culinary master. Hot dogs! I can't believe you."

Grace laughed, and tossed her hair back over her shoulders. Her turquoise eyes sparkled with a blazing intensity as she nodded.

"Okay, Mr. Chef Boyardee. All of my pots and pans are still in boxes, so I'll take you up on your offer. But I warn you, I want my lunchables cold."

"Lunchables! Lunchables!" Damian waved his hands through the air. "That's it, that was the last straw. I'm pulling out all the stops. You have talked yourself into a dining experience!"

"Okay, we'll see," said Grace smiling at Damian's handsome face.

Damian nodded. "Yeah, we will see. Well, here is my telephone number." He handed her an embroidered business card from his wallet. "Call me."

"I will."

"I look forward to it," and with that, he took her hand into his, and kissed it gently. "Have a good night."

Agent Moore watched Damian glide off to a group of impeccably suited young men and join in their conversation.

"Damian, I see you've stumbled into Jonel," Dante told his brother.

"How do you know her?" Damian asked.

"I saw her seated at the bar. Actually, I saw her when she first walked in. She's like that. A chocolate-colored honey with turquoise eyes!"

Damian nodded, "Well, she and I have a dinner date."

"Damn," Dante said. "I knew I should have made a play for her. I'll tell you what, let's make a deal."

Damian shook his head. "No."

"I'll tell you what, you can have her."

"Giving up that easy?" Damian asked. "That's not like you."

"I just looked at my watch, and she didn't look at hers. Now you try it."

Damian raised his wrist and looked at his watch. Across the room, Grace looked at hers too.

"Well bro, looks like she's watching you," Dante told Damian. "I guess she's all yours. I'll start checking her out tomorrow."

"Dante, don't be so paranoid all of the time," said Damian already knowing his brother had her under investigation.

"That's what I'm here for," Dante said with a smile for his older brother. "That's why you love me."

Damian Reigns threw his head back in laughter. He took

22

his left hand and rubbed it through his brother's hair, pressing down on his waves.

"Dante."

"What?"

"Make sure that this time they can identify the body. Tyrone's family are real good people. At least let them be able to give him a funeral."

"I did. I took care of it personally."

"Good."

Chapter Four

The hollow, gurgling sound of the V-12 rapidly turned into a high-pitched, raspy sounding whine as Damian depressed the car's aluminum gas pedal.

"C'mon," he told a shocked and speechless Agent Moore, while nodding his head toward the empty passenger seat. "Get in, dinner is in the warmer."

Grace Moore had seen pictures of Lamborghinis before, but she had never actually seen one up close, let alone ridden inside of one. Damian's Lamborghini Murciélago was a deep, luscious red with a saddle-colored leather interior. It was the top of the line, a VT roadster, with a removable roof panel and all-wheel-drive. Its state of the art Alpine stereo system and 22-inch aluminum racing wheels were standard along with the car's 200 plus mile-per-hour top speed.

Agent Grace Moore reached down and pressed the doorknob of the two hundred and fifty-thousand-dollar car, and marveled as the door swung forward in a scissors type motion.

"Nice car," she told him.

"Thanks," Damian nodded his head and allowed himself a sheepish grin. "It gets me from point A to point B."

Grace Moore slid inside of the vehicle's passenger seat, and placed her arm on Damian's shoulder. "I'll bet it does. And fast, too."

Damian allowed himself a good laugh before shifting into gear and propelling his exotic car rapidly forward.

Agent Grace Moore had never been briefed on Damian's residence. In fact, she had never even been shown pictures. However, nothing could have prepared her for what she saw.

Damian Reigns' white mega-mansion sat on a bluff, overlooking a massive, crystal blue lake that touched his gently sloping back yard. The clear blue sky served as a beautiful, almost surreal backdrop to the stucco and glass, Mediterranean-style mansion. Surrounded by gigantic, luscious evergreens, a variety of neatly clipped and trimmed bushes bursting colors of pink, red, and white, along with splashes of yellow, violet, and blue, the home and its accompanying flora could easily have been lifted right from the pages of *Architectural Digest.*

Agent Moore entered the massive, all glass double doors of the mansion and again found herself having to keep her jaw from dropping. The floors of the immense foyer were covered in rich, luscious colors of deep burgundy, emerald green, snowflake white, and creamy beige Italian travertine marble. Their mirror-like finish reflected the gigantic crystal and platinum chandelier, providing the room with a double shot of light.

Agent Moore walked carefully over to the center of the foyer where a heavy marble pedestal held a similarly large and undoubtedly priceless vase, which in turn held a prohibitively expensive silk floral arrangement. She examined the arrangement and then turned and examined the room.

To her right was a massive freestanding sculpture by Botero, which was positioned under an extremely large oil painting by the same artist. It was the left side of the foyer that piqued her attention, however. A large, lit, crystal and marble waterfall occupied the entire left side of the foyer. Its delicately cascading flow glided smoothly down each of its crystal layers until coming softly to rest inside the white marble base. The running water provided a soft, relaxing, and melodic ambience to the entrance and set the stage for the opulent luxury found throughout the rest of the mansion.

"Come on in," Damian gestured toward the interior of the home with a nod of his head. "My home is your home."

I wish, Agent Moore thought to herself as she followed her impeccably dressed host into his family room. The smell of Grey Flannel cologne wafted through the fabric of his finely tailored Brioni suit, leaving a sweet, seductive trail in his wake.

"My father used to wear that," she told him, while rubbing her hand across his right shoulder, and feeling out the material of his jacket.

"Excuse me?" He stopped and turned to face her.

"Your cologne," she smiled. "My father used to wear it."

Damian smiled politely. "Well, your father is a man of impeccable taste."

Grace Moore returned his smile, and then turned away to examine the room. "Either that, or you have the taste of an old person."

Damian's mouth fell open as he feigned shock. "Alright, you've been inside of my home for less than five minutes and you're already insulting me."

Grace smiled at him again as she rounded the large, emerald-colored, leather sectional which sat facing the one-hundred-and-twenty inch screen projection television.

"What, am I being irreverent?" she asked him. "Am I disrespecting the great Damian... whatever your last name is?"

"Reigns, my last name is Reigns, and yes, you are being irreverent." Damian strolled over to the marble and glass coffee table, which sat directly in front of the leather sectional, and lifted a remote. "Usually, when a person is a guest in someone's home, they are a little more polite."

"A guest?" She smiled. "I thought you said that your home was my home?"

Damian returned her smile. "I'll bet your co-workers hate

26

you."

"Actually, the feeling is mutual. I work at a bank."

"Really? Which one?"

Agent Grace Moore seated herself on the sectional.

"Citibank."

Damian walked up to her, and extended his hand, inviting her to take it.

"I can't imagine them allowing you to interact with customers."

Grace laughed uncontrollably as she took Damian's hand, and allowed him to pull her up off the sectional.

"I see you bite back."

Damian pressed a button on his smart home remote. Instantly, the lights dimmed, the fireplace came alive, and soft music began emanating from the hidden speakers which surrounded the room.

Grace was impressed at the home's automation, and surprised by the song he selected, 'Spend My Life With You', by Eric Benet and Tamia.

She punched him gently on the shoulder. "This is one of my all time favorite songs!"

Damian pulled Grace close, wrapped his arms around her, and began dancing slowly. "I like this song too."

"Do you do this to all the girls? Is this how you seduce them?"

"Yes," he said, no need in lying to anyone.

Startled by his bluntness, she blushed for several moments. "You could have lied and said no," she told him. "At least tried to make me feel special."

Damian pulled his head back, and looked into Grace Moore's eyes. "No, I couldn't have. I'll never lie to you, Jonel. Never, lies have a way of coming back to people. And this, this is too important for me to blow."

Grace swallowed hard and quickly leaned her head against his shoulder to avoid his eyes. "When's dinner?" she asked softly.

"When do you want it?"

"Now."

"Then it's ready now. Your wish is my command."

Damian took her hand and led her into the massive dining room. Again, her breath was taken away.

The dining room was sixty feet by forty feet, with a thirty-foot mahogany dining table seated beneath a massive, antique, crystal chandelier. A large, black, marble fireplace abutted one wall, while an immense, intricately carved mahogany and beveled glass china cabinet commanded the other.

Damian waved his hand at a seat near the head of the table.

"Mademoiselle."

"Ah, parlez vous Français?"

Damian snapped his head toward Grace in surprise. "Mais bien sur. Je parle Français."

"Oui, ausez-vous appres?"

"Ma mere enseignait le Francais, et na 'forcer a' apprendre la langue. Et vous ou vous apprais?"

"Mon pere travaillait a L'ambassade a' Paris," she told him.

"Comme je vous l'ai dit je sois propreitaive du plus beau chateau qui existe dans La Loire. Eh vous devez venir le voir."

"Mas bien sur. Sounds great," she told him.

"So, how long was your father a diplomat?" he asked.

"We spent eight years over there. So, what's for dinner?"

Damian's hands meandered magically through the air before he clapped them together forcefully.

"I have the most wonderful meal in the world prepared for you: curried shrimp and pasta salad, peach chicken breast, rice pilaf, lemon green beans, walnut sweet potato pie, and a bottle of chilled Chateau Lafite."

"Sounds great, but how does it taste?" she asked with a

sarcastic smile.

"You'll just have to see for yourself."

Agent Moore stopped at her apartment door and turned to face Damian. "I had a wonderful evening. I haven't laughed or danced that much in a long time. Thank you."

Damian extended his arm and took her hand into his.

"No, thank you." He raised her hand slowly to his lips, where he kissed it gently. "You're a wonderful woman, Jonel. I really enjoyed your companionship this evening."

Agent Moore blushed. "I still don't believe you cooked that meal."

"I did," Damian told her. He raised his right hand into the air. "On my honor."

"What's that, scouts honor?"

"No, my honor."

"Your honor as a gentlemen? As a male chauvinist?"

Damian slapped his hand across his forehead. "My goodness! Are you back to that? Did I open the door for you? I mean, I even wore an apron when I served you!"

Grace laughed and poked Damian in his chest with her finger.

"You were being sarcastic. And, yes, you did open every door for me and you did walk me to my door."

"I walk everyone to their door. I have a friend, he's six foot nine, two hundred and twenty pounds, and I walk him to his door too!"

"Get out of here!"

"Okay, I'm just kidding," Damian raised his finger. "But that was not a chauvinist act."

"Okay, and I think that apron looked cute on you."

"Ha, ha, real funny. So, would it be chauvinistic to ask you out to dinner on Wednesday?"

"No, besides, if you didn't, it would probably have gotten you a kick in the shin."

Damian threw his head back in laughter. "Well, I'm really glad I asked."

"Not as glad as I am," Agent Grace Moore leaned forward, and wrapped her arms around Damian's neck. She pulled him close to her, where she kissed him firmly.

"That was nice," Damian told her. "Are you always this aggressive?"

"Only when I'm going after something I want."

"It's nice to be wanted."

Grace nodded and smiled. "Oh, you're wanted alright. I'll bet half the women in this city are chasing after you."

Damian smiled, lifted her hand, and once again kissed it softly. "Au revoir. J'espere vous revoir bientot."

"Moi aussi. Bonsoir."

Chapter Five

Dante maneuvered the mouse around the soft, gray pad until the arrow on the computer screen came to rest on the stop button. Two clicks on the mouse caused the computer's MIDI to stop the playback of the previous night's dinner conversation between Damian and Agent Moore. Dante then began to tap rapidly at the computer keyboard, entering the notes he took from the conversation onto the computer's hard drive. His work was interrupted by Damian's entrance.

"Finished?" Damian asked.

Dante looked over his shoulder at his brother. "Almost. Just have a few more notes to take."

Damian smiled, laid his hand upon his brother's shoulder, and stared at the computer screen.

"I don't know how this thing does it."

"It's really quite simple," Dante told him. "The computer controls every function inside of the home including the digital music system. Since the computer plays the music and does the audio recording, I can simply tell the computer to remove the digital music from the recording, which leaves only your conversation."

Damian shook his head and smiled. "Dante, you do love your toys. Find anything interesting?"

"The computer's voice stress analyzer detected nothing," Dante again turned toward Damian. "Either she's telling the truth or she's a pathological liar."

"There's one other possibility."

"Oh yeah? What?"

"She could just be really good at lying for a living."

"That remains to be seen," Dante seriously noted before he turned back to the computer screen. "Net search came up empty. I'm about to tap into the university's database and pull up her college file."

Damian patted his brother's shoulder.

"Good."

"No, it's not good," Dante stopped, and turned toward Damian. "This is just the beginning. Call her and invite her to dinner, my treat."

Damian smiled at his brother and nodded his head slowly. He didn't know what Dante had in mind, but he did know that Dante was good. No, change that, Dante was the best and Damian was glad Dante was on his side.

"It's already done," Damian informed his older brother and shot him a look letting him know he was on his job. "I anticipated that you would want to interact with her. Look, I have to make a quick run. If anything pops up, call me on the scrambled cellular."

"Roger," Dante told him. He turned, lifted the cordless phone from its base, and rapidly dialed a number from his memory.

"Hello?"

"Angela!" Dante greeted the voice cheerfully. "How would your sexy tail like to go out for dinner?"

"Dante?"

"Yes, of course. Who else?"

The voice on the telephone exhaled heavily, and after a brief pause asked sharply, "What is it now, Dante?"

"Dinner, dinner and a movie."

"What do you really want?"

"I have someone I want you to meet," he told her. "In fact, you should already know her. She's an old classmate of yours from the university."

"Uh-huh," Angela suddenly caught on. "Well sure, Dante, dinner with you and an old friend, how could I resist? Besides, I know how you like to spend money and impress, and I stress, lots of money."

"But of course," Dante smiled. "I know you wouldn't have it any other way, Angela."

"Good bye, Dante," she said sharply.

"Good...bye..." The line went dead before he could finish his sentence. Dante smiled at the fact that Angela still hated him, yet still couldn't deny him, ever in this life.

"**H**ello?"

"Hey, Liz, this is Grace," Agent Moore greeted Special Agent Holmes over the telephone. "I'm just checking in."

"Roger," Holmes yawned loudly over the telephone. "So what's the word?"

"Well, I've been to his mansion, I've ridden in one of his exotic cars, I've danced with him, and he's cooked dinner for me."

"Ooh, dinner. Aren't you the lucky one."

"Actually, he's quite an accomplished chef. That wasn't in his file."

"Well, you know how Intel is," Agent Holmes replied in her usual nonchalance. "They usually miss most of the small things."

"Which usually turn into big things down the line," Grace retorted. "And also, he speaks French, fluently, I might add. Why wasn't *that* in the file?"

Agent Elizabeth Holmes breathed heavily over the telephone and removed her glasses. She placed them on the tiny, wooden nightstand by her bed.

"Look Grace, I'm going to give Henry a call back in D.C. and see if we can get some better Intel. But at any rate, you're going to have to play a lot of it by ear. Just do the best you can, and if you feel things are getting out of hand, pull out."

"Gotcha."

"When's the last time you did a check on the emergency rescue button on your ring?"

"Yesterday. Nathan had me test it before Damian picked me up."

"Good, good. If things get hairy, hit the button. The guys will come in with guns blazing and rescue you."

"Has this emergency rescue stuff ever been used before?"

"No, you're the first."

"Oooh, that's just great."

"Good luck, sweetie."

"Bye."

"Bye."

Grace Moore hung up the telephone and rolled over in her bed. The darkness of the room allowed the moonlight to illuminate the white miniblinds hanging over the windows, giving off a warm, soft glow.

The mini-blinds had come with the apartment, as did several other amenities. A gated entry, an alarm system, a carport, two large swimming pools, individual washers and dryers inside the apartments, two fireplaces, three tennis courts, a basketball court, several racquetball courts, picnic tables, and a private park. There was even a clubhouse that had a private gym, sauna and steam room for tenants only. However, despite all of the luxurious amenities, Grace Moore now called into question the solidity of the apartment buildings themselves, especially tonight, when the walls were exceptionally thin. Tonight when she was all alone inside of a cool, dark bedroom with no warm body to hold her, to comfort her, to warm her, especially tonight, when the seemingly super thin walls allowed her to hear her neighbors' passionate lovemaking. The high pitched screams of the woman and the guttural grunts of the man caused a warm tingling sensation between her legs.

Grace Moore could feel the blood flowing inside of her body, swelling in places that had not been excited in a very long time. She could time her neighbor's rhythmic thrust by the intervals between the woman's passionate cries. She was lonely, so very lonely. It had been at least six months since she released those same pleasurable moans and felt the warmth of companionship. As her mind recalled her own experiences, she could feel herself becoming moist. Grace breathed heavily and crossed her legs, only to realize that her hands were now resting on the inner part of her tightly closed thighs. She didn't want to go there. In fact, she hadn't masturbated since she was a teenager back in high school. No, she wanted the real thing.

The building cries of her neighbors only exacerbated the situation. Grace knew it was feeling good to them and that it was getting better with each passing moment. Her warm wetness increased to the point where she could feel it trying to escape from inside of her. Throbbing rapidly, she rolled over and grabbed the pillow from the other side of the bed, placed it between her legs, and rolled over onto her side.

No, no, no, don't do it. Stop thinking of it and it will go away. She couldn't stop though. She masturbated every night before falling asleep and she told her self she was going to stop. *Get men out of your mind Grace,* she told herself. She didn't have time for a relationship, let alone the dating that came with it. Her assignments around the world prevented it. Sure, she could settle down and marry, but first she would have to find the time to actually meet someone who she wasn't trying to bust. Then there was the question of children. She just couldn't do the mommy thing right now. How sexy and attractive would she be with a belly extending out two-feet from the rest of her body? And then the question of baby-sitting, of child-care, day care, and all the other forms of rug-rat care that parents had to contend with. Children were out of the question for now, no children. That would leave her with a marriage to a husband whom she could rarely see because of her worldwide assignments, and it would leave him with an absent wife and no children around to fill the household. No, marriage was out of the question for right now. So again, she found herself back at square one. Was her career with the Bureau worth giving up so much? Was it that rewarding? Something inside of her said yes, but then again, something inside of her cried no.

It was only during moments like these when Grace found herself questioning her commitment to her career. For as far back as she could remember, she had always wanted to be a police officer. As she grew older and more emotionally mature, her ambitions simply matured with her, police officer to police detective to FBI agent to FBI director. That was what she wanted, to carry a gun, to carry a badge, to have the law on her side, and the power to make the streets safe for law-abiding citizens.

As an FBI Director, she would be able to do so much good. She would be able to bring down hundreds of Damian Reigns, all across the country. Yes, it was worth it all. The lonely nights, the empty motels and apartments, the midnight flights to nowhere. She would make the streets safe for kids, for the elderly, for families...

"Families..." she whispered softly into the darkness of the room. "Families..."

Grace Moore could tell the most convincing of lies, and could pull off the most convincing of deceptions. She could be a bag lady, a cashier in a grocery store, and an airline stewardess on a commercial flight. In fact, she had disguised herself as all of those things and many more. She could deceive the most cunning of thieves, the wisest of drug dealers, and the craftiest of crooks, but the one person she could not deceive was herself. That loneliness caused an emptiness inside her as vast and dry and burning as an Arabian Desert. Her soul, her heart, her humanity needed someone to love, to hold, to help, and to cherish. She needed someone to confide in and someone to confide in her. It was that ever reaching yet always unfulfilled need to embrace. Yearning is what it was called and she, in the deepest, darkest of the night is when she yearned for someone to love.

Grace Moore crossed her arms and turned over in her bed. She could hear the last piercing cries of her neighbors as the coupling culminated into a bursting, gut wrenching climax. Their release caused Grace to release a liquid of her own. Her burning tears of loneliness cascaded down her soft cheeks, and came to rest upon her pillow.

Chapter Six

The elevator's speed never ceased to amaze Dante. On average, it took less than two minutes to get from his penthouse apartment to the subterranean garage, just below the basement, and that included all of the annoying little stops to pick up and deposit all of the building's well-to-do, silver haired patrons at their various destinations.

The elevator doors opened and several members of Dante's entourage stepped off with their hands inside of their coats. They looked around for several moments to make sure that no surprises were lurking in the shadows before allowing their boss off the elevator. Dante only left the elevator when Riley, the head of the personal security detail, waved him an 'okay' with the nod of his head.

Riley was good, one of the best. He had come to Dante with excellent credentials and had been a gift from the Reigns family's friends down south. They had wanted to keep Riley for themselves, but sending him to Dante served two purposes. For one, they were able to create good will between Dante and themselves, and second, they were able to keep Interpol from closing in on him. Riley had once been Captain Raul Villarosa, a commander in the El Salvadoran Death Squads.

Dante summoned his security men as he walked toward his waiting vehicle.

"Riley, I'm to go alone, that was the condition of the meeting. They may have someone watching, so I want two guys to wait twenty minutes, and then use the GPS system to hone in on my location. Once I'm inside of the apartment, if I hit the emergency transmitter on my watch, come in blazing."

"Si, Señor Reigns," Riley nodded.

Dante stopped and reached for the door handle of his black S600 Mercedes.

"And, Riley..."

"Sir?"

"Leave no one alive."

A smile spread slowly across Riley's weathered, olive-colored face.

"Si, Señor Reigns."

It was something he was good at. The smile and look of delight on Riley's face made Dante lower his head and laugh. It was then when he saw it.

The garage was as well lit as it should have been considering the exorbitant cost of residency, yet a garage was still a garage, which meant darkness, and shadows, and reflections of all sorts. Beneath the big, black, Benz was a green light reflecting off the concrete. It was a light that in and of itself was harmless, but it was a light that should not have been there.

"Bomb! Run!" Dante turned and sprinted as fast as he could away from the vehicle. If Brooks Brothers lacked a sportswear line, Dante had just invented one for them. He sprinted across the garage in his three-button suit as though it had been made for a track meet. He dove over the hood of a white Lincoln Town Car just as the explosion ripped through the garage.

"God dammit, Princess!" Dante reached inside of his coat and pulled his ten-millimeter, glock handgun from inside of his shoulder holster. Slowly, he stood.

The bulk of the black Mercedes was thirty yards away from where it had once been parked, and it was now flipped on its roof, burning like a cord of firewood. Burning pieces of the vehicle were scattered all over the garage.

"Boss, are you okay?" Melvin asked. Melvin was one of Dante's bodyguards. He had been with Dante since the beginning.

"Yeah," Dante nodded. He shook his head to relieve some of the ringing sensation inside of his ears and then holstered his weapon.

"Where's Riley?"

Melvin shook his head. Another bodyguard approached.

"Riley's dead. So is Chi-Chi," he told them.

Dante removed his pocket square, and placed it over the bleeding bodyguard's eye.

"Ron, you're bleeding bad. Hold this over your wound."

Ron took the now crimson pocket square and held it in place. "Thanks boss. Hey, we gotta get you outta here."

Dante turned toward the stairwell. "I'm leaving. The plan goes through as follows. Get a hold of Damian and let him know what happened."

Dante jogged to the door leading toward the steps and opened it. He turned back toward what was left of his bodyguard.

"And sanitize this place. The cops will be here any minute."

Princess placed the telephone back inside its cradle and turned to her room full of associates and smiled. She lifted her glass and bowed her head slightly toward Patrick O'Limerick.

Patrick was her explosives expert, her top hit man, and occasionally, her lover. Patrick was good. So good, that for many years he gave the Ulster Constabulary Forces in Northern Ireland sheer hell. For a while, he even managed to make number one of Scotland Yards most wanted list. It was a source of great personal pride with him, and it all came from doing what he loved to do—what he LIVED to do—which was blowing things up.

"Congratulations," Princess said with a smirk of twisted evil across her face.

Patrick lifted his champagne flute into the air, acknowledging her toast. Several others inside the apartment did the same.

"Now dat Don-te is smithereens, when are ye gone ta let me blew Damian in he's arse?" Patrick asked with his thick Irish accent. He and Princess shared a laugh. She waved her hand toward another suited gentleman.

"Marlow here will be arranging that." Princess sipped at her champagne. "I'd like to catch him on the way home from Dante's funeral."

Everyone inside the room laughed.

Princess closed her hand, turning it into a tiny fist, and pounded the air.

"My God, I would have loved to have been there! I would have loved to have seen Dante fall to the ground in little, tiny, burning pieces!"

Patrick walked to where Princess was standing and wrapped his arms around her.

"Don't worry me luv, I'll be sure ann let yer see Damian go boom." His blue eyes sparkled as he spoke his words.

Princess returned his smile, and then ran her hand through the curly, orange hair that matched the freckles dotting his face. Princess often told him how his curly hair and soft freckles gave him an innocent looking baby face. The only thing that gave away his thirty years was the long scar that ran down the left side of his face. Patrick often told her the story of how he later blew up the English sniper who gave it to him.

There was a knock at the apartment door.

Patrick's hand left Princess' shoulder, and slid down her back where it came to rest on her behind. He squeezed firmly as his fingers reached in between her legs before letting her ass go.

"Don't go anywhere, me luv," he told her.

41

Patrick turned and walked to the door, where he looked out of the peephole. "It's the mediators."

"Damn interfering Colombians!" Princess turned, and examined herself in the large, gilded mirror that hung just behind her.

"Open the door. We'll inform them of Dante's unfortunate accident. Let them know that the situation has been resolved and get rid of them."

Patrick nodded and opened the door.

In walked Jesus Alcantar, Jose Barrientes, Miguel Cantu, and Frederico Hernandez, the Colombian's handpicked mediators.

Everyone was anxious to avoid a war. A war among the Reigns family would disrupt the distribution network, bring heat down on everyone, and put a severe dent in everyone's profits. It was for that reason the Colombians and their Mexican middlemen wanted the situation resolved quickly and without bloodshed. A drawn out war could potentially cost them billions, and the 'B' word got everyone's attention.

Patrick started to close the door, but found it being pushed back open.

"Oh me Lord!" His eyes flew open wide as nickels and he gasped as if he had just seen a ghost.

"No, but as close as you will ever get," Dante said as he walked in.

Princess' eyes flew wide and she gasped. "Dante!"

Dante walked casually to the coffee table, which sat in the middle of the apartment, and lifted a green apple from the fruit bowl sitting on top of it.

"What's the matter, sis?" he chomped down into the apple. "You two look like you've seen a ghost."

Princess lifted her hand and placed her palm on her chest. She swallowed hard.

"Dante, welcome... welcome, come on in."

"Wow, you're acting like you're surprised to see me," Dante told her with a smile. "You weren't expecting me? Am I a surprise?" he said lighting up his eyes with a smile.

Princess cut her eyes toward the Colombian mediators, and then back to Dante.

"Of course I was expecting you." She swallowed hard, and then ran her hand across her tight French roll hair-do. "Well, let's get down to business."

Princess strutted across the floor and seated herself in a chair adjacent to the couch. She motioned for her guests to be seated. "Gentlemen, please, make yourselves at home."

The Colombians sat.

Dante maneuvered past Patrick and whispered into his ear, "You missed."

Patrick smiled back at him. *I won't the next time.*

Dante seated himself in a tan, overstuffed, Italian leather recliner. To his left was the door, which was guarded by Patrick. To his right sat a sofa full of powerful and respected Colombians, and directly across from him sat the most dangerous person of all: his sister.

Princess crossed her smooth, silky, chocolate-colored legs and ran her palms across her long, black, Prada skirt.

"To get right to the point, Damian is going to cut you off," she told her guests from the South. "In the next few years, our family will be completely out of the business. Where will that leave you? I, on the other hand, want to expand. I will increase our relationship and business arrangements tenfold."

Jesus cleared away the lump which had formed in his throat. "Tenfold?"

"Tenfold," Princess repeated. "Imagine our secure distribution lines, our reliability, and our contacts in charge of the entire South. We could unify all southern business arrangements under one umbrella. That means greater security, greater efficiency, and the reliability you've come to expect from the Reigns family."

"Dios Mios!" Jose leaned forward. "Do you have the capability to do such a thing, the capacity, the manpower, the facilities, the contacts? What you speak of is a great undertaking."

"And Florida?" Jesus asked. "You would leave Florida out of course. We have our own people in Florida."

"Yes, I know," Princess nodded. "Your nephew, the one who agreed to work for the DEA this morning."

"What?" Jesus stood. "How dare you!"

"He was busted last week. The charges were conspiracy to distribute ten tons of cocaine, running a continuing criminal enterprise, first degree murder, conspiracy to commit murder...need I continue?" Princess lifted her drink from the table and sipped seductively. "He just walked out of a federal courthouse in Miami three hours ago. Our people said he cut the deal."

"Lies!" Jesus shouted.

Miguel raised his hands and patted the air, "Sit down, Jesus."

Jesus seated himself and stared at Princess fiercely.

"My people in Miami are prepared to take over all of your operations in Florida," Princess smiled at Jesus. "And neutralize all informants."

"Princess, what if we took Florida from Don Alemendez and gave it to you?" Miguel asked. "Would you be willing to relocate to Miami and run things there?"

"She would only expand from Florida toward Texas, instead of from Texas toward Florida," Dante told them. "Her goal is to get control of the South. Once she controls the entire South, she controls almost all of this country's entrance points. Then she will turn her eyes toward New Mexico, Arizona, and California, and get absolute control over all of the country's entrance points. Her thirst for power is unquenchable. Her appetite for destruction is insatiable. Eventually, after she controls all of the distribution in the United States, she will decide that she no longer needs you either. She'll decide that she wants to grow and manufacture her own commodities."

Princess frowned and rolled her eyes at her brother.

"Dante, we called this meeting because our Boss does not want another interruption in his distribution chain. The last interruption cost us billions and nearly exposed our methods."

"Miguel, I'm here on behalf of Damian to apologize to your Boss. His personal interest in our welfare will not go unnoticed. We have prospered together and will continue to prosper. We thank El Jefe for sending you, but again, we see no peaceful solution to our sister's aggression."

"Dante, can't you give her something?" Frederico asked.

Frederico was the oldest and fattest member of the delegation. He was also the highest ranking, the most reasonable, and at the same time, the most treacherous.

Dante bowed his head slightly. "Señor Frederico, I would give anything to stop the bloodshed. I do not know what we could give. We only control Texas and portions of Oklahoma, Louisiana, New Mexico, and Arkansas. She wants more than we have."

"Señor Frederico, what my brother says is only partially true," Princess spoke up. "I do want to expand. But the expansions will bring your operations in the South under control of one distributor. It will minimize your exposure and bring savings and efficiency to us all. I need Texas as a base from which to expand."

"But couldn't you expand from Florida?" Miguel posed.

"Theoretically the expansion could be done from Florida, but it's not practical. The Jones family controls Mississippi, so using Gulfport as a wellhead is out of the question. The McGuiness family controls Virginia, so Hampton Roads is a non-starter. The Douglases control Georgia, and they're pretty strong. The Coast Guard and Custom Service are all over Florida, which means I would have supply nightmares. No, Texas is the place to start."

Frederico leaned forward. "Dante, your brother did discuss with us the possibility of shifting his focus from our operations to his other business operations. Why not shift them to your sister?"

"El Jefe was consulted about this possibility, however, in the end all parties agreed that it would not be in our best interest. Princess' previous time at the helm left everyone with a bad taste in their mouths."

Again, Princess rolled her eyes at her brother.

Frederico nodded and turned toward her. "What is it that you want?"

No longer in the mood for any pretense, Princess continued to scowl at her brother as she answered. "Don Frederico, what I want is simple. I want the world, and everything in it."

"Princess..."

"Don, I thank you for coming," she said. Princess rose. Her guest did the same. "Once I am the head of the Reigns family, I am going to make El Jefe rich beyond his wildest dreams. And I am going to forget the fact that the commission sided against me and gave control of a family that I built to my brother."

Princess waved her hand at the door. Patrick opened it while Marlow walked behind the Colombians, herding them through it. Dante walked behind Marlow, and his sister just behind him.

Once at the door, Dante turned, and came face to face with his sister.

"I received your little present today, sis. Are we attacking each other in our homes now?"

"Dante, I don't know what you're talking about. Our homes, just like our parent's homes, are strictly off-limits. They're safe zones, remember?"

"Yeah, well the garage underneath my penthouse looked more like a war zone than a safe zone."

"Laddie, your home is safe. Your carriage is a horse of a different color," Patrick told him with a smile.

Princess allowed herself a grin.

"I lost two good men today. I lost Chi-Chi and Riley," Dante said before he quickly pulled out his weapon and pointed it at Patrick. He squeezed the trigger, shooting Patrick in the throat. He quickly turned the gun on Marlow, and shot him in the middle of his forehead. Their bodies fell on top of each other.

"Dante, noooo!" Princess screamed as she dropped down to the floor and grabbed Patrick.

"You son of a bitch!" she said glaring daggers at her brother.

"I lose two good men, you lose two good men," Dante stared at the remainder of Princess' stunned and ducking entourage. None of them moved. He holstered his weapon, turned, and walked down the hall.

Chapter Seven

The high-pitched whines coming from the rear of Damian's Fiorno Red, Ferrari 360 Spider, were more distinctive than the thrashy gurgles of his Lamborghini Roadster. The Ferrari's engine sounded peppier, and the car's smallness reminded Grace Moore of her brother's tiny Hot Wheels toys that they played with while growing up.

Grace wondered which of the two sports cars were faster, although she never wanted to personally experience either car's top speed. She smiled as she opened the Ferrari's door and sat down.

"So, which one of your toys goes the fastest?" she asked.

Damian smiled and pressed down on the car's gas pedal, causing the engine to rev loudly.

"My Lambo will eat this thing up," he told her. "But don't get me wrong; this car's no slouch."

Grace placed her hand over Damian's hand, which rested on the car's shifter. "I didn't take you for one of those guys who likes his cars fast."

"Fast toys, and..."

"Fast women?" she replied, before he could finish his sentence. Damian smiled, shifted his car into gear, and pulled off.

"I like fast cars, fast planes, fast boats, fast horses, and even fast food sometimes. But..." turned and smiled at her, "I like my women slow."

Grace peered out of the car's lowered passenger side window, and admired the scenery that was flying rapidly by them.

"Old fashioned, just as I suspected."

She turned back toward Damian with a smirk. "You want them in the kitchen, barefoot and pregnant too, I suppose?"

Damian laughed and turned away. "Now what's wrong with being old fashioned? You say it like it's a dirty word."

"It is, when it's old fashioned male chauvinism."

"Not that again?" Damian asked. He shifted gears once more and sped up to enter onto the highway. "I like and maintain old fashioned values: hard work, belief in education, love of family, and service to my community. I mean, what's wrong with wanting to work hard, go to church, and raise a traditional, well-balanced family?"

"Nothing, especially if you're willing to let your wife come out of the basement on some of the really important holidays."

Damian slapped his hand across his forehead and laughed heartily.

"What am I going to do with you?"

Grace rubbed Damian's hand once more and slipped her hand up the cuff of his finely tailored Kiton suit. She accidentally pulled his jacket sleeve back and exposed his Swiss chronometer. It was a Girard Perreguax.

"Do you really want those things, Damian? I mean... do you really believe in those things?"

"In what things?"

"In going to church, in serving the community, in education, in hard work, in old fashioned family values?"

"Of course, what else in life is there?" Damian turned and stared into Grace Moore's blue-green eyes. "Jonel, back in my grandparents' days, people worked hard, saved up, and moved ahead. They believed the best way to advance was through a good education. My grandparents fought for

49

that right. They were beaten, bitten, spat on, and washed away with fire hoses, just so they could learn. Just think about the fear, the firebombs, the cross burnings, the lynchings. My grandparents are my heroes. Heck, all of our grandparents and parents are heroes. And you know what, they didn't do it for themselves. They did it for future generations, with no pay, no profit, no glory—just dedication, perseverance, courage, and sheer self-sacrifice."

Agent Moore stared out of the window and contemplated Damian's last statement. *Community,* she thought to herself. *How can he lie so convincingly? Either he truly believes that the drugs he peddles are good for the community, or he is a very convincing actor.*

"Jonel, I know a lot of guys pay lip service to helping our people, but I don't just talk the talk, I walk the walk," he told her. "I sponsor five adult learning centers, eight children computer learning centers, five Little League baseball teams, six Pee-Wee football teams, four community centers, and five community parks. I sponsor some five hundred kids and offer five hundred full scholarships to economically disadvantaged high school kids who otherwise could not afford to go to college. This doesn't include the things that my foundation or my family's foundation does. Jonel, I'm serious about my commitment to my people."

Who does this Negro think he's talking to. He's nothing more than a drug dealer. Grace Moore wanted to yell at Damian Reigns. She wanted to call him a lying, drug dealing, murdering bastard, and she wanted to scream it at the top of her lungs. She wanted to hit him, and then find a gun and shoot him. *Kids? Has he any idea what his drugs are doing to kids? The parks he sponsors is probably where he sells his drugs. Doesn't Mr. Intelligent, Harvard MBA, All-American, drug dealing superboy realize that if all the kids are dead from his drug-related violence then there will be no one left to wear his precious, Pee Wee football uniforms, or attend his computer learning centers, or go to his Goddamned baseball games! Doesn't he understand that?*

The arrival at the restaurant broke Grace's chain of thought. Damian turned toward her with his ever-ready smile.

"We're here," he announced. "I'm sure you'll find the cuisine to your liking."

Grace Moore returned his sly smile, "And if I don't?"

"Then I'll fire the chef," he laughed. "I own the restaurant."

Chalk up another one for the Intel guys, she told herself. *This place isn't on the list.*

The restaurant was very upscale in its accoutrements, yet modern enough to be called trendy. It boasted several bars, two stages, and numerous elegantly decorated dining tables. Contemporary, slow, urban music flowed soothingly through the restaurant's club like stereo system, joining the dimmed lighting and candlelit tables to create a romantic, urban adult dining experience.

Grace marveled at the restaurant's massive crystal chandeliers and marble flooring that welcomed the guests at the entrance.

"Nice, really nice," she told him.

"Of course it is. I told you I own it," Damian replied meaning every word he spoke. He extended his arm with a sweeping gesture, gallantly inviting her into the establishment.

The restaurant was busy, yet not overcrowded. Amidst the intimate ambience, guests spoke to each other in subdued tones. Subdued *romantic* tones, she guessed, noticing that most of the patrons were seated two to a table, smiling flirtatiously and holding hands.

Grace Moore spotted Dante and a female guest seated at a nearby table. Upon seeing them, Dante rose, and extended his arms toward his brother.

"Hey, Bro," Dante greeted Damian. A smile and firm hug accompanied his salutations. "How's everything going?"

"Pretty good, if I may say so myself," Damian answered. He turned and smiled at Grace. "Jonel's just giving me a real hard time. She's still accusing me of being a chauvinist."

Dante laughed heartily, throwing his head back slightly. "My brother is a male chauvinist pig. He believes that women belong two steps behind their men, so you continue to give him a hard time."

Damian's hands extended from his sides as he shrugged his shoulders. "How else can they be the true wind beneath our wings? Our motivation, our inspiration, our..."

"Walking board?" Dante's date interrupted. She and Grace smiled at each other and exchanged high fives.

"Tell him again, sister," Grace said glad to have someone on her side for a change.

"Excuse my manners," Dante told them. He waved his hand toward his date. "Jonel, I would like to introduce you to my dear friend, Angela. Angela, this is Jonel."

Agent Moore extended her right hand and firmly gripped Angela's.

"Pleased to meet you," she told her softly.

"Likewise," Angela replied with a friendly smile.

Damian waved his hand toward the awaiting table. "Ladies..."

Grace Moore sat across from Damian, while Angela sat across from Dante. The table was intimate, like all of the others inside of the establishment, and it's seclusion in the far right corner of the restaurant added to their privacy. The group could converse without worrying about bothering the next table or being over heard.

"So, Jonel, tell me a little bit about the woman who has swept my brother off of his feet," Dante said teasingly.

Grace Moore blushed sheepishly before composing herself for a witty reply.

"Well, he hasn't told me much about her," she smiled toward Damian. "But I would sure love to meet her."

"Ha, ha. Real funny," Damian replied. He shifted his gaze

toward his brother. "And you, you talk way too much."

"Me?" Dante placed his hand on his chest, and feigned shock. "You're the one who can't stop talking about her."

"Do you guys always behave like this?" Grace asked them.

"Only in the company of beautiful women," Dante replied. "So, back to my original request, tell me about the woman inside of the exquisite package. Is she just as beautiful?"

"Well, let me see. I'm twenty-five, single, no children, no pets, and I work for an overbearing, unappreciative boss, that about sums up my life."

"Where are you from?" asked Angela.

"I just moved here from Virginia, but I'm originally from Atlanta."

"Atlanta!" exclaimed Angela. "What a coincidence, I'm from Georgia also. I was raised in Savannah."

"Really?" asked Grace. "I've been to Savannah many times. I just love that little French restaurant on Eighteenth and Main. It is *so* cute!"

"Yes, yes girl!" Angela bounced up and down in her seat and gave Grace Moore a high five. "I know exactly the one you're talking about. They have this fine, I mean, super-fine brother from Senegal working there as a maitre d'."

"Yes, that's the one!" Grace agreed.

"So, did you go to school in Atlanta?" Angela asked.

"No, I went to school in Nashville."

"Girl, don't say it," Angela replied.

Grace Moore nodded. She knew her cover was airtight. The Bureau was experts at creating fictitious identities. They had been extra, extra careful with hers. For this assignment, she was utilizing the name, and background of a real person, air tight.

"I went to Fisk," Grace Moore told her newfound friend.

"Girl, I went to Fisk too!" Angela told her. "We're about the same age, so we must have been there about the same time. I just don't remember seeing your face. What dorm did you stay in?"

"I stayed in Livingston Hall."

"Oh, over there off Herman Street."

Grace Moore recalled a street being named Herman, during her reconnoitering of the campus. So she shook her head emphatically, "Yeah."

Angela slapped her across her hand lightly. "Girl, I used to hate it when I lived in Livingston. We would have to walk all the way across campus to Sixteenth Street, just to get to the library. It was super scary at night."

"Oh yeah, I know what you mean, they really needed some better lighting," Grace agreed.

"Jubilee Hall wasn't any better," Angela continued, "dangerous, just plain dangerous."

Grace Moore nodded and smiled silently in agreement.

The dinner date went well, with the girls exchanging college stories while Damian and Dante interposed with compliments, quick wit, and college stories of their own.

The boys escorted the ladies out of the restaurant into the cool evening air where they exchanged good-byes. Damian and Grace quickly disappeared into the brisk, star-filled night, while Dante wrapped up his business with Angela.

"So?" he asked, as the tail lights from his brother's Ferrari faded into the darkness.

Angela turned toward Dante and allowed a smile to slide across her gorgeous face.

"Well, for one, Livingston Hall is on Seventeenth and Jackson, not on Herman Street. Two, Jubilee Hall is off Meharry Boulevard, not Herman Street. Three, the library is on Seventeenth and Jackson, not Sixteenth Avenue, and finally, we wore white dresses during our induction ceremonies, not pink ones. Ms. Thang did not go to Fisk, has never set foot on a black college campus, and was definitely not raised in the South."

"Are you sure?"

"Dante, I'm a Southern belle, the only Georgia peach you've ever tasted in your life, trust me, we recognize our own. That bitch is from Iowa or Nebraska or from some lily white place in the Midwest where they grow a lot of corn. Ask her about Huckleberry Fin; she might know something. But she damn sure don't know nothing about the South. I bet she never has been to Georgia.

Dante folded his arms and shifted his weight to one side.

"And how do you know that?" he asked her.

"Listen to her voice, her speech patterns, darling. Historically black, she is not. Southern raised, not in this lifetime!"

"Angela, this is important. Are you sure?"

"Dante, I'm the best. I'm a speech pathologist, with a minor in sociology. And I went to Fisk, remember? If that bitch went to Fisk, then my father is Jefferson Davis. I don't think so!"

Dante turned and stared down the roadway in the direction in which his brother's car had just traveled. The thought of Damian riding off into the darkness alone with the unknown caused a tingle to creep up his spine. He quickly found himself frowning.

The coolness of the evening, the gentleness of the breeze, and the calming, melodic song of the whistling, rustling leaves did little to mitigate his quickly overheating body. It was a calm, cool, and collected anger—an intelligent, controlled, calculating anger. It was one of his 'they will never in this lifetime find your body' types of anger.

Staring into the darkness, Dante found himself able to mutter only a few whispered, seething, brooding words. They oozed from his mind and rolled slowly off his tongue like balls of poisoned molasses.

"Dead bitch..." He shook his head slightly. "You're...a dead bitch..."

Chapter Eight

Grace Moore watched as Damian gracefully strolled up the sidewalk to the door of her apartment. He looked like he was floating—no, gliding—across the concrete as though he were on rails. His bearing was dignified, noble, statuesque. His regality fit hand-in-glove with his impeccable manners and flawless wardrobe. He was the prince of the city.

Today Prince Damian wore a charcoal gray, wool, three-button-suit with black lace-up shoes to match. His only accessories were a pocket square, a set of platinum cuff links, and a plain, yet outrageously expensive, platinum Cartier diamond bezeled wristwatch: elegant, understated, tasteful.

Grace counted fifteen seconds after he rang the doorbell a second time before she opened the door. She didn't want to seem excited by his arrival.

"Hello, Damian," she said in a playful, seductive tone. "What a pleasant surprise."

Damian smiled because of the tone of her voice. He blushed at its suggestiveness, even though he knew that she was just teasing.

"Hello, Jonel," he replied after extending his hand.

Grace took Damian's hand into hers and shook it as she pulled him inside.

"Are you just going to stand out there, or are you going to come in?"

"Well, you were blocking the door, and an invitation to come inside would have been nice to hear first."

"Oh, excuse me, I forgot." Grace shook her head toward the ceiling. "Mr. Manners."

"Are we going to have this discussion again?"

"Of course not," Grace told him. She placed her arms on his shoulders and slid them down to his chest, feeling the fabric of his suit.

"Nice suit."

"Thank you."

"Well, I'm almost ready."

She whirled, and headed for the bathroom. "Make yourself at home, I'll be out in a minute."

Damian glanced around Grace Moore's sparingly furnished apartment: a sofa, a love seat, a small portable CD player resting on a cheap black plastic and glass book shelf. No pictures, no trinkets, no odds and ends that said I lived here and there and I'm a single, educated black woman.

Damian ventured into the bedroom, which hosted a bed, a nightstand, an alarm clock, and a small, cheap, wooden dresser. A book rested on the dresser next to a small, thirteen-inch Magnavox television. Again, no odds and ends, no gaudy gifts from parents, aunts, siblings, or sorority sisters. Just rooms that screamed, 'I've just moved in and hastily assembled some furniture'.

The thought that slid across Damian's mind made him smile. *Either she's running from someone or the big boys are getting careless.*

"Hey, I see you're finding your way around my humble abode," Grace said as she entered the bedroom. She sat on her bed, and lay across it, spreading her arms across the large, green, down-filled comforter. "This is my bed," she smiled teasingly.

Again Damian blushed. "I see," he nodded. "I was kind of hoping that it was your bed seeing that it's inside your bedroom."

"You know Damian, I'm going to tease you every chance that I get." Grace Moore sat up in her bed. "I see that I can embarrass you and make you blush. Your male chauvinist butt is in trouble."

"So," Damian spread his arms through the air. "Is this everything?"

Grace Moore looked around her bedroom and nodded slowly.

"Yeah it's everything, everything that I own."

"Why is that?" Damian asked.

"Well, a really sleazy boyfriend for one. He cleaned me out, and took everything. Not just the things that we bought together, but everything. My pictures, my elephant figurines, my college degree, even my toothbrush. What kind of sick bastard steals your toothbrush?"

"Just recently?" he asked.

Grace Moore dropped her head into her hands and nodded. "Recent enough, that and some really terrible investment advice, and well, voila."

Damian walked over to the bed where she sat and kneeled down in front of her. He caressed her head gently, which caused her to look up.

"Jonel, I'm your friend now. Don't ever worry about anyone stealing from you or hurting you like that again."

"Oh, you're going to protect me now, Mr. Damian Reigns?" Agent Moore asked as she let out a slight grin.

"Of course."

"And just how do you intend to do that? Are you going to throw your pocket square, briefcases, and fountain pens at all those nasty guys that are out there?"

Damian laughed, and caressed the side of her face. "If I have to. But I'd rather use my head. First things first: I'm going to make a phone call and I'm going to have you moved into a high-rise, with gates, armed guards, and cameras everywhere. Right after that call, I'm going to take you shopping, and we are going to purchase all new furnishings

58

for your apartment and a new fall and winter wardrobe for you."

"Damian...I..."

"Then, I am going to go over your finances. We are going to redo all of your investments, we're going to look into some promising new IRAs and some pretty solid blue chips which I think are on the verge of some tremendous growth."

"Damian, I..."

"Trust me Jonel. I know that I told you that I had an MBA in business management, but I also have one in economics and finance. I know what I'm doing."

"Damian, I don't know what to say. I..."

"Don't say anything. Or better yet, just say that you'll be ready to leave after I make the phone call."

North Star Mall

"**S**o, when did you get your degree in finance?" Grace asked.

Damian swung her hand through the air as they strolled through the mall like two teenagers in love.

"I got my MBA in finance first. I went to the University of Pennsylvania's Wharton School, then I went to Harvard. You seem like a very quick study, and you seem to have a great interest in the world of finance. Why don't you go to B-school?"

"Me?" Grace shook her head emphatically. "No, I'm through with school for now. Besides, I'm so rusty."

"I could help you study for the GMAT. It's not as hard as they make it out to be. I could definitely help you pass it so that you could get into a good business school."

"Thanks, but not right now. Later, maybe, but not right now...." Grace Moore's eyes flew wide open when they turned the corner, and she spotted the elegant white Lexus sitting in the middle of the floor. "Look, a raffle!"

She pulled Damian at full steam toward the car, and

immediately started filling out entry forms. She turned, and looked over her shoulder at him.

"If I could win something like this!"

Damian peered through the windows of the car and smiled. "It looks real nice," he told her.

"Nice? Nice? Are you insane? Do you know what a car like this does for a girl's personality? It is definitely a pick-me-up!"

"You like this, huh?" Damian asked, as he removed his tiny cell phone from his coat pocket.

"Like it, I'd go crazy over it. Everything but the color."

"What color do you like?" Damian asked, punching digits into his phone.

"Burgundy, with a white interior, of course."

"Yes, Jacqueline, this is Mr. Reigns. Call Lloyd over at Lexus of San Antonio, and have him deliver a fully loaded, LS 430 to Ms. Jonel McNeal at the Towers over San Antonio. Yes, it's the address I gave you earlier. Yes, wonderful. Ah, I believe she wanted it in burgundy with a white interior. Yes, yes, charge my black card. Okay, thanks Jackie; you're a doll."

Agent Grace Moore had frozen in place when she heard Damian speak into his cell phone. The hairs on the back of her neck stood at attention when she realized that he was having his secretary order a car for her. Even now, the lumps remained in her throat as she turned to face him.

"Damian, you can't....I can't...."

He grabbed her arm and led her into a nearby store.

"We've purchased your furniture, we've purchased your wardrobe, we've had your hair and nails done, but we've forgotten one of the most important things, a jacket."

Grace Moore turned and examined her surroundings, and then quickly backed toward her benefactor.

"No!"

"What are you talking about now?" Damian asked. He flashed the quick, innocent grin that she was quickly becoming accustomed to.

"Damian, this is Lillian's. This is a furrier—one of the most expensive furriers in the world. No!"

"You need a coat!" he insisted. "How about this one?"

Damian walked over to a full length fur coat that the store had on display. Grace shook her head.

"No."

"It's nice, isn't it?"

"Yes."

"Come and try it on."

Hesitantly, Grace walked over to where Damian stood with the coat. She allowed him to place it on her, and she quickly became lost inside it.

"Hmmm," she purred. "Feels like heaven."

"You want it?"

"No," she answered firmly. Grace held up her wrist and examined the price tag. "Oh my God! They....they....they put too many damn zeros on this thing!"

Damian looked at the price tag, and then let out a slight laugh. "Do you want it?"

"Damian, no! Take this thing off me. This is a seventy-five-thousand-dollar Russian sable. No!"

Damian helped her remove the coat, and then grabbed another.

"How about this one?"

Playing it smart now, Grace reached for the price tag before allowing herself to try the coat on. It wouldn't do any good to torture herself.

"Damian, lets go!" she told him.

"What's the matter?"

"This is a sixty-thousand-dollar Russian lynx. If you insist on buying me a coat, we can go right down the hall to Dillards or Foleys or Nordstroms."

"I want to buy you a coat right now. This store is close to the exit, and I don't feel like walking all the way back down the hall to Dillards or Foleys or Nordstroms. I'm getting old you know," and again, the smile came.

"Damian, I will not allow you to buy me a coat that costs the price of someone's home!"

"Okay, deal! I will not buy you one of these coats."

Damian turned toward the white, middle-aged, impeccably dressed saleswoman. She jumped at his beckoning.

"Yes, Mr. Reigns?"

"Dorothy, she refuses to allow me to buy her one of these coats. Therefore, we'll buy them both."

"Yes, sir, Mr. Reigns."

Chapter Nine

Princess strode across the Italian travertine marble floors of her four-story, Mediterranean style palazzo, clicking her Manolo Blahnik heels with each confident step. She ventured past her two-story, French double doors and into her backyard paradise, where she headed for her large, white, Victorian-style gazebo. The meeting was to be on her territory today.

Princess' multi-million dollar estate sat just on the edge of Palm Beach County, nestled between the old-world enclaves of Palm Beach and Boca Raton. It was a twenty-acre, horticulturist paradise. Azaleas, daffodils, roses, pennyroyals, and numerous other blossoms burst with color and scent, creating a sweet, aromatic, and visual paradise.

Today's meeting would take place beneath the pavilion, near the azalea garden. It would give the commission members a chance to take in the fresh ocean breezes, the abundant floral fragrance wafting off her numerous flower gardens, and the gentle rays from today's beautiful sun. It was truly a wonderful day for a meeting. Not a cloud inhabited the soft, baby blue sky, and yet the southern Florida temperatures were not expected to rise above the seventies.

Princess lifted her hand to her white St. John blouse and smoothed the fabric out as if she were posing next to Marie Gray herself. Her guests were already beginning to arrive, and she wanted to look her absolute best. Two white suited servants carried a large, sterling silver tray of Escargot à la Bourguignonne into the garden. They were followed by another set of servants carrying a large, sterling silver tray filled with various French cheeses.

Princess waved her hand toward a large, elaborate buffet table off to her left.

"Set the trays down next to the scampi," she ordered. She extended her hand and gripped the elbow of another white clad servant who was leading a group of similarly dressed gentlemen to a second table. "What is that?"

The group of sommeliers stopped and stared at each other.

"It's Chablis, mademoiselle," one of the wine porters answered nervously.

"Chablis?" Princess waved her finely manicured hand through the air, dismissing the porters. "We're having shrimp, which is a shelled fish, you imbeciles. Take the Chablis away, and bring several bottles of Pinot and Riesling."

The porters bowed and retreated back into the residence. Princess exhaled loudly, adjusted her oversize St. John hat, and walked to the nearby pavilion, where she seated herself in a large, white, lace wicker chair. Soon, she spied her husband, Marcus, leading her guests down the stone pathway, through the gardens, toward the pavilion. She had finally found something he could do.

"Señorita Reigns!" Don Ferdinand greeted her cheerfully.

Princess rose.

Don Ferdinand clasped her soft, mocha-colored hand and slowly brought it to his lips, where he kissed it gently. "Hola, Señorita Reigns. ¿Como esta?"

"Bien, gracias, Don Ferdinand," she responded with a slight bow and a polite smile. "Y tu?"

"Marvelous!"

Don Alemendez of Florida smiled politely. Officially,

64

Princess was one of his regional chiefs and his underboss for strategy and tactics. Her portfolio included running the affluent Palm Beach County area. Unofficially, however, she controlled the area from Palm Beach County all the way up north to Jacksonville, and was constantly expanding and making war against the Don and his other underbosses and regional chiefs. Unofficially, he hated her and wanted her dead.

"Señorita Reigns," Don Alemendez greeted her with a smile. He leaned forward and kissed her hand politely.

Princess bowed her head slightly. "Don Alemendez, how wonderful to see you. You're looking well." *Unfortunately,* she thought to herself.

Princess waved her hand toward the group of sofas and chairs arrayed throughout the pavilion. "Gentlemen, please make yourselves at home. I thought it wise that we conduct business first and then we'll enjoy ourselves."

Don Frederico seated himself on the wicker couch next to Princess' chair. Although fifty-five years of age and suffering from a variety of physical ailments, he still loved to be in the company of beautiful women. He smiled at Princess, flashing his crooked, brown teeth.

René Tibbideaux seated himself on the wicker couch, next to Don Frederico. He used the Don as a buffer between himself and Princess, the woman he despised more than anything on the planet. It had been his territory that Princess had conquered first, during her reign at the head of the Reigns organization, and it was Princess who had killed his older brother. René feared that if he seated himself too close to her, he would be tempted to reach out and choke the life out of her.

Chacho Hernandez of New Mexico seated himself on another sofa across from Don Frederico and René Tibbideaux. He too was no fan of Princess Reigns. She had taken over large swaths of his territory as well. In fact, she had managed to extend her reach all the way into Santa Fe before she was finally ousted from the commission. In New Mexico, Princess Reigns had followed a scorched earth, take-no-prisoners policy. Chacho still had bad memories to go along with the bad taste she had left in his mouth.

Raphael Guzman of Oklahoma seated himself next to Chacho Hernandez. He hated Chacho, but he despised Princess even more. She had utterly humiliated him during her time at the head of the Reigns family, and had obliterated his entire army. Adding insult to injury, she had elected to make him not the underboss for the state of Oklahoma, not a regional chief for one of the state's major subsections, and not even an area chief for one of the major cities. She made him the area boss of Muskogee.

Barry Groomes seated himself in a chair as far away from Princess as possible. He knew for a fact that he would ring her scrawny little neck if he got close enough to her. One of Princess' Irish lover's car bombs had taken his pregnant wife, seven-year-old daughter, and three-year-old son away from him. He would avenge them if it was the last thing he did. Fuck business, it *was* personal.

Julian Jones of Mississippi squeezed onto a sofa near Princess. Julian had been far enough away from her during her reign to be safe from her aggressive expansion. He was one of the few men in the group who didn't hate her. In fact, the opposite was true: he wanted to love her. He wanted to *make* love to her. Julian had often wondered how far he could rise with a woman like Princess by his side. He thought that they could own the world. It puzzled him how a woman like Princess could get tangled up with such an un-ambitious, simpleton husband like Marcus, especially when a handsome, young, African warrior like himself was available. Princess needed a lion, not another butler. She needed someone who could conquer her jungle and tame her. Julian walked his eyes up Marcus' frame and scoffed haughtily at him.

Emil Douglas of Georgia seated himself next to Don

Alemendez, on another one of the wicker sofas. He, unlike the others, had no idea what this meeting was about. The fact that neither Dante nor Damian was present, and Princess was, made him nervous.

Don Ferdinand seated himself on one of the large, overstuffed, wicker chairs. He coughed, signaling that he was ready to bring the meeting to order. Princess lifted her hand into the air, and waved away her group of servants. Her husband retreated back into the house along with the white-clad workers. Julian Jones laughed quietly.

"We called this meeting to discuss some very serious issues," Don Ferdinand told the assembled group. "Although all of the members of the commission are not present, I have spoken with the others, and they have assured me that they would support whatever decision we make today."

Emil lifted his palms into the air, turning them skyward. "Wait a minute; where's Damian?"

Princess frowned and rolled her eyes. She had known that Damian's mirror, Emil, would be a pain-in-the-ass today, but she hadn't anticipated it would come this quickly.

"It is not necessary for Damian to be here today," Don Alemendez told him. In fact, the reason we have convened today is to decide whether Damian should continue his association with this commission," Don Ferdinand added.

"What?" Emil asked loudly. He turned toward the only other African American in the group for support, but Julian was too busy smiling and winking at Princess to notice anything other than her print exposed from her St. John pants.

"Emil, it is no secret what Damian is planning to do in the next couple of years," Don Frederico told him. "He is going to pull the Reigns family out of the business. He is separating his books as we speak, and in the next few years, he will announce that he is retiring from the commission."

"So?" Emil protested. "This is not a lifetime contract. None of us want to do this until we die."

"That depends, monsieur, on how soon one dies," René Tibbideaux told him with a smile.

The commission members arrayed around the pavilion laughed.

"The Reigns family's departure will leave a vacuum, and potentially expose our operations," Don Ferdinand observed. He leaned forward. "Emil, in case you have forgotten, Texas is responsible for seventy percent of the commission's commodities. We lose Texas and the commission is through."

Don Frederico crossed his legs, interlaced his fingers, and reclined back on the sofa. "Not to mention the fact that if Damian pulls out, we lose more than just a secure border area, we also lose his distribution capabilities. Does anyone care to venture a guess as to how long it would take to replace those capabilities?"

Whistles flew throughout the pavilion. Barry Groomes of Arkansas leaned forward and frowned. "Let me get this straight," he told them in his deep, southern drawl. "You are suggesting that we remove Damian and replace him with Princess?" Barry shook his head, sending his long curly red hair all over his face.

"Have you people forgotten that we took away Princess' seat on the commission and gave it to her brother? Have you people forgotten why? I will not support such a move!"

"What of our territories?" Raphael Guzman shouted. "She's a warmonger! She'll immediately begin attacking us again!"

Don Ferdinand lifted his hands and silenced the murmuring of the commission members. "That was then, this is now. Times are different. People are older, wiser, and more mature now. Let us hear from Princess."

Princess rubbed her hand over her white pants, smoothing out the fabric and drying her now moist palms. "I sincerely regret some of the actions that I've taken in the past. I was younger then, and foolish. This time, however, things will be different. There will be no more war, just peace and cooperation."

"Empty words from a puta!" Chacho Hernandez shouted. He turned and spat on the ground.

Princess shook her head. "They are not empty words, Chacho. I won't attack."

"Why should we believe you?" Raphael asked.

Princess lifted her hands. "Look, here's the deal. Damian is going to pull out and leave you all shit-out-of-luck. As we all know, when a commission member is attacked by someone outside of the circle, we all join together and attack back. If you lose Texas, this commission loses close to fifty percent of its strength. You'll be sitting ducks without a powerful, unified Texas. I am going to give you that, and I'm going to give you a reliable distribution chain *and* I'm going to pull all of my family's remaining soldiers out of your territories. I am going to leave Florida, and, as insurance against future aggression, I am going to send my husband Marcus to work for Don Alemendez. If I make a wrong move, Don Alemendez has my husband."

"Actions speak louder than words," Raphael Guzman told her.

"And why are we to believe that you give a shit about your husband?" René Tibbideaux asked her.

"Then we shall send Marcus to work for Raphael," Don Alemendez told the commission members. "And if Princess attacks, Raphael can deal with Marcus."

Don Alemendez desperately wanted this deal to go through. He would be able to rid himself of Princess and concentrate on unifying his unruly territory. A unified Florida, with its own adequate supply and distribution channel through the Keys was something that he desperately wanted to give to his sons.

Señor Frederico interlaced his beefy fingers and rested them on top of his large paunch. "And remember, you will all get your territories back from the Reigns family once Princess is in charge. This change will mean significantly greater profits for all of you."

The profit word commanded the commission members' full attention. Their unquenchable thirst for power was only overshadowed by their insatiable greed.

"North Carolina, South Carolina, Tennessee, Alabama, and Virginia are all in favor of it" Don Ferdinand informed them.

"Of course they are! None of them would share a common border with this woman," Raphael sneered.

Don Ferdinand turned to Julian Jones, whom he knew would be in favor of giving the Reigns seat on the commission back to Princess.

"Julian, what do you think?"

Julian smiled at Princess and ran his hand over his short, wavy hair. "I think that bringing Princess back into the commission is a wonderful idea."

"I concur," Don Alemendez told them.

Don Ferdinand tuned to René Tibbideaux, "René?"

René lifted his hand to his long Parisian styled mustache and twirled it. He shifted his face to the ground for several moments before returning it to Princess. "And you will remove all of your men from my territory?"

Princess nodded.

René exhaled and then turned to Don Ferdinand, "Oui, monsieur, bring her back."

Don Ferdinand turned to Raphael.

Raphael stared at Princess, "And you will reduce your army?"

Princess closed her eyes and nodded solemnly.

Raphael turned to Don Ferdinand, "Si."

Emil Douglas stood, "No! I will not stand for this! Damian has been loyal to the commission. He has brought peace and stability to our organization. Is this how we repay loyalty?"

Princess snorted, "For crying out loud, Emil. Grow up!"

Chacho Hernandez spat on the ground and affixed

Princess with his fierce black eyes, "Mi madre always told me that if a perra bites you once, don't stick your other hand out to her," Chacho shook his head, "No tres nada, puta."

"Gentlemen, Damian Reigns is putting our organization at risk," Don Alemendez told them. "If he pulls out, we lose Texas and our distribution capabilities."

"We can reshift our entrance points back to Florida!" Emil told them. "We can use Gulf Port, Savannah, and Hampton roads, as well as increase our operations in Arizona and New Mexico. These places aren't as good as Texas, but combined they'll make up for the loss."

"The dissent matters little at this point," Don Ferdinand announced. "The majority rules, Princess Reigns will replace her brother Damian Reigns as the head of our Texas territory."

Princess smiled and bowed her head slightly toward Don Ferdinand.

"This is crazy!" Emil shouted.

Don Alemendez smiled, "Emil, we are in America. Democracy has prevailed."

Several of the commission members laughed.

Princess lifted a sterling silver bell from a nearby table and rang it. "Gentlemen, please enjoy your selves."

White-coated servants streamed out of the mansion carrying food and wine, while a white suited orchestra began to set up on the lawn. The servants and orchestra members were followed by dozens of voluptuous, scantily clad young women.

Barry Groomes clapped his hands together, "Alright! Let's get this party started!" Two long-legged beauties quickly occupied his lap.

René Tibbideaux began stuffing his face with crab cakes.

"Have you people forgotten something?" Emil asked the partying commission members.

"What's that?" Don Alemendez asked, while rubbing his hand across the bottom of a tanned, toned, South Florida coed.

"Dante!" Emil shouted.

Don Frederico smiled and stuffed several jumbo shrimps inside of his mouth, "Don't worry about Dante. Let me handle him."

Chapter Ten

Dante waved his hands through the air, guiding the steel beam into place. When finished, he pushed back the powder blue hard hat that rested on his head and lifted his Motorola two-way communicator to his mouth.

"Hey, Bart, swing her over to the right a little more. And watch out for Charlie and his crane."

Getting out of the office and being with the guys was something that Dante loved. He had always had a fascination with building and construction for as far back as he could remember. It wasn't so much that he loved the physical work as he was simply mesmerized by the tools involved. From hand-held drills to massive cranes and bulldozers, it all fascinated him. Damian could have his high-dollar business jets and fancy Italian sports cars, but Dante would settle for a wrecking ball and bulldozer any day.

Dante unlatched his safety belt and walked across the massive, red-iron beam that constituted part of the seventieth floor of the eighty-story office tower that Reigns Enterprises was currently constructing. The black-glass office tower, would eventually house the Reigns family's latest venture, Energia, a global oil exploration corporation.

"Hey, Boss, how about those Spurs last night?" Charlie asked over his two-way radio.

Dante smiled and lifted his radio to his lips, "Sorry Charlie, maybe next year your T-wolves will do better."

"Next year?" Charlie shouted into his radio. "Hell, this is our year!"

Dante lifted his head toward Charlie's eightieth floor crane, and placed his hand over his eyes to shield the sun's bright rays. He smiled and shook his head, "Not as long as we have Little Timmy."

Charlie laughed and keyed his two-way radio twice, signing off. Dante turned and walked to where members of his seventieth story crew had assembled and were trying to maneuver a massive, crane-hoisted, red iron beam into place by hand. He joined in.

"Bring the beam left," he said loudly, as they grunted and struggled to maneuver the iron into place. "We need to stand this one up. This beam is for an up weld."

Dante turned to the crane operator, and lifted his thumb up into the air, indicating that the beam needed to be brought into an upright position. The crane operator obliged.

Jeff, another one of the construction workers, tapped Dante on the shoulder and pointed off into the distance. "Is the boss coming for a visit today?"

Dante turned and squinted in the direction in which Jeff was pointing. Again he pushed his hat back on his head, and this time, wiped away the thick beads of perspiration that had aMassed on his forehead, "Not that I know of."

The helicopter continued to get close to the work site.

Dante squinted and followed the helicopter. The sun's bright rays were playing havoc on everyone's vision today.

"It's not one of ours, it's too small," Dante told them. "It looks like a bell or something, probably just some local newbies."

The small, white, Bell Textron Helicopter turned and headed around a nearby skyscraper, where it disappeared.

Jeff pushed his hardhat back on his head, "They've dipped below the hard line, and are winding their way in between the buildings. That pilot must want to lose his license or something."

Dante nodded, "It's the newbies; they'll do anything for a story."

The Bell helicopter darted around a nearby skyscraper and slid in sideways. Dante and his men quickly grabbed onto anything that was bolted down. The rotor-wash from the helicopter's blades threatened to sweep them off the building.

"Fucking idiots!" Jeff shouted. He and several of the workers began to wave their hands through the air, shooing the helicopter away.

Andy, one of the construction foremen, grabbed a bullhorn. "Hey! You in the helicopter! Your rotor-wash is endangering my men! You are too close! Get out of here, before we report you to the FAA!"

The door on the right side of the small helicopter swung open, and a rifle with a telescopic sight came out.

"It's a hit!" Dante shouted. He buckled his safety harness to one of the cables connected to the safety system strung throughout the eighty story structure, released the iron beam to which he had been clinging, and ran for his life.

The M-16 assault rifle in the helicopter opened up. Sparks flew off the steel girders as the 7.62 millimeter bullets struck. Joel was the first one to fall. The bullet struck him high in his chest, causing him to fly backwards off the steel structure. His body dangled between the sixtieth and fifty-ninth floors, where his safety cable stopped him.

"God dammit, Princess!" Dante shouted. He climbed onto a set of steel spikes imbedded into one of the side girders, and quickly began to descend. He felt his only chance at survival was to make it to the ground. Other than that, he'd be a sitting duck like the rest of his men. Jeff's bullet riddled body flew past him, on its way to the ground some seventy feet below.

The helicopter swung around the building as the gunman tried to get a better aim at the running, ducking, and hiding workers. Dante jumped back onto one of the beams and hid behind a girder as the small chopper flew past him. Sparks popped off of the girder he was hiding behind as the gunman continued to spray the building.

Dante's mind raced. The fact that the helicopter had not keyed in on him told Dante that the hit man could not differentiate him from the workers. He was wasting his time by taking out everyone on and around the seventieth floor. Additionally, the fact that the gunmen knew in advance that Dante would be here today working on this particular floor told him that they had a source inside of his organization as well as someone inside a nearby building watching him, which building, he would never know. But whoever it was had definitely lost track of him once the shooting started. For that, he was grateful. But still, the fact that this was a professional hit meant only that Princess was behind the attempt. And if that was the case, it meant that the shooter wasn't going to stop until everything within a ten-floor radius was dead. Climbing down those spikes would be useless. He wouldn't make it past the sixty-fifth floor. He needed something faster. He needed the lift.

Dante turned and eyeballed the elevator that ran through the center of the building. It had been mounted where the permanent elevators would be. He ran for it.

On his way to the elevator lift, Dante was tripped by a big, beefy hand.

"Uh, uh sweet cakes, where do you think you're going? That elevator will just get you killed."

Dante rolled over from his face down position on the landing, turning toward the voice he recognized. She smiled at him.

"Nice day for this shit, huh?" she asked, with her crooked, toothless smile.

It was Anne Maddox, one of his site supervisors.

Anne was a big, bulky, white woman from Nashville, Tennessee. She could out drink, out curse, and even out lift most of the men working for Reigns Enterprises. And by some inexplicable miracle, she could also piss farther. It was rumored that Anne had lost her front teeth in a bar brawl in Georgia, although she denied it. Others say that she lost them while working the oil fields of west Texas. Anne had told them she lost them in a pick up football game at the trailer she had lived in while doing railroad construction work in Arkansas.

Dante knew her, he'd put his money on the bar fight rumor. "Yeah, it is a nice day to die," Dante told her.

"Or kill the sons-a-bitches in that helicopter!"

Dante smiled, "That's who I was talking about. I know you didn't think that I'd be the one doing the dying."

Anne laughed. She scooted her massive, scared, pink body closer to Dante. "Well, whatever it is you got planned, you'd better hurry. I imagine they're running out of targets on the other floors just above us."

"Why do you say that?"

"Listen. The amount of time in between the gun fire is increasing."

She was right.

A loud thud struck the beam just behind Dante, causing him to duck. He turned quickly, only to see the body of one of his men hanging upside down. It was the body of Marti Jacobs, his on-site architect. Marti's eyes were still open, and blood ran down from the holes inside of his chest to his neck, and on to his face, where it dripped down to the ground.

"Fuck!" Dante banged at the plywood floor that made up the sixty-eighth floor landing where he was lying. Suddenly, the blades from the helicopter grew loud, and he looked up to see a smiling rifleman aiming in his direction.

"Anne! Look out!" Dante rose, and sprinted to an opening in the floor of the landing, where he dove through it. He landed hard on his feet on the sixty-fifth floor landing and rolled, sending pain shooting up his spine. He could hear

Anne cry out in pain amid the sound of bullets ricocheting off metal. Anne's bulky frame soon came crashing down onto the landing.

"Anne!" Dante scrambled toward her bloody body. His back felt as though it were on fire. "Anne!" He took her hand into his.

Anne Maddox opened her big, bulging, frog-like eyes and smiled at her boss. Blood ran down from the corner of her mouth, down her fat rotund cheek.

"Dante..."

"I'm here Anne, I'm here..."

"Dante..."

"Anne I'm still here. Don't talk, just try to hang on."

"Dante... Kill those sons-a-bitches..." Anne Maddox' head fell to the side, and she closed her eyes.

Dante lowered her hand to her chest and gently released it. It was then when he heard his radio crackle.

"Son-of-a-bitch!"

He pounded his fist into the palm of his hand. "The crane!" He had forgotten about the crane. He quickly grabbed his two-way and keyed the talk button. "Charlie, are you there?"

No one answered.

"Charlie, this is Dante, are you there?"

There was still no answer.

"God dammit, Charlie, answer me. I know you're there, your stupid ass accidentally keyed the radio!"

"What?" Charlie screamed into his radio.

"Where in the fuck are you?"

"I'm in Kansas right now playing with Dorothy and Toto!"

"Charlie!"

"Okay, I wish I was in Kansas. I'm hiding like a scared bitch inside the crane."

Dante smiled. "Alright, Charlie, listen to me. The guys in the chopper brought plenty of ammo. The motherfuckers haven't stopped shooting yet. That means one thing, they are going to kill us all, Charlie, unless you and me do something about it."

"Okay, Boss, first of all, I have a crane. Not an Apache Attack Helicopter, not an F-16 Fighter Jet, but a fucking crane! Second of all, there is nothing here to fight back with. And finally, but most important of all, you said *we*. You don't pay me enough to be no fucking hero!"

"Charlie, Anne's dead."

"Boss, that's terrible. I feel bad for Anne, and I feel bad for her family. I'm going to let them know that when I go to her funeral."

"Charlie, Anne's dead, and so is Marti, and so is Joel, and Danny, and Jeff, and probably most of the others. You and I will be joining them if we don't do something! And if we don't do something and you and I manage to survive this thing, you'll be dead. Do you understand me?"

"Do what?"

"I have a plan. Is that beam still attached to that cable on your box?"

"Affirmative."

"I'm going to lure the helicopter over toward your box. When it gets close enough, you swing that son-of-a-bitch over, and you drop it on that motherfucker. Do you hear me?"

Charlie keyed the mike twice on his two-way, signaling affirmative. Dante rose, he would have to make it to the other side of the building, and get the helicopter to swing around the building and chase him. The trick to doing it was to still be alive once the helicopter swung around the building after him. He'd just have to avoid the ten-rounds-per-second spray that the machine gun would send his way.

His back was still killing him from the fall he took earlier, but he'd rather put up with an aching back than a bleeding heart, a punctured lung, a ruptured spleen, and maybe a ventilation system in the top of his head. He could hear the helicopter making its way down to the sixty-fifth floor. It would be on him any second.

Dante walked to the center of the landing, lifted his arms into the air, and waved to the helicopter pilot. The pilot's eyes flew wide. Dante lifted his right hand into the air and shot the pilot his middle finger. The pilot frowned, turned, and shouted to his companion. He quickly angled the helicopter so that the gunman could get a clear shot. Dante ducked behind a steel beam.

Although the bullets could not penetrate the red-iron beams, one, or a few of them, could ricochet off of some of the metal, and strike him in any of a million places that would ruin his day. Besides, having hundreds of flying pieces of steel striking a narrow beam inches from his face was not something Dante particularly enjoyed. Sparks popped off the steel beam between Dante and the helicopter, sending tiny flames and pieces of metal filament around his closed eyes. The gunfire soon stopped. Dante knew what it meant. The frustrated pilot and gunmen had realized that they could not get him from the angle in which they were firing. He listened as the blades from the helicopter increased power in order to maneuver the craft around the building. They were going to try to slide in behind him and get off a good shot. He quickly ran and ducked behind another beam.

The helicopter slid into position just behind the spot where Dante had once been. He could see the frustrated pilot curse, and pound his hand. Now came the dangerous part. He had to fix the helicopter into one position long enough for Charlie to work his magic. Dante stepped from behind the beam in which he had been hiding. The pilot's eyes flew wide open.

"Be still, you son-of-a-bitch!" Dante told them through clenched teeth. "Charlie I hope you're paying attention."

The helicopter pilot wheeled his machine around, so that the gunner would be facing Dante. Dante waved at the gunman, and continued his approach toward the helicopter. His walking toward them had them puzzled. Didn't he know that he was going to die? They were stunned into inaction. Dante smiled when he heard the crane moving.

The rotor-wash from the helicopter's blades threatened to sweep Dante off the building. But still, he forced himself to keep walking toward the small helicopter. He could hear the whistling of the crane's steel cable, as the red-iron beam free fell toward the chopper. It was then that he realized the plan was flawed.

The beam was a multi-ton piece of steel. When it struck the small helicopter, it would not send it plunging straight into the ground as Dante had thought. Instead, it would cause the helicopter to explode with the force of a train hitting an eighteen wheeler full of gasoline. The helicopter would detonate, and pieces of the blades would fly throughout the building, slicing up anything in their path. They all saw the shadow of the beam, just before its impact.

"Fuck!" Dante turned, and sprinted for the center of the building. This time, he was not aiming for another landing; he wanted to fall through a couple of floors. "I hope this fucking safety harness shit works!"

Dante leaped through the center of the building, just as the massive steel beam struck the small helicopter. The explosion from the collision sounded as if a bolt of lightening had stuck a tree just outside of his window, but even louder, and more violent. Fire, fiberglass, and burning, twisted pieces of aluminum and titanium shot through the area.

"Whoopee!" Dante shouted, and broke out into laughter, as his safety harness began to slow his descent. He came to a soft stop just between the fiftieth and forty-ninth stories. "Charlie, I love you!"

Hanging in the center of the skeletal structure, some fifty odd stories above the ground, Dante laughed and swayed with the breeze. He grabbed his radio and lifted it to his lips. "Charlie, are you there?"

"Yeah, Boss."

"Tomorrow, I'm going to make a call to the T-wolves' front

81

office."

"What, are you treating me to a game, Boss?"

"Charlie, I'm going to buy you the fucking T-wolves."

Chapter Eleven

Damian took Grace's hand into his as they strolled down along the edge of the football field. When the kids on the sideline recognized him, he was surrounded.

"Mr. Reigns!"

"Mr. Reigns!"

Damian lifted his hands, "Whoa, slow down. One at a time, now. What's up?"

One of the kids raised his hand. Damian pointed at him.

"What's up, Timothy?"

Timothy stepped forward, pushing his way through the crowd.

"Mr. Reigns, we just want to say thanks for the new uniforms!"

"Yeah! Thanks, Mr. Reigns," several of the kids shouted in unison.

"Hey, it was my pleasure. We've got to look good when we make it to the city championships!"

The kids broke into cheers.

Another one of the Pee Wee football players raised his hand.

"What's up, Ernie?" Damian asked.

The empty spaces where Ernie's two front teeth should have been, caused him to speak with a lisp.

"Mr. Reigns, do you really think that we can beat Shaint Matthewsh?"

"Of course you can!"

"But they've won three years in a row!"

83

"Yeah!" the group concurred.

Damian lifted his hands and calmed them. "Guys, you can beat them."

Another little one pushed and shoved his way to the front. He turned and faced the group. "You guys are afraid of St. Matt's and we haven't even gotten to them yet. We still have to play St. Luke's."

Groans went through the crowd.

Damian kneeled down on one knee and gathered in the purple and white clad youngsters.

"Look guys, this is St. Vincent's year. Don't worry about those other teams. We just have to play the best we can. If we do that, then we'll beat everybody."

Ernie turned and pointed to the opposite side of the field.

"But look at them. They're some big bitches."

"Ernie, you aren't supposed to use that kind of language!" Damian said throwing his head back and laughing with the kids.

Grace couldn't help but laugh with them.

"Hey guys, don't worry about how big they are. They're just St. Luke's Lions. But us, we're the St. Vincent Vikings! And you know what?" Damian asked standing up. "A Viking can beat a Lion any day! Come on guys, when I count to three, we'll all yell 'Vikings!' Are you ready?"

Nods went through the crowd.

"One, two, three!"

"VIKINGS!"

"Who are we?"

"VIKINGS!"

"Who's going to win?"

"VIKINGS!"

"Who's the best?"

"VIKINGS!"

"Let's get 'em!"

"Yeah!"

The crowd of purple and white uniformed youngsters

took off and charged the field. Damian looked up in time to see a slim, tanned, white-aired priest approaching. A smile spread across Damian's face and he extended his arms.

"Father O'Connell!"

The priest wrapped his arms around Damian and hugged him tightly. "Damian! It's good to see you." Father O'Connell released Damian, leaned back, and stared at him. "Let's see, I haven't seen you in a month of Sundays or Saturdays or Fridays or Wednesdays or any of the other days of the week for that matter. What, are we boycotting Mass or something?"

Damian laughed. "Never that, Father, I have bad memories." Damian lifted his hand to his earlobe, and began rubbing it.

Father O'Connell laughed with him. He turned to Grace. "Did he tell you about that? Well, if he did, he exaggerated. I only dragged him to Mass by the ear twice. And it wasn't snowing outside, and it was only for half a mile. The story seems to grow every year. I've heard your stories of ten miles and in a freezing blizzard," Father O'Connell joked.

"Father, please excuse my manners." Damian waved his hand toward Grace. "Father, this is Jonel McNeal. Jonel, this is Father O'Connell."

Grace extended her hand and Father O'Connell shook it firmly.

"Father O'Connell taught calculus and chemistry at my old high school. He is also my mentor. Without him, I'd be dead or in prison or in the streets somewhere."

"Aw shucks, you know I was getting on you about Mass, and so you throw me a compliment to butter me up. It won't work," Father O'Connell winked at Grace, and then leaned in close to Damian. "I see your brother Dajon, and his lovely family at Mass twice a week. I see Princess and Marcus at Mass every Saturday. I want to see you and Dante at Mass this coming week, or else. And this time Damian, it will be several miles, and it just may be in a hurricane or tornado or blizzard. I still have my super secret ear grip, ya' know."

Damian laughed, "I will be there, Father."

Father O'Connell patted Damian on his shoulder, "Tell your mother and father that I said hello. And tell her that I said thanks again for the wonderful cake she gave me after Mass last Friday. It was delicious." He turned toward Grace, "It was nice meeting you."

"Likewise."

"Well, I have a team to cheer for," Father O'Connell told them as he stalked off.

Damian took Grace's hand and led her into the stands. They seated themselves at midfield, halfway up the old, wooden, green-painted bleachers. Grace turned to Damian and smiled.

"I've never been to a Pee Wee football game before."

"Never?" Damian asked in mock astonishment.

Grace shook her head, "No, never."

"Aw man, Jonel, you should have warned me."

"Warned you about what?" She sat on the edge of her seat.

"Warned me that you have never been to one of these Pee Wee football games. Trust me it's not for the faint of heart."

"Damian, stop being silly," Grace slapped him across the arm.

"No, seriously, Pee Wee football is one of the most violent, grotesque, graphic, sexually explicit sports that you could ever imagine."

"Yeah, right."

"No, seriously, watch," Damian pointed. "See that fat lady down there in the front row?"

Grace's eyes walked across the front row, "Which one?"

"My point exactly!" Damian smiled. "Those cows down there are Pee Wee football mothers. They're not petite, polite, dainty suburban soccer moms, Jonel. They are violent. I once saw a referee make a questionable call, and he got trampled. They had to call in a back hoe and dig around him just to free him from the field."

Grace laughed and rested her head against Damian's shoulder.

"And the men, oh my goodness, the men! They are Pee Wee football dads. They are a special breed of human beings. They are pot-bellied, Monday-morning quarterbacks who wear super tight T-shirts that ride up over their stomachs when they stand up and cheer. I mean it's the most disgusting thing you ever want to see in your life!"

Grace clapped her hands together and laughed. She pointed at Damian's stomach, "Be careful, that's how you'll be looking in ten years."

"Never!" Damian shook his head. "Not in a million years!"

"I'm sure that's what they said."

"And you, are you going to look like a Pee Wee football mom, or a soccer mom?"

"Hmm... I don't know. How does a Little League baseball mom look?"

Damian shook his head and looked down. "The worst of all, they're mutts. They're a cross between football moms and soccer moms."

"How is that?" Grace asked, propping her elbows on her knees and resting her chin on her tiny, tightly balled fist.

"Well, Little League moms are not as fat as Pee Wee moms, but they're not as skinny as soccer moms. However, they are the wildest, raunchiest of the bunch. Their language would make a sailor blush. Another thing you have to remember is that soccer moms operate in dens, football moms move in herds, but baseball moms operate in packs."

"I like that," Grace nodded. "I think I'll be a cross between a soccer mom and a baseball mom."

"There is no such breed!"

"Then I'll invent one. You sure are an authority on these things."

"Well, you sponsor enough of them, and you come to learn the distinctions."

"So, why do you sponsor them? What's the real reason?"

"I guess, to give back and to keep these kids from running the streets and getting involved in negative activities. You give them positive groups to belong to, and it fulfills their need to belong. It prevents them from fulfilling that need by joining negative groups, like gangs."

Grace nodded, and turned her head toward the football field. "It helps the families too," Damian told her. "It gives them something to cheer, something to focus on, and it takes their minds off of their bills, their jobs. It brings them all closer together as a family, too. Plus, Father O'Connell would pull my ear off if I did anything less."

Grace laughed. She turned toward him, "So, you buy all of their uniforms?"

Damian nodded, "I buy all of the uniforms for the majority of the teams in the league. Other private sponsors buy the rest. Thirty-two teams, sixteen teams per conference, four teams per division. The teams get to play for their division, then their conference title, and finally, the city championship. The winning team and their families, get to go to Disney, on me of course."

"Wow!"

"Same thing for the soccer league, the basketball league, ditto for the baseball league. Father O'Connell has one heck of an ear twister on his wrist."

Grace laughed again.

Damian examined his surroundings and then turned his attention toward the sky, "It's beautiful out here today."

Grace nodded, "I agree. One thing I've noticed about this city, it has some beautiful days."

Damian stood suddenly, and began to clap.

"Go, Ernie! Run! Run, run, run!" Damian jumped up and down in the bleachers. "Touch down! Yeah, Ernie!"

Grace laughed and clapped as she watched a tiny, fully padded little boy do the dirty bird in the end zone. Damian sat back down next to Grace.

"Did you see him?" he asked proudly. "That kid is a future pro-bowler, just watch," Damian said as he stared at Grace. "I went to school with his mother. She had Ernie when she was a junior in high school."

"Oh really? Wow, that must have been hard."

"It was for me because I liked her so much. Ernie's not really mine, but I've always helped to take care of him. I used to give her my lunch money to help out."

"That was sweet!" Grace placed her arm around Damian.

"Yeah, but some days I really wanted those hamburgers, or that pizza."

Grace laughed heartily, "Well, now you know what it's like to be a parent. Parents sometimes have to make sacrifices for their children."

"Yeah, I didn't know it then, but Ernie would become my full responsibility. I pay for him to go to St. Vincent's Boarding School, I give him money, pay all of his bills, buy him clothes and stuff. I take him on vacation with me every summer, after summer camp is over. He's a great kid."

"Really?" Grace raked her hand through her hair, sending it over her shoulder, another Intelligence failure, a pleasant one, but a failure nonetheless. "Where's Ernie's mother?"

Damian peered out over the field.

"She's dead...she overdosed on crack cocaine two years ago."

Grace turned toward the field, and spotted a tiny Ernie smiling and waving at Damian. She felt her eyes moisten, and once again, she hated Damian.

Chapter Twelve

"**O**kay, what have you learned?" Special Agent Elizabeth Holmes asked, as she strode across the living room floor of the poshly decorated town house the bureau had provided for her. Her cover as Grace Moore's aunt called for decidedly better accommodations than that which her co-worker received. Besides, after forty plus years of government service, she always got what she asked for.

"Well, I haven't learned much about anything," Grace answered uneasily. "If he's dirty, he's definitely got it together. No bragging, no boasting, no showboating, no nothing. I haven't seen anything."

Special Agent Holmes stopped in front of a large, gilded, gold leaf mirror, where she ran her thin, well-manicured, diamond laden fingers across her tight, French roll hairdo. The wisp of gray twisting through her hair corresponded elegantly with the large Mikimoto pearls nestled within her diamond rings.

"You said, 'if' he's dirty?" she turned sharply and faced her fellow agent. "Damian Reigns is definitely dirty."

"Okay, he's dirty, but he's also extremely intelligent. Too intelligent for me to be able to waltz in there, smile at him, and have him lay bare his entire organization. It's going to take some time."

"Are you enjoying the Lexus?"

Grace froze. She knew that there was no way she would have been able to keep the car a secret, or even keep the car, for that matter. Well, maybe after they busted him and sent him away for a nice long time she could grab it at the private FBI auction. But that came later. The fact that the Bureau was watching her every move frightened her. She was supposed to be one of them, one of the good guys.

"He bought a car for me," Grace answered defensively. She turned and walked to the window, where she stared out at the nearby duck pond. "Isn't that what you wanted? Isn't that what the Bureau wants? You want me to get close to him right? You want me to bring him down?"

"The Bureau wants results. Not agents riding around in seventy thousand dollar cars, wearing eighty thousand dollar furs and ten thousand dollar suits and dresses."

"That's reserved only for you!" Grace spun around to face Elizabeth. "I'm sorry Elizabeth, am I stepping on your toes? The Bureau is only allowed one spoiled black woman at a time?"

"Agent Moore!"

"No, Elizabeth, how dare you follow me! This is supposed to be a deep cover assignment! No tails, no wires, no surveillance, just deep cover, with a rescue team on standby! Yet, you have been doing just the opposite. If the other shit works, then pull me out now!"

"Henry ordered surveillance; I didn't! So if you have complaints about it, talk to him."

"Why, Elizabeth?"

"Grace, we've lost several agents trying to penetrate this organization. The Reigns family is dangerous. Damian is extremely intelligent, extremely charming, extremely handsome, and extremely deadly. Don't let his manners fool you. Behind those thousand dollar suits and million dollar smiles lies a cold, heartless, soulless monster. He will devour you."

"I'm an agent of the United States Federal Bureau of

Investigation. I'm a professional. I know the risk. I knew the risk when I signed on in Washington, why now?"

Elizabeth Holmes exhaled loudly, and settled herself on the arm of the love seat.

"Why what now?"

"Why the change? Why the surveillance?"

"Grace, Henry and I have been around a long time, a very long time. You're a young woman, unmarried, uncommitted, un..."

"You think I'm going to fuck him?"

"Grace, the United States attorney doesn't want any taint in the case."

Agent Moore stumbled forward and seated herself on the sofa across from Elizabeth Holmes. She placed her hand over her heart and felt it beat several times, before she spoke again.

"Oh my God, you do think that I'm going to sleep with him, you do...."

"Grace, in this job, we are all under a tremendous amount of pressure. The stress, the decisions that have to be made on the fly, the...."

"I'm a Goddamn professional!" she screamed sounding like Jennifer Lopez.

"Professionals make mistakes too."

"Have you?" Grace asked her.

Elizabeth rose from the arm of the love seat, and walked to the window where Grace stood. She stared at the duck pond, and the deep, thick, pink clouds that loomed beyond.

"We've all made them," Elizabeth said in a tone that was barely audible.

"I said, have you?" Grace asked with force.

"Yes."

"Have you ever slept with a target?"

"Yes," Elizabeth lowered her head and turned her body in the direction of the sofa. "A long time ago, that is why I cannot let you make the same mistake."

Grace rose from the sofa and tried to close her mouth, which had fallen open upon Elizabeth's revelation.

"How did you... I mean... your job?"

Elizabeth smiled, and allowed herself a laugh as she thought of events past. "Times were different then. People were different. People listened, people understood."

"And Bureau policy?"

"Was whatever J. Edgar said it was!" Elizabeth walked slowly to the coffee table and poured herself a strong cup of rich, black coffee. "Sure they tried to hang me out to dry. They tried very hard. But there was this very young senator from Massachusetts who wouldn't let them. He listened, and he believed."

Grace Moore nodded and lowered her head. She had heard parts of this story before, as well as many others surrounding Elizabeth Holmes, and her friend, the young senator. It reminded Grace that she was in the presence of a living legend.

"Is he... is he why you later joined the secret service?"

"I was the first black female special agent of the FBI, and I later became the first black woman ever to join the Secret Service," Elizabeth declared, with lots of pride. "They were very trying times."

"Were you in Dallas?"

"I was."

Grace noticed the quiver in Elizabeth's lips when she answered that last question. She had heard stories of how that tragic event had affected members of the secret service until they drew their last breaths. It obviously had an affect on her fellow agent as well.

"Elizabeth, I..."

She was interrupted by the raising of Elizabeth's hand.

"Grace, I believe you. I believe in you. I believe in you because I believe in me. You are me forty years ago. I paved the way, but I paved it very roughly. It is now your road to smooth out. There are those who are still watching to see if

93

we belong on this side of the criminal justice system. There are those who feel that we cannot be trusted to enforce the law when it comes to our own people who break it. Grace, don't let their actions get you down. Just do the best job that you can do. The fact that they are watching you just means that they'll have plenty of material to support your next promotion."

"Elizabeth."

"What?"

"Is it true what they say, about why you haven't retired?"

"I haven't retired because I do not want to retire."

"Do you have files on everyone?"

Elizabeth's smile told Grace that she was the real deal, and she knew where the bones were buried.

"Grace, if perhaps over the years I have come to learn things about certain people who are now in power, it is only because they let me. One cannot know of skeletons, if there are none to be found. Remember that."

"I will."

"Henry is being pressured in Washington. He needs some results. You concentrate on getting those results, and I'll keep the dogs at bay as long as I can. Get Damian Reigns!"

"**I**'m headed that way anyway," Dante told Damian, as he paced the marble floors of his 60th floor penthouse. "I'll just take a little detour, swing by Nashville, and see what I can come up with."

"Concentrate on Miami. I need for you to reassure our friends in Colombia that we are with them. If our friends in Mexico want to break away and do their own thing, that's their business. Tell them that our sun still shines from Colombia."

"Gotcha."

"And Dante..."

"What?"

94

"No bodies. I don't want a war with our friends in Colombia, and I don't need a war with our friends in Mexico."

"Strictly business, big Bro, it'll be strictly business," Dante smiled, and clapped his hands on Damian's shoulder. "Now, about Nashville."

"Dante, don't get caught up on that."

"I'm not, but she's no more from the South than the Queen of England!" Dante turned away from his brother and walked to the massive glass window, where he stared down into the city. "I think we need to know what we're dealing with."

Damian walked up behind Dante, and patted him on his back. "Of course, you're right."

Dante turned and faced his brother, "I want to go to Nashville and see what I can dig up at the University."

Damian slid open the massive glass door and walked out onto the terrace. The wind was blowing and the air was nippy at this time of the evening, but the view was incredible. Dante's penthouse overlooked the city, and on a decent night, you could see clear to the hills that surrounded the city. The view was indeed breathtaking.

"A long way down," Dante said from inside of the apartment.

Damian stepped closer to the wrought iron railing, which surrounded the terrace, and stared down at the street below. It was indeed a long drop, a deadly drop. He wondered if Dante had ever dropped someone from this height before. *Is this how he will kill her, if she isn't who she claimed to be? A free fall from sixty stories?* Damian shook his head to clear those thoughts from his mind. How his brother chose to go about his business was not his concern. As long as the job got done, and got done in a way that could not be linked back to them, it didn't matter. He could picture the petite little Jonel flapping her arms trying to fly or glide or soar or do anything to save herself before her pretty little face crushed against the concrete. For some reason, the thought brought a half smile to his face. He turned to his brother.

"Dante..."

"What?"

"Your detour to Nashville is approved, just hurry back and be careful."

"Always."

Chapter Thirteen

She estimated the warehouse to be about one thousand feet by two thousand feet, considerably larger than a football field. Had the roof been a little higher, one could have installed seats, lighting, a scoreboard, and made themselves a nice, indoor stadium.

Grace smiled when Damian squeezed her hand, smiled at her, and gave her a tour of one of his family's warehouses. This was one of the larger ones, he'd told her. It was also one of the newest—highly automated, very secure, and virtually fireproof. *This is the perfect place to hold and distribute large amounts of pure Colombian cocaine*, she thought uneasily. Had she actually found the warehouse? Was she actually inside of his primary distribution center? With the passing of each stack of crates, she could feel the tiny hairs on her neck stand up at attention. She knew that this was the place. *It has to be the place,* she told her self.

"And the high level of automation means tremendous savings from the cost of having to maintain high levels of personnel," Damian told her. "We can operate this warehouse at a fraction of the cost of the older ones. And the fire suppression systems are all automated state-of-the-art setups."

"Sounds fascinating," said Grace as she thought to herself all the possibilities.

"That's nothing, watch this," Damian told her. He clapped his hands loudly, "WANDA!"

Over the loudspeakers, a computerized voice came alive. *"Yes, Mr. Reigns?"*

Grace Moore's eyes went wide. "What in the hell is that?"

Damian smiled proudly, "It's WANDA. Warehouse Automation and Distribution Algorithmic," Damian lifted his head toward the ceiling. "That will be all, WANDA."

"Yes, Mr. Reigns," the feminine computerized voice replied over the warehouses loud speakers.

"Wow!" Grace clapped her hands. "That's neat. Where did you get that from?"

"Dante and a college buddy of his from India designed the program. She, or it, controls every function in the warehouse."

Grace turned toward him. "So, what do you keep here?"

"Well, we keep all sorts of products and supplies for our various businesses. We primarily utilize this one as a hub for our trucking company because of its highly automated distribution capability, though. We have to make sure the goods get to where they are supposed to, when they are supposed to."

I just bet you do, she told herself. *Can't let the kids in Houston run out of cocaine; how else could they make their crack?*

Grace reached out her hand and lifted a wooden lid that had been pried off of a crate marked, 'Authorized Personnel Only'.

"What's in here?" she asked.

Damian grabbed Grace Moore's hand with such speed and firmness that she suddenly became frightened.

"It's um... a secret," Damian nodded his head, motioning for her to follow. "C'mon, I'll show you around the office. The computer that controls the warehouse is in there."

Grace pulled her hand away from Damian's. The hairs on her neck were buzzing now. She knew that she had hit the mother lode.

Special Agent Grace Moore! She liked the sound of that.

More importantly, she now realized that Damian was a monster. *He did have something hidden inside of him that could burst out and hurt others.* The thought made her rub her wrist again. *After today,* she told herself. *After today, Damian Reigns will never ever be able to hurt anyone else again.* She would handcuff this monster personally.

"Uh, Damian? Before you show me your big toy, I need to use the little ladies room."

"The little ladies room? I never thought that I would ever hear such a thing come from those beautiful lips of yours. And to think, if I would have said such a thing, you would have jumped all over me. I would have been a male chauvinistic, Neanderthal, pinheaded, pea-brained pig!"

Grace smiled and winked at him. "Yes, you would have. I can say it, but you cannot!"

Damian slapped his hand across his forehead, "You need to write an instruction manual on how to be politically correct when it comes to dealing with the female gender."

Grace stepped forward, and rubbed her hands on Damian's shoulders. "I don't want to write a manual, I want to break you down, and mold you. That way I know it will be done right."

Damian threw back his head in laughter.

"Now where is the ladies room?" Grace asked him again.

Damian pointed to it. "It's just around the corner. When you are finished, I'll be over there underneath the stairs, leading to the upstairs office. Waiting to take you up those stairs, and, as you put it, show you my big toy."

Grace threw her head back in laughter and stalked off to the ladies room.

Once inside, Grace checked beneath each stall to ensure that she was alone. Once she was certain, she quickly pulled out her cell telephone and dialed the number to the field team.

"Number one-one-one-two-five, code gold, I repeat, code gold, blue jay reports status gold, activating the transponder on my cell phone now."

Grace hung up the phone, folded it, and put it back inside of her small, black purse. She then used the restroom, washed her hands, then rinsed her face. She studied herself in the mirror. *It was almost over*, she told herself. *It was almost over, and she was still alive.*

Grace dried her hands and dabbed her face gently, so as to not disturb her lipstick. She breathed in deeply, held her breath, and then exhaled, while studying herself in the mirror. She had never actually been in a raid before. Well, at least not inside the establishment while others did the raiding. Usually, she was part of the entry team. Never had she fired her weapon during a raid, nor had most of the agents she knew, but this was certainly a special situation. *Would Damian and his workers resist? Would he get hit, and go down in a hail of gunfire? Would some of her fellow agents? Would she?* Never before had she missed her gun as much as she missed it now. It was showtime.

Grace gave herself the once-over-once again in the mirror, breathed out heavily, and headed out of the restroom. She saw Damian standing near the stairs waiting for her. As usual, he wore that spellbinding smile.

"Wow, I didn't know the restroom was that big. Maybe I should have digital maps put in there."

"Well, sometimes we ladies take a little longer to do what we have to do," she told him as she approached. She was almost near him, when she saw the first agent.

He wore an all black uniform, with black boots, black shin guards, black knee and elbow pads, and a black, Kevlar helmet on his head. His face was covered by a black balaclava, while black goggles covered his eyes. He wore black gloves, a black gas mask hanging around his neck, and a black, tactical vest with all sorts of nasty weapons hanging on it. She could also tell by his bulging midsection that he wore a thick application of body armor beneath his uniform. Why he needed it, she couldn't tell, because the massive, black body shield he carried protected most of his body. Whatever didn't protect him, his black HK MP5 submachine gun would.

"Get down on the ground now!" he yelled. "FBI, search warrant! FBI, search warrant! Get down on the ground now!"

Even though he had a black, communications headset sticking out from underneath his helmet, she knew that he wasn't screaming to the other federal agents. He was talking directly to her, and pointing his machine gun at her chest. The red dot on her left breast told her so. She got down on the ground immediately.

My God, do I look that scary when I'm suited and booted? she wondered.

Red dots swam all over the warehouse, giving it the eerie feeling of a deadly discotheque. Black clad FBI agents seemed to appear like roaches from every nook, cranny, crack, and crevice, yelling, shouting, pushing, and shoving. Grace Moore could smell the adrenaline flowing through the warehouse. She could also feel herself being handcuffed.

"Clear!"

"Clear!"

"Clear!"

She could hear shouts coming from all over the vast interior of the warehouse, as agents shouted to one another that their areas were secure. She felt relieved that the situation was quickly placed under control, and even more relieved that not a shot had been fired.

"Get up!" A burly officer yelled at her, as he lifted her up by her arms.

The first thing that she saw was Damian staring at her and shaking his head.

"Sorry you had to go through this, Jonel. But, I promise you my attorneys will make them regret it. And dearly, I might add."

His eyes told her that he was sincere. A little embarrassed, but mostly they showed concern for her. It had been a long time since a man had showed any concern for her welfare. She was slightly touched.

"I said, are you sure you're alright?" Damian repeated.

Grace snapped out of her wondering thoughts, and focused in on Damian.

"Huh? Oh, yeah... I'm fine," she said.

That's what was missing, she thought to herself. *I'm a banker. I'm supposed to be nervous.* "Damian, what are all these people doing here?"

"They are the FBI, Jonel. I know there are all kinds of crazy thoughts going through your head right now, but just bare with me. I'll explain everything later."

"No, Mr. Reigns, I'd like to hear your explanation right now," a suited gentleman declared, as he approached from across the room. "Explain how you rationalize bringing in tons of cocaine each year, so it can poison our children. I'd really love to hear it."

It was Nathan Hess, the special agent in charge of the San Antonio field office. Grace had met him in Washington several times, during preparation for her undercover assignment. Nathan came across as a no-nonsense, old-school Bureau type who cut straight to the chase.

"Nathan!" Damian called out cordially, as if greeting an old friend from the golf course. "I thought I smelled you and your cronies in here. You know, you really should have called first. I could have prepared a little something for you."

Damian's smile told everyone in the room what he meant. And they knew that his surprise would have been for all of them as well. Grace Moore had never seen Damian smile like that. It seemed to underline the subtleties of his words. Unlike his usual smile that made her tingle in secret places, this one made her shiver all over.

"Damian, I'm sure that you would have liked to have prepared something for me, just like I would love to have something prepared for you. Like a one hundred count federal indictment, followed by a conviction, followed by a

102

trip to Terra Haute, and a nice, SHORT stay on Federal Death Row!"

"Wow, Nathan, I'm hurt. I never considered you to be an advocate of the death penalty."

"It's monsters like you who make me not only support it but cherish it!"

Damian laughed for several moments before regaining his composure.

"Nathan, I want to call my attorney. Then, I want you and your goons to get off of my property immediately."

"We have a federal search warrant, Damian," Nathan told him. "We'll leave when we're ready. As for your attorney, I called him before I walked in. He should be on his way."

Nathan turned to several of his black-clad agents. "Take Mr. Reigns and his female companion up to the office. Gather the rest of the warehouse workers in the center of the warehouse and post a guard on them. I'll be upstairs with Mr. Reigns in the office. Let me know when the agents from the IRS and the customs service arrive. That will be all."

"Customs? IRS?" Damian laughed. "You boys are really getting desperate. IRS just audited me last month. The boys from customs were here last week. Nathan, Nathan, Nathan, what am I going to go with you?"

Nathan Hess turned to his officers. "Let me know when you find something. Take these two upstairs!"

Four Hours Later

A black-clad FBI agent peered into the office. "Mr. Hess?"

Nathan quickly rose to his feet. "What is it?"

"The warehouse is clean, sir," the agent informed him.

"Damn!" Nathan stomped the ground, and then turned toward Damian. "Today, you got lucky again. But I will catch you, and I will destroy you, your demonic brother, and that psychopath sister of yours! You can count on it!"

Damian, knowing when to bow out gracefully, reiterated his stance.

"Nathan, if you ever find anything, it will be because your agents put it there. I have never, and will never, engage in any criminal activity. I am a law-abiding citizen. I vote, I pay my taxes, and I resent your agency's accusations stating otherwise. Now, if you'll please remove these handcuffs and remove yourselves from the premises, I can continue to run my corporation."

Chapter Fourteen

Dante loved south Florida: the sunny weather, the moderate temperatures, the clear, blue, water, the beautiful beaches, and the absolutely drop-dead gorgeous women. It's what kept him coming back. He and his cousin Kevin were currently preoccupied with two of the latter.

Two voluptuous, scantily clad Latinas had themselves wrapped around them. Dante kept company with the longhaired Dominican in the yellow, two-piece string, while Kevin held onto the short haired, Puerto Rican bombshell with the red, two-piece string.

Dante ran his hand down the string bikini, pulling it from between her cinnamon-colored buttocks. She slapped his hand away.

"Dante, stop!"

"Naw, let me see, just a lil' bit," he laughed and leaned forward to kiss her on her neck. She pushed his head away.

"You're moving fast, aren't you?" She smiled. "I mean, how about getting to know each other first?"

"I'm trying to get to know you, just a lil' bit," Dante said really laughing at his 50 jokes. He rubbed his hand across her ass. Kevin released his South Beach beauty, and tapped Dante on his arm. Dante looked up, and Kevin pointed toward the water.

"Here they come," Kevin told him.

Dante lifted his hand to his newfound friend's chin, and lifted her face toward his.

"So, why don't you give me your telephone number? That way we can hook up later?" Dante asked.

"You have something to write with?" she asked holding her hands in the air, revealing nothing but body and no place for a pen.

Dante ran his tongue across his front teeth, and then smiled at her. "What do I look like? You think I can't remember seven numbers?" he grabbed her ass again. "As good as you look, do you think I'd forget your telephone number?"

The small, white motorboat pulled up along side the pier. Two large Cubans, in white cotton Guyabera shirts climbed out and stood on the pier. They waved at Dante.

Dante nodded, acknowledging their presence, and then turned his attention back to the string bikini.

She smiled, "555-2996".

"I'll call you tonight," he told her. Dante turned toward his cousin Kevin.

"Showtime."

They headed for the motorboat, which took them to Don Alemendez' yacht. It was his territory that Princess had been making inroads into. It was also his territory that Don Frederico had offered to Princess during the mediation. To say that Dante felt uncomfortable about the meeting would be an understatement.

The Reigns family was the wealthiest of all the distributors by far. Their control over all of Texas including the boarder entrance points gave them a powerful voice on the commission. The sheer size of the Reigns empire, and the number of workers they employed, made their army the third largest in the commission. All of this was true despite the fact that Damian employed the minimum number of soldiers required to keep things running smoothly. He encouraged his underbosses and area chiefs to do the same. Still, because of the Reigns empire's sheer size, the numbers they employed were staggering.

The Douglas family of Georgia operated the second largest army. They were continuously at war with their underlings in Atlanta and with their chief in Savannah. They were weak politically and constantly in danger of being overthrown.

Señor Alemendez himself boasted the largest army. He had enough soldiers to last days, and certainly needed them. Princess had an army in his territory, the Dominicans, the Jamaicans, the Haitians, the Colombians, the Mexicans, the Italians, and even the Russians were all thick, and all waiting for the opportunity to take over. Dante could sympathize with him.

Don Alemendez' yacht was a large, two-hundred-foot Christensen. It was his second yacht, and as such, he spared no expense. Gold sinks and faucets, Persian carpets, crystal chandeliers, and state-of-the art everything. He had named it Snowflake, thumbing his nose at the DEA. The trade had been good to him.

Dante stepped onboard Don Alemendez' yacht and was quickly escorted below deck, where the rest of the distribution commission was seated around a large, mahogany conference table. One of Don Alemendez' large, hulking bodyguards pulled a chair out for him and seated him.

"Glad to see you again, Señor Reigns," Don Alemendez told him. Alemendez was seated at the head of the conference table, while Señor Ferdinand was seated at the other end. Don Ferdinand was El Jefe's personal representative and the nominal head of the Distribution Commission. He interlaced his fingers, and leaned forward.

"Now that we're all here, let's get down to business. First, the Boss wants me to congratulate you all for a very productive third quarter. As you all know, next quarter is the Christmas bonus quarter."

Several members of the commission smiled greedily. Don Ferdinand continued.

"This year, the discount will increase by five-percent, all the way up to a full fifteen!"

Several members of the Distribution Commission whistled, while all of them clapped. Julian Jones of Mississippi cleared his throat.

"Fifteen percent is quite generous," he spoke to Don Ferdinand. "I think I speak for the entire commission when I say, long live El Jefe!"

The members lifted their champagne glasses, Dante lifted his water glass, and they toasted the Boss.

"Now, Julian, what is going on in Gulfport?" Don Ferdinand asked.

"Nothing anymore," Julian adjusted his yellow and gray silk Hermes tie. "The disturbance has been quelled."

"Good."

Ferdinand turned toward Emil Douglas of Georgia. Emil was a young, gifted African American with a law degree from Yale. Everyone liked to tease him about being Damian's rival. To the contrary, Damian and Emil were very good friends.

"How is the Savannah situation?" Don Ferdinand inquired.

Emil squirmed. He was Intelligent, efficient, and thorough, but he was not ruthless. In Dante's eyes, it was his only flaw.

"We are in the process of restoring relations and restarting the free flow of our materials."

"Emil, you have negotiated and reopened the free flow of your 'materials' three times in fifteen months," Don Ferdinand told him. "Can you not handle the Savannah section of your organization?"

Emil bowed his head slightly toward the Don.

"Señor Ferdinand, our structure in Georgia is a little different from the others. I merely sit at the head of many quasi-independent organizations, things take time."

"Emil, unify your organization," Don Ferdinand waved his hand around the table. "The commission will help you."

Dante cleared his throat. "Don Ferdinand, if I may?"

The Don nodded.

"The Reigns family will personally finance, oversee and conduct the operation against the Savannah factions. With one phone call, I can put one hundred soldiers in the air to fly down and take over the hostilities. Within a month, that number will grow to three hundred. All with Emil's approval of course."

"That is mighty generous of you, Mr. Reigns," Don Ferdinand told him.

Dante nodded to him. "That will allow Emil to focus on solidifying his home base in Atlanta. The Atlanta opposition he faces has grown tremendously strong." *It will also keep the rest of you sons of bitches out of his territory,* Dante thought to himself.

"Dante, I thank the Reigns family for its generosity. Your assistance would be greatly appreciated," Emil said to him.

Emil knew that his territory was in no danger. Forgetting his friendship with Damian, the Reigns family were simply not expansionist. Their soldiers would leave Georgia after the Savannah hostilities had ceased.

"Well, that leaves us with one other important matter... Dante, what is the Reigns family going to do about Princess?" Don Ferdinand asked Dante.

"She has over three hundred people in south Florida! She is constantly engaging my men," Don Alemendez spoke up and announced forcefully.

Dante lifted his hands to silence Alemendez and looked at them wanting so badly to scream 'I told you so'.

"When this commission backed Damian's take-over, we could have taken care of her then. You said that you needed muscle in Florida to help you against all of your enemies. You asked for her, and you made her one of your regional chiefs. Don't blame the Reigns family for the snake you invited into your home!" said Dante as polite, yet 'I told you so' as he could be.

"You can get her!" Don Alemendez shouted. "You can destroy her!"

"We made that offer in the beginning. You and this commission allowed her to live. You wanted her, and you got her. You destroy her!"

"And if I do?" Don Alemendez lifted an eyebrow. "What happens then?"

"Absolutely nothing," Dante told him, "In fact, I'm sure that everyone in this room would be very relieved." *I can't be any clearer. Please someone kill Princess, please,* he prayed this to himself hoping someone would take care of her and soon.

"Dante, that brings us to another matter," Don Ferdinand told him. 'The offer your sister made to Don Frederico."

"Señor Ferdinand, you can't really be considering that offer!"

Dante looked around the table at the faces of the other members. He saw smirks and smiles. René Tibbideaux of Louisiana, Raphael Guzman of Oklahoma, Chacho Hernandez of New Mexico, and Barry Groomes of Arkansas, all looked extremely pleased. This was a result of the Reigns family's control of pieces of their territories. They failed to realize that it was under Princess that those territories were taken. Their looks told Dante two things. One, that they had discussed the matter before his arrival, maybe even prior to this meeting. Two, they had probably approved of Princess' proposal.

"Señor Dante, El Jefe was very attentive to your sister's idea," Don Ferdinand told him.

"El Jefe does remember what happened the last time Princess was in control, doesn't he?" Dante stared around the table. "That's how we came to control other areas outside of Texas." The smiles left the faces of several commission

110

members.

Don Ferdinand's smile widened. "As I recall, you were her number two. Dante, you can temper her activities."

Dante shook his head. "Once she gets started, trying to stop her is like trying to stop a hurricane with a paper towel."

"Dante, think about it," Don Alemendez told him, "We're not saying that you have to kill Damian. He could assume other responsibilities in your family."

Dante rose and jabbed his finger forcefully on top of the table as he spoke, "When Damian took over he stopped the war! He reduced our army and he even gave certain members of this commission some of their territory back. And this, *this* is how you repay him?"

"Dante, sit down," Don Ferdinand told him. He waved his hand toward the chair in which Dante had been seated. "Please, just listen. Hear me out."

"Don Ferdinand, I will not support such a thing. Neither will our area chiefs. Our people in Houston, Dallas, and San Antonio will make war with Princess. They are fiercely loyal to Damian!"

"You can control them, Dante," Don Ferdinand said.

Dante reseated himself. He placed his arms on the table and interlaced his fingers. "Does everyone understand what is going on here? Obviously from your smiles, you understand the first part. They want Princess to take over the Reigns organization. The second half comes after that. Once in control, she is to expand and take over the entire distribution network."

The members seated around the table began to stir. They all turned quickly and looked at a now smiling Don Ferdinand.

"Is this true?" Don Alemendez asked. His eyes were wide, and his neck bulged against his collar.

"Of course it's true," Dante told them. "No more commission, no more commission members. Just El Jefe,

Don Ferdinand, and Princess," Dante smiled. "I suspect that shortly afterward, there won't even be a Don Ferdinand, just an El Jefe and Princess."

"This is betrayal!" Raphael Guzman shouted. He banged his fist on the conference table to emphasize his point. "We were with you in the beginning!"

"Welcome to the commission," Dante told them with a smile.

"Look who's talking!" Don Ferdinand told Dante. "You think it's a secret that your family is leaving the commission? You have Price Waterhouse Cooper going over your books. You're separating them, even as we speak! Who is really the betrayer?"

"How we run our organization is no one's business. We pay, you deliver. I think you overestimate your power and you underestimate ours," Dante told him, staring him boldly.

"What?" Don Alemendez' voice trembled with anger. "Do you challenge the power of El Jefe?"

"The Reigns family is not a family of punks. We refrain because we want peace, not because of fear."

"How dare you speak this way to me! I am the personal representative of El Jefe!" said Don Alemendez as he rose above everyone seated as Dante rose behind him.

"You know what? Fuck you, and fuck that fat son of a bitch in South America! You forget Juarez is closer to San Antonio than Medellin! Nuevo Laredo is closer to San Antonio than Cali! Monterey is closer to San Antonio than Bogotá! There are suppliers who would love to make billions with our family!" said Dante, letting him have it.

Don Alemendez then rose. "They will make them without you!" He snapped his fingers and the suited gentlemen standing against the walls of the conference room pulled weapons from underneath their coats. Dante looked around the room, saw the weapons, and reseated himself. He broke out into a slow, deep, steady stream of laughter. His laughter made the commission members nervous. They thought he was mad.

Dante now had firm confirmation of his suspicions. Don Alemendez had sicced his men on him because of a confrontation between himself and Don Ferdinand. This, even after he had explained El Jefe's intentions to replace the entire commission with just Princess. This meant that Don Alemendez was set to benefit somehow from that arrangement. Dante turned his attention to the members of the commission.

"Before I left San Antonio, my brother made me promise that there would be no bodies. That is the only reason I don't kill you," Dante continued his laughter.

"I think that you are mad my friend," Don Alemendez spoke to him. "You are in no position to decide life and death."

"Whenever the commission meets, its members' safety is supposedly guaranteed," Dante reminded them. "I suppose that is no longer valid?"

"You are no longer a member of the commission. From this moment on, your sister is. You my friend are shark food," Don Ferdinand said to him.

Dante laughed even harder. He lifted his hand into the air and snapped his fingers. Don Alemendez' men turned their weapons on the commission members.

"Who the fuck do you think we are?" Dante asked them.

Don Alemendez choked realizing his own men where on Dante's team.

"I anticipated that one day these neutral meetings would no longer be neutral." Dante turned to Kevin. "Get a hold of Damian, and tell him what has just transpired. But first, escort these sons-a-bitches topside and throw them overboard."

Kevin nodded toward the stairs leading to the top deck. The commission members stood, and one by one headed upstairs.

After the last one had exited the room, Dante reached into his pocket and removed his tiny cell phone. He punched in a local telephone number.

"What?" The voice on the other end of the line asked.

"Luke! What's up baby?"

"Who dis?"

"Your boy, Dante."

"Oh, what up dog?"

"I'm in Miami, and guess what?" Dante asked, "I got us a two-hundred-foot yacht to play with."

"No shit!"

"Yes, sir! Call up some of them stripper hos you know and let's get this shit crunk!"

"Bet!"

"And Luke..."

"What up?"

"Tell 'em to leave the boa constrictors at home this time. I only got twenty-four hours."

Chapter Fifteen

Damian shifted the gears in his red Ferrari 360 Spider and sped up to merge smoothly with the traffic already speeding down the highway.

Grace rubbed the black mark on her wrist where the cuffs had bruised her. After this assignment was over, she was going to make that idiot agent who cuffed her so tightly pay dearly. She turned toward Damian.

"So, what was all of that about?" she asked as innocently as possible.

"A long story, but I do owe you an explanation. Jonel, a lot of people in this world have blinders on. And a lot of those people fear what they can't understand. What's so crazy is that they don't even try to understand. They have preconceived notions about everything and everyone, and if those people don't fit into their preconceptions, they try to make them. I refuse to be who the FBI or Nathan Hess wants me to be!" Damian pounded his steering wheel forcefully with his fist. "I'm young, educated, and successful. Under any other circumstances, I'd be held up as a role model, as all that is right with America. But you see, I also happen to be black."

"But, Damian, what do those things have to do with the FBI accusing you of selling drugs?"

"They have everything to do with it, Jonel. Because I'm young, educated, successful, and black, they feel that I just have to be doing something illegal!"

Grace held her hands up to her face and sobbed.

"But, Damian, why you? Of all the successful, young, black men in the country, why are they targeting just you?"

"Do you know how many times I've asked myself that very same question? Why me? What have I done to warrant such treatment?" Damian let out a half laugh to go along with a hurt smile.

Grace noticed them both; the hurt on Damian's face appeared real to her. Either he was an excellent liar or he was telling the truth. Grace believed that it was the former.

"Damian, what's funny?"

"I was just thinking something crazy, that's all."

"Well, I...I like to tell myself sometimes that they're mad at me because of my youth programs, because I'm spending millions of dollars a year on various programs to keep kids from going to prison," Damian's voice became edgy. "Because my programs are messing up the western Texas plantation system. The more young black kids I keep from going to prison, the less they will have to work at their federal prison factories! If they can get rid of me and seize all of my money, then they can stop the programs. They can ensure their supply of young, healthy, black prisoners to work in their damn factories!"

Damian balled his fist, and pounded the air in front of him. "I won't let them, Jonel! I won't let them," he said softly.

Grace Moore leaned her head against his shoulder. She was unsure of everything for several moments, unsure because Damian Reigns sounded so convincing. Never had she met a drug dealer who spends millions on his community to keep kids in school and out of trouble. She had seen drug dealers do a lot of things with their money, but never that. There were just too many paradoxes, too many pieces that didn't fit, too many loose ends that needed tying together. For the first time in her career, she just wasn't sure about the solidity of her case.

"And you know what's so bad about the whole damn thing?" Damian asked her.

"What?" Grace asked staring at him with intense eyes.

"Nathan is a black man. They use our own people to destroy us!"

Grace turned her head and stared out of the window. She wanted to be anywhere but inside of that car, at that moment. She wanted to fly away. She was almost certain she could.

Nashville

Dante flashed the picture of Grace Moore that Damian's security cameras had provided, and again, no one at the school's registrar's office recognized her. He did, however, get a hit on the name.

"Yeah, Jonel McNeal, she stayed over in Livingston." The young coed snapped her fingers as she tried to recall bits and pieces of information. "She had a roommate named..."

The young coed turned her head, sending her thick, African style braids flying over her shoulders.

"Gina! What was that girl's name that used to work here last year? The one in professor Marquez' graduate applied science class?"

Gina shrugged her shoulders and then shook her head.

"Tammy, I don't know who you are talking about. What girl in professor Marquez' class?"

"The one I didn't like. The one who thought she was all that just because her daddy was the mayor."

"Mayor?" Dante held up his hands. "Did you say mayor?"

"Uh-huh," Tammy smacked her lips and waved her hand through the air. "Just because her daddy was the mayor..."

"They were roommates, she and Jonel?" Dante asked interrupting the girl.

117

"Yeah."

"Could I get her address from you?"

"Well, we really don't give out..."

Her sentence was interrupted by Dante's counting. He peeled off bill after bill, while her eyes bugged out of her head. She had to swallow to keep from drooling.

"Well, for you, I'm sure I could look it up. Just give me a quick minute!" she told him.

Thank you," Dante said with a smile. He handed her the wad of twenties.

Tammy tapped rapidly at the computer keyboard in front of her for about two minutes. She knew the mayor's last name had been Tillman, and that gave her a last name to go on. She quickly cross-referenced Tillman with the list of graduate students, past and present, and came up with an address. She smiled when she found it.

"Shelisa Tillman, 6519 Parkland, North Nashville."

Dante quickly wrote down the address, thanked her, and headed out the door. It was time for business.

The neighborhood was nice, old, and settled, the type that would produce offspring that would venture out into Fisk, Howard, Spelman, and all of the other bourgeois institutions of higher learning. Dante laughed at the thought that he too, had once been a bourgeois African American. His family's wealth had afforded him the luxury of attending several upscale private schools while growing up.

"If Father Domingo could see me now," he said to no one in particular. Dante had no illusions. He knew he was bound for hell.

The door opened slowly, and before Dante stood a middle-aged woman on the mature side of her forties.

"May I help you?" she asked.

"Yes, Mrs. Tillman?" he questioned wondering was it her.

"Yes?" The woman answered hesitantly.

"Hi, it's so wonderful to finally meet you!" Dante said extending his hand and releasing a warm smile.

Confused, Gloria Tillman took his hand and accepted his greeting.

"I'm a friend of Shelisa's, from Fisk."

Gloria Tillman's hand clasped her chest in a gesture of relief.

"Oh, I see. I thought something terrible happened to my daughter," she stood aside, and made a broad, sweeping gesture with her hand. "Won't you please come in."

"Thank you," Dante said, with a slight, graceful bow. He had gambled correctly. Judging by the home, the car, and their prominence in the community, he guessed that they might hold filial connections to the university. In all probability, Gloria Tillman had not only met her husband there but both of their parents had as well. His mentioning of the university had gained him entrance, but more importantly, it had gained him acceptance. She would now speak openly and freely.

"So, you went to Fisk with my daughter? I'm sorry, your name is?"

"Matthew," he told her. "Matthew McCray."

The click clack of Gloria's high heels ceased as she stopped her strutting across the highly polished marble floors and turned to face him.

"I'm sorry," she told him in a deep, southern drawl, "I just cannot recall my daughter mentioning a Matthew McCray." Gloria Tillman smiled broadly at her guest with perfect mannerism. "And with a good biblical name like Matthew, along with a face as handsome as yours, I'm almost certain Shelisa would have talked about you nonstop."

Dante tried to subtly match her accent. "I dated Jonel at the time."

"Jonel! Well I do declare! Beth Ann kept you a secret! I will get on her about that the next time we have our annual convention!" Gloria squealed

Beth Ann, the name threw him, but he kept an open ear.

"Yes indeed, that little devil. And I'm so surprised, because Beth Ann could never keep a secret, even when we were roommates at the university! So how are she and Jonel doing?"

Dante quickly deduced that Beth Ann was Jonel's mother.

"Oh, well, I haven't seen much of either of them lately," he told her.

Gloria reeled back in shock. "You mean Jonel let you get away?"

"I'm afraid so. In fact, that's kind of why I'm here. I'd like to reestablish contact with Jonel, Shelisa, and all our other friends from the university."

"Well, my daughter is now working in Memphis. Arnette...you do remember Arnette don't you?"

"Of course, who could forget Arnette?" Dante nodded, not having a clue.

"Well, she is married to a doctor from Georgia. They live in Savannah now. And Jonel, well, she's still bouncing around from job to job. She hasn't settled down, if that's what you're interested in," Gloria said with a mischievous smile.

Dante pretended to blush and go along with the flow of the conversation.

"Well, I have to admit, I was wondering. So, where is she now?"

"Texas, last I heard, she took a job in Texas. Can you believe that, a nice Southern girl, from a decent family, wanting to live in Texas?"

"Is she still working in the accounting field?" Dante asked.

"Accounting?" Gloria Tillman threw her head back in laughter. "Now can you imagine dainty, prissy little Jonel doing anything with numbers? You and I both know that she wasn't exactly the brightest thing this side of the Mississippi. Add to that the fact that she would have to be using a pencil or tapping at a calculator or keyboard all day! No way! I once saw Jonel wear gloves for seven days because she broke a nail!"

"So, what is she doing with herself nowadays?"

"Why, she's still into theatrical arts. The child has no direction, no purpose. She just goes from theme park to theme park, managing and directing their stage shows. Oh, her poor mother. We just knew Jonel was going to be a cardiovascular surgeon. I mean, with those dainty little fingers of hers. Well, that's what happens when you don't study and spend all of your time primping in the mirror. You end up working for a circus. That's why I told my girls, get an education."

Dante pulled out the picture from Damian's security camera and stared at it.

"I can't wait to see her again."

Seeing what he held in his hand, Gloria strode over to where he was standing, and took the picture from him.

"Who is this?" she asked.

"You don't recognize her?" Dante asked with a concentrated frown.

"No, I don't. I thought we were discussing Jonel McNeal."

"We are."

"Son, this is not Jonel. I went to school with her mother. She and I are sorority sisters. We pledged AKA together. I practically helped raise Jonel, not to mention the fact that she and my daughter are the best of friends. This creature is not Jonel McNeal!"

Dante took the picture back from her and glanced at it.

"Oh, I'm so sorry, wrong picture. This is Tammy. Well, I'm certainly sorry to have taken up so much of your day," said Dante hearing all he needed to hear and ready to leave.

"Shelisa's friends are always welcome, especially ones as

handsome as you," Gloria told him, placing her hand on his rear, and giving him a slight squeeze.

"I take it our dear mayor is out and about making sure this fair city remains a place where people of decent morals and values can live without fear of sin?" Dante said watching Gloria Tillman smile wickedly up at him.

"But of course," she said her hand caressing slowly from Dante's rear to his waist, resting on the front of his trousers. "We must all do our duty to ensure that our city remains a bastion of morality, a place that people of good, Southern values can be proud to call home."

"Speaking of calling home, please excuse me for a second," said Dante breaking the spell.

"But of course."

Dante removed his cell phone, and dialed Damian's private number.

"Hello?" Damian answered.

"Yes, I'll give you three guesses, and the first two don't count."

"Come home."

"I'm there," Dante said coldly. He disconnected the line, and turned back toward Gloria Tillman. "Again, I thank you for your hospitality, ma'am."

"Must you be going so soon?" she asked, again fondling him near his zipper.

Dante sucked his teeth, "Ma'am, you seem like a fine southern lady in distress. And as a gentleman of the South, it is my duty to assist you."

"Thank goodness for chivalry," Gloria told him, as she kicked off her heels and dropped her dress to the floor.

"Magnificent!" Dante exclaimed. "However, there is one, tiny, little thing."

"What is that?" she asked, standing before him, completely nude.

"Put the heels back on."

Chapter Sixteen

Grace pulled her foot away from Damian's hands and kicked him softly on the shoulders.

"Hey, I resent that! Don't think that just because you got me out here in this beautiful field, lying on this blanket while you give me a foot Massage, that you can get away with being a male chauvinist!"

"What did I say?" Damian asked with a smile. "Just because I said that this is the way things should be, a man taking care of his woman, Massaging her feet, feeding her strawberries, pouring her champagne..."

"Nope, you are living out your Wild Wild West fantasies, sir," Grace said to him. She motioned toward the horses lying near by. "You have me out here in the middle of your ranch, riding horses, wearing cowboy boots and a cowboy hat, and now you're talking about a simpler life, open campfires, wide open ranges, and all of that Wyatt Earp crap."

"How is that being chauvinistic?"

"Because the part about men shooting the buffalo and taking them back home for their wives to cook was a bit much, Mr. Damian. A foot Massage will allow you to get by with some things, but the part about the men doing the hunting and the women doing the cooking was a little too much, buster!"

"Didn't I make the sandwiches for the picnic?" Damian laughed

"I'll grant you that, and they were very delicious," Grace nodded. "Thank you very much."

Grace reclined back onto the blanket once again and placed her foot inside of his lap. "You may continue pampering me, but without the caveman dialogue."

Damian laughed and provided the smile that she had become enamored with. "So, let's talk about something else then."

"Like what?" Grace asked. She arched her foot and wiggled her toes, as Damian's thumbs massaged her arch in deep, circular motions. "Ummm, that feels so good."

"Well, we could talk about you, for example," he told her.

"Me?"

"Yeah, you, my favorite subject."

"Oh really? And when did that take place?"

"What?"

"When did I become your favorite subject?"

"The first night I met you," Damian told her. "I haven't been able to talk about anything else since."

"Oh, I liked that one. You're a smooth one, Damian Reigns, I'll give you that. You are a smooth one," she said giving him an applause.

"So, why is it that some lucky man hasn't snatched you up?"

"Who said that I wanted to be snatched up? Do you think I sit around all day, waiting for some man to come and save me? Do you think that I need to be saved?"

"Yes."

"What?" Grace opened her eyes and stared at him sharply.

"You need to be saved, collected, protected, and cherished. You're beautiful, Intelligent, and funny. You're a very special woman, one who should be locked down. You make a man become selfish, Jonel. I for one know that you've made me become very selfish. I don't want to share you with anyone or anything."

"Okay, wait a minute," Grace held up her hand. "Red light, Mr. Damian. Now, why are you still available?"

"I asked you first."

Grace shrugged her shoulders.

Damian laughed and gently twisted her ankle a little. "You're not getting away with a shoulder shrug, don't....I mean, please don't think that."

"Okay, okay," Grace said, as she pulled her legs away from Damian and sat up. "I'll explain."

She paused for several moments of deep thought, and then stared into his eyes.

"Do you believe in love, Damian?"

"I do."

"I mean, true love? That deep, comfortable, secure, ever lasting love? That I-love-you-for-who-you-are and I'll-always-love-you-regardless-of-what-you've-done type of love?"

Damian squinted and nodded solemnly, "I think I know what you're talking about."

"Well, that's what I'm looking for. That's why I'm still single."

"You mean to tell me that you have yet to meet anyone who was willing to love you like that?"

Grace nodded and then turned her face to the sun. It was bright, warm, caressing. It contrasted nicely against the clear blue-sky and the crisp, cool, fall breeze.

"So what about you?" she asked him. "Where is the love of your life?"

Damian laughed and stared off into the meadow where the two black Arabian stallions grazed.

"Have you ever noticed how one partner always loves the other more?"

Grace nodded.

"Have you ever been in a relationship where it was all

games? Where you would have to pretend like you didn't really care in order for the other person to show you that they cared?" Damian turned, and stared into her eyes. "Jonel, I gave so much of myself that I had nothing left."

Grace could see the hurt, the pain, in Damian's eyes. Instinctively, she reached out for him, pulling him close. "I know, I've been there before. I've been there before, a couple of times. That's why I'm still single."

"Don't want to get hurt again?"

"You got it," she told him.

"That's no good." Damian shook his head. "Life is about love. It's about joy and pain, hugs and hits, laughter and tears. You have to keep trying, I know I will. I'll never give up. I'll never stop myself from falling in love. Love is the most wonderful feeling in the world."

"Yeah, when it's right. When everything is going good, it's good. When things are not going right, then everything is all wrong."

"You still can't ever give up on love or being loved."

"Damian, all my life, love has been like trying to hold onto a handful of water. Every time I think I have it, it slips through the cracks of my fingers. I try to grab it, squeeze it, hold it, cup my hands to try, and hold onto it, but it always slips away."

Damian took his hand, placed it on Grace's chin, and turned her face toward his.

"That's because you have to feel it inside of you. You have to immerse yourself in it and then drink it. Let it live inside of you. Then it can't slip away."

Grace closed her eyes and felt herself drifting forward slowly. She could feel the warmth of his breath, and smell the sweet aroma from the wine he had sipped just seconds before their lips met.

Their kiss was firm, passionate, and stimulating. Grace felt herself tingling in places where she knew she shouldn't be. She felt all those lonely nights disappearing with a kiss.

Not here, not with Damian, not with the man I've been sent here to bust..

"So, how did you come to know so much about love?" she asked him as she parted her lips from his.

"I learned from my grandmother," he said.

His smile shifted from her to the comforter on which they sat, as his thoughts returned to the woman he loved more than life itself.

"She and I are extremely close. We could always talk about everything. When I was young she always told me to follow my heart, that I would know the signs of true love once they showed themselves."

Grace Moore rubbed his head and laughed. "Sounds like wonderful words of wisdom."

"My grandmother—you haven't met her yet, have you?"

Grace shook her head.

"Well, what are we waiting for?" Damian said, as he jumped and stood up.

He led off and gathered the horses, which stood nearby grazing. He helped Grace mount her stead, quickly mounted his own, and entered into a slow gallop across the fields, away from the setting sun.

Grace surveyed her surroundings and found them to be breathtaking. The horses were well-muscled Arabians, imported from Egypt. The sun shone on their flawless, jet-black coats, making them glisten like reams of soft, black silk. They were truly magnificent creatures.

They came across a small, white, wooden bridge that crossed the beautiful Guadeloupe River, which ran through the property. The lakes, the hills, the duck ponds, the small creeks and streams and the abundance of wild life, all came together to form a private, South Texas paradise. Grace Moore had never felt so free.

Soon, they came across a small area enclosed by an intricate, wrought-iron fence. Damian quickly dismounted and Grace followed suit. She watched as he unlatched the small gate and reverently began to make his approach toward a massive, rose and gray colored gravestone. Her heart fell to her knees as he began to sing.

I went, to the house where I used to live.
The grass had grown and covered the porch.
A man across the street said I know who you came to see
But she, she don't live here anymore-
She's somewhere around god's throne.

Damian fell softly to his knees just in front of the headstone.

She's somewhere around god's throne.
So I'll keep searching and searching until I find her,
For she's somewhere around god's throne.

Damian began pulling weeds from around the headstone, and cleaning up the area around it.

I went to the church where I used to go.
The preacher was still there, he met me at the door.
He said, I know who you are, and who you're looking for,
But she, she don't come here anymore.
She's somewhere around god's throne.
I said she's somewhere, around god's throne.

Damian sniffled several times as the tears streamed down his face.

So I'll keep searching and searching until I find her,
For she's somewhere around god's throne.

Grace Moore wiped the tears from her eyes and cupped her hands over the lower half of her face. She stood at the gate with her body shaking and convulsing as she bawled her eyes out. Damian, still on his knees, turned his face toward her.

"My grandmother loved that song. I would sing it for her every Sunday after we left church on the way to grab something to eat."

Grace nodded fervently, her hands still covering the lower half of her tear-filled face. He was not a monster. They had it all wrong. They had to be wrong.

128

"Excuse my manners," Damian waved his hand toward the grave stone. "Jonel, this is my grandmother, Telly Mae Perkins. Grandma, this is Jonel."

Grace walked softly into the small family cemetery, toward Damian. She didn't know what to say, or what to do, but she did know that she wanted to be near him.

"Grandma, I won't break down and cry this time, especially in front of our company. I know it wouldn't be proper, you taught me that." he said with a slight smile, "But I do want you to know that I love you so much and that I still miss you."

Damian broke down into tears despite trying not to.

"They say it takes time, that the pain will go away in time, but it still hurts, Grandma. It hurts like it was only yesterday. I have a great big hole inside my chest where my heart is supposed to be, and it hurts."

Grace knelt down and wrapped her arms around Damian, while he bawled like a baby. He cried for several minutes before regaining his composure enough to speak coherently.

"I'm sorry," he apologized to Grace, and then turned toward the gravestone. "I'm sorry Grandma. I just wanted you to meet her. You always told me that I would know the signs when the true love bug hit, and I think I've seen a couple of them."

Damian took Grace's hand into his hand and sniffled several times. "She's just like me, Grandma. She's been through the ups and downs of life, and she's been hurt a few times. She's tough, though, resilient and she doesn't take any mess. A strong woman, Grandma, just like you. I know you would approve. She's gonna take good care of me, Grandma, and I'm gonna take good care of her. I remember all the things you told me: Don't hit women, always give respect, work hard at the relationship, communicate, and all of the other things. Well, G-lady, that's about it for now. You know I'll be back Sunday, same time. You be good, I might sneak us a little sherry out here. I love you Grandma."

Damian rose from his knees and Grace rose with him. She stared at him in silence as he closed his eyes and entered into prayer. She then closed her eyes and began to analyze her situation.

Here stood Damian Reigns: young, black, talented, educated, kind, committed, church-going, and handsome. A true gentlemen who dressed impeccably, loved and respected his grandmother dearly, was unafraid of love or commitment, sponsored youth programs to help young black kids, had no criminal record, and was probably the best thing that had ever walked into her life.

Millions of women worldwide would die to meet and marry a Damian Reigns, yet here she was standing by his side and gaining his trust so that she could find evidence of wrongdoing—evidence which up until this point the entire FBI, DEA, BATF, Customs Service, and IRS had been unable to find. *Is he guilty? Is he that good an actor? Is anyone? What is it that I'm feeling inside, and how did I come to feel this way? Am I falling for Damian? Could I actually bust a man whom I'm falling in...love with? Love? Is it love? Could I really arrest him if he's guilty? Could I?*

Grace Moore knew that it was a question that she would one day have to come face to face with. It was a question that she desperately hoped not to have to answer, at least not anytime soon. She needed to sort her feelings out first. Grace opened her eyes and stared at the side of Damian's head. *God damn you, Damian Reigns, you'd better be innocent*, she said to herself. Deep down, she knew that it wasn't that easy. Deep down, she knew that he wasn't.

Chapter Seventeen

The Lakes of Compaignion was the most exclusive community in all of Louisiana. It was gated, guarded, and patroled by roving pairs of security guards in trucks and on foot.

The Lakes, as it was known to insiders, was a private resort community, complete with its own fifteen-million-dollar country clubhouse and a trio of golf courses designed by Greg Norman, Tom Fazio, and Jack Nicklaus. The Lakes were nestled among the finest acreage in the state, with first-rate equestrian facilities, twenty-acre lots, and multi-million dollar estate homes constructed by the finest custom home builders in the country. It was a community for Louisiana's finest.

Being able to afford an estate within the community would by no means guarantee one's entrance. One's money not only had to be abundant, it also had to be old—very old.

The Tibbideaux clan had made its original fortune in France in service to the king. Their service had also been rewarded with a patent of nobility, vast tracts of land, and eventually the ire of the Estates General. The Tibbideaux fled France after their beloved king was deposed. Unlike most of the French aristocracy, however, the Tibbideaux' were able to escape with their wealth.

The family's subsequent fortunes were made in the colonies, dealing in cotton, sugar, and slaves. The large swath of Tibbideaux plantations that ranged up and down the delta, on both sides of the great river, was the stuff of legends.

René Tibbideaux' forty-thousand-square-foot, plantation-style mansion in The Lakes would have made his ancestors proud. His choice of a bride, however, was something else entirely. He was certain that many of his forebearers were rolling over in their graves.

Anjouinette Tibbideaux was undoubtedly a mulatto, although not the kind the Tibbideaux ancestors fell over themselves to get to—at least not in public. She could not pass for being white, Creole, or even Octoroon. Her skin was clearly that of a half-negro.

Anjouinette's mother had been a tall, elegant, full-blooded Cherokee from the state of Oklahoma and her father had been a tall, dignified, former ambassador to Washington from the French speaking African nation of Senegal. As a result, Anjouinette had been born with luscious pink full lips, and a deep, burnished, coppery-red skin tone that resembled a fiery red penny. She had also inherited her mother's high, distinguished cheekbones, thin, sharp nose, thick, naturally groomed eyebrows.

Anjouinette's jet-black hair fell down her back and past her knees, where it hung like strands of fine silk. Anjouinette was as beautiful as the sun was hot. Her beauty was captivating but in a sad manner, reminding everyone of an elegant but captive ibis unable to fly. It was the beauty of a rare, black butterfly that had been caught inside a crystal cage.

Anjouinette had fell into the hands of the Tibbideaux clan at the age of fourteen. She had given birth to René Tibbideaux' daughter at the age of fifteen and a son at the age of sixteen. Another daughter came at the age of twenty-four, and more recently, a second son six months ago. Anjouinette was thirty-four with a daughter in her second year at LSU.

"The baby's crying," René told her, as he woke her from her sleep on the couch.

"René, I'm tired, can't you go and get your son?"

"I'm a man; tending to children is women's work."

"René, I have ze flu," she reminded him, in her thick, melodic, French accent.

René Tibbideaux extended his hand to her face, where he slapped her full, red lips.

"That's a warning."

Anjouinette shuddered at his raised hand.

"What did I tell you about talking back?" he asked sticking his finger in her face.

Anjouinette rose from the couch and turned her back toward her husband.

"Le cochon," she whispered.

"What did you say?" René asked her.

Anjouinette shook her head. "Rien."

"Yes, you did. You said, le cochon. You called me a pig; didn't you?"

"Non!" she said shaking her head.

The baby began to cry even louder.

René Tibbideaux loosened his belt and pulled it from his trousers.

"No, René, please!" Anjouinette lifted her hands, and began to back away from her husband.

René snapped his belt. "I'm a pig, huh?"

"No, René, please. Les enfants, ze children, they are upstairs. I'll get Philipe. I'll get his bottle, please."

"Hush li'l baby, don't say a word, Dante's gonna buy you a mocking bird, and if that mocking bird don't sing, Dante's gonna buy you a diamond ring..."

René and Anjouinette Tibbideaux turned toward their massive, wrought-iron staircase, and watched in horror as Dante Reigns descended the stairs, cradling their six-month-old child. Several of Dante's suited bodyguards followed just behind. Anjouinette closed her eyes and began weeping. Her

133

children were upstairs, from where Dante had just came.

René felt a sharp pain shoot through his stomach, and suddenly it felt as though his heart had fallen to his knees. The fact that Dante Reigns was inside of his home meant that all of his bodyguards were dead. The fact that he had come from upstairs where his children were inside their rooms studying, or playing their video games, meant that his children were quite possibly dead as well. He knew he was going to die.

Dante rocked a cooing Philipe Tibbideaux back and forth in his arms.

"And if that diamond ring don't shine, Dante's gonna buy you a bottle of wine. And if that bottle of wine gets broke, Dante's gonna buy you a billy goat."

Dante shifted his gaze from little Philipe to René.

"What comes after the billy goat?"

René swallowed hard, and his gaze fell to the floor. The leather belt he held in his hand also fell to the floor.

Dante shook his head. "Ah, it doesn't matter." He shifted his gaze back to the baby.

"And if you don't like that billy goat, Dante's gonna slit your daddy's throat."

Several of the hulking body guards laughed. Quietly, they fanned throughout the living room, where they took up various posts around the room. Dante nodded toward Anjouinette, greeting her. She closed her eyes. Dante shifted his gaze to René.

"Hello, René."

"Dante, please tell me that my children are okay," Anjouinette sniffled, as the tears continued to stream down her face.

"Anjouinette, your children are safe. The doors to their rooms were closed, and I never opened them."

Anjouinette's body shuddered as she began crying heavily. "Thank you, monsieur. Thank you."

Dante nodded, and shifted his gaze back to her husband.

"So, René, what exactly were you going to do with that belt?" Dante lifted his finger and shook it toward the Frenchman. "You know how I feel about domestic violence—or any kind of violence for that matter."

Several of the bodyguards snickered.

René lifted his palm into the air. "Dante, please. It was not my wishes to betray you."

"Aw, c'mon now René, you're one of the loudest, most vocal members on the commission. And if the commission wanted to replace my brother they would definitely have to overcome you, and Raphael's and Barry's objections. I mean, you guys are the ones who would have to live next door to Princess."

"Dante, it wasn't me. I voted for Damian to remain."

Dante shook his head.

"Do you know what it's like to hide behind a steel girder, while some idiot in a fucking helicopter tries to turn you into an NRA recruiting commercial?"

"It was not me! I told them that giving Mademoiselle Reigns control would be madness! Don Alemendez and Don Ferdinand pushed the commission to replace you."

Dante smiled wishing the old man would stop his lying.

"I talked to Emil. I also talked to Raphael." Dante made the sign of the cross on his chest. "God rest his soul. They told me everything. Well, Emil told me a lot, but Raphael, well, let's just say he spilled the beans...and his guts...and his entrails... and kidneys...and live and learn...and, well, you get the point."

"Don Frederico is the one who put the hit out on you, not me!"

Dante lifted an eyebrow.

"Oh, did he? So, Fat Freddie wants to play with helicopters, eh?"

"Dante, please, spare me."

Dante looked down and shook his head.

"René, you know I can't do that. Didn't you see that

movie Shaka Zulu? Nande said, 'never leave an enemy behind or one day he will fly back at your throat' or it was something to that effect. I don't remember, but I do know that it was very good advice," Dante smiled.

René Tibbideaux fell upon his knees. "Dante, I will give you one-hundred-million dollars if you let me live."

Dante turned and walked to a plush, leather, wing-backed chair, where he seated himself. He leaned back in the chair and crossed his legs. His Armani trousers rode up, exposing his silk, Hermes socks.

"René, you know that money means nothing to me."

"Power is what you crave? I'll give you all of Louisiana!" René interlaced his fingers and held his hands into the air. "I'll leave the country, and you can have all of Louisiana."

Dante shook his head and smiled.

"René, once I kill you, I'll have all of Louisiana anyway. Your underbosses are dead. Your area chiefs are dead. You're the last man standing, and after tonight, Louisiana will be mine for the taking."

René Tibbideaux dropped his hands back down to his sides, and began to weep.

"Dante," Anjouinette called out to him softly.

Dante shifted his gaze toward her.

"I knew what my husband did for a living. I accept my fate, as I know that you cannot leave any witnesses. But my children have not seen your face, nor the faces of your men. I have never asked you for anything, but I beg you now to please spare the lives of my children."

"Anjouinette, you know this is business, and you know our code. Are you going to call the police on me once I am gone?"

"Monsieur Dante, if you were to leave me with my life, I swear before God, that I would not give any testimony against you to the authorities."

"What?" René Tibbideaux rose from his knees.

Dante lifted his hand and pointed his finger at

Anjouinette, "If you do, then my men will come after you, and the lives of your children will not be spared."

"I would do nothing to endanger the lives of my children, monsieur."

"I know. Anjouinette, you and your children are in no danger here."

Anjouinette Tibbideaux bowed her head slightly and then shifted her gaze to her husband, as she continued to address Dante.

"When you do what you have to do, monsieur, would it be possible for you to do it in such a way that would not traumatize my children?"

"What?" René shouted. "You ungrateful bitch! They can kill me, as long as they do it quietly?"

Anjouinette turned her nose up. "At least die like a man, René."

René Tibbideaux lunged forward and slapped his wife. She gasped, and lifted her hand to her nose, where she wiped away the blood.

"Je desire tu mort!" she told him through clenched teeth.

"You want me dead?" he frowned. "This is the thanks I get?"

"You bastard! I hate you!" Anjouinette hissed. "For twenty-years, I have waited for zis moment!"

René recoiled.

"I was fourteen years old, you perverted son-of-a-bitch. You raped me! For fourteen years, you raped me! Now die!" Anjouinette turned to Dante. "What is going to happen to René's seat on the commission?"

"Nothing."

"And my husband's territory? To whom will le commission give it?"

"They cannot give away what they no longer control," Dante answered.

Anjouinette walked rapidly to where Dante was seated, and kneeled down before him.

"Then you can give it to me?"

"What?" Dante leaned forward. "Do you really know what you are asking Anjouinette? Do you really think that you have the stomach to do what we do? It is a ruthless business, Anjouinette."

"Dante, I am a mother, with children to feed, clothe, and shelter. There is nothing that I would not do to protect my children. René has made a lot of enemies. I need to protect my family."

"Anjouinette…"

"Dante, the one thing zat monster did do was allow me to attend university. I have a masters from Dilliard and my bachelors in business from Xavier."

Anjouinette lifted Dante's hand to her lips, and she kissed his ring. "Monsieur, if you give me Louisiana, I pledge my eternal loyalty to your family."

Dante smiled.

René Tibbideaux flew into an uncontrollable rage.

"Oh shut up René," she told him. "The children will hear you."

Anjouinette rose and turned to her husband. "You are the one who chose this life. Your family had money, power, and connections, René. You did not have to become the monster that you became. And now, you leave me with four children, two who are in the university. I have to pay their tuition, René. I have to pay for this house, our other homes, the boats, the planes, and all of the workers who depend on us to feed their families."

Anjouinette turned back to Dante. "Have him remove his clothing, and then drown him in the swimming pool. It's quiet and it won't arouse suspicion. I can explain it to my children as being a terrible accident. I will wait until one hour after you have been gone to find his body. I go now, to look after my children." Anjouinette turned and glided up the stairs, where she disappeared.

Dante shifted his gaze to a shocked, sulking, and

defeated René. "She's one hell of a woman."

René nodded.

"Very beautiful, very strong," Dante added.

"And very gullible, if she thinks that you are going to leave this house with her alive."

Dante stretched and yawned, "You know, René, I once had a woman by my side just like Anjouinette."

"I remember. Le field marshal Angelique. She was very beautiful, very deadly."

Dante nodded. "And very loyal."

Dante shifted his gaze to the staircase upon which Anjouinette had disappeared.

"I think I will give her control of Louisiana. I think that Anjouinette will work out fine."

"You add insult to injury!"

"At least I'm not going to torture you."

René nodded.

"I'd love to chat with you, René, but I really must be going. I have other commission members to kill."

René laughed.

"Such power. What does it feel like, to have that much power, Monsieur Reigns? We all started out together, and now, you are like Amerique. The lone super power."

"It feels good René. But as you know, all good things must one day come to an end," Dante said before he rose from the chair.

"Only yesterday, I was invincible. Only yesterday, I had the mayor over for dinner to discuss his gubernational ambitions. Yesterday, I had soldiers, hundreds of them. And billions of dollars."

"And today?"

"Today, or tonight rather, it appears as though I have seen my last moon." René extended his hand, and Dante shook it.

"Congratulations monsieur. The best man has won."

Dante shook his head.

"No, René. The most ruthless man has won."

Dante turned toward his men.

"Take him to the pool and strip him down to his boxers. When you're done with him, call Anjouinette on her cell phone, and let her know that it is done. I'm on my way to the airport, I have to go and pay my respects to our friend, Don Frederico."

Chapter Eighteen

Damian lifted his arm, and again began to point things out to Grace.

"Over there is Mr. G's soul food restaurant, and to my left is the community center that I built last year."

Damian and Grace walked down the narrow community street, touring the neighborhood. His one hundred and twenty inch Mercedes stretch limousine followed just behind them. Behind that were three heavily armored black Ford Excursions filled with armed men. In front of Damian and Grace walked six hulking men in long gray and black overcoats.

"Damian, why do you have all of these men with you?" Grace asked. "Why do you need them?"

Damian smiled his easy smile, and then stuck his hands inside of his long gray cashmere over coat.

"Jonel, you know I have a lot of money, don't you? I mean, it should be obvious by now. Well, cars aren't the only thing people in neighborhoods like this hijack. They also kidnap people. You know that, don't you?"

Grace nodded her head slowly. His reason was plausible.

Damian started laughing. "Can you imagine Nathan having to track down my kidnappers and rescue me?"

The thought of Nathan having to do so made Grace laugh. Again, Damian had been right on the money. Not

141

everyone who needed bodyguards was a drug dealer. And Damian was certainly wealthy enough to present a legitimate target. Heck, she had investigated the kidnappings of people whose families had only a fraction of Damian's wealth.

"I think my case would be one of those that makes for a good Geraldo Rivera special. I can see it now," Damian spread his hands across the sky. "What happened to Damian Reigns, the young scion of a wealthy industrial family?"

Grace laughed and placed her arm in his.

"C'mon, let's go check out this community center of yours," she said pulling him by his arm toward the building.

The building was a large structure, encompassing roughly one hundred thousand square feet spread over two floors. Its exterior was made up of hewn stone of a light brown shade and black-tinted, steel-framed windows. The materials served to minimize the building's maintenance requirements, and to ensure its beauty and durability over a considerable period. It would stand for generations.

Damian stopped at the building's entrance and turned toward Grace. "I would open the doors for you, but I don't want to risk being called a male chauvinist."

"I was waiting to see if you were going to open them so that I could jump all over you. I see you're learning," Grace said as she pinched his cheek.

Damian waved his hand, and one of his hulking men in suits pulled the glass door open and held it.

"Smart, real smart!" Grace laughed and nodded.

"Now you can't accuse me of being a chauvinist," Damian laughed, grabbed Grace's hand, and entered the building.

The interior of the community center was cool, clean, and surprisingly quiet. The floors were covered in a low maintenance beige stone tile, the walls were covered with a thick, heavily textured beige wallpaper, and even the lighting fixtures looked as if they were made to last a lifetime. They were made of stainless steel.

Damian walked through the center, pointing things out

142

to Grace.

"Over here is the video arcade and the music center where the kids can go and learn to play an instrument."

Grace nodded as she looked at everything he pointed out to her.

"And over here we have the basketball courts, the fitness center for aerobics, and a fully equipped gym. There's also a wellness center with a dietician to teach the community about obesity, food preparation for diabetics, and things of that nature."

"Wow!" Grace had to admit she was impressed.

"We bring in speakers and doctors, and people from other organizations and government agencies to talk to the community about various issues. We have a nice size auditorium here. We also use it for the community playhouse's local talent shows and things of that nature. Planned Parenthood used it the other day to talk about teen pregnancy."

"Damian, this is some place you have here." Grace ran her fingers through her hair, sending it back over her shoulders. "How many of these centers do you have?"

"Right now, twelve. We're building three more as we speak. They've had a tremendous impact on the communities they serve. We link ourselves with other groups and quadruple our effectiveness. For instance, we hold clothing drives here for Goodwill and for various churches. We sign up volunteers here for Habitat for Humanity. During the winter months we open up our auditorium, bring out the cots, get the kitchen going, and feed and shelter the homeless. We get a bit of overflow from the churches and the shelters, but not enough to overwhelm us. We've managed to do some really good things, but, the best is yet to come. Follow me."

Damian nodded his head toward a wide stairway and headed up. Grace followed closely behind.

"So, what about staffing?" she asked him, as they

reached the second floor. "Is it hard to find and maintain staff?"

"Glad you asked. We maintain a relationship with the Texas Employment Commission and the Texas Rehabilitation Commission. They use our auditoriums to reach the communities and help provide jobs for the people they send us, who live in the communities. We also maintain a relationship with Alamo Community College. We allow their students to intern at our center. They send people out to the centers to teach Adult Continuing Education, to help people earn their GEDs, to tutor kids still in school, and, more importantly, to teach computer skills. And I'm not just talking about computer literacy. I'm talking about programming, software design, computer graphics, all the advanced stuff."

Damian stopped and opened one of the doors to a computer classroom not in use. Grace followed him inside.

"Nice set up," she told him. Grace tapped at the keys of a computer keyboard. She lifted her head and stared at Damian. "They're new."

"Of course," Damian lifted his hands into the air, and spun around slowly. "In order to learn cutting edge technology, you have to have state-of-the-art equipment."

"How much did all of this cost?"

Damian shook his head. "You don't want to know."

"Mr. Reigns!" A voice called from the doorway.

Damian and Grace turned.

"Mrs. Hathaway!" Damian smiled and outstretched his arms as he walked toward her. They embraced.

Grace guessed her to be about fifty. She wore long, cheap, synthetic braids with her natural gray hair showing visibly at the roots. Judging from her clothing, she was local.

"Mr. Reigns, it's so good to see you!" she told Damian.

"Mrs. Hathaway, it's nice to see you," Damian replied. "What brings you to the center at this time of the morning?"

"Well, I took your advice. I got the results back from my

GED test yesterday, and now I'm here registering to take vocational nursing classes!"

Damian hugged her again.

"That's wonderful!" he leaned back and stared at her. "I take it you got your GED?"

"I sure did," Mrs. Hathaway smiled. "I couldn't have done it without you!"

"What did you score on the test?"

"I scored a one hundred and fifty! I needed to average fifty points, and I did it!"

"That's wonderful!"

"Oh, Mr. Reigns, thank you. Thank you so much for everything."

Damian nodded as if it was nothing.

"How's Martha? Is she still clean?"

"No." Mrs. Hathaway looked down. "She's back in rehab."

Damian tilted his head to the side. "I'm sorry to hear that."

"It's not your fault, you tried."

"Mr. Damian!" A large, gruff, pot-bellied gray haired man in coveralls walked up to them. He extended his hand and Damian shook it. He turned to Mrs. Hathaway. "Betty, how you doing?"

"Jeremiah, I'm fine. I'm just on my way out the door. How's Sally Sue?"

"Oh, she's fine. Just at home fussing and cussing at those grand kids."

Betty Hathaway laughed. "Tell her that I'm gonna call her tonight. I got some good gossip for her and it can't wait till Sunday!"

"I'll tell her," Jeremiah laughed.

"You two, take care. Thanks again, Mr. Reigns," Betty Hathaway turned and walked away.

"So, Mr. Cooper, how is everything going?" Damian asked. "Oh, and Mr. Cooper, I'd like you to meet my friend

Jonel. Jonel, this is Mr. Cooper. Mr. Cooper teaches the saxophone, the trombone, the tuba, and the trumpet here at the center. He makes a saxophone talk so seductively sweet that you'd swear Billie Holiday was whispering in your ear."

"Aw, now there you go, Mr. Reigns. I ain't that good."

"Mr. Cooper, you are the best. The best!"

Mr. Cooper cleared his throat and looked down. His hands began fumbling with the old, worn, baseball cap in his hands. Damian knew the signs. He knew when Jeremiah Cooper had something on his mind that he wanted to talk about.

"So, what's on your mind, Mr. Cooper?" Damian asked.

"Well, ah, well...it's about Junior."

"Is he in trouble again?" questioned Damian, his face contorted.

"No, far from it," Mr. Cooper twisted his tattered, red, baseball cap even more. "Well...a...I don't know how to say it."

"Mr. Cooper, is everything okay?" Damian said frowning his face with wonder.

"Yeah, and that's what I want to say." Mr. Cooper looked up at Damian. "It's cuz of you that my boy is doing okay. He ah... well, whatever it was that you told him when you took him to that New Orleans Saints game, it worked. He ain't running with those other boys no more. He's getting his lessons and he's even talking about going off to college."

"That's good!" Damian slapped Jeremiah Cooper across his broard shoulder.

"Yeah, it's real good. I don't know if I can afford college, but I'd rather squeeze up and afford college, than squeeze up and afford a funeral. Aw, shit, what I'm saying is thanks, son."

Mr. Cooper extended his hand, and Damian gripped it tightly.

"You are welcome, Mr. Cooper. And when it's time for Junior to go to college, let me know. It's on me."

Jeremiah Cooper shook his head. "Nope. You've done enough already. You gave him back to me, got him talking things out with me, and that's good enough. I'm going to enjoy every minute of struggling and paying my boy's way through school."

Damian smiled and nodded. "I know what you mean. But either way, remember there are plenty of scholarships out there for him. Just tell him to work hard and study hard, and later on he'll be able to chill and take it easy."

"Will do, Mr. Reigns," Jeremiah Cooper released Damian's hand, and waved at Grace. "Nice to meet you, Mrs. Reigns," he said before he turned and walked away.

"Mrs. Reigns?" Grace lifted an eyebrow.

"I didn't say it; he did," said Damian smiling from ear to ear.

"You didn't correct him, either," said Grace looking serious.

"You didn't either."

Grace turned away to hide her smile. She stepped out of the classroom and into the hall. Damian closed the classroom door.

"So why do you do it?" she asked.

"Do what?"

Grace lifted her hands and waved them around. "This. All of this. What's it all for? I mean, really for? And don't tell me it's because of Father O'Connell's super secret ear twist either."

Damian smiled. "It's for my people. I'm a black man, Jonel. I'm a wealthy black man at that. I have a responsibility to make things better. Do you know where our race would be right now had we not been forced into slavery? Do you know where our race would be had we been compensated for slavery? We would have no projects or ghettos or hoods to have to live in, struggle in or fight in. We'd be equal in our education system and financial wealth."

Damian started down the hall, with Grace walking along

147

next to him as she listened to him speak.

"I once read a novel about the Hitler Youth. I remember this one particular passage, where it said that those kids had been born to die for Hitler. And I always remembered that phrase, born to die. And later I thought about us, and about the conditions many of us grow up in. There are kids out there that are born to go to prison, kids that are born to die for their neighborhood gang. It's ridiculous, Jonel and a complete waste of life, a waste of potential, a waste, period. I don't know, maybe I'm trying to challenge fate, maybe I'm trying to change something that's already written, but hell, I just can't help it. I just can't accept the fact that these kids are born to go to prison, that they are born to grow up into killers, that they are born to die! Something inside of me just won't accept that. Is that wrong, Jonel?" Damian stopped, and turned toward her. His eyes met hers.

"Am I doing wrong?"

Grace shook her head and looked down. Her unfaithfully eyes could not bare to face his.

"No, Damian. You're not doing wrong. You're not doing wrong at all."

Chapter Nineteen

Utah's Wasatch and Uinta ranges of the great American Rocky Mountains are one of the country's best-kept secrets. The ranges are home to fifteen of Utah's ski resorts, some of which are the best in the country. The Utah ranges receive, on average, over five hundred inches of the lightest, fluffiest, and softest snow in the world. Add to that, the majestic vistas provided by the Rockies, and affordable prices for everything a skier could possibly want, and the ranges' close proximity to Salt Lake City, and one can understand why the Wasatch and Uinta ranges are a true skier's paradise. It was because of all this that Don Frederico kept coming back year after year. Where else could one treat oneselves to an abundant seven-course-meal for less than one hundred dollars, and do it all in total anonymity?

The slopes were nearly empty and the snowfall was fresh. With less than six-percent moisture content, the snow promised to be powdery and provide a very soft, ski-friendly slope. The fat Don couldn't wait to try it out. To him, breaking in a fresh hill was reminiscent of breaking in a fresh woman. Sadly for him, it had been years since he had done the latter; virtue was hard to find in America and virtually nonexistent for men of his age and girth.

"American women," the Don snorted. "So easy with their virtue, but so full of money."

In Colombia, it was the opposite. The women had virtue,

but very few had money. And money could easily buy virtue. It was one of the things he missed about the old country.

One of his men approached.

"Don Frederico, everything's ready. We're all set up on a hill just north of here. The hill's pretty empty, and we've taken care of the lift operator. You're going to have the hill all to yourself, Don."

Frederico folded two large pancakes, dipped them into the syrup that was pooled on his plate, and stuffed them into his already full mouth.

"Good, good," he mumbled with a nod of his fat head. He pushed his chair away from the large, elaborately decorated table, rose, and bounded out of the restaurant. His men dutifully followed.

The morning promised a beautiful day. The sun was just starting to peek over the horizon. The air was crisp, cool, and soothing, and the sky radiated a deep, fluorescent blue, framing the majestic, white mountains.

Don Frederico seated his four-hundred-pound frame on a nearby chair at the slopeside restaurant. The establishment was empty this morning, reserved for him and his men. It had cost him three thousand dollars to have the owner open the restaurant up this early in the morning, all so he could enjoy fresh snow and virgin slopes.

One of the Don's bodyguards knelt down before him, and proceeded to put on the Don's skis. It had been a long time since he had been able to tie his own shoes, let alone put on his own skis. It was a concession he had to make for enjoying the good life.

With his skis firmly in place, the good Don rose and ambled his way toward the ski lift. His obedient entourage followed. The lift for this particular hill consisted of an open air, bench type with seating for two, the type the Don loved. The chair provided him with unobstructed views of the ranges and the majestic valleys below.

Don Frederico plopped himself down on the lift chair

while one of his men climbed into the seat and sat next to him. The rest of the Don's bodyguards climbed aboard three additional lift chairs behind him to rendezvous with the men already positioned on the slopes. A person of the Don's importance couldn't be too careful. He was El Jefe's personal mediator, messenger, and voice to the Distribution Commission not only in the United States and Mexico, but in Colombia, Panama, Costa Rica, Nicaragua, El Salvador, and Honduras as well. He liked to think of himself as being the Oliver Wendell Holmes of El Jefe's borderless empire. And a Chief Justice of an empire couldn't be too careful. He turned to his assistant.

"Did you bring the pump?"

The assistant quickly fumbled through the pockets of his down-filled ski-jacket until he located Don Frederico's asthma medicine. He shook the inhaler and handed it to the Don. Frederico placed the asthma pump to his mouth, pressed down upon the top of the inhaler, and sucked in the medicated crystals. The high altitudes combined with his four hundred plus pounds were cause to play havoc on his lungs. He held his breath, waited for sixty seconds, and inhaled another dose of medicine. Don Frederico tossed the asthma pump back to his assistant.

The view of the valley far below the lift gave Don Frederico a tremendous amount of sensual pleasure. Peering over the bench down into the valley spiked his adrenaline in a way that could only be rivaled by the very best cocaine. He was hundreds if not thousands of feet in the air. He swung his fat legs back and forth through the air and enjoyed the rare feeling of weightlessness upon them. He often found himself enjoying the lift ride as much as he did the downhill journey, and sometimes even more so. The Don's enjoyment quickly came to a jolting halt when the ski lift suddenly jerked to a stop.

Don Frederico turned and glanced back over his shoulder toward his men, who were riding in the other lift chairs. "What the hell is going on? We're in the middle of the valley!"

Several of his clueless men shrugged their shoulders, and lifted their palms into the air.

"Well, get on the walkie-talkie and call back to the lift operator!" the Don shouted. "Tell him that he has three minutes to fix this thing or his wife will be a widow by lunch time!"

One of the bodyguards lifted his two-way radio to his lips, and spoke rapid Spanish into it. He listened for the answer, and then called back to the Don.

"Don Frederico, they say there is a problem, but it was not Enrique who answered."

"Not Enrique, then who is it?"

The bodyguard again spoke rapid Spanish into the two-way communicator. His face turned ashen when he looked back up at the Don.

"He says that he is the angel of death."

"What?" Don Frederico turned red with anger. "You tell the fool on the other side of that thing that he has just signed his death warrant! Tell him that I am Don Frederico Ponce Hernandez de Silva, and that *I am* the angel of death!"

The bodyguard again spoke into his walkie-talkie. His face turned red, and he peered up at the Don again.

"Well, what is it?" the Don demanded.

"He said...he said..."

"Spit it out!"

"He said he knows who you are, Fat Boy!"

Heat bled into Don Frederico's face, turning it beet red. It was then when they heard the whir of the helicopter blades.

The big, black and gold Sikorsky made its way through the valley until it came to a hovering stop some eighty yards from the stranded skiers. The massive, black rear door of the helo slid open to reveal a smiling Dante Reigns.

Dante lifted a large, white and blue bullhorn to his lips.

"Hey, Fat Boy! You wanna play with helicopters and

machine guns, huh? That's fine, as long as you recognize it, when you see it comin'!"

Dante turned and sat the bullhorn down. In its place, he lifted a large, black, M-16 assault rifle, with a large, black scope on it. Don Frederico's men pulled out their handguns and started firing.

Dante chambered a round from the M-16's magazine, and set the weapons rate-of-fire selector on full-auto. He lifted the assault rifle to his shoulder, and began to squeeze the trigger.

Don Frederico's bodyguards on the first lift bench, turned into a large haze of blood, smoke, and feathers from their down jackets. Dante shifted his aim to the second bench, and again squeezed the trigger. The machine gun burped rapidly, and the bodyguards seated in that bench fell into the valley below. Fortunately for them, they were already dead before they left the bench. Dante removed the now empty, one hundred round drum lip from his machine
gun, and inserted a full one hundred round drum magazine. He lifted the machine gun to his shoulder, and turned the bodyguards seated on the third bench, into a Mass of blood, wooden bench splinters, down feathers, and smoke. The bullet-ridden bench collapsed from beneath the bodies of the men, sending them plummeting into the snow filled valley below. Dante leaned back and smiled, as he observed his handy-work, only the Don and his assistant were left.

Don Frederico unbuckled his seatbelt, and tried to lift his body high enough to extend his hand and grab the overhead cable. His shifting weight caused the bench to tilt dramatically forward, almost spilling him out into the cold, crisp, mountain air. He quickly abandoned that idea and put his seat belt back in place.

Dante turned and sat the M-16 down inside the helo. In its place he lifted a Barrette, fifty-caliber, sniper rifle. Dante chambered one of the massive fifty-caliber rounds, and then took aim and squeezed the trigger. The head of Don

Frederico's assistant exploded, causing blood to fly all over the Don's clean, white, snow suit. The Don screamed.

Dante lifted his bullhorn again.

"Hey, Fat Boy! I'll tell you what. If I can't hit the cable in three shots, I'll leave. If I do, then you'd better hope all that blubber cushions your fall!"

Dante lowered the bullhorn and again lifted the massive rifle. He aimed through the scope, and put the cable into the crosshairs. Dante exhaled fully and then held his breath and squeezed the trigger.

The massive, fifty-caliber round tumbled through the air and tipped the thick wound steel cable that carried the lift chairs. The sound of metal striking metal rang out, and the cable vibrated violently. Don Frederico grabbed the bench and held on tightly.

Dante shook his head at the near miss and lifted the bullhorn to his lips again.

"That's one!" He lowered the bullhorn, lifted the rifle, and took aim again.

The booming sound of the fifty-caliber rifle echoed throughout the valley for a second time as Dante held his breath and squeezed the trigger. This time, however, he missed the cable entirely.

"Shit!" Dante pounded his fist against the carbon fiber butt of the rifle. Firing from a helicopter and trying to strike a four-inch cable with a single round was a lot more difficult than he had anticipated. He turned to his pilot.

"Bring us in another twenty yards."

The massive Sikorsky slid itself within sixty yards of the terrified Don, and again, Dante lifted his rifle and took aim.

Dante brought the cable directly into the center of his electro-illuminated crosshairs, adjusted his breathing, and squeezed the trigger. The fifty-caliber weapon cracked loudly, and the massive bullet tumbled through the air. It missed the first cable, but sliced through the second. The lift chairs plummeted violently for several feet until the cable became

154

caught back at the lift station. Dante cursed and Don Frederico threw his hands into the air.

"That's three!" The Don shouted, while holding three fingers in the air. "That's three! I live señor! You gave your word, and that's three!"

The lift chair was connected to the cable by a five-inch thick metal bar that was itself connected to a metal pulley with six wheels that glided the chair along the cable. Dante lifted the rifle to his shoulder, and aimed for the thicker, metal bar. He squeezed the trigger and watched with delight as the massive round disintegrated the metal bar. Don Frederico's chair plummeted some twenty-two-hundred feet to the valley below. Dante lifted his bullhorn.

"Don Frederico, I forgot to tell you. I can't count!"

Chapter Twenty

Grace Moore could feel butterflies in her stomach every time the helicopter hit a down draft. She placed her hands over her stomach, gripping it tightly, while silently hoping that all of those butterflies flapping around inside would somehow give her the ability to fly should something go wrong.

Fortunately, there were no signs that anything would go wrong. The overstuffed Connelly leather seats, full entertainment center, and crystal champagne bar inside the cabin reassured her that she was flying in the very best helo that money could buy. *The best*, she told herself. *Nothing but the best.*

Grace Moore leaned back in her seat and closed her eyes, as the helicopter began its descent toward the landing pad at Reigns Industrial Complex Number One. Traveling by helicopter was frightening, but traveling in sheer luxury every time she left the penthouse, well; she could get used to that. The though of her burgundy Lexus made her smile.

"We're here," Damian told her. He rose, opened the door to the helicopter, and climbed out. Grace watched as he brushed himself off, straightened out his Armani suit, and then turned and out stretched his hand to her. "My lady."

"Thank you," she said, clasping his hand tightly and climbing out of the big Sikorsky. She too straightened out her attire once she was on the ground. It was more out of habit than anything else.

The industrial park was massive. Vast expanses of brick buildings interspersed among corrugated steel ones, stretched as far as the eye could see. Giant smokestacks pierced the skyline, billowing steady, white streams of steam and smoke. Grace Moore was impressed.

"The park stretches from here until you get to Interstate 37 South, and from loop 410 South all the way back until you get to FM 70." Damian spread his arms wide, and turned slowly. He was the master of all he surveyed. "Welcome to Reigns Industrial Complex Number One."

Grace Moore smiled and nodded. "Impressive, how long did it take to build all of this?"

Damian placed his hand on her lower back and guided her toward the entrance of the industrial complex.

"Actually, it started off as an old cement manufacturing plant and my father moved his construction company onto the premises. We refurbished and renovated the cement manufacturing plant and then added warehouse after warehouse along with consolidating all of our heavy industries and manufacturing here. We kept adding and buying up adjacent plots of land until one day we woke up and realized we owned the largest industrial complex in Texas."

"Wow!"

Damian tossed his head back in laughter and then glanced at Grace. "Is that all you could come up with? Wow?"

"That's all I could manage to come up with," she told him in between her short spurts of laughter. "Of course, a few profane words popped up in my head first, but..."

"I'll take the wow," Damian said.

Grace turned her palms up toward the sky. "So what exactly do you manufacture here?"

"We manufacture construction equipment, bus shelters, lots of light commercial and industrial tools and equipment, and cement."

"Cement?"

"Yeah, just enough to supply all of our commercial construction needs. Most of the cement for our industrial projects comes from the Portland Cement Company, though."

Damian led Grace through a massive set of metal doors into a vast warehouse filled with people, forklifts, pallet jacks, and pallets of cement bags, buzzing to and fro. Again, Damian lifted his arms and turned slowly, surveying his domain.

"This is ground zero. This is where the project headquarters will be for the new highway construction contract that the state has just awarded us. It's a fifteen-million-dollar project that will eventually turn into a thirty-seven-million-dollar contract once we win phase two of the bidding!"

What? A thirty-seven million dollar contract with the state, all going to Reigns Construction? Why, if he's a suspected drug dealer, that certainly doesn't make sense.

Grace Moore walked away from Damian and strolled up to a pallet of cement bags.

Thirty seven million dollars, she thought to herself. She reached out and ran her hand over the bags of MCC cement. *Thirty seven million dollars,* she couldn't help but think of all that money.

Her fingers traced the bold black letters on the cement bag that proudly proclaimed that this product was "Hecho en Mexico". *NAFTA,* she thought to herself. *Was the Reigns family getting rich off of free trade in more ways than just cement?*

"Hey, did you hear what I said?" Damian asked. He hugged her from behind. His touch startled her, causing her to jump.

"What? I'm sorry, what did you say?"

"I said I'm going to celebrate the contract by taking you to the Caribbean!"

"The Caribbean?!" Grace turned and faced him. "Are you serious? I've never been to the Caribbean before!"

Damian lifted her light frame and spun her around. "Of

158

course I'm serious! Oh, Jonel, we are going to have so much fun!"

Grace squeezed Damian's neck tightly and laughed giddily. A free trip to the Caribbean was fine with her. She just hoped that the Bureau wouldn't giver her static about it. They weren't especially pleased with the fur coats and the brand new Lexus, nor the penthouse, the clothing, the furnishings, or jewelry. But they did want her to get close to him, didn't they? All of the gifts were just girlfriend perks, weren't they? I mean, the Bureau would get them all in the end, wouldn't they?

Grace lifted her hand and peered over Damian's shoulder at her finger. The flawless, ten-carat, princess-cut diamond sparkled like a new star, even under the artificial lighting of the warehouse. *Sure, the Bureau would get most of the stuff. But not all,* she thought, smiling.

"So, who's going with us?" Grace asked, "Will Dante and his girlfriend be joining us?" She had not seen nor heard anything about Dante in the last few days. It would be good to keep track of his whereabouts.

Damian shook his head. "No, Dante will be taking care of things while I'm away. It'll just be you and me, the ocean, the stars, and about ten thousand other tourists."

Grace laughed and punched Damian on his shoulder. "You sure know what women want to hear!"

"What, ten thousand tourists including all their screaming kids isn't romantic?"

Grace laughed and again glanced at the ring on her finger.

Dante's Penthouse

Damian stood at the bar and sipped at his cognac. His back was toward his brother. "I'm listening."

Dante leaned back on his crème colored, Italian leather sectional, and crossed his legs.

"I talked to Jonel McNeal—the real one. She lives in Texas, but a banker she is not. She is a good lay though."

"Stick to the facts."

"Our little Jonel is not the real Jonel. That, my dear brother, is a fact."

Damian sipped again, then turned, and headed for the glass wall of windows, where he peered out into the city. He loved this view, especially at night when the city lights twinkled against the darkness. It was his shining city. His Camelot. He turned and faced his brother. "FBI?"

Dante ran his hand over his Canali trousers, smoothing out the gathered pants leg. "More likely than not. Her cover is deep, real deep. In a twisted sort of way, she even resembles the real Jonel."

"How do you know they resemble one another?"

"Jonel's roommate's mother led me to the real Jonel. Always the big things they forget. They're notorious for perfecting the small things, but something as obvious as a roommate and her mother, they let slip."

"She'll be dead by midnight," Dante rose sharply.

Damian lifted his hand, motioning for Dante to stop.

"No, don't. Let's not be like them, let's think this thing through."

"There is nothing to think about, she's a goddamned FBI agent! I'm burying her... tonight."

"Like you did all of the others?"

"Yes."

"And look what happens. They just keep on coming!"

"Of course, they're going to keep coming, it's their job! What you think this little cat and mouse game we play with the FBI will ever go away, my brother?"

Damian sat his glass of cognac on top of one of Dante's end tables and began a slow pace around the room.

"It's the FBI's job to bust criminals. We have not been

160

caught doing anything. They have absolutely nothing on us, yet they keep on coming," Damian said, stopped his pace and wheeled toward his brother. "No, Dante, this is personal. By now they would have pulled the plug. Somebody in Washington has a bug up their ass, and they've made it personal."

"Duh? How many agents have they lost trying to bust us? Don't you think those agents had buddies in the Bureau? Families who turn knobs and apply pressure?" Dante sat back down on his sofa and took a drink from his glass of ginger ale. "I can just picture the letters. Dear Congressman Blowhard, My husband was killed in the line of duty and the FBI will not give me any information about his death. Our unborn son, Little Timmy, will never know what happened to his father while he was serving our country trying to make the streets safe for him."

Dante enjoyed a good hard laugh and leaned forward staring Damian eye to eye.

"Brother, let me take care of our problem, before our problem takes care of us."

"Dante, I don't know; I got a feeling about this one."

"I'm sure you do, I get a throbbing feeling whenever I'm around a beautiful woman too."

"Not like that! Not that kind of feeling. She's not exactly a real veteran at this. She's not playing it right. She's not snooping, asking questions, being very FBI-like," Damian said shaking his head.

"Of course not; she's good. They wouldn't have allowed her to go in this deep if she weren't."

"No, no, she's in over her head. She doesn't know what she's doing."

"What are you saying?"

"I can lay her."

"Good, then do it. All of the evidence she's obtained will be inadmissible. Our lawyers would eat her up."

"It's more than that. It's the way she looks at me, the

hugs, the caresses, the conversations. I can look into her eyes and tell she's really into me."

Dante turned on the couch and faced his brother again. "Are you saying she's in love with you?"

"Maybe."

"Whoooaah, wait a minute. Damian, are you clear on this? You're talking about looking into her eyes, and deep conversations, and her looking into your eyes. Are your feelings clear on this?"

Damian smacked his lips and tilted his head toward one side. "Come on now, Dante. You know me better than that. What I'm saying is that I can turn her."

"Turn her? Damian have you gone mad. She's the fucking FBI. She is here to destroy you. She's not in love, she's acting, it's what they do. She's a cop—a federal cop at that. She gets paid to lie. It's how she makes a living and how she gets to live when people catch her."

"Dante, what's the going price for a federal agent?"

"Millions."

"I can get us one for free."

"You're playing a dangerous game."

"The game has always been dangerous and it was started by them. They sent her to me. Besides, she's already here, it costs us nothing. I'm already taking her to the Caribbean. I'm going to get her to fall in love with me."

"And then?"

"And then she's going to defend me against those bastards. She'll go back to them and swear up and down that we're squeaky clean."

"She's going to have to tell them that anyway."

Damian folded his arms and smiled. "Love will make her tell it to them more passionately."

Dante laughed at him, *Damian must be in love with her. Doesn't matter; the bitch won't destroy us. I won't let her.*

"We'll keep her close," Damian told his brother. "Having a girlfriend in the Bureau will be like having a shield, a pit

162

bull, and a permanent alibi all rolled into one."

"Mmm hmm, and eventually we could spoon feed her information on our opponents. Let her overhear staged conversations from the table next to ours. Oh man, we can do all kinds of things!"

"You see, and you wanted to kill her."

"That's why you're the yin to my yang."

"Now, about the club. How did she know I was going to be there?"

Dante folded his arms and lifted his thumb and index finger to his chin. "Hmm. It would have to be someone who had your itinerary for that night. Who?"

"My driver, Lenny, knew. My cook, Ernestina, I told her that I would pick up something to eat at the club."

Dante shook his head and frowned. He had preached to Damian over and over about operational security.

"Oh yeah, the head of my personal detail, Steve," Damian added.

"Are you taking security with you when you go to the Caribbean?"

"Of course, a few hidden trailers, nothing major."

"Steve's not going," Dante told him. "Get a new head of security."

Damian nodded. He understood what Dante was saying; poor Steve. He actually liked Steve.

"Take care of everything while I'm gone."

"Of course."

"And don't go crazy."

"I'm not. I'm just going to take care of the leak, that's all. When do you leave?"

"Day after tomorrow," Damian replied eyeing his brother skeptically.

"Have a good trip, Bro," Dante said with a wide grin.

Chapter Twenty-One

The air above Ochos Rios was thick with humidity. The sun beamed brightly, its fiery orange glow providing a brilliant contrast against the cloudless, baby blue sky. The warm rays tickled the faces of everyone they touched, especially the people closest to them.

"It's so beautiful up here," Grace told Damian. She took his hand and held it tight. "The water looks as blue as the sky from this height."

Damian peered over the basket in which they were riding and examined the clear blue water below. *It is absolutely beautiful*, he thought. The water was so clean, so clear, and so blue.

"Take us a little higher," he told the balloon operator.

The operator pulled the lever controlling the balloon's altitude, adding helium and heat simultaneously, and the balloon rose even higher.

"Damian, I hope this thing doesn't pop or deflate, or do whatever it does when things go wrong," Grace Moore said grabbing onto Damian and holding his arm tightly against her.

"Relax Jonel, I've done this a hundred times, and the balloon has never popped."

"Oh, a hundred times, huh?" she pinched his forearm. "Is this where you take all of your girlfriends?"

"Oh, now you're my girlfriend?"

Grace blushed and turned away from his wide smile. "Look at that cruise ship. It looks so tiny from up here."

Damian knew that he had made her blush. He wasn't going to let her off that easy. "Are you my girlfriend?"

Grace pulled away from him, and leaned lightly over the edge of the basket, while cupping her hand over her eyes to shield them from the sun's brightest rays. "Look at those palm trees! They look like toothpicks!"

"Oh, so now you want to ignore me." Damian stepped closed to Grace, and pressed his body against hers. "It's Ignore Damian Day, huh?"

"Okay, you got me, I slipped," Grace laughed. "Now are you happy?"

"No," Damian said before he wrapped his arms around her and squeezed her tightly. "I have a question."

"What is that?"

"Are you comfortable with me now, now that you've started thinking of me as your boyfriend?"

Grace broke Damian's hold and turned around to face him. "What do you want me to say?"

"Yes."

"No. I'm not comfortable." Grace closed her eyes and folded her arms nervously. Their closeness made her fidgety.

"You're lying." Damian leaned forward and kissed Grace softly. Her hands dropped to her sides and then rose to his shoulders. Her lips parted, and she felt his warm tongue glide in her mouth. Her hands slid down to his waist and then rose up his back as she wrapped her arms around him.

Grace felt the warmth of the sun on her back, the warmth of Damian's body next to hers, and the warmth of his tongue continuously sliding across hers. She felt the moisture between her legs, and she knew that the true fire lied within. It had been a long time. A long, long time, too long. By the time he released her, her body ached and she was on fire.

"Damian..." her voice purred softly. Grace swallowed hard, and cleared her throat. "Damian..."

Damian placed a finger over her lips, silencing her. "Don't speak. Just let me hold you."

Grace nodded, wrapped her arms around him, and watched the beauty of the Caribbean, through her tear-filled eyes.

Dante strode into Damian's kitchen and sat the grocery bag on top of the black, granite, counter top. "Ernestina!"

Dante opened the massive double doors of the refrigerator and examined its contents. After a few seconds of studying, he leaned down, opened a produce drawer, and removed a large, ripe tomato.

"Ernestina!" he shouted again.

"Coming, Señor Reigns," a voice called out in the distance.

Dante sat the tomato on the counter, and removed a razor sharp peeling knife from a black knife holder underneath the cabinet just in front of him. Damian's cook strode into the room.

"Yes, Señor Reigns?" she asked, wiping her hands on her pink and white uniform.

"Ernestina, my dear Ernestina," Dante lifted the tomato, sliced a piece of it off, and then tossed the slice into his mouth. "You know what I haven't eaten in a long time?"

"What is that, señor?" Ernestina's heavy Spanish accent, made every question she posed seem provocative. It didn't hurt that she worked out everyday and had a body that would put most models to shame.

Dante smiled. He knew what Ernestina was thinking, and he really would have liked to indulge her, but this was business. *What a waste*, he thought, as he shook his head and ate another slice of tomato.

"No, my dear, not you," he told her. "Although it has

been awhile."

Ernestina laughed and placed her hands on her hips. "Well, you know I'm at your service, Señor Dante," she told him.

"I'll keep that in mind." Dante ate another slice of tomato and ventured over to the butler's pantry. He opened the door, walked inside, and grabbed several boxes of lasagna before returning to the kitchen counter.

"Oh, Señor Dante!" Ernestina clasped her hands. "You're not going to treat me to some of your famous lasagna, are you?"

Dante smiled and nodded.

"And the special cheese?" Ernestina turned toward the large paper sack sitting on the counter. "Oh, you got the cheese!"

Dante pulled a large pot from a rack hanging over the center island in the middle of the kitchen.

"Hand me the cheese. I'll get the tomatoes."

Ernestina opened the grocery bag and stuck her hand inside, fumbling around. She felt something hard and alive, just as she felt multiple bites. She started screaming and snatched her hand out of the grocery bag.

"Señor Reigns! Aaah! Oooh! Something bit me!"

She fell to the floor holding a bloody arm toward her stomach. "Help me!"

Dante helped her up, and set her down on one of the stools in front of the center island. He pulled a towel from a nearby drawer and handed it to her.

"Apply pressure with this."

"Señor, what is the meaning of this?"

Dante reached inside of his pocket, and pulled out a tiny glass vile.

"This is the anti-venom. Without it, you will die. Do you understand?"

"What is the meaning of this?" she asked again, in between her sobs, nodding her head to him.

"Inside that bag is a very young, very poisonous snake. Young snakes cannot control the amount of venom they pump out. They just let it flow. So it is important that you stay calm, understand?"

Ernestina's face was flush, while her arm had swelled visibly. He throat was already becoming dry.

"Why, Mr. Reigns? Why me?"

"Ernestina, did the FBI come and talk to you?"

"Besides the two times that I told the other Señor Reigns, no."

"Ernestina, are you telling me the truth?"

Ernestina's tears began to flow heavily. "Yes, Señor. I always tell you when they come."

"Okay, I didn't think it was you. Stop crying, now."

"Oh... oh...kay," said a frightful Ernestina.

Dante removed a syringe from his coat pocket, and plunged the needle into the tiny vile he held in his hand. He pulled back the stopper on the syringe, drawing in several cc's of thick, clear liquid. "Here, give me your arm."

Ernestina stood, and raised her red swollen arm, exposing three, double-pronged bite marks. Dante stepped closer, grabbed her arm, and injected the needle into one of the bite marks.

"Thank you, señor," she told him with a sigh of relief.

Dante removed the needle from her arm and sat it on a nearby counter top. Ernestina grabbed her chest.

"Señor, it hurts!"

Dante nodded and smiled, "I know."

Ernestina stumbled backwards, and grabbed for the granite countertop to her right.

"Señor, help me!" Her arm accidentally swept all of the crystal and ceramic jars off of the counter.

"Ernestina, what I gave you, speeds up the effects of the venom. It's untraceable, so it will look like you died from the venom of the snakebite. After you are dead, I'm going to have your body taken to your home, and placed outside in the garden. Then, I'm going to release the snake into your garden, so that the Animal Control Officers can eventually find it."

Sweat poured down Ernestina's face, mixing with the tears from her eyes. Her chest hurt intensely, and increasingly she found it harder and harder to breathe.

"Why... my family in Mexico... they need me..."

"I know. Your family will be taken care of." Dante lifted the knife and tomato, and sliced off a piece for himself. "I always liked you, Ernestina. That's why I wanted your death to be easy, free of pain."

"It...it hurts..."

"But not for long." Dante lifted his hand and snapped his fingers. Two of his suited bodyguards quickly stepped into the kitchen. "Help her to the car. She should be dead by the time you get her to her garden."

Ernestina held out her arms for the bodyguards to grab. They quickly supported her. Dante stepped forward and kissed Ernestina's forehead.

"Goodbye my love," he whispered softly.

Quietly, Ernestina was led from the room.

Grace pulled her knees close to her body and wrapped her mocha arms around her legs. She rocked back and forth ever so slightly. Her wrap around skirt blew gently in the cool, Caribbean breeze as she sat alone on the rickety, old, wooden pier. The crispness of the breeze helped her to focus her thoughts as she tried to bring order to the chaos that was now overtaking her life.

Damian is the most perfect man, I've ever met, she thought to herself. He was young, black, charming, educated, wealthy, polite, sensitive, and caring. He was everything that she had ever wanted in a man, and more. He was a dream come true, and yet...

Grace ran her fingers through her hair, raking it out of her face. She stared into the blackness of the ocean before her and exhaled loudly. It was that and yet... that was killing her.

All of her adult career she had learned to trust her colleagues, trust herself, trust her gut feelings. The FBI Academy had instilled that self-confidence inside her. It had instilled in her the institutional belief that her fellow agents would never let her down. Those same agents included those in the Intelligence department who had told her that Damian Reigns was a ruthless, cold-hearted, cold-blooded, drug dealing murderer. It was written in black and white across the case file, the psyche reports, and all of the other supporting documents. But what about what she had seen? What about the man she had come to know? What about that? And what do you do when the trust you have in yourself and the trust you have in your fellow agents contradicts the trust that you have in your heart?

Grace stretched out her legs and wiggled her toes to get the blood flowing again. Slowly, she stood. She stared off into the distant sky and allowed her thoughts to wander. The moon was full tonight; its gorgeous ecru color nicely complimented the clear, bright, sparkling stars in the sky. The twinkling stars and the pitch black night reminded her of diamonds lying on a black velvet cloth. Diamonds...

Grace stared at her right wrist and gently rubbed her left hand's index finger over the diamond tennis bracelet wrapped around it. Damian had given it to her after the balloon ride over a candlelit dinner. It was then when he had told her that he was falling in love with her.

Grace folded her arms and swayed her body from side to side. She could still see the look he had on his face when he told her that he was falling in love with her. His eyes...his eyes had been sincere.

Grace Moore's own eye's denied her the ability to hide her true feelings. The swift Caribbean breeze that blew by her caught the tear rolling down her cheek and carried it off into the wind. Her future, like the tears, was uncharted, uncertain, and quickly traveling toward some dark, unknown fate.

Chapter Twenty-Two

Damian wore a yellow suit with a white helmet while Grace wore a pink suit with a pink helmet. Together, they ran and leaped off the cliff.

The wind was perfect today—it carried their handglider over the island with ease, like a paper airplane. From the height at which they soared, they were able to see things that the balloon ride had missed.

"I can't believe I'm doing this," Grace told him. "I can't believe I let you talk me into this."

"C'mon, we're going to turn to the left," Damian told her.

Together they shifted their bodies and guided the colorful glider to the left. Damian pointed. "Look, over there is the Volcano of Love."

"The Volcano of Love? How exactly does one equate a volcano with love?"

"Legend has it that two slaves found out that they were about to be sold off to different masters. The night before they were about to be separated, they ran off. The overseer and his posse of men and bloodhounds tracked the young lovers to the top of the volcano and had them surrounded. Instead of going to their master and enduring their separation, they held each other tightly, kissed, and leaped into the fiery bowels of the volcano."

"Oh, that's terrible!"

"Not so fast, supposedly a hand came down from the sky,

caught the falling lovers, and lifted them safely out of the volcano. The massive cloud-like hand sat the young lovers down on a supposedly semi-deserted island owned by the Dutch, who had already outlawed slavery. The young couple is said to have lived out the rest of their lives happily ever after."

"Oh, Damian, that's beautiful!" Grace told him. "They loved one another so much that they were willing to die for their love. But God saved them."

"Look, there's Queen's Valley, and Prince Edward's River," Damian pointed to his left.

Grace looked down into the lush, tropical vegetation of the mountains and valleys and admired a beautiful blue and white river snaking through it. "Oh, Damian, it's beautiful. Jamaica is so beautiful."

Dante, his cousin Mina, Damian's head of security, Steve, and several other hulking, suited gentlemen stood at the door to the garage. Dante unlocked the door and twisted the knob.

"I can't believe you're buying this place," Steve told him. "Your penthouse living room is bigger than this whole house."

Dante walked into the garage, followed by his entourage. Thick, white sheets of plastic covered the entire garage, from floor to ceiling. Steve lifted his hands and spun around slowly.

"What, are they painting the garage, or something?" He bent over and lifted a piece of the plastic. Dante waved his hand frantically.

"Careful, don't mess up the plastic. I don't want to get blood on the floor."

Steve dropped the plastic and stood erect. "What blood?"

"Yours."

A large, muscle bound bodyguard placed a stun gun to Steve's neck and squeezed the trigger. The shock from the high voltage gun made Steve instantly go limp and black out. The bodyguards standing behind him caught his limp body.

Steve awoke to find himself naked with his arms outstretched above his head and chained to a steel beam that ran across the garage ceiling. He tried to focus his vision on the people standing
around him.

"Dante, what's this about?" he asked.

"Steve, I'm just going to be honest. You're going to die. Now, how you choose to die is entirely up to you. It can be painless, or it can be excruciatingly painful."

"Fuck you Dante! Do it however you want to. If you think I'm going to beg your sick ass, you've got another thing coming."

Dante shook his head and looked down. "Tsk, tsk, Steve. I'm ashamed to hear you say that. I thought you were smarter than that."

Steve tried to spit on Dante. His blurred vision made him miss.

"I never liked you Steve. Damian hired you because he said you had balls. Well, Steve, I guess he was right, you do have balls. Too bad you won't be needing them anymore. By the way, I want you to meet your replacement. Damian's new head of security will be my cousin, Mina."

Mina Reigns stepped forward. She held in her hand a pair of vise-grips.

"I don't have any balls, Steve, may I borrow yours?"

Mina lifted the vise-grips to Steve's testicles, and clamped down. Steve's testicles exploded. He screamed and jerked.

Mina and Dante laughed.

"Oh, come on now, Steve. The fun's just getting started. If this weren't a brand new housing development, someone would definitely hear you." Dante turned and walked to a generator that his security men had brought in. "Too bad for you that it's a new development. Too bad for you we don't have any neighbors," Dante said starting the generator.

Mina grabbed a pair of jumper cables connected to the generator, and walked back to where Steve was hanging. She clamped one cable to his right nipple, and the other to his left. He screamed.

"Dammit Steve. I haven't even hit the juice yet! You scared the shit out of me screaming like that," Dante told him. "At least wait until the juice flows before you scream."

Dante adjusted the voltage knob, which regulated the amount of electricity that would flow through the cables. He didn't want to kill Steve just yet. When he was sure the right amount of current that would flow, he hit the power button.

Electricity flew into Steve's body, causing him to arch his back and let out an inhuman scream. Strands of his hair began to smoke, and tiny sparks of electricity danced across his teeth. The garage smelled of burning flesh, new paint, and singed hair.

"Okay Steve, now, can we dispense with the billy-bad-ass act?" Dante asked. "I have some questions, would you like to answer them?"

"F...f...fu...fuck...fuck you."

"Wow," Dante said, clapping his hands. "I'm really impressed, Steve. I can't believe you took all that and you're still in a mood to resist. Steve, if I would have known you were this fun to be around, I would have done this a lot sooner."

Dante adjusted the voltage on the generator, setting it a little higher. He pressed the appropriate button and gave Steve another jolt.

Steve arched his back and howled a deep, guttural cry. Blue and orange sparks popped across his front teeth, and sections of his hair caught fire.

"Steve, you use Afro sheen don't you?" Dante asked. "And all this time, I thought your hair was just naturally soft and shiny. You cheater."

"F...Fu...F...Fuck you."

"Steve, you really are a guy after my own heart. I can't believe your tolerance for pain. You know what? I haven't met many guys like you, Steve. By now, most guys would be telling on their grandmother. You know what Steve? I want to see what you're made of. I want to see what makes you stand tall when others would have fallen weak."

Dante turned to Mina. "Pass me the skil saw."

Mina handed Dante a large skil saw and plugged it into the generator. Dante pulled the trigger, and revved up the motor on the saw.

"Would you like to answer my questions?"

Steve remained silent.

"Incredible!" Dante pulled the trigger and saw the blade rotate up to speed. He ran the blade across Steve's knees, until he had created a neat but bloody box surrounding Steve's kneecaps.

Dante handed the bloody saw to Mina, lifted a butcher knife from the top of the generator, and pried away the bloody flesh covering Steve's knees.

"That's how you're able to stand up to me!" Dante smiled. "Your knees are pretty strong."

Dante inserted the knife into Steve's leg, and pried off his right kneecap.

Steve screamed in agonizing pain.

Dante walked to the generator, lifted a pneumatic nail gun, and returned to where Steve was hanging.

"Steve, oh Stevie boy?" Dante placed the nail gun on Steve's ankle and pulled the trigger.

Steve cried out.

"Don't you die on me!" Dante yelled. "You die when I'm ready for you to, and not a moment sooner! Do you understand me?"

Steve said nothing.

Dante hit him in the shin with a nail from the nail gun. Steve cried out.

"Shit! He's losing consciousness, he's bleeding to death!"

Dante fired a nail into Steve's stomach. "God damn you, you stubborn sonofabitch! I just wanted to ask you a few questions, but no, you couldn't cooperate! You had to be a bad ass, you motherfucker. Okay, fuck you, go ahead, and die. But the leak will be plugged, Steve! Do you hear me?"

Steve said nothing.

Dante paced the floor of the garage frantically for a few moments, mumbling to himself. He returned to where Steve was hanging.

Dante slapped Steve's bloody kneecap over his knee, and then lifted the nail gun and drove a nail through it, to hold it in place.

"Here Steve, here's your damn knee back!"

Steve cried out in pain, and then fainted.

"Fuck!" Dante turned to Mina. "He's through. Take care of him, and then get this place cleaned up."

Mina nodded, then lifted the skil saw, revved up the motor, and then began to cut.

"That was fun!" Grace told Damian. She unbuckled the straps that had held her safely to the glider. Damian did the same.

Their landing had been in a large field, in a valley next to the cliff from which they had taken off, not to far from Round Hill. The field was green and purple with violets.

Grace removed her helmet and let it fall to the ground. Damian followed suit.

"Damian, thank you for bringing me here, this place is so beautiful. I've done so many things I had never thought of doing before. I've conquered fears I never knew I had. Thank you."

"You're welcome, Jonel. And trust me, it's been my pleasure."

Damian took Grace by the hand, and led her across the field.

Grace ran her hand through her hair, sending it back

over her shoulders. "Where are we going?"

"The waterfall we passed just before we landed. I want you to see it."

"No! You're taking me to a waterfall?"

"Yes." Damian turned and stared at her. "Is there something wrong with that?"

"Yes, everything!" Grace lifted her arms, turned, and spun slowly. "Look at this place, Damian. It's beautiful. Every girl dreams of a place like this. Every girl dreams of waterfalls, unicorns, and a handsome prince," Grace shook her head. "Don't do it to me, Damian."

"Too late, we're here."

Grace turned, and saw the crystal blue water falling gently into the river before them.

"Damian..."

Damian placed his finger over Grace Moore's lips, turned, and led her into the waist deep waters. They waded delicately through the gentle flowing river, until they came to rest in the white foam created by the waterfall.

"Irish legend has it that whoever kisses under a blue waterfall will be in love forever."

"What makes you think I want to be in love with you forever?" Grace asked.

"Who says that it has anything to do with you?" Damian replied with a smile. "Maybe *I* want to be in love with *you* forever."

"Even if I don't love you back?"

"Does love have conditions?"

Damian turned and waded into the waterfall. Once beneath it, he turned back to Grace and smiled.

"Hey brown skin, bring those green eyes over here so I can fall in love with them forever."

Grace smiled and waded under the waterfall.

Chapter Twenty-Three

Damian emerged from the water, removed the snorkel from his mouth, and took in deep gulps of uninhibited air. No matter how many times he'd done it, breathing through a tube wasn't something he couldn't get used to. He removed the goggles from his face, and ran his hand over his face, clearing away the warm Caribbean water. Grace Moore rose just behind him.

"The coral reef is breathtaking," she told him while removing her goggles.

"It is quite spectacular," he replied. "The flora and fauna is something you never get used to."

"I saw a shark."

"Just one?"

Grace ran her hand through her hair, sending it back over her shoulder. "Yeah right, quit playing!"

"You mean, you really didn't see that pool of sharks near that sunken galleon?"

"Damian, quit playing. That wreck is just a hundred yards to the west of us."

"And what does that mean?"

Grace looked over her shoulder toward the spot in the water where the wrecked French galleon was submerged. "Besides, sharks don't swim in schools."

Damian pulled Grace close. "Schools? I didn't say they were swimming in schools. I said it was a small group of sharks swimming near the wreck. They were probably feeding off of the schools of fish that inhabit the wreck."

Grace turned and peered over her shoulder toward the wreck. Damian quickly submerged, grabbed her leg, and pulled her underneath the water. He could hear Grace scream just before she went under.

The bite was swift, and mind numbing. Blood gushed from Lenny's hand in rhythmic spurts. One could tell by the quick intervals between the spurts that his heart was beating rapidly.

Dante's wicked laugh carried through the crisp, cool, evening air, mingling with Lenny's screams and the tiger's snarls.

"That was Boo-Boo Kitty," Dante informed Lenny.

Dante leaned forward and adjusted the blindfold covering Lenny's eyes. "No cheating! I want to see if you can tell them apart. Now, meet Fluffy."

Dante waved his hand and Lenny the chauffeur was once again lowered into Damian's tiger pit.

Fluffy, a rare, white, 900-pound Bengal tiger leaped from the boulder on which he had been standing and slashed violently at Lenny's head. His razor sharp claws tore into the side of Lenny's face, leaving five, deep gashes across his right cheek. Lenny screamed.

"Oh, shut up, for crying out loud," Dante told him. He waved his hands, motioning toward the surrounding estate. "No one is around to hear you. Watch."

Dante let out a high pitched scream and waved his hands like he was trying to scream his head off, and followed it with a heavy burst of laughter. He waved his hand, and Lenny was lifted out of the tiger pit.

The pit was actually an elaborate preserve, filled with rocks, waterfalls, and much of the natural flora and fauna that the tigers would find in their natural habitats. The sunken preserve encompassed some two hundred acres, and was located in the middle of Damian's twenty thousand acre South Texas ranch.

Dante waved his hand, the crane operator hit the appropriate lever, and Lenny's dangling body was moved closer to Dante.

"Lenny, oh, Lenny."

Lenny held his hand tightly. The pain from Boo-Boo Kitty's bite was worse than the pain from Fluffy's claws. "Dante...I didn't..."

"Oh, stop it Lenny, just stop it," Dante said, then removed the blindfold from Lenny's eyes. "Look, you know you're going to die. So, why don't we make it quick and painless? Why don't you just be honest and tell me what I want to know."

"Dante...I...didn't..."

Dante shook his head. "Yes Lenny, you did! I know you did, you know you did, and everyone else knows you did. So stop playing on my Intelligence! Who was it? FBI, DEA, Customs? Who? When? Where?"

"Dante..."

Dante stepped closer to Lenny's bloody face. "I just killed the best piece of Mexican ass from LA to Miami for no reason at all. I'm pissed about that, Lenny. I don't like wasting good pussy! Now, who, when, where, and what are they after? And what is their angle, Lenny?"

Lenny shook his head, "Dante, I didn't."

Dante waved his arm, and the crane operator swung Lenny back over the tiger pit.

Tied at his ankles and dangling upside down, Lenny began wiggling profusely.

"Dante, no!"

Dante nodded, and once again a screaming Lenny was lowered into the tiger pit.

Boo-Boo Kitty was a white, 950-pound Malaysian tiger with a voracious appetite. Boo-Boo Kitty beat Fluffy to the punch, tearing Lenny's skin away, all the way up to his elbow. Flesh was shredded like cheese and bone was snapped like dry spaghetti. Lenny's screams stopped when he fainted. Dante had him pulled up from the pit.

"Lenny, if you're going to be a girl about it, then I'll just kill you right now."

Lenny said nothing.

Dante extended his hand to a nearby bodyguard. "Alcohol."

A bottle of green rubbing alcohol was quickly placed in Dante's hand. He removed the top, placed the bottle under Lenny's nose, and squeezed. Lenny came to with a cough.

Just for good measure, Dante dashed some of the alcohol on the deep gash across Lenny's face. Lenny screamed.

"Lenny, that's not fair. You're letting Boo-Boo Kitty and Fluffy have all the fun. Tabby and Snowball haven't been able to play."

Lenny coughed, "Dante...please...no more..."

"Talk."

"Deal... I wanna make a deal."

"I'm listening."

"I live. I wanna walk away from this one. I'll tell you everything. I want my life."

"I could say yes, and then kill you anyway."

"Please, Dante, I was loyal for many years," Lenny began crying. "Let me talk to Damian. Please..."

"Damian can't help you," a female voice called out from behind.

Everyone turned.

"Princess! What are you doing here?" Dante asked.

"Just visiting."

Princess adjusted her black Ferragamo hat and then removed her short, black, silk gloves. She handed her gloves, along with her small, black Chanel handbag, to one of her massive bodyguards positioned just behind her. She rubbed her immaculate, French manicured hands over her black, form fitting Chanel skirt, and then brushed away some imaginary lint from her matching Chanel jacket top. She looked up at Dante.

"The question is, my dear brother, what exactly are *you* doing here?"

"I'm taking care of business," Dante answered.

Princess walked to the edge of the railing which encircled the preserve and looked down. Boo-Boo Kitty snarled at her with his blood-covered mouth. Princess raised her hands to her lips, and blew the tiger a seductive kiss.

"What do you want, Princess?" Dante asked her.

Princess turned and faced her younger brother. "Actually, I'm here on business. I have a proposition for you."

"I'm in the middle of something."

"I'll wait."

Princess strolled back to her entourage of bodyguards, turned, and stood just in front of them. Dante scowled at her as she walked past him. He turned his attention back to Lenny.

"Lenny, speak!"

Lenny looked at Princess, and then back at Dante. "I...I can't."

Dante motioned to the crane operator, who swung the boom around, placing Lenny back over the tiger preserve.

Lenny shouted, still holding his arm. "No! Dante, later."

"Who?"

"FBI!"

"When?"

"Two months ago!"

"Where?"

Lenny broke down into tears again. "When I went to visit my brother in prison. Dante...they were gonna reduce his life sentence. Please..."

"Who arranged it?"

Lenny looked at Princess, and then back at Dante. "Abrahams! Henry Abrahams! And...her."

Lenny's head jerked back violently when the bullet

struck. His body immediately went limp. Dante turned in the direction from which the shot came. To no one's surprise, Princess was blowing smoke away from the tip of a chrome, forty-caliber Beretta.

Princess shrugged her shoulders and smiled. "Hell, if the truth is going to come out, I may as well tell it myself."

"You can't kill him so you send him to prison forever?" Dante growled.

Princess shrugged her shoulders a second time. "It sounded like a winner at the time."

"And me?" Dante asked angrily. His voice rose, filled with passion. "You bitch! What about me going to prison forever?"

Another shrug. "Collateral damage."

Princess walked over to where the crane operator sat.

"Lower that thing into the pit," she told him. She turned back to her large contingent of bodyguards. "Snitches. They tell once; they tell twice."

"If Damian kills you..."

"Don't worry about Damian," said Princess flagging her brother.

"What's that supposed to mean?"

Princess smiled. It was the same smile that she always gave when she was hiding something. It was a smile that Dante knew well. He turned to one of his men.

"Get a message to Damian. Code red it. And get some more men down there ASAP!"

Princess frowned.

"Why do you protect him?" she asked angrily.

"Besides the fact that he's our brother?" Dante asked. "He's leading our family in the right direction."

"Dante, join me."

"Princess, we tried that already. It didn't work then, it won't work now."

"Things will be different this time Dante. Strictly business."

Dante shook his head and took a step toward his sister.

"What's the matter with you? You have all the money you could ever want! This is about ego, Princess, nothing else. You want to be the big fish, the head honcho, the big cheese! Cut the bullshit, Princess!"

"Dante, there will come a time when you will have to choose between me and Damian." Princess stepped closer to her brother, and leaned forward so that her lips almost touched his ear. "Choose wisely," she whispered.

"I already have."

Princess fumed. She spun rapidly and stormed away. Her entourage of hulking men-in-black followed obediently.

Dante turned toward his men.

"Clean up that mess when they are through with it. Then clean up the cats." He turned and watched as Princess stormed into the house.

"One more thing, start recruiting some soldiers. There's going to be a war."

Chapter Twenty-Four

Damian took Grace Moore's hand into his as they walked along the deserted black sand beach. They could feel the breeze growing cooler as the evening progressed. Grace unfolded the blanket she carried inside of her arms and wrapped it around her shoulders.

"Are you cold?" Damian inquired. "Would you like to go back in?"

"Are you kidding?" Grace asked. "We rented that Rover just so we could find some privacy. We find a beautiful, deserted, black sand beach, and you want me to give it up? I knew you were a sadist."

Damian laughed. His laughter was infectious and Grace joined in.

"Let's stop here," she told him.

"Right here?"

Grace nodded, spread the blanket onto the sand, and plopped down. Damian joined her on the blanket. He unfolded the blanket he carried in his arms, and wrapped it around the both of them.

Grace repositioned herself so that she could be seated between his legs with her back against his chest. She leaned back and rested her head against his right collarbone.

"Damian, listen to that," she told him.

Damian sat in silence for several moments before finally speaking.

"Hear what?" he asked. "I don't hear anything but the ocean."

"I know, doesn't that sound wonderful? Nothing but the sound
of the waves crashing against the beach."

Damian nodded.

"This has always been my dream," she told him. "To live on a beach, watch the sun rise, and paint the sunsets."

"And drink out of coconuts, wear grass skirts, and live in a little grass hut?"

Grace thrust her arm back, elbowing Damian in his stomach.

"I'm serious, silly!" She turned her head slightly and looked up at him. "Don't you have any dreams? Haven't you ever wanted to get away from it all? I mean, just live how you want to live? Where is your perfect place, your perfect world?"

Damian exhaled, and sat silently for a few moments to collect his thoughts.

"I don't know, I mean, I...well..."

"C'mon, spit it out."

"You might think it's silly. You might laugh."

"I won't laugh."

"Promise?"

Grace raised her hand with two fingers and her thumb extended. "Scouts honor."

"Oh, so you were a scout? Did you used to be one of those annoying little, don't-take-no-for-an-answer cookie peddlers?"

Grace nudged him again. "Stick to the topic at hand."

"Okay, okay, let's see. Well, I guess that in my perfect world, my perfect place, I would be with the woman I love, and we would travel and see the world."

"Get out of here! That's so lame, I can't believe you!"

"I'm serious. See, that's why I didn't want to tell you."

"Okay, okay, I'm sorry. I didn't mean to down you. I just

don't understand what's so special about that."

"Well, it's more than just traveling. It's about being with someone who you love, someone who loves you. Two people who pledge to spend their lives with one another, traveling the world, seeing all of the wonders. We would go to Paris and hold each other as we look over the city from the Eiffel Tower. We would go to India and see the Taj Mahal. We would go to Great Britain and visit all of the castles and palaces. We would go to Egypt and see the pyramids. To Senegal and see the door of no return. To China and see the great wall. To Mexico and see the steep pyramids. To Italy and take a gondola ride down the canals of Venice. We would go to Greece and visit the Parthenon. We would spend our lives traveling, climbing mountains, sailing the seas, seeing the sights, hiking the outback, traipsing through the jungles and rain forests, seeing Burma by elephant, the Sahara by camel, I mean living! We would never walk by a flower without stopping to smell it. We would never hear a song playing without dancing. We would never see food being prepared without tasting it. I would take the love of my life, and enjoy every waking moment with her. Together we would celebrate love, life, and being alive, by actually living. Sounds crazy?"

Grace shook her head and stared off into the distance. "No Damian, that doesn't sound crazy. It doesn't sound crazy at all. It's beautiful," she whispered.

"And you, Jonel, what's your dream? How would your perfect life and your perfect world be?"

Grace drew her legs close, and wrapped her arms around them. "I don't know, well...I mean, now that I think about it, it's kind of the same. The sun's especially beautiful when you have someone to watch it with. A coconut drink is just a drink unless you have someone to share it with."

"So you're looking for Prince Charming?"

"Honestly, at this point, I'm looking for prince breathing. As long as he's alive, I'm game."

Damian and Grace shared a laugh.

"Wow, those are some standards."

Grace shrugged. "I don't know, sometimes you're just ready to settle. Sometimes, you're just tired of battling life and loneliness, but I'm not going to settle for just anything."

Damian wrapped his arms around Grace tightly, and pulled her even closer. "Are you lonely, Jonel?"

"Have you ever been so lonely that you cry yourself to sleep at night?" she asked.

"Why are you lonely, Jonel?"

"I don't know. I don't know whether my expectations of others are too high or whether their expectations of me are."

"You're a beautiful, young, educated woman, Jonel. You're funny and fun to be with. You're sharp, witty, Intelligent, and drop-dead gorgeous."

Grace Moore turned and looked into Damian's eyes. It had been forever since she had been complemented like that.

"It's not you, Jonel, trust me," he whispered.

"Then why am I..."

"There's a difference between being lonely, and being alone," he told her. "If I had my way, you'd never be alone again."

Grace closed her eyes and lowered her head. Damian placed his finger underneath her chin and lifted her head.

"What is it, Jonel?" he asked. "Let me help you find whatever it is that you're looking for. Let me help you chase away whatever is tormenting you. Let me help you."

Grace Moore caught herself. She turned and faced the sea once again.

"How can you help me?" she asked him

"I can start by listening. I can start by just holding you tight and always being there for you."

Damian's words cut through Grace Moore like a sword to her stomach. She knew that his words were sincere. He cared for her. He wanted to fill the empty spaces in her life, to bring light to the dark spaces in her soul.

She was an agent, he was her target, but he was the first man in a long time she felt she could really love, the first man in her life who really cared deeply for her. And the entire relationship was built on deception. Grace closed her eyes to keep from tearing up. It was then when she felt his warm breath against her neck and his warm kiss.

"Damian, don't."

Damian pulled his lips away from her neck. "Is it someone else? You're committed to someone else aren't you?"

Grace threw her head back in laughter. She laughed hard for several moments while Damian stared at her with a look of confusion.

"What's so funny, Jonel?" he finally asked her.

"Damian, it's not another man, trust me. My God how I wish it was, but no, that's not it."

"What is it?"

"Damian, it's hard for me to explain." Grace turned her head around and faced him once again. "Damian, have you ever been in a situation that was so complex that it defied explanation?"

"Yes, and you know what I do?"

"What?"

"I stop being logical. I stop being over analytical."

"Huh?"

"I stop using my head, and I follow my heart," he told her.

Grace again faced the rolling waves. She lifted her hand and caressed the side of Damian's face. "And what if you can no longer trust your heart?"

"Jonel, you can always trust your heart. Your head is about living, your heart is about being alive."

"And if your heart had betrayed you?"

"It can never betray you."

"If it led you to look for love where there was none? What if it keeps leading you on? What if you keep using your heart and keep coming up short?"

"Coming up short on what?"

Grace turned and stared into Damian's eyes. "On love."

"On love?"

"It's elusive. Every time I think that I've found it, it slips away. What do I do about that?"

Damian lifted Grace's hand from off of the side of his face and kissed it gently. "You keep on trying to grab onto love, that won't work. Drink it, Jonel. Let it become a part of you."

"I'm scared."

"You never have to be scared when I'm with you, Jonel. So that means you'll never have to be scared again."

"You'll always be with me?"

"If you let me. No, change that. If you let me; if you don't let me; it doesn't matter. I'll always be there. I love you."

The words struck Grace like an ice pick through the heart. She wasn't prepared to hear them. Not here, not now, not while everything was just so right.

Grace Moore closed her eyes and floated away. Damian leaned forward and kissed Grace softly on her lips. Grace kept her lips together for the first few pecks, but then found them opening slowly. Their tongues touched softly, caressing one another, feeling each other out.

Grace fell back onto the blanket, while Damian leaned forward on his knees kissing her. Their tongues tumbled, mingled, and danced, stroking the fires that burned within. Grace took Damian's hand and placed it on her breast. He obliged by rubbing, caressing, and removing pieces of her clothing intermittently.

Grace soon found herself lying back naked on the blanket, on a deserted black sand beach outside of Ocho Rios, Jamaica. She was about to make love to a man she was simultaneously committed to bringing down and a man she was in love with.

On fire, she took his hand and placed it near her place of desire. He removed his hand and did her one better. He went into her.

191

For the first time in a long time, Grace Moore made love. She made love, while being in love, and while feeling loved. Under the blue Caribbean moon, Grace Moore embraced Damian tightly, and pulled him as far into her as she could. She wanted to drink from within, immerse herself in him. She wanted to pull him into her soul.

As the night progressed, their lovemaking became blissful, a thing of pure ecstasy, an exercise in unadulterated carnal fulfillment. Somewhere during the night of passion, a tear-filled Grace Moore rubbed gently on the sweating, naked back of her target, her love, Damian Reigns, and swore to herself that she would never leave him. She would love him, care for him, and protect him, no matter what came their way. Even if it cost her her job. Even if it cost her her soul.

Chapter Twenty-Five

"**O**kay, Dante, what mission requires me to wear this skimpy, two-piece, string bikini?" Angela asked placing her hands on her Halle Berry hips.

"I'll explain the mission perimeters once we're out on the water," Dante told her.

Angela shifted her weight to one side, and folded her arms. "What mission requires that you have to tell me about it in the middle of Canyon Lake on a jet ski?"

"Angela, I just want to talk to you, okay? Can we just go out on the lake and talk?" Dante exhaled.

"Can't we talk here? Dante, you know how things are between us. Why do you want to go there?"

Dante frowned and shook his head. "Angela, you are one headstrong..."

"Bitch?" Angela unfolded her arms and placed her hand on her hips again. "Is that what you were going to call me? You seem to like that word when I don't bend to your will. You like calling me whatever you want, when I don't give in to you."

Dante lifted his hands. "Okay, okay, you win. I just thought I could talk to you."

Dante turned and walked to the lift mechanism. He slammed the lever forward, activating the hydraulic lift for the Jet Ski. The arm attached to the Bombadier jet ski lifted it out of the water again.

"Dante, what's the matter?"

"A lot."

Angela walked to where he stood. She placed her tiny, well-manicured hand on his cheek, and turned his face toward hers.

"This is important to you?"

Dante frowned and turned his head away. Angela reached around him and activated the hydraulic lift, lowering the jet ski back into the water.

Dante watched as she climbed onto the large, two-seat watercraft. Angela was as shapely as ever. She was built like a brick house, solid. She had enough ass to divide between three women, and it was all as solid as a rock. Her stomach was so flat and tight you could lay a marble on it and it would sit still. Angela wasn't runway model fine, she was raised in the south, cornbread-fed, whipped with a belt across the ass, American beauty fine. She could put on a potato sack and make it look provocative. Angela turned and peered over her shoulder at Dante.

"Are you coming?"

"I used to love it when you would ask me that."

Angela smiled. Dante climbed onto the jet ski and sat behind her. He placed the gun he held in his hand inside of the compartment just to the rear of the seat. Angela throttled up the engine and they sped off onto the lake.

"So, what's the matter, Dante?" she asked.

"Everything. We're having problems with everyone."

Angela peered over her shoulder, "Princess?"

"And the commission."

"What's going on with the commission?"

"They want Princess to replace Damian."

"What?" Angela throttled back and zigzagged to bring the jet ski to a stop. Once this was done, she turned and faced Dante. "Are they crazy? Are they suicidal now? Don't they know they'll be signing their own death warrant?"

"Well, actually, it's the boss who wants her in charge. He

wants to unify his distribution network."

"It makes sense theoretically, but in reality, he loses power. With different states under different people's control, no one can become too powerful and he can play the heads of the organization off against one another."

"Like he's been doing."

"And, under one umbrella, the head of this unified network could just say fuck him and buy from someone else."

"Angela, I don't know what he's thinking."

Angela tossed her now wet hair over her shoulders. "And the commission is backing their demise?"

"No, once it was exposed, they went wild."

"So why are they tripping with you?"

"Well, the meeting turned bad, and I had them thrown overboard..."

"Overboard?"

"The meeting was on Alemendez' yacht."

Angela laughed. She lifted her hand and caressed the side of Dante's face. "Dante, what am I going to do with you?"

Dante placed his hand over Angela's, and rubbed her hands. Their eyes locked. Angela turned away.

"Dante, let's not go there."

"I know," he lowered her hand from his cheek to his lips, where he kissed it. "I just wanted to talk."

"So, the family and the commission are at war. Once you recruit and call up all of your reserves, you're almost as strong as the entire commission united. You have more money, more political connections, a larger manpower base, and better generals. You'll win and El Jefe has what he wants, a unified commission." Angela smiled, and caressed Dante's cheek again. "He started this war on purpose. He's forcing you to wipe out the commission and take over."

Dante grinned and stared off into the distance. "I didn't see that. Damn, woman, you're brilliant."

"Still brilliant," she told him with a smile. "Let me help you."

"How?"

"Give me an army, and I'll wipe out the commission. I'll solidify your hold on Louisiana, Oklahoma, New Mexico, and Arkansas. I'll take Mississippi, Arizona, Missouri, and Kansas. I'll make Emil one of your regional chiefs and then I'll crush Don Alemendez and give you all of Florida in time for your birthday. That will make you untouchable. El Jefe will beg for your forgiveness."

Dante smiled. He knew that she was serious, and he knew that she could do it. He knew that she *would* do it. Angela had been his and Princess' top general. She had planned the family's wars and had personally taken Arkansas and Oklahoma, while he conquered Louisiana and New Mexico. She was Dante in a crimson red, two-piece string. Unfortunately, she left when the family drew down its army and changed directions. Dante would give anything to have her by his side again.

"No, Angela. I can't let you come back in that capacity."

"Or, if you like, I could take some men and smash Princess for you."

Dante shook his head. "I offered to send Emil one hundred men to help make Savannah part of his organization. I sent two hundred. I have another hundred laying low in Atlanta and a hundred men scattered throughout Florida, keeping an eye on Don Alemendez. Our boys in San Antonio, Houston, and Dallas have been given the order to recruit, and they've already gotten pretty big. I want you to organize, strategize, and conduct operations from here."

"Why not let me go into the field and conduct operations from there? It's more efficient, and besides, you know I'm a hands-on type of operator."

Dante shook his head. "You're too valuable to risk."

"Too valuable?" Angela recoiled. "Dante, this is me you're

talking to. Besides, I'm an independent contractor, aligned with the family. I'm not one of your day-to-day people. Nothing will suffer if I catch a hot one."

Dante stared into Angela's eyes. "I will."

Angela frowned at first and then turned away. "No, Dante, let's not go there. You know better." She turned back toward him. "I thought we weren't going there."

"Angela, what happened between us?"

"Dante, you know what happened."

"Did you love me, Angela?"

"You asked me that in the past tense." Angela leaned back and rested her head against his shoulder. "Dante, I still love you, I never stopped. I don't think that I ever will stop loving you, but we can't go there, understand?"

Dante leaned forward and kissed Angela's neck. He followed that kiss with another and then one on her cheek. He made his way to her lips.

Angela turned her head. She stared into Dante's eyes and slowly, their faces drifted toward one another. Dante's tongue glided across Angela's tongue as they sat in the middle of the lake.

"Dante..." Angela whispered.

Dante quieted her by kissing her again.

Angela pulled away. She stood and turned around on the jet ski, and then reseated herself facing him. She climbed on top of Dante's lap and slid her string bikini to the side. Dante pulled his swimming shorts down and entered inside of her.

Angela moaned and wrapped her arms around Dante's neck, stuck her tongue inside his mouth, and began rolling her pelvic area in a forward thrusting motion. Dante closed his eyes, tilted his head back, and placed his hands on her thick, firm ass. He could feel her muscles contracting and expanding as she rode him.

"Dante, where's your gun?" Angela moaned.

"It's inside you," he replied.

"Dante, sweetie, unless you want to go before you cum,

you'll get your gun," Angela continued her thrusting.

"Angela, what are you talking about?"

"I'm talking about three men on jet skis bearing down on us."

"What about them?"

"Men on jet skis don't wear black ski masks," Angela said still riding him.

Dante turned around and saw the men bearing down on them. He grabbed his gun out of the compartment as Angela rose and turned around on the jet ski. She quickly started it, throttled it up to speed, and took off.

Dante and Angela sped into the recreation section of Canyon Lake. Other jet skiers, sailboats, large water trampolines, fishing boats, and tubers were spread throughout.

The ski masks kept coming.

"They're gaining on us!" Dante shouted.

"No shit!" Angela answered. "They have fast one-seaters and we're on a two-seat, waterborne pig!"

"You know what that means?" Dante shouted. He lifted his glock into the air and cocked it.

"It means, my Lord, that we are about to enter into an old fashioned joust."

Angela turned the jet ski around, skidding it across the water violently.

Dante shook his head and held on tightly to her waist. "No, Angela, that's not what it means!"

"Too late!" she brought the machine up to full throttle.

"Dammit!" Dante reached over her shoulder, aimed his weapon, and fired.

The jet ski rider in the middle flew backwards off of his machine. The other two masked gunmen returned fire. Two lines of water skirted by Angela and Dante's jet ski as they passed in between the two gunmen.

"Dammit, Angela! You don't play chicken with three guys with guns! Head for Damian's house!"

"Where in the fuck do you think I'm going?"

Dante peered over his shoulder. "They'll be catching up to us again in about a minute or two."

"Well, here's the plan. Once they get close enough, I'm cutting. That means the idiot on our right can't blast us without risking hitting his partner."

"And what if he doesn't give a shit about his partner?"

"Then we're all up shit's creek!"

The gunmen closed steadily and once they were within fifty yards of Dante and Angela, they opened fire.

Angela ducked her head.

"Shit!"

She turned the jet ski toward the left, bringing it across the path of one of the gunmen. Dante took aim and nailed the gunman on the right just as their jet ski collided with the gunman's on the left. The impact from the collision sent them all flying through the air. The jet skis themselves exploded into a fiery shower of fiberglass and metal. Pieces of the machines rained down on the area as Dante and Angela surfaced from beneath the water.

"Angela, are you alright?" Dante asked, as he swam toward her.

Angela nodded, as she doggie paddled toward the shore. Once she reached a shallow enough part of the lake, she stood and stumbled onto the shore, where she collapsed on the banks of the lake. Dante soon joined her.

"What happened to your plan?" he said, still holding the water-filled glock.

Angela sat up and stared at him. "You mean it didn't work?"

Angela broke out into a wild, uncontrolled frenzy of laughter. Dante quickly joined in. They laughed until they saw the gunman stumbling down the shore of the lake toward them. Dante lifted the weapon and pulled the trigger. The gun popped and the gunman fell.

"Dante! You should have taken him alive, so he could tell

us who sent them."

"I know who sent them."

Angela looked in the direction of gunman, who lay on the ground holding his chest, and writhing in pain. "It could have been the commission or Princess or..."

"Angela," Dante interrupted, "Right now, they're all one and the same."

Chapter Twenty-Six

The Gulfstream G-IV was met on the tarmac by a phalanx of men in black. Stepping out of the plane, Damian was startled by the sheer number of large men in dark suits surrounding him. A few he recognized, many he didn't. But there was someone he did recognized.

"Mr. Reigns."

"Niccolo," Damian said shaking his hand.

Damian turned and grabbed Grace Moore's hand. "Niccolo, this is Jonel. Jonel, this is Niccolo."

Grace extended her hand to Niccolo, who shook it gently.

"A pleasure to meet you," he told her. He turned to Damian. "A limousine has been arranged for Ms. McNeal."

The fact that Niccolo knew her last name told Damian that he had been briefed by Dante. The fact that Niccolo had personally met him at the airport told him even more.

"Very well, where's the limo?" he asked.

Niccolo signaled with his hand and a long black super stretch pulled around the plane.

"What's wrong? Is everything okay?" Grace asked as she turned to Damian.

"Of course," he said placing his arm around Grace. He escorted her to the limousine. "I'm sure that it's just factory business."

Grace peered over her shoulder. "But all of these men?"

The driver opened the rear door of the limousine for Grace. Damian leaned forward and kissed Grace on her cheek.

"Don't you worry your pretty little head. Roger here is an excellent driver. He'll take you home and I'll call you tonight."

Damian helped Grace into the limousine and shut the door. He blew her a kiss through the dark black tint as the stretch Lincoln pulled off. As he turned to Niccolo, his expression changed instantly.

"What is it?" Damian asked.

"We have a royal situation," Niccolo told him. He raised his hand into the air and waved two fingers. "It's critical, Dante's waiting at the penthouse."

A massive, heavily armored, black Ford Excursion whipped around the G-IV. Two large bodyguards opened the door and stood just to the right and the left of the opening.

"Shit!" Damian pounded the air with his fist.

"I'll brief you on the way to the penthouse," Niccolo told him.

Damian climbed into the Excursion and stared angrily out of the thick, bulletproof window, as the nine-vehicle caravan wound its way through the airport.

"How was your trip?" Special Agent Elizabeth Holmes asked.

"It was fun. I had a lot of fun," Grace nodded.

"Fun? That's it? Just fun?"

"Yeah, we were met at the airport by a lot of people. Anything going on I should know about?"

Elizabeth Holmes rose from her leather covered Queen Anne chair and walked to the cherry wood desk which sat in the corner of the room.

"Yes, Grace, a situation has developed. Intelligence thinks that a major power struggle is underway and that a major intra-family war is imminent. Princess Reigns is

202

recruiting, and so is Dante. We're trying to get someone inside the ranks on both sides."

Grace removed a book from the shelf and studied it intensely. Her heart was racing rapidly. *How much did Intelligence know? Was Washington still following her? Did they know about the beach?* Her hand began to tremble visibly. Grace placed the book back into its proper place on the shelf and folded her arms. Not ready to face her fellow agent, she continued to face the shelf and pretended to look at the books.

"Grace, the war is going to get bloody. Bullets flying, car bombs, assassinations in broad daylight, we can't protect you in this type of situation. You could catch a stray round, or, if Princess thinks that Damian has feelings for you, you could become a target."

Grace Moore turned and faced her fellow agent. "Wonderful, I go deep undercover to keep from catching a hot one, and now I'm in danger of catching a hot one because I'm deep undercover. Can we arrest her?"

"No, she hasn't done anything. At least, she hasn't done anything that we can tie to her and take to a grand jury. Director Abrahams says that it's your call. We're proud of everything you've accomplished so far. We can reassign you, get you out of there, and maybe after things clear out, bring you back."

"So they're expecting Damian to win?"

"Intelligence says that Dante is going to win. Psych thinks that he's going to kill her entire organization. Psych also thinks that he's going to kill her too this time."

"And we're just going to sit here and let this happen?" Grace's arms flew through the air. "Excuse me, I thought we were the FBI?"

"We are, and we use our heads. That's why we are going to get him," Elizabeth Holmes said, then rose from the cherry desk upon which she had seated herself. Her right hand stroked the pearl necklace she wore as she peered out of the window into her flower garden. "We can't stop this from taking place, Grace. We have to choose our battle, choose our moment, and then capitalize when he makes a mistake."

"Why can't we get them for murder?"

"If it were that easy, we wouldn't have lost the last six agents. Grace, pull out. There's no dishonor in it. You've gotten further than any other agent we've had on this case."

Grace walked to the window and stared into the garden with her friend and fellow agent. She didn't want to make a decision just yet. Grace knew that she wasn't ready to leave the assignment, she wasn't ready to leave Damian.

"Liz, did the techies hook your computer into the Bureau's ID database?"

"Yes, why?"

"Could you check a name for me?" Grace asked.

"Yes, of course," Elizabeth turned and walked to her computer desk and sat down. She tapped rapidly at the keys for several moments before looking up at Grace.

"What's the name?"

"Niccolo."

Elizabeth typed for several moments, then looked up at Grace again.

"No."

"Try last name unknown, first name unknown, hell, it could be an alias, I don't know."

Elizabeth saw Grace Moore's frustration, and she understood the importance of finding the name.

"Grace, give me a minute, I'll find him. I promise."

Grace recrossed her arms and rubbed her forearms, wrinkling the light blue, knit sweater she wore over her blouse. Her gaze focused on a family of bright red Cardinals living in Elizabeth's garden birdhouse. *Family,* she thought, *family.*

Grace lowered her hands and rubbed at her belly softly. She drew in air and inflated her stomach, and then turned to the side to examine her reflection in the window. She was unaware that Elizabeth had stopped tapping at the computer and was now watching her.

"Grace."

Elizabeth's voice startled her. Grace quickly dropped her hands and turned toward her friend.

"Huh?"

"I've found him."

Grace strode rapidly across the cherry hardwood floor to the rear of the computer desk. She peered over Elizabeth's shoulder at the computer generated photo of the gentleman who she had met at the airport. Elizabeth tapped her finger against the photo on the computer screen.

"There he is," she told Grace proudly. "And it was an alias or nickname rather. I know him."

"You know him?"

"Yep, a real bad boy. His name is Nicanor Moreno Mata. A black Cuban, one of Castro's golden boys. Served in the Cuban Special Forces and the Cuban death squads. Russian Spetznaz trained, served in Mozambique, Angola, and Namibia. Trained in torture, an explosive expert. The Angolans called him 'Carne Cero.' It means 'The Butcher'. He has an international warrant for his arrest. The international court of justice in The Hague wants him to stand trial for war crimes."

Elizabeth peered over her shoulder at Grace Moore.

"Do you know where he is?"

"No," she whispered as she shook her head in the negative.

"Grace, I know him, because many years ago, he shot me. He also killed my partner. We were helping the Secret Service investigate an alleged Russian counterfeit ring, and we came across him. Now tell me, how do you know him?"

"I heard the name."

"Where? From who?"

"I just overheard it, that's all."

Grace stood erect and slowly made her way back to the

window.

"Grace, is Moreno Mata in Texas?"

"People like that, what do they get out of killing?"

"People like that have no soul, they have no limitations. It all boils down to money, but they have no sociological impediments to the way they obtain it. They are monsters, Grace. Dante is one of them. Damian Reigns is one of them."

Grace Moore turned rapidly and stared at Elizabeth Holmes. There was a frown on her face.

When Elizabeth Holmes saw the look on Grace Moore's face, she exhaled loudly, and shook her head. She knew that Grace knew more than what she was saying, and she could tell that Grace didn't like the fact that Damian had been called a monster. Elizabeth recognized it all.

"Grace, do you know why I was given this assignment?"

"Yes, because of your political connections, your field experience, your..."

"I was given this assignment because I was once a young,

lovely, female FBI agent. I was once used to lure criminals into lowering their guard and slipping up. I was once very good at doing what Tom Peoples and Henry Abrahams asked you to do."

Elizabeth Holmes stood, walked around her desk, and faced Grace Moore.

"It's a slippery slope, Grace. The monsters can be charming, very handsome, very alluring. They can spend their way into your heart, Grace. They pay attention to you, romance you, send you flowers, and treat you like you are the only woman in the world. They are not the knights in shining armor, Grace. They're the dragons. Do you understand?"

Grace Moore folded her arms and her face contorted. She began sobbing.

"What happened in Jamaica, Grace?" Elizabeth asked.

Grace shook her head.

"Did you fall Grace? Did you slip?"

Grace nodded her head slowly.

"Are you feeling okay on this?"

Grace Moore broke down and began crying heavily.

"It's over, Grace. I'm pulling you out." Elizabeth turned toward the desk and lifted the telephone from its cradle.

"No, Elizabeth, please..." Grace said through her sobbing.

Elizabeth hesitated for a moment, and then lowered the phone and set it back in its cradle.

"Elizabeth, please..." Grace called out to her again.

Elizabeth Holmes turned and stared at a crying, shaking Grace Moore. She had been there before. She knew what Grace was feeling. Elizabeth walked to where Grace was standing and wrapped her arms around her.

"How bad is it?" she asked softly.

"I don't know Liz," Grace told her through a torrent of tears. "I don't know..."

"So, how bad is it?" Damian asked.

"She's recruiting," Dante answered. "Our people say she's having trouble getting big quick because people still remember the last war. We smashed her pretty bad last time."

"How long before she moves?"

"Any day now. But, we have a month, maybe two, before the major shooting starts."

"Fuck!" Damian removed his coat and then loosened his necktie. "I do not need this shit right now! Not now!"

Dante raised his hands in a calming motion. "I'll take care of her. At least enough to buy us some time."

Damian walked to the glass wall and stared out at the city below. "I'm listening."

"Marcus, her husband. He'll have a real bad car accident. One, that will show her we're serious. Two, it'll slow her down."

"Approved," Damian told him. "When did Niccolo arrive?"

"I sent for him three days ago. I had him fly straight to the Caribbean."

"The Caribbean?"

"I quadrupled your bodyguards in Jamaica. I had him supervise."

Damian smiled, "I didn't notice."

"You weren't supposed to," Dante walked to the bar and poured a drink for Damian. He also poured himself an orange juice.

"So, how is the other situation coming along?"

Damian turned and walked to the sliding glass door, which lead to the outside terrace. He opened the door and stepped out.

Dante walked out onto the balcony and handed his brother the drink.

"Scotch?" Damian asked.

Dante nodded.

"Thank you."

Damian stared out over the city. It was dusk outside and the lights were beginning to twinkle all across the city—his favorite view. "She's compromised."

"The beach outside of Ocho Rios?" Dante lifted an eyebrow.

"How did you know?"

"I quadrupled your bodyguards," Dante smiled. "What else happened?"

Damian leaned forward and rested his arms on the balcony railing. "She told me she loved me."

"Really?" Dante shook the glass of orange juice which he held in his hand, twirling the ice cubes around inside. "Interesting, very interesting."

"I thought so, it sounded like she meant it, too."

"And what did you do when she told you that?" Dante asked.

Damian stood up straight and brushed his hand across his eggshell colored, silk, Kiton dress shirt to remove the dust that he had picked up from leaning on the railing.

"I told her that I loved her."

Dante threw his head back in laughter. "Capital!"

"I think that it's time to settle down, old boy," Damian told his brother. He slapped Dante on his back. "I think I'll hang up the old player license and jump the broom."

"A wonderful idea!" Dante laughed. "I'm just sorry that I didn't think of it first."

"Do you think that we could have the reception in the Hoover Building?"

"I don't see why not. After all, we will be part of the family," Dante laughed.

"You'll be my best man, won't you?"

"I'd be honored. I thought for a second that you would want to ask Nathan Hess to stand by your side during the happiest moment of your life."

"The cake, Dante, what about the cake? A nice, six-tiered deal, shaped like a badge?"

"And don't forget about the tux. FBI blue? DEA blue? Or, a nice Justice Department blue?"

"Decisions, decisions, decisions. Now I see why wedding planners make so much money!"

The brothers broke out into a long stream of laughter.

"My sister-in-law, Special Agent Reigns," Dante said, "I love the sound of that."

"I thought you would."

Dante placed his arm around Damian's shoulder.

"So tell me, brother, how is FBI pussy?"

"Arresting!"

Chapter Twenty-Seven

Grace Moore rubbed her hand across Damian's back, feeling the fabric of his dark gray, Luciano Barbera suit. She had chosen the suit herself because she loved the way it looked on him. She could get used to this life, she told herself. Being the girlfriend of a billionaire businessman certainly had its perks. The seventy five thousand dollar, white, full length Siberian sable that she was wearing along with the seven hundred thousand dollar, ten-carat, diamond and platinum ring that sat on her finger could testify to that.

Murdering drug dealer or not, Damian Reigns knew how to spoil a woman. The eighty thousand square foot, Mediterranean style lake front home, the two hundred and twenty foot Palmer Johnson yacht, the pair of thirty five million dollar gulf stream jets, the in-home chef, the private boxes at the opera, the one hundred thousand dollar ball gowns, the million dollar diamond pieces from Harry Winston, the chauffeured one hundred and twenty inch, stretched Lincolns and Mercedes, the endless charity balls, and ever flowing rivers of expensive wines and champagnes, all of this would overwhelm even the most discerning of debutantes. Grace knew that Damian was a keeper. Too bad she would have to send him away for life.

Grace stared at the ceiling of the warehouse, allowing her mind to wander. She thought back to Elizabeth's den

210

and the conversation that she had with her friend.

Elizabeth hit the nail right on the head, Grace thought. She had known everything that was being thought without it being said. Loneliness, when combined with a handsome, Intelligent, wealthy and charming young bachelor who provided much needed attention, had proved to be a dangerous combination.

Grace still felt something for Damian, though she could not put into words exactly what it was. She had a job to do. If Damian was guilty of doing the things that Bureau Intelligence had him doing, then she would arrest him. If not...

It was the 'if not' that troubled Grace. What if she couldn't find anything? What if she could not find anything to incriminate him, but he was *still* guilty? What about her fellow agents, the ones whose lives had been taken away by this man? What about their families? Their children? But...what if he was innocent? What then? What about her life, her job, who would she say good-bye to? Would she even bother to say good-bye? What would her superiors say if she continued seeing him secretly and they caught her?

"What do you think?" Damian asked. He waved his arms through the air to showcase the warehouse's expansiveness.

"Huh?" Grace asked. She had been caught off guard.

"I said, what do you think?"

"Oh, yeah it's nice, nice and big," she smiled at Damian, and again rubbed her hand gently across his back.

"That's it? Just nice and big?" Damian placed his hand upon his chest and feigned shock. "I'll have you know that this is a four-million-square-foot, state-of-the-art distribution center. Everything is computerized. Everything that comes in is tagged, routed, and tracked electronically. This warehouse is one of the premiere warehouses for global distribution."

The words 'global distribution' grabbed Grace's attention. From here, distributing cocaine throughout Texas would be a piece of cake. Something inside of Grace told her that this was the place. This was the fountainhead from which the Reigns family spewed its intoxicating poison. Grace felt her legs become wobbly.

"Damian, what exactly do you distribute from here?" she asked.

"Well, just about everything. This is one of the premiere shipping and routing locations for NAFTA traffic. Anything—well, change that—just about everything that comes up through Texas from Mexico is routed through here. Our North American Free Trade Agreement warehouses receive thousands of trucks per day alone."

Tiny microstrands of hair stood up on the back of Grace's neck. It was his largest, most high tech, and most capable distribution center. Would an Intelligent person like Damian use his flagship distribution center as a front for the base of his narcotics distribution? Wouldn't it attract too much attention? Wouldn't it be the first place the DEA would look? Would Damian's confidence get the best of his Intelligence? Was this place so obvious that it would be overlooked?

Grace rubbed her hand across the back of her neck, to rid herself of the tingling sensation. She had to focus her thoughts. Thousands of trucks a day came up from Mexico. No customs, no tariffs, no inspections, very few regulations, just open road and opportunity. Somewhere out there, thousands of trucks were using this country's arterial highways as arteries for distributing their narcotics throughout the American heartland. And this place, this massive, technological monstrosity, was the heart that pumped them out.

Grace felt herself becoming nauseated. She lifted her hands and placed them on her stomach, which had become upset. She cold feel the glands inside of her mouth begin to produce more saliva as her head began spinning. She felt as though she were about to collapse. The mental stresses and strains that she was enduring were too much. Damian was guilty. Damian was not guilty. She loved Damian. She did not love Damian. This was a warehouse. This was not a warehouse. Grace cupped her hand over her forehead and wiped away the beads of perspiration. She swallowed hard to keep from vomiting.

"Grace, are you alright?" Damian asked.

Grace took an additional step before she stumbled forward. Damian caught her, and she snapped back into semiconsciousness only to find herself in Damian's arms with him peering down at her. She screamed.

Thoughts flashed rapidly through Grace's mind, too rapidly to be coherent. Scenes from throughout her life rushed through her mind without any form of organization: FBI school in Quantico, her roommate Jackie's smile, her meeting the director at graduation, busting a pair of scraggly looking bank robbers in Omaha, the meeting in Washington DC, Elizabeth's motherly smile, her warnings about Damian. Damian, the man who had his arms wrapped around her. Damian, the man who killed her fellow agents. Damian, the monster. Grace Moore panicked. Then she remembered the ring.

The signal flowed quickly from Agent Moore's ring to a van parked several blocks down from the massive warehouse. Inside of this maroon van sat two technicians at a large bank of computer terminals with a digital encrypter and highly advanced communication sets. One technician removed his headset and quickly grabbed for another. This one was a small earpiece with a microphone attached to it. He inserted it into his ear.

"Code blue! Code blue! I repeat Sigma signal from Bluejay. Sigma signal from Bluejay."

The EH-60L black hawk communications helicopter flying high above the city received the transmission first. Its advanced quick-fix system and thermal-imaging radar pinpointed Grace Moore's exact location within the warehouse. The helicopter's systems operator let everyone else know where she was as well.

"Hawk One, this is Eagle Eye, over."

"Eagle Eye, this is Hawk One, go ahead, over," responded Nathan Hess.

"Hawk One, there are sixty five chickens in the coop. I repeat: sixty-five chickens. Bluejay is inside at point six, four, two, point eight, nine one. Over."

"Eagle Eye, I copy, sixty-five chickens. That is sigma fox chicks. Bluejay is inside at point six, four, two, point eight, nine, one, over."

"Affirmative."

"Eagle Eyes, HRT is in route. Update Bluejays position every thirty seconds. Over."

"Roger that Hawk One. Eagle Eye out."

Nathan keyed his digital radio twice, signaling that he understood. He then lifted it to his mouth again.

"Raptor One, this is Hawk One. Do you copy Bluejay's position? Over."

"Hawk One, this is Raptor One," replied Special Agent John Mobley, leader of the FBI's hostage rescue team, "Blue Jay is at point six, four, two, point eight, nine, one, over."

"Affirmative, Raptor One," Nathan replied. He lifted his hand and massaged his temples. Years of hard work were about to culminate in the arrest of one of the country's most notorious drug dealing families, or he was about to lose another agent. Nathan prayed that it was the former. He lifted his radio again.

"Raptor One, what's you estimated time of arrival? Over."

"Hawk One, Raptor's ETA is two minutes. I repeat we are T minus two minutes to entry. Over."

"Roger. Hawk One out."

The explosion from the entry team knocked Damian and the rest of his entourage to the ground. Grace, already on her knees, looked up in time to see a rope fall from the roof and a black clad agent slide down on it. The laser beam from his infra-red sight painted a red dot across her head several times, before finding a home somewhere else. Nevertheless, the red laser beam pierced her field of vision enough to cause her to vomit. She heaved several times, before bending over in gut-wrenching pain, and lost her breakfast.

"Get on the floor! Federal agents! Get on the floor! FBI! Get down on the floor and place your hands where we can see them!"

The heavily armed, black clad agents fanned throughout the warehouse, securing the facility and gathering its occupants.

Damian felt himself being handcuffed. The flash from the stun grenade knocked him off balance and weakened his coordination. Bright white dots still appeared in his vision, and his ears rang. His disorientation did little to abate his anger.

"What the hell is going on here?" he shouted.

Nathan walked in just as the question was being posed. With his long, beige, London Fog coat, impeccable dark suit, and black Motorola radio in his hand, he looked the part of an FBI agent.

Damian saw him approaching.

"I should have known!" Damian shouted. "God dammit, Nathan, you're way out of line on this one! I'll have your badge for this!"

Grace lifted herself from the floor. The hand she placed on her forehead was quickly removed and placed behind her back. She was handcuffed like the others.

The fact that she had stood on her own, and was not handcuffed while on the ground escaped Damian's attention at first. He was preoccupied by his anger, his disorientation, and his focus on Nathan.

Although her vomiting had cleared her head considerably, she still felt terrible. Damian's shouting had woken her up and she knew where she was. She remembered her role.

"Damian, what's going on?" she asked.

Nathan stepped closer to Damian, and the two started their fierce stare-down. "Your boyfriend here is a murdering, low-life, drug dealer. That's what's going on."

"Leave her out of this, Nathan."

"Why, you mean you haven't told her what you really do for a living?" Without removing his eyes from Damian's penetrating gaze, Nathan began addressing Grace.

"Your boyfriend's real job has nothing to do with construction, shipping, restaurants, internet services, or any other legitimate business. He's really just a highly polished, highly refined, Ivy-league coated drug peddler."

Grace's mouth fell open and she turned toward Damian. "Damian, is that true?"

"Yes, yes it is true," Nathan responded, "Tell her, Damian. Tell your girlfriend how you sponsor youth sport leagues, Cub Scout jamborees, private school vouchers and scholarships, and then you turn around and pump drugs into the communities."

Although handcuffed, Damian started toward Nathan, "Now, wait a minute!"

Black-clad FBI agents restrained Damian.

"No, *you* wait a minute!" Nathan shoved his finger into Damian's face. "You self-righteous sonofabitch! You walk around here with your thousand dollar suits, all of your fancy manners, and your Harvard-educated, New England accent, and you poison the world!"

Several agents gathered around their boss and restrained him.

"You are the lowest life form on this earth. You're the pride and joy of your community and you use your brilliance to destroy your own people!"

"Nathan, this is not about my community or drugs or any other grand cause!" Damian shouted. "This is personal! This is about a daughter who was left standing at the altar. Your daughter! She forgave me, Nathan, why can't you?"

"This is not about her, Damian. This is about you. I was

216

there at your graduation! I know your family! I watched you grow up! How dare you do this to us, Damian! How dare you!"

"This is about Stacia. It's about your precious, little, broken-hearted, debutante slut!"

"You sonofabitch!" Nathan broke free from the surrounding agents and threw a wild punch at Damian. His right fist struck Damian on the left side of his face, sending him reeling to the floor. The nearby agents grabbed their boss and held him tightly.

Damian shook his head and stared up at Nathan from the ground.

"You're the judge and jury now, Nathan?" he asked in a calm, serene tone. "Where's your gun? Pull out your gun, Nathan. You may as well be the executioner too."

Nathan tried to slide his hand into his coat, but his entourage prevented him. Another agent approached.

"Sir, we've found nothing."

"Look again!" Nathan shouted at the agent.

"Sir, we've pulled every canine team in south Texas. We've stripped Lackland Air Force Base clean. We have Border Patrol dogs, Houston, Austin, and Corpus Christi's DEA, FBI, and ATF canine units, as well as all of the locals from the six surrounding counties. Sir, they want their dogs back. The National Guard guys have opened every box, every crate, and every carton. They're tired, sir. There's nothing here."

Nathan resisted the urge to look at Grace. Instead, he frowned at a smiling Damian.

"There's nothing here, Nathan. There has been nothing here the last fifteen times. There will never be anything, Nathan. I'm innocent."

"You're going down! And when it goes down, I hope you fight back."

"You want to kill me now, Nathan?" Damian asked. "What happened to my rights? What happened to being innocent until proven guilty?"

"They're dead. They died when the first crack baby to overdose on your product died. You're a disgrace, you know that? You make me ashamed to be a black man."

"Is that what this is about? Us Negroes is makin' you look bad to Massa? Who gave you the right to judge? Who gave you the right to decide who is fit to be black and who is not? These people you are so concerned about, when's the last time you left your nice, plush, federal office building, and went to go and see them? I was there yesterday. How many black kids have you sent to college? I've sent over five thousand. How many black families have you fed? I employ over ten thousand. The only thing you've done for the black community and those little old ladies who you claim to be protecting is to send their grandchildren to jail! Grandchildren who are out hustling so they can feed and pay the bills of those same little old ladies because the government that you work for lied to them about slavery, social security and everything else! Don't ever preach to me again about a community that you have long since forgotten about!"

Several federal agents grabbed Damian and lifted him up off of the ground. Nathan Hess stepped closer to Damian until they stood nose to nose.

"I'm going to bring you down," he whispered through clenched teeth.

"You'd better hurry," Damian whispered back. "I have a thirty-six year plan. In thirty-six years, my children will be senators, congressmen, governors, and ambassadors."

"Over my dead body," Nathan told him.

Damian smiled. "Is that all?"

218

Chapter Twenty-Eight

Palm Beach Florida has long been known as the Beverly Hills of the East, and for good reason. It boasted more millionaires per capita than any other community in the United States. The streets inside of the old world enclave were flawless, as trash pick up occurred daily. The only objects inhabiting the sides of the broad, well-paved avenues, were the tall, green and brown palm and coconut trees that stood sentry over the wide sidewalks and pathways.

Palm Beach was also home to the internationally acclaimed Worth Avenue, Palm Beach's version of Rodeo Drive. The high number of exorbitantly expensive specialty shops, five-star restaurants and hotels clustered on and around Worth Avenue made it one of the premiere shopping destinations for the world's rich. Billionaire businessmen, international glitterati and European and Middle Eastern royalty could all be seen floating in and out of the various emporiums, bistros, and hotels throughout Palm Beach. Most of course, were accompanied by their first, second, third, or fourth wives, as well as an equally sizable contingent of nubile, young mistresses. Don Alemendez could not even begin to fathom calling any other place home.

The sun was shining brightly, bringing the temperature to a scorching ninety-two degrees. In this type of weather, the residents limited their activities to one of five things: shopping, golf, shopping, swimming, or shopping. Don Alemendez had decided to pursue the first.

Annecy Du'Bourgoune, his latest conquest, was from Belgium. She was twenty-three with light, cloudy blue eyes, thick, pouty, pink lips, long curly golden hair, and long, sultry, sinewy legs that looked to be a quarter mile long. She had told the Don that she was an aspiring actress and part-time model. He had discovered her working in a local restaurant. That was over a month ago and now Annecy Du'Bourgoune had another job. In exchange for her brand new, nine-thousand-square-foot penthouse and brand new, off the show room floor black Jaguar XK8 convertible, all she had to do was keep her Don happy. And that was something she had proven to be truly gifted at.

Don Alemendez was no fool, and he certainly was aware of his age. Particularly his declining vigor, and shriveling parts, and yet, Annecy had managed to make him forget his sixty-five years and feel like a young man again. Her passionate cries, her clasping and scratching of his back during their blissful lovemaking, her constant compliments, all made her patron feel taller and stronger. Annecy's dainty figure, her soft femininity, and the way she melted inside of his arms when their bodies merged had captivated the good Don's attention. His wife, Marie, was from the old school. She believed in taking a skillet to the good Don's head whenever he didn't act right. She also believed in cooking and cleaning for herself, despite the fact that the Don employed three housekeepers and two cooks. Marie insisted on preparing beans and rice everyday for dinner, along with those heart clogging flour tortillas that she spent most of the day preparing. She also believed in walking around their sixty thousand square foot Mediterranean-style mansion barefoot, and wearing those loud, frilly, Mexican style house dresses. For Chrissakes, the woman once dug a hole inside of their well-manicured backyard and barbecued a pig's head in it, wrapped in foil! A pigs head! Marie had about as much class as Rodney Dangerfield, but Annecy...sweet, petite, elegant, young Annecy. She was a woman's woman, and she could write a manual on how to make a man feel like a king!

It was because of all this that Don Alemendez had decided to present her with the necklace he now held in his hand. It was a timeless piece. A five-tiered, cultured pearl necklace with twenty one carat diamonds clustered around a flawless, twenty five carat stone. The pearls had been extracted from the South Sea while the diamonds had been discovered in South Africa. The raw diamonds had been flown to Tel Aviv where they had been painstakingly cut into breathtaking jewelry. They were then airlifted to Amsterdam, where they would be sold on the open market. These particular stones had found their way to Cartier, where they were transformed into the exquisite, million-dollar piece he now held in his own bejeweled, well-manicured hands. Annecy would look like a goddess tonight at the opera. His favorite design house, Oscar de la Renta, had designed a dress to match the platinum, pearl, and diamond necklace. Now all he needed was to find a pair of earrings to match.

Don Alemendez leaned forward and pressed the intercom button on his limousine's door. "Arturo, I've changed my mind, take me back to Harry Winston's."

"Yes, sir," said the driver.

Arturo Venegas wheeled the long, black, Lincoln stretch limousine around, and headed back toward the fabled Worth Avenue. The Don's decision to head to the avenue today made Arturo smile. It was a gorgeous day, and the well-to-do women of south Florida would be out in droves. He relished the thought that he may get to pick up a few while the Don was shopping. Arturo lifted his Motorola two-way communicator. "Hey, guys, the Boss wants to head back to the Ave."

The bodyguards driving in front of him and in back of him, in two separate Lincoln Town cars keyed their devices, acknowledging the transmission. Soon, the three car caravan came to a stop at an empty Palm Beach intersection. The only other vehicles around were a pair of black, Ford Excursions that were stopped at the intersection, just to their left. A black Hummer H2 was stopped at the intersection, just to the right of them. The Don's caravan had reached the intersection first and so they proceeded to cross the quiet, neighborhood street.

The first Excursion barreled into the Don's lead car, while the second smashed into the Don's chase car. They sandwiched the Don's limousine in between them.

Dark-suited men poured from the massive, black trucks like ants from a trampled ants' nest. They swarmed the two smashed Lincoln Town cars and poured semi-automatic gunfire into them, taking out the passengers that remained alive.

Dante emerged from the black H2 Hummer. Wearing black sunglasses, a black suit, a long, black, trench and black, leather gloves, he looked sorely out of place in colorful, sunny, south Florida. He didn't give a shit.

His business here today would be brief, as he had come to Florida for one single purpose: to kill the man who had sent the assholes on jet skis. It was business, but at the same time, it would be a pleasure.

Dante strode to where the trapped limousine sat and pulled out his black, ten-millimeter, glock handgun. He slowly walked around the long, black Lincoln and blew out its tires. When finished, he turned to his cousin Kevin, and extended his hand.

Kevin Reigns opened the maroon backpack that he had slung over his shoulder and pulled from it a large, half-cylindrical device, which he placed inside Dante's waiting hand. Dante took the device, turned it flat side up, and peeled from it a long, broad swath of paper, revealing sticky, yellowish goo. He turned and pressed the gooey material against the car's window, sticking the device to the car.

Dante smiled as he pressed a small, red button on the side of the device. A small, green light began blinking. Dante turned and extended his hand so that Kevin could hand him another.

Don Alemendez was no fool. He had ordered his limousine from a German armoring company that specialized in manufacturing vehicles for foreign dignitaries, heads of states, and various VIPs. The company had guaranteed him that the vehicle's armor would protect him from land mines, heavy assault rifles, and even rocket-propelled grenades, should they ever become a weapon of choice for Florida carjackers. But the manufacturers had never guaranteed that the transparent armor that made up the limousine's windows would be able to withstand a shape charged plastic explosive applied directly to them. The Don watched in horror as Dante walked around his vehicle, sticking large plastic explosive devices on the windows.

Dante knew that Don Alemendez' vehicle would be equipped with the heaviest armor possible and that it would do no good to waste bullets firing at the car. It was for this reason that he had decided to dispense with the preliminaries and go straight to the heavy stuff. Twenty pounds of Pentalite plastique, mounted on each of the Don's windows, should definitely be enough to ruin the good Don's day.

Seeing the charges being placed on the car's windows, Alemendez' driver was no cool customer. He opened his door and tried to sprint down the street. Dante grabbed Arturo by his throat, placed his glock to his head, and squeezed the trigger. Arturo's brains flew onto the limousine's roof.

Alemendez hit the intercom button. "Dante, let's reason together. You and I could come to an agreement. We could take over the commission together."

Dante released Arturo's throat, allowing the driver's body to crumple to the ground. He climbed in the limousine and placed one of his explosive devices on the glass divider that separated the driver and the passenger compartments.

"Dante, let's be reasonable men," Alemendez shouted over the car's intercom. "Dante, this is not business, this is personal! Look, let's all talk this thing over!"

Don Alemendez lifted his tiny cell phone and rapidly dialed a set of numbers. "Look, I'm calling Damian! We're going to work this thing out!"

Dante's cell phone rang. He removed it from his pocket, flipped it open, and placed it to his ear. "You have reached Dante's psychic hot line. This call costs ninety-five cents a minute. You will probably get a bill for thirty-two cents, because you won't be able to talk for an entire minute. I foresee your miserable life coming to an end in the next twenty-seconds. Oh yeah, in case the FCC is listening, this call is for entertainment purposes only." Dante flipped close the tiny cell phone.

Alemendez hit the intercom button again and shouted, "Dante, I have in my hands a million dollar necklace. It's yours. And I will go with you to a bank of your choosing and transfer all my money to your account. Please..."

Dante paused. "Let me see the necklace."

Don Alemendez fumbled open the jewelry case, and held the necklace up to the window with his shaking hand.

Dante nodded, "Okay, deal."

"Your word!" Don Alemendez shouted. "Give me your word!"

Dante lifted his hand into the air. "I give you my word. May my children have to live the life I lead, may my unborn son become a monster like me, and may people curse and spit on my family's name if I break my word."

Don Alemendez opened the door and climbed out of the limousine. Dante's men grabbed him by the arms.

Dante removed the necklace from the Don's hand, and held it up to the sunlight.

"This is gorgeous. It'll make a wonderful present for Boo-Boo Kitty," Dante said before he turned and walked to the driver's side door, opening it. He turned to his men. "Bring the good Don over here."

Dante grabbed the last of the plastic explosive devices from Kevin Reigns' backpack and place it inside the limousine, under the driver's seat. His men brought the Don forward.

Dante pointed at the driver's seat. "Sit him down inside the car."

Kevin passed Dante two sets of handcuffs. Dante took the first cuff and placed it around the Don's small, wrinkled wrist. He then placed the other cuff around the left side of the steering wheel, securing the good Don to it. He repeated the procedure with Don Alemendez' right hand.

"But, you gave me your word!" Don Alemendez shouted.

Dante stopped and stared at the bewildered Don. What, do I look fucking Italian to you or something? Dante shook his head and closed the car's door.

"Don, we're in a school zone. If your asshole flies out of the top of your head at more than ten miles per hour, you could get a ticket. Clinch your butt cheeks together."

Dante's bodyguards laughed. Dante reached his hand inside the limousine and ruffled the Don's hair. "Don't look so depressed. Look at it this way. If by some miracle you are going to heaven, this explosive underneath your seat will get you halfway there and save you the trouble!"

Dante turned and walked back to his Hummer H2 while his bodyguards piled into a pair of brand new GMC Yukons.

"To the airport," Dante ordered his driver. He lifted from the floor of his Hummer a small, black box and extended the small antenna mounted on top of it. After the Hummer turned the corner and was a safe distance away from the Don's limousine, Dante pressed the large, red button that sat in the center of the black box. The limousine's explosion could be heard for miles.

Chapter Twenty-Nine

"**T**wo bogus raids, millions of dollars in resources and manpower down the drain, and for what? So that Damian Reigns can make me look like an idiot!"

Nathan Hess' voice boomed throughout the mahogany paneled conference room. It made Grace Moore cringe. Assistant Director Thomas Peoples lifted his hands in a calming motion.

"Calm down, Nathan," he told him. "We just have to resist. We'll pause, let Grace keep digging, and eventually, we'll get him."

"I will not calm down, Tom!" Nathan stood just behind Grace, who was seated at a large, rectangular, conference table with several others. He shouted down at the back of her head. "I had two hostage rescue teams, one on the ground, one in the air. I called in every law enforcement agency in existence, from the panhandle to the Gulf, I borrowed blackhawks from the army, national guardsmen from the governor, and crowbars from five local hardware stores so we'd have enough to open all of those goddamn crates! And guess what? I get a bill from Damian Reigns' goddamn lawyers!"

"Nathan..." Grace started to speak, but was quickly silenced.

"Shut up! Just shut up!" Spittle flew from the corner of Nathan's mouth. He bent over so that he was right next to

226

Grace's ear. "Do you know the difference between the transmitter on your cell phone and the one on your ring?"

Grace nodded.

"Bullshit! I don't believe you do! The cell phone is to alert agents of a drug find. The ring means that you are in imminent danger. The ring tells us to rush in and save your stupid ass!"

"Nathan that's enough!" Elizabeth Holmes told him firmly. "She made a mistake, that's all. We've all made them."

"I'll say when it's enough!" Nathan exploded. Elizabeth jumped. "Her incompetence is inexcusable! And expensive! I don't like getting bills from fucking drug dealers!"

Nathan Hess pulled Grace's chair away from the conference table and spun it around so that she could sit facing him.

"Do you have anything to say for yourself?" he shouted.

"I messed up," Grace said, turning her palms up toward the ceiling. "I'm sorry, I...I don't know what happened."

"You don't know what happened? What the hell do you mean you don't know what happened? Are you using what we're looking for? Is that why we can't find it? Have you used it all?"

"Nathan that's not fair," Elizabeth told him from the other side of the conference table. "She's doing the best that she can."

"I can't tell. She's had six months, and all we've gotten are bills!" Nathan turned and took several steps away from Grace before spinning on his heels and once again turning to face her. "Maybe you're enjoying that Lexus a little too much. Maybe the apartment that he has you in has become a little too comfortable!"

"Nathan!" Elizabeth Holmes stood.

"Look, I'm doing the best job that I can do," Grace told him. "I can't find anything!"

"Hell, are you even looking?" Nathan shouted.

"Of course I am!"

"Then tell me something!"

"Tell you what?" Grace exhaled, and leaned forward in her chair. She lifted her hand to her temple and began messaging it. "I don't know...I don't know anything to tell," she said softly.

Nathan stared at her coldly before he spoke, "Exactly! That my dear, is the problem."

"Look, sir, I'm investigating. You want me to investigate, dig up hard facts, and bring down his organization? That's what I'm doing."

"Grace, you have to understand. We're all a little frustrated here," Thomas Peoples told her. "You've been in deep for more than six months. Surely you should have come across something by now, I mean...something."

"Sir, I thought this was the Federal Bureau of Investigation, not the Federal Bureau of Make Something Up!" Again, Grace's palms were turned toward the ceiling. "I've found nothing. Nothing."

Thomas Peoples leaned forward and rested his forearms on the large wood conference table. "Nothing?" He interlaced his fingers and lifted an eyebrow.

Grace swallowed hard, and turned her chair back toward the conference table. Nathan walked to the head of the table where Assistant Director Thomas Peoples was seated and stood next to him. Grace alternated her glance between the two.

"I've found nothing. I don't know whether he's just extremely careful or if he's just not doing anything."

Murmurs flew throughout the conference room as its occupants stirred in their seats.

"Do you realize what you've just suggested?" Nathan asked her. "Several people in this room have lost very close friends who were investigating the Reigns family at the time of their disappearance."

Grace shifted her glance and stared at a section of the table just in front of her. "Maybe we need to start preparing ourselves for the possibility that maybe, just maybe, we're wrong."

"Wrong!" shouted Nathan. "I've lost six agents from this field office alone! What do you mean wrong? What the hell is wrong with you?"

Thomas Peoples raised his hand to silence Nathan.

"Let's hear her out," Tom said nodding at Agent Moore. "Grace, please continue with your theories."

"I mean, there is the possibility that Dante, or this evil sister that I was briefed on, may have done things without Damian's knowledge," Grace lifted her head and stared at the assistant director. "Have we investigated the possibility that the criminal side of Reigns Enterprises could be something totally separate from the legitimate side ran by Damian?"

Thomas Peoples lifted his finger to his face, and pushed his glasses further up on his nose. He sat back in his large, dark brown, winged back chair and whistled.

"Damian, innocent? You gotta be kidding me?" Nathan asked incredulously. "Agent Moore, are your feelings okay on this? I mean, sometimes deep cover agents have a tendency to lose their neutrality. They become too close to their targets, too emotionally attached. They bond and develop an admiration, sometimes even a legitimate friendship. It happens sometimes."

"What are you saying, sir?" asked Grace frowning her face.

"I'm asking, are you too fucking close to the goddamned trees to see the forest?"

Grace sat up straight. "Are you?" she asked. "What was all of this stuff about the community, your daughter, a wedding? Why wasn't I briefed?"

"Headquarters felt that this was irrelevant, Agent Moore," Tom Peoples told her. "Nathan's daughter and Damian Reigns' previous relationship was inconsequential."

"Bullshit!" Grace stood. "I see what's going on here. I was sent in blind on purpose." Grace shifted her gaze to Nathan

Hess.

"You knew it would come up. And if I didn't know, I would be surprised and shocked. I would even question Damian about it later. You and your damned psychologist played on the fact that I was a woman to help boost my cover, you son of a bitches."

"Grace," Elizabeth called to her softly, in order to calm her down.

"No, they used me. We were supposed to be on the same team, but they used me," Grace said, her eyes glaring at Nathan. "What else did you leave out? What other surprises?"

Nathan smiled. "You seem upset. Does the fact that Damian slept with my daughter upset you that much?"

"No, it doesn't upset me, does it upset you? Tell me, did you use her to bust him, like you're using me, you sick son of a bitch!" Grace gathered up her purse and her personal effects from the table.

"What did you call me?" Nathan asked.

"I called you, a sick, son of a bitch...*sir*," Grace said calmly and accurately before she turned, stormed out of the room, and headed down the hall.

"Grace! Grace!" Elizabeth called out to her, racing after her.

She caught up to Grace at the water fountain in the massive lobby of the federal building.

"Grace, don't let them get to you," Elizabeth told her.

Grace Moore leaned up against the wall next to the water fountain. She sighed. "They know, Elizabeth. They know about me and Damian."

"They don't know, Grace."

"They do, Elizabeth, you heard them. Those bastards were counting on it. They knew I'd sleep with him." Grace lifted her hand to her face and covered her eyes.

"Grace, we don't do things like that. We are the FBI, not the KBG, and this is America, not Russia," Elizabeth told

230

her.

Tears fell from Grace Moore's eyes. "Bullshit!" She removed her hand and stared Agent Holmes in the eyes. "Liz, why was I chosen?"

"Because, you can do the job, Grace. You're smart, you're strong, and you're a good agent. No other reason."

Grace Moore shook her head. "They know. Did you know about Nathan's daughter?"

Elizabeth Holmes looked away, "I wasn't briefed on it."

"But you knew! Elizabeth, you knew!"

"It was a rumor, that's where I heard it. Just Bureau scuttlebutt."

"Is this Nathan's own personal little war, Liz?"

"Grace, we all have our own personal wars to fight. If Nathan's brining down a major drug dealer who left his daughter hanging out to dry, then what does it matter?"

"Because it does. What if he's innocent? What if Nathan's wrong? What then?"

"Is Nathan wrong, Grace? Use your head, Grace. Is it possible for Dante to run a parallel drug empire without Damian knowing?"

"I think he's innocent, Liz. I can't find anything, Nathan can't find anything, and none of the other agents could find anything. Maybe there isn't anything to find."

"Grace, how are your feelings on this?"

"I'm clear, Liz. My feelings are clear," Grace told her, but her thoughts were otherwise.

Elizabeth Holmes placed her hands on Grace's shoulders and looked her fellow agent straight in the eyes.

"Are you sure?"

"No," Grace smiled, and let out an uneasy laugh as tears fell from her eyes. She folded her arms as she laughed and cried at the same time.

Elizabeth pulled her close and hugged her. "You want out?"

"I can't get out, I'm trapped. Either he's innocent and the

world is going to know it or he's guilty and I'm going to bust him. Either way, Liz, I'm trapped. I'm trapped."

Chapter Thirty

The Alamo is the shrine of Texas' independence. It existed before there was a San Antonio. It existed before there was a Texas. It existed before there was even a United States. The Holy Church of the Immaculate Conception existed before that.

When the Spaniards moved north from Mexico to establish a mission outpost, they constructed a small church which they christened the Holy Church of the Immaculate Conception. The Spanish mission later ventured out to find suitable ground, near a reliable water source, where they could establish a more permanent settlement. This suitable ground was to be found to the west of the current settlement, on the banks of the San Antonio River. The majority of the mission relocated to the new ground, christening it, Mission San Antonio de Valero, and thus the Alamo was born.

The mission conception expanded and grew and eventually became the cathedral conception. It was a massive structure, which brought together High Gothic and Spanish Imperial Colonial architecture into one imposing, authoritative work. Vaulted ceilings, Florentine Renaissance frescos, Spanish Imperial gold leaf, and Imperial Spanish furnishings, along with the cathedral's sheer size, made it an awe inspiring place. Its age and pristine condition would have made it the church of the city's white elite. However, the cathedral conception was located east of the Alamo, which itself was on the eastern edge of the city's downtown. The cathedral conception was located on the city's predominately black, east side, and for this reason had become the exclusive province, pride, and joy of the city's black Catholic elite—an elite of which the Reigns family were very prominent members.

Grace's breath was taken away when she stepped inside the Cathedral's two-hundred-year-old gold leaf double doors.

"My God, Damian," she said then interlocked her arms inside of his. "This place is so big. It's like an ancient, medieval castle."

The more Grace looked around and examined the church and its occupants, the more she began to fidget. The church was filled with immaculately dressed patrons. Grace thought it looked as though it could be a St. John, Escada, and Chanel convention.

Damian began waving, shaking hands, and introducing Grace.

"Mr. and Mrs. Jackson, Mr. Ridgeway, Mr. and Dr. Parks, Mr. and Mrs. Washington, Dr. and Mrs. Franklin. Mrs. Eubanks, Councilman Barret, and Mrs. Baret. Judge Martin and Mrs. Martin, Dr. Lowe and Mrs. Lowe, Dr. and Mrs. Carter, Councilwoman Nelson and her husband, Mr. Nelson, Congressman Newby and Mrs. Newby, Senator Hawkins and Mrs. Hawkins, Congressman Taylor and Mrs. Taylor, Commissioner Johnson and Mr. Johnson, Drs. Lloyd and Caroline Smith, Director Rice and Mrs. Rice, Judge Terrance and Mrs. Terrance.

The introductions were staggering.

Fathers O'Connell and McKee approached. Father O'Connell wore a deep purple robe with gold embroidering. Father McKee, a young, African American priest, with a short, tapered haircut and deep brown eyes, wore a snow-white robe with gold embroidering. Father O'Connell extended his hand first.

"Damian, good to see you, finally," he said. The finally

was said with a raised eyebrow. "You couldn't get Dante to join you, eh?"

"Actually Father, he will be here shortly," Damian replied.

"Wonderful!"

Damian shook Father McKee's hand.

"Father McKee, good to see you."

"Likewise," said Father McKee nodding solemnly.

"Damian, Father McKee is no longer assigned to Mission Conception on a permanent basis," Father O'Connell told him.

"Oh, leaving us, are you?" Damian asked. "We will certainly miss you."

"Actually, he is leaving us for an even greater mission, to educate young minds." Father O'Connell wrapped his arm around Father McKee's shoulder. "As you know, Father McKee here has a PhD in education from Georgetown. Well, the diocese is going to let him put that brilliant mind of his to use. We are going to re-establish St. Gerard's High School on the city's eastside, and Father McKee is going to be the principal."

"Wonderful!" Damian became excited. "The diocese's decision to close it took us all by surprise. I think opening St. Gerard's up again is a wonderful idea."

"I thought you would. Now, the question is, how much of a good idea do you think it is?" Father O'Connell asked hoping for a donation.

"Father, your sales pitch is as smooth as ever. The time you spent as a missionary in Africa was certainly well spent. You obviously took in a great deal of the outdoors, especially observing wildlife."

Father O'Connell looked puzzled, "Why do you say that?"

"Father, only one who has observed the cheetah could pounce as skillfully as you."

Together they laughed.

"Damian!"

235

They turned to see an exquisitely dressed young lady approaching. She wore a fuchsia colored jacket and skirt with matching high heels, and an exceptionally large fuchsia colored hat. Her outfit screamed Coco Chanel, as did her purse and her perfume. Her diction, walk, and attitude were distinctly Spelman College, with a trace of Ivy League grad school. Her skin was a deep, rich, flawless pecan brown, her eyes a walnut brown, and her hair almond brown. Her hair hung from beneath her tilted hat tied into a neatly pressed, flouncing ponytail, while her figure was shapely, healthy, provocative. Grace hated her instantly.

"Hello, Fathers!" She turned toward Grace and waved. "Hi, hi."

She turned back toward Damian, wrapped her arms around him, and planted a kiss on his lips. "My sugar bear, boo-boo cakes, how have you been?"

"Stacia, it's been a long time," Damian responded nervously.

"Well, it certainly has been," she told him, "You know better than to stay away this long."

"Uh, Stacia, I'd like you to meet my friend, Jonel."

Stacia turned and stared at Grace. Her eyes started at Grace's shoes, and walked themselves slowly up Grace's body until they came to rest on Grace's eyes. Her look was one of contempt, disdain, and haughtiness. It was as if she had been introduced to Damian's gardener. Again, Stacia lifted her hand and waved at Grace. She quickly dismissed Grace and turned back to the priests.

"I'm going to steal my sugar bear from you, just for one moment."

The priests smiled and nodded.

Stacia grabbed Damian's arm and stalked off. She took Damian into the cathedral's sitting room and pulled him into a secluded corner.

"Stacia, I have a guest" Damian told her. "This is rude."

Stacia waved him off, "Oh, forget about her. As a matter

of fact, that's why I dragged you in here. She's Bureau."

"What?" Damian acted surprised. "She's FBI?"

Stacia nodded, "One-hundred-percent Hoover girl. They have a new operation against you. It's called Sunshine—Operation Sunshine. They've pulled out all the stops and green-lighted the whole package."

Damian cut his eyes to the side and leaned forward. "Stacia, are you sure?" he whispered nervously.

"Oh, of course I'm sure. My husband works in Intel and my father is the special agent in charge of this field office. In fact, my father is the coordinator for the entire operation. Damian, it's serious this time."

"Stacia, what's the deal with my sister and her little Florida operation?" Damian asked.

"It's still the same; she's shopping up territory. And there's a third party making major moves. And not just in Florida, they're taking over territory all across the South."

"That's us," Damian told her. "I got into it with the commission. We're in an all-out war."

Stacia nodded. An older couple walked by, and she turned and smiled at them. "Dr. Benson, Mrs. Benson, how are you? Mrs. Benson that dress is lovely!" She turned back to Damian after the couple passed. "You're winning. You're taking over chunks of territory. Damian, how did you get into a war with the entire commission?"

"I've asked myself that question a thousand times. You know what? I'm starting to think that it was all planned. Angela came up with the idea first, and now it looks as though she may have been right. El Jefe knew what would happen and he knew we had the money, the political connections, and the manpower base to take on the entire commission. He threw Princess out there as a decoy, knowing that we would defend ourselves and destroy the entire commission as a result of the meeting in Miami. That treacherous bastard counted on it; now he gets what he wants."

Stacia tilted her head inquisitively to the side. "Which is?"

"His distribution network unified." Damian shook his head. "We're going backwards. We're supposed to be pulling out, but instead…"

"Give me El Jefe's location."

Damian shook his head. "No one knows it. Not even me. But, I'll tell you what. After this is over, I'll get my people to find it," Damian smiled. "Trying to throw the old husband a bone, huh?"

Stacia smiled seductively. She placed her hand on Damian's chest and rubbed the fabric of his finely tailored suit. "We might as well. He's done so much for us."

They both shared a laugh.

"I'll tell you what, I'll throw him several bones, the commission members and turn up the heat on them. I'll let you know which ones, and when. That way I can pull my people out so they won't get caught up."

"Of course, I was already going to suggest that. Anyone who attacks my sugar bear is my enemy and my enemy is the enemy of the Bureau."

"Stacia, do you realize what we're doing?"

Stacia smiled. "We're using the FBI to get rid of your enemies and help you take over the distribution of fifty percent of the cocaine coming into the country."

"Stacia, you are wicked."

Stacia looked around to insure that no one was watching, and then leaned forward and kissed Damian passionately.

"You made me wicked." Stacia grabbed Damian's private parts. "You turned me out, Damian Reigns."

Damian shook his head slowly. "I think you have it backward. It was you who turned *me* out, Stacia Hess."

"You couldn't stay a virgin forever."

"Stacia, we were twelve!"

"I know, I can't believe I waited twelve whole years to give you this cat," she laughed seductively.

"Stacia, we're in a church."

Stacia Hess tilted her head. "Damian, you and I both know where we're going."

"Stacia!"

Stacia and Damian turned in the direction from which the voice came. It was Nathan Hess.

Nathan extended his hand. "Sweetheart, come on, leave that monster alone."

Stacia turned and walked to her father. She wrapped her arms around Nathan, kissed him, and then walked back into the chapel. Nathan approached Damian.

"What are you doing here?" Nathan asked.

"I go to church here," Damian replied.

"God expeled Lucifer from heaven; he didn't want him polluting his angels. Lucifer was disobedient, unholy, and evil." Nathan lifted his arm, and pointed toward the door. "Can't you take a hint?"

Damian lifted his hand and shook his finger toward the special agent in charge. "Nathan, judge not, lest ye be judged. Besides," Damian spread out his arms and smiled. "I'm here to repent."

"Ha, there is no amount of contrition that would satisfy the Lord!"

"Nathan, the Father told me that my sins were forgiven. I had to do twenty Hail Marys, and twenty Our Fathers. Don't tell me they were all in vain."

"Does the Father know that you're a police killer?"

"I make confession every week. Why don't you ask him?"

"You son of a bitch!"

Damian walked to the door leading to the chapel and stopped. He turned back toward Nathan.

"Nathan, you're still looking for your missing agents?"

Nathan frowned.

"Bug the confessional, Nathan; bug the confessional." Damian laughed, turned, and walked out of the room.

Chapter Thirty-One

World famous R&B singer Faith Evans waved her hand to the capacity crowd, still on its feet applauding her performance. She lifted the microphone to her flawless lips.

"Thank you! Thank you so much! You're such a wonderful crowd and it's been a tremendous pleasure performing for you. We'll have to do this again sometime."

The crowd went wild.

Faith had to wait a full minute for the whistles, shouts, and thunderous applause to subside before she could begin speaking again. She hushed the crowd.

"I want to say hello to an old friend of mine who's in the audience today," Faith said, lifting her tiny cream-colored hand into the air and waving. "Hello Damian. I'll see you on the slopes, enjoy the concert."

Grace grabbed Damian's hand and turned toward him. "You know Faith Evans?"

Damian smiled and nodded. "Yeah, she's an old friend."

Grace didn't like his smile. She frowned. "How *well* do you know her?" she asked.

Damian laughed at her frown. "I plead the fifth."

Grace released his hand, and turned away from him. She folded her arms and stared at the stage.

"Jonel, you know I wasn't a hermit before we met. I did have a life."

"Yeah, like that FBI's daughter?" Grace again turned her

gaze on him. "Why didn't you tell me about her?"

"What did you want to know? I mean, what, am I supposed to tell you about every woman I ever dated?"

"She was your fiancée!" Grace questioned forcefully. "There's a big difference!"

Damian placed his arm around her shoulder and pulled her close. "Jonel, they are old; they are the past. You on the other hand, you're my future."

Damian placed his thumb and forefinger underneath her chin, and lifted her head. He leaned forward to kiss her but Grace turned away.

"I don't know, Damian." She turned back toward him. "What else is there? What else do I not know about you? What other secrets are going to pop up tomorrow, the next day, the day after?"

Damian smiled, lifted his hand, and motioned to a bodyguard who immediately disappeared.

"No more secrets, Jonel. I promise. You mean everything to me. You're my everything."

Onstage the superstar R&B singer Tyrese was just about to begin one of his love ballads. He walked to a stool just in front of the microphone stand and placed the microphone in its holder. He sipped at a glass of ice water that sat on another stool just to his right. Then he cleared his throat, sat down on the stool, and adjusted the microphone.

"How ya doing?" he asked the enthusiastic crowd.

The crowd erupted with screams, whistles, and applause.

"Good. I got a song that a good friend of mine asked me to sing to a special lady friend of his tonight. Yeah you know it; it's one of my biggest hits. Jonel, this is from Damian. He loves you a lot, and he wanted me to tell you that you're his everything."

The superstar R&B artist caressed the microphone, pulled it close, and in a silky smooth, sexy, sultry voice, began singing to Jonel.

By the time the song was finished, Grace was bawling uncontrollably. With her hands covering her tear filled face, she ran from the crowded stadium to Damian's waiting limousine. He ran behind her and ordered the driver to take them back to his place.

Grace arched her back and squeezed Damian tightly. She felt his body go rigid and then she felt him throbbing inside her. She began kissing his hulking shoulder as she rubbed her hands across his muscular back. She could taste the salt from his perspiration and feel his body slowly beginning to relax. He tasted good to her. He felt good inside of her. Grace closed her eyes and continued to hold him tight. She wanted to savor this moment, to hold onto him as long as she could.

The gray, silk sheets felt good against her naked body. The light from the fireplace danced across the vaulted ceiling of Damian's bedroom and provided a radiant glow across their faces. Grace could still taste the nutty sweetness from the bottle of Chateau Petrus that she and Damian disposed of earlier. She could still taste Damian.

Damian tried to lift himself from off of her, but she quickly wrapped her legs around him and pulled him back inside of her.

"Where are you going?" she asked softly.

"Nowhere, I was just going to lie next to you."

Grace shook her head. "I want you right where you are." She kissed his neck.

"I'm not heavy?"

Again, Grace shook her head. "Uh-uh, you're just right."

"So, how do you feel?"

"Confused," she said lightly. She couldn't believe how easy it came out.

"Confused about what?" Damian leaned forward and began kissing her lightly all over her face and neck.

"About life, about us, about where this is going."

242

"I'm not scared of commitment, Jonel, if that's what you're worried about. I'm the kind of guy that you can take home to mother," Damian snarled and began biting and sucking on Grace's neck.

She screamed and broke into laughter.

"That tickles," she told him. "Stop, it's time to be serious."

"I don't want to be serious, I like being Damian."

"Why?"

"Why what?"

"Why do you like being Damian? Who is Damian, and what's so special about him?"

"He's real fly. He's handsome, educated, and wealthy. Dresses well, has impeccable taste, and knows how to make toe-curling love. Who wouldn't want to be Damian?"

"Well, five out of six isn't bad."

"Excuse me?" Damian went for her neck again, this time biting, licking, and snorting.

Grace laughed uncontrollably. She slapped him across his right shoulder with her right hand.

"Stop, silly! I knew you were a pig!"

"Which one did I get wrong?" He started tickling her sides. "The handsome part, the impeccable taste, or the toe-curling love?"

"Okay, okay, I was kidding!" Grace shouted in between bursts of laughter.

"That's what I thought. You had better be kidding."

Grace smiled and stared into Damian's eyes. "What are we going to do, Damian?"

"About what?" he asked, and began kissing her face with tiny little pecks.

"About us," Grace sighed. "What are we going to do, Damian?"

"If God blesses us, we'll grow old together, Jonel."

"Damian, don't say that unless you mean it. Don't play with me, don't play with my feelings."

"Jonel, since we've met I haven't been the same. My life has changed. My days are brighter, the air I breathe seems fresher, and my legs seem lighter. Jonel, I love spending time with you, I love being around you. I could just sit in an empty room and stare at a blank wall and I would have a smile on my face because I'd know you're near me."

A tear fell from Grace Moore's eye, "But do you love me?"

Damian lowered his head and kissed the tear trolling down the side of her face. "I love you so much that it hurts sometimes. Jonel, I want to marry you. Will you marry me?"

Grace broke out into an uncontrollable stream of tears. Her body shook and she wrapped her arms around him tightly. Damian held her in his arms, and again they made love.

Chapter Thirty-Two

Damian walked to the window and stared out over the lake. It was beautiful out there today. The lake was calm, serene, and peaceful. It was much like the lake his mansion was situated on.

Lake Travis was a massive blue-green lake situated to the north of Austin, Texas. It was here that Damian owned one hundred sixty acres of lakefront property and an eight thousand square foot, seven bedroom log cabin. He and Dante were currently discussing business inside the master suite of that rustic, early-American cabin.

"Damian, it's not that bad," Dante told him.

"It *is* bad," Damian lifted his Budweiser long neck to his lips and took a long swig. "We're supposed to be pulling out. Now look at us. We've taken Mississippi, Alabama, Florida, South Carolina, North Carolina, most of Virginia, all of Tennessee, with the exception of Memphis, all of Arkansas, New Mexico, Arizona, and parts of Colorado. That's brought us into a war with the guys in Kansas and Missouri."

Dante shrugged his shoulders. "So we'll wipe them out too."

Damian turned and faced his brother. "Then Chicago steps in. Maybe even Nevada, and New York. If Nevada steps in then we are at war with not only the Italians, but the Russians. New York steps in and we're at war with the

Sicilians. We take Chicago, and everybody will come after us. We're messing around with the old ones now, Dante."

"Damian, we didn't start this war." Dante pointed east. "They did! We just finished it."

Damian nodded. "I agree. And now what do we do with all of this territory?"

"Reward our guys, give them chunks of territory, let them pacify the conquered territory and make it loyal to you."

Damian lifted his beer and drank from it. "And then?"

"And then we carry plane loads of money to the Caribbean while we separate the books. We don't even worry about integrating the new money or cleaning it. We just fly it out and continue to extract ourselves from the dirt we currently have."

"It's not worth the risk."

"The risk is not all that great. We'll let the area bosses be responsible for getting the money to the Caribbean. Their people get popped, then they get the heat, if there is any. If they're defeated, then it's no loss—one less area to worry about."

Damian exhaled and nodded slowly. "Put it into effect. Reward our people, and as soon as they are secure, pull back our soldiers. We need to start to build down, and we need to have an accountant set us up in the Caribbean. Get the money rolling and continue to separate books."

"So, we agree to the truce that the remaining members of the commission are proposing?"

"Yes, and then kill them anyway."

Dante smiled and nodded.

"About the Princess situation..." Damian turned and stared out of the window again. "How's that coming along?"

"I have an idea."

"Let's hear it."

"We make her an offer. We offer her control of the other side of our family enterprises."

"And what does that do?" Damian asked.

"It makes her stop recruiting and it makes her stop attacking. I mean, right now, it's like a bat attacking an elephant. We are way too strong for her. But, like you said, we need to build down. This will allow us to do so, and it will buy us time while we pull out. It also allows us access to her—it enables us to kill her in such a way that it will look like an accident."

Damian took another swig of his brew. "How do you know she'll bite?"

"How could she resist? It gives her the power that she craves."

Damian nodded. "Approved, make the offer."

Dante nodded.

"Anything else?"

"I promoted Mina. She's your new head of security."

Damian lifted an eyebrow. "Oh really? Dante, do you honestly think she's ready?"

"She's been tailing you and covering your ass. I have a couple of guys watching her and they say she's been doing a really good job."

"If you say so." Damian nodded, turned, and walked to the bedroom door. "It's your call."

He opened the door and walked out into the living room where his guests were occupying themselves.

"Mr. Damian, I've found your little treasure trove," Grace told him.

"What are you talking about?"

Grace lifted a picture from Damian's shelf. The shelf was made from large buck antlers and glass. She turned the picture toward him and raised an eyebrow.

"That's Daphanie," Damian told her with a smile.

Grace turned the picture back toward her and smiled at it. "Hi, Daphanie." She looked up at Damian, "And where is Miss Daphanie now?"

"Her father made her a goodwill ambassador, so she's

probably running around Europe somewhere."

"Her father made her an ambassador? And who exactly might little Miss Daphanie's father be?"

"He's a Nigerian king. I forget which tribe."

Grace turned and lifted another picture of Daphanie from the shelf. In this one, Damian stood just behind her with his arms wrapped around her.

"Oh, Miss Daphanie is a princess!" Grace smiled, and turned the picture toward him. He could tell that her smile was hiding her anger.

"That was taken in St. Barts," he told her nervously.

"Oh, so she's a skiing, jet setting, Nigerian princess!" Grace turned and lifted another picture of Daphanie.

"The Sahara," Damian told her.

Grace replaced the picture of Daphanie and lifted one of another woman. She turned back toward Damian and held the picture up.

"That is Marjorie."

"Another princess of yours?" Grace asked.

"Actually, yes."

Grace's mouth fell slightly open.

"Well... she's not exactly my princess, a... well, she is a princess. Her dad is a chief, and well, he's the oldest, and her grandfather is the king, and well... she's from Senegal. *Was* from Senegal. Actually she is from Senegal, but now she lives in Paris. She's a model now." Damian tried desperately to clean things up. "Ahh, you're my princess now."

Grace frowned, turned, and replaced the picture. She began examining the others.

"I know her, I hated her last movie," she said to the first. "I've seen her in magazines," she said of the next. "And I loved her last album," she said of the third. At the fourth group of pictures, she turned back toward Damian with a raised eyebrow. "Wow, more pictures of the modeling princess?"

Damian laughed. He wrapped his arms around Grace

and tried to kiss her. Grace pushed him away, and broke free of his hold.

"Jonel, what are you tripping about?"

"I'm not the one tripping."

Damian placed his hand against his chest. "I'm not the one tripping."

Grace nodded, "Yeah, you're right. You're not tripping; I'm the one tripping. I should have known better."

"Jonel, what are you talking about?"

Grace pointed at the pictures. "Why do you still have them? What do you expect me to say? How do you expect me to feel, Damian? I come here and there are pictures of women all over the place!"

"Jonel, they are old. You are new."

"Bullshit!" Grace stormed out to the far wall of the cabin and pointed at a massive poster-size picture of Stacia Hess in a bikini, seated on a jet ski. "What is that bitch still doing here?"

"Jonel!"

Grace lifted her hand. "Damian, if you still love these hos, then let me know. Let me go!"

"Jonel!"

"No, Damian! I love you, but I'm not going to play games. That shit Stacia pulled at the church hurt me, Damian. And then the concert, when Faith told you that she would see you on the slopes?" Grace began crying. "Damian, I don't have the money they have or the pedigree or the fame. I can't compete with them. I can't."

Damian walked to where Grace was standing and wrapped his arms around her.

"Jonel, you don't have to compete with them. I never asked you to. They are who they are. You are who you are. You're going to become Mrs. Reigns. You're the one who I chose to spend the rest of my life with. They can't compete with you, Jonel. They don't hold a candle to you."

Damian kissed Grace on her forehead and then turned to

one of his men. He nodded at Stacia's massive picture.

The bodyguard removed it.

"Throw that thing in the lake," Damian winked at his bodyguard. "I don't ever want to see it again."

"Yes, Mr. Reigns."

Grace sniffled, and looked up at Damian, "You're going to do that for me?"

"Jonel, I would do anything for you. Don't you know that by now?"

Grace sniffled and hugged him tightly.

Chapter Thirty-Three

Damian eased into the parking space, shifted his Cadillac Escalade into park, and cut off the ignition.

"I can't believe His Majesty is actually going grocery shopping," Grace told him.

"Ha, ha, real funny," Damian opened his door, and stepped out of the large, black, SUV. Grace did the same.

Gone were the tailored English and Italian suits, expensive shoes, and custom-crafted wristwatches. Today, Damian wore baggy black jeans, large clunky suede hiking boots, and a red and black flannel shirt. An oversize, black, down-filled parka, along with a large, thick, black knit beanie cap also helped to keep him warm. He looked as though he could have been torn straight from an Eddie Bauer or Lands End catalog. Grace was dressed in a similar outdoorsy style.

"I'm just saying," Grace extended her hands out to her sides and shrugged her shoulders, "no limousines, no body guards, no entourage, just you and I? It's creepy. It's almost as if we have miraculously managed to become a regular couple."

"We *are* a regular couple."

"Damian, regular couples don't have three maids, a cook, a chauffeur, a butler, three grounds keepers, and dozens of bodyguards."

"You make it seem as though having money is a curse."

Damian wrapped his arm around her as they walked toward the grocery store. "Jonel, we are a regular couple. We do everything that other couples do. Besides, I didn't bring any of those people to the cabin with us did I?"

Grace shook her head.

"It will be you and I and Dante and Angela, hanging out and having fun. Tomorrow, the temperature will be back up into the sixties, and I am going to barbecue for us." Damian leaned over and kissed Grace on her forehead. "You are in for another culinary treat. My barbecue falls off of the bone and my sauce..." Damian kissed the tips of his fingers. "C'est magnifique!"

"We'll see," Grace told him. "But one thing bothers me."

"What's that?"

"You said, another culinary treat. When was the first?"

"Oh, that did it! That is it! You are going to pay for that one!"

Grace grabbed a shopping cart and raced down the aisle. "You'll have to catch me first!"

"What, you think that I won't?" Damian took off after her. He chased her down one aisle and up another.

"Damian, stop! You're going to make me run over somebody!"

"I didn't tell you to insult me and then run!"

Grace stopped her speeding cart and turned back toward him. She raised her arms in a gesture of surrender.

"Okay, okay, I quit!" Grace said, breathing heavily. "The meals that you have prepared have been delicious."

"That's it? Just delicious? For the past seven months I have treated you to meals that would make five star chefs envious. Now all you have to say is they were delicious?" Damian shook his head. "No, a hamburger from McDonald's is delicious. A flame-broiled whopper is delicious. What I prepare are masterpieces."

Grace threw her head back in laughter. "Well excuse me, Picasso. I didn't know you were sensitive about your cooking."

"Call it what you want to call it, but I do know one thing. I was considering sharing some of my culinary secrets with you, but you obviously can forget about that now."

"Okay, okay," Grace lifted her hands into the air, and began to bow. "Oh great one, please teach me your secrets."

"Your sarcasm is the reason that you can't cook toast."

Grace laughed again. She and Damian turned down the grocery aisle. Halfway down it, they noticed that two men in dark overcoats had stepped in front of the aisle, blocking it off. Damian quickly turned and peered over his shoulder, only to find that two more suits were blocking the rear of the aisles. Grace saw them too. She grabbed Damian's arm.

"Damian, what's going on?" she whispered nervously. Deep down, she knew the answer. The men in suits were not Damian's men. Grace knew that there were many ways to die in the line of duty. It was the perpetual risk, of being an undercover agent. Usually, however, that risk came from being careless, from being discovered and caught. Never had she heard of an agent being killed because they had concealed their identity too well. Never had she thought she would go down in a hail of gunfire because she had been caught in a turf war. A knot formed in her stomach.

"My dear brother."

Grace and Damian turned.

She wore an expensive, navy colored wool skirt with a matching jacket and hat. Her navy Manolos clicked as she walked along the highly polished tile floors of the store. Grace recognized her from the briefing photos. Her name was Princess.

"Funny catching you here," she laughed, and pressed her well-manicured hands against her chest. "Excuse me, I meant, funny meeting you here."

"Oh, so this is a coincidence? Great, well, nice seeing you, Sis. You look well," Damian grabbed Grace's trembling hand and began to walk away. "See you later."

"Yeah, right. You know better than that Damian," Princess told him. Two of her hulking men folded their massive arms and maneuvered themselves just in front of Damian and Grace. Princess smiled, leaned down and stared into the shopping cart, "Barbecue? You know how I just love your barbecue. Is that what you'd like for a last meal?"

"Actually, I'd like a nice Norwegian sturgeon. Unfortunately, those can only be found in the Barents Sea. But, I'm willing to wait of course."

Princess smiled, "Even in death you maintain your sense of humor. Admirable."

Princess shifted her attention to Grace. "Now, what do we have here?" Princess lifted her hand and grabbed Grace by her cheeks. She turned Grace's face to the side, examining her. Grace snatched her head back. Princess shook her head

"Dear, dear brother, slumming again, are we?"

Grace frowned.

"What is your name?" Princess asked her.

"It doesn't matter, Princess, she has nothing to do with anything. Let her walk away."

Princess laughed. She turned to her entourage of large, dark suited men, and they laughed as well. She turned back to her brother.

"Let her go? How noble of you. But alas, that I am afraid, is impossible."

Grace turned, and stared at Damian. Her heart fluttered at the fact that he was trying to save her.

"She's not involved in this, Princess. Let her walk away," Damian uttered through clenched teeth.

Princess stepped closer to her brother. She frowned, and tugged forcefully at his jacket. "No one let Patrick make it. And what about my first fiancé, did anyone let Dillon make it?"

Princess turned and examined Grace with contempt. She lifted Grace's down filled parka, and walked her eyes down

254

Grace's body. Princess stuck her hand inside Grace's jacket and felt her breasts. Grace screamed, knocked Princess' hand away, and wrapped herself around Damian. She began crying.

"Damn you, Princess!" Damian shouted. "Leave her out of this!"

Princess laughed, "She dresses poorly, but her figure is outstanding. Not bad at all. Does she have a nice pussy, Damian?"

Princess lifted her hand and grabbed a strand of Grace's hair. "Does she have some good pussy, Damian? Is it nice and tight and pretty?"

Grace shivered and began crying harder. She was naked without her weapon. She was surrounded, helpless, and violated.

"That's enough, Princess!" Damian told her.

Princess leaned forward and whispered into Grace's ear. "You're going to die, sweetie. That is, unless you are willing to take those pretty green eyes home with me. Do you hear me, Green Eyes? Come home with me, and let me taste that pretty brown skin and I might let you live."

Grace shivered, buried her face in Damian's chest, and began crying harder.

"Okay Princess, let's just get this over with," Damian told her. "You're not going to torture her. If you're going to do it, then let's get it over with."

"Oh, come on now, Damian. In the middle of the grocery store? I don't think so. I have a car waiting outside. You and your girlfriend are going to have a terrible accident."

Princess waved her hand and her two suits guarding the top of the grocery aisle moved. The suits standing around her surrounded Damian and Grace.

"I'm glad you're being a sport about it, Damian," Princess told him. "You understand it's nothing personal. In fact, you continue to be a good sport, and I promise you, I won't make your girlfriend suffer. She'll get one clean bullet through the

255

head." Princess turned and smiled at Grace, then added, "I'll do it personally. Unless, of course, we come to other accommodations after you're dead." she smiled at her brother.

"I thought we were going to have an accident?" Damian asked.

Princess waved him off. "Oh, of course you are. I'm just teasing Green Eyes."

Princess and her entourage walked out of the store, and Grace reached for the emergency transmitter on her ring. Before she could, however, they were all quickly surrounded by another group of men in suits and overcoats.

This second group began to disarm Princess' men. The disarmers, Grace did recognize. They were Damian's.

Mina Reigns quickly approached from the parking lot.

"Damian, take the limo." Mina waved her hand, and a large, white, Mercedes stretch limousine wheeled around the corner. "I'll have someone drive your Escalade home." Mina turned toward a fuming Princess and smiled. "Hello, Cousin, nice to see you here. We'll talk after Damian is gone."

Damian turned, and smiled at Princess. "Well, it's been fun, I'll see you at Mom and Dad's on Thanksgiving." He motioned toward Princess' entourage. "I don't want to see them at Mom and Dad's on Thanksgiving," he whispered to his cousin.

Mina nodded understanding his orders exactly. It was the same strategy that worked so well the last time. It was why Princess had a hell of a time recruiting anyone to work for her; it helped to keep her ambitions in check.

A suit opened the rear limousine door for Damian and Grace. They climbed inside and the door was closed. The black, tinted, power window lowered smoothly, and Damian stuck his face out of the window.

"Mina, you've really come a long way. Good job." Damian winked at Princess. The limousine pulled away smoothly, taking Damian and Grace back to the safety of the cabin.

Mina smiled, turned back toward her men, and nodded. They escorted Princess' condemned soldiers off to a group of waiting black Ford Excursions. Mina, turned, blew Princess a kiss, and walked into the parking lot toward her waiting vehicle.

Chapter Thirty-Four

Princess opened her legs wider and placed her hand on her husband's ass. She pressed down hard, and counter rotated against his pelvis. Marcus raised up and pulled himself out of her. He lifted her ankles to his shoulder, leaned forward, and re-inserted himself. It felt good to her. She let out a continuous barrage of moans and gasps, as her nails dug into his arms.

"Oh, Marcus! Harder, harder!"

Marcus continued to thrust forward violently, and bang away.

"That's it, baby, that's it!" she told him. "Right there."

Marcus continued to bang away in this position until Princess stopped him.

"Hold on," she told him.

Marcus was breathing heavily and sweating profusely. He lifted his hand, and wiped away the beads of sweat on his clean shaven head. Princess gently pushed him away and turned over. She lifted herself onto her knees, and peered over her shoulder at him.

"Well, what are you waiting for?"

Marcus, still very excited, re-entered his wife. Princess gasped but then let out a watery cry of pleasure. She took her hands, placed them on her being, and spread herself apart. Marcus placed his hands on his wife's hips, and continued thrusting.

"Oh baby, oh baby, you know how I love this position."

Princess lowered her head into her silk sheets and bit down on them. Marcus was working overtime tonight. In fact, he hadn't been quite this pleasing in some time. Or maybe she hadn't been quite as easy to please. Patrick had been hung for a white boy, and he had been quite accomplished in giving oral sex. There had been many nights when she'd sworn that his tongue was twelve inches with it's own personal refrigerator. It stayed cold—long and cold.

Marcus began thrusting forward violently. His deep penetration made Princess gasp and grab for the bed sheets.

"Oh, Marcus! Oh, Marcus!"

The last couple of thrusts did it for her. She reached a climax and felt herself releasing a torrid of fluid. Her explosion was followed shortly afterwards by Marcus'. She could feel him throbbing inside of her, filling her up. Thank God for birth control.

She and Marcus did not have any children. They had never talked about children and it was all for the best—at least for the moment. Maybe children would have come at a later time, maybe. But that was a big maybe for Princess. She had little time for labor and even less time for a shitty assed, snotty nosed, wailing baby. But then again, she would have to leave her empire to someone, an heir. The thought intrigued her, a son. Who would take over and be her shield, in her old age? Who? She would have to give serious thought to that issue in the future. *Kids.* Was that why she felt the way she did about her husband? Would having children have changed her feelings? Would looking at them, and seeing herself and her husband, have made her feelings different? She cared about Marcus; she cared deeply for him. That was why she had to do what she had to do tonight. But why didn't she love him? Could she love him? Could she love anyone?

Marcus pulled out of his wife and collapsed on the bed next to her. Princess rose, reached for her see-through lace nightie, and put it on. She walked across the thick maroon carpeting of their master bedroom, to the marble bar, which sat in the corner of the room. Princess walked to the rear of the bar and grabbed the remote that sat on the counter. She pointed it at the marble and glass electric fireplace, and pressed the appropriate button. The fireplace came alive. It filled the room with warmth, and a nice, cozy ambience.

Marcus rolled over and faced her. "Sweetie, could you fix me a gin and Seven-up?"

Princess nodded. She sat the remote down on the counter and placed two glasses on the bar. She opened the refrigerator underneath the bar and removed a half-filled bottle of Chateau Margaux. She filled the two champagne flutes on the bar with the chilled champagne and then replaced the bottle. Princess grabbed the champagne glasses and walked to the king size bed, where she handed her husband a glass.

"Honey, I wanted gin."

"This is better for you, Marcus."

He stared at her stoically. "Princess, I'm a grown man. I know what's good for me and what's not."

Princess exhaled. "Marcus, lets not fight. We need to talk, okay?"

Marcus sat his champagne glass on the nightstand, "I knew this was coming."

"Knew what was coming?"

"This...this talk," Marcus sat up in bed. "Look, P, I know that neither one of us has been exactly faithful to our marriage, but lets try to work things out. Let's not just rush into a divorce."

Princess laughed, and shook her head, "Marcus, we're not getting a divorce," she said softly.

"Oh," Marcus breathed out a sigh of relief. "What is it then?"

"Marcus, I'm at war with my brothers."

"I know, Princess." Marcus placed his arm around his wife and kissed her on the top of her head. "We're going to get them, P. Is that what you're worried about?"

Princess shook her head. "Marcus, I'm at war. And the reason I am at war is because I am trying to take over, me, Marcus, not us. I'm in charge."

Marcus frowned. "I know who's in charge, Princess, you don't have to keep reminding me!" He rose.

"Marcus, it's not that, just sit down and listen!"

Marcus began putting on his underwear, "Dammit, Princess! You're my wife, not my mother! I understand you run your own little organization, but treat me with some goddamned respect!"

"It's not a little organization anymore, Marcus," Princess told him softly. She folded her arms. "I've done a lot of recruiting."

"Oh yeah? How, where, when?"

"Florida, Mississippi, Louisiana, Alabama, New Mexico, Arizona, Oklahoma, all over. My brothers failed to take into account the fact that not everyone in the organizations they defeat would be very happy working for them. People lost brothers, cousins, and friends. I've picked up a lot of soldiers, Marcus. A lot of angry, experienced soldiers."

"That's good!" Marcus finished putting on his pants and walked over to her.

"I know it's good, Marcus, but..."

"But what? We can go after them with a vengeance."

"But, there are still loose details to tie up."

"Like what?"

Princess looked down, and a tear fell from her eye, "Like you."

"Me?"

She nodded.

"What the hell are you talking about?"

Princess turned and pressed the intercom button on the

telephone. "Guys, could you step inside?"

The door to her master bedroom suite swung open, and three hulking, suited men walked inside. Princess turned back to her husband.

"Marcus, I know my brothers. I know how they think. They are going to kill you in order to slow me down. I won't have time for a funeral or to wait until all of the police investigations are done to resume the war. Time is on their side. They would use that time to consolidate, to re-group, to strategize, and get more soldiers into the mix."

Marcus stared at the men standing behind him. He didn't recognize any of them. She had, in fact, done some recruiting. She had placed these strangers inside the residence and removed the ones whom he had become friends with. The bitch had planned it all out. Marcus turned back toward his wife.

"So, why can't I just go and hide in Europe or Asia or even Africa?"

Princess tilted her head to the side, "from Dante? You know better than that. He would find you and kill you." Again she looked away. "Trust me, I've thought of all these things."

"So, you're going to kill me. You don't want them to kill me, so you're going to kill me? Dammit Princess, I'm your husband!" A tear fell from Marcus' eye.

"Marcus, you think I wanted it to come to this?"

"Then don't do it!"

"I don't have a choice!" Princess shook her head. "I don't have time for funerals, for investigations, for your family to fly down and be all over my home, and all in my business!"

"Taking over a drug empire is more important to you, than the man you chose to spend the rest of your life with?"

Princess looked down and nodded, "Yes, it is." She unfolded her arms. "Marcus, I'm going to get this out of the way, have your funeral, and take care of all the other details, and then go to war with my brothers. I know them, they're ruthless. I can't leave anything to chance this time."

"They're ruthless?" Marcus leaned forward. "You're calling them ruthless? You're all sick. Your whole family is sick! You're all demented, pathological psychopaths!"

"I'm going to take care of your mother," Princess told him.

"Don't you go near my mother!" Marcus shouted. "Don't you send her a goddamned dime!"

"Marcus..."

"No! In fact, send my body up there, and let them bury me. Get me the hell out of this place!"

Princess nodded and turned to the guard. "Take him to the clean house. I'm going to shower and dress. I'll be there shortly."

Marcus frowned. "Until death do us part, huh?"

Princess turned cold. "Marcus, our marriage vows have always been a joke. Don't try to take them seriously now."

Marcus turned and stormed out of the bedroom. One of the guards nodded at Princess and then closed the door gently as they left the room.

Alone, Princess sat down on the edge of the bed and wept.

Chapter Thirty-Five

Bob's Barbecue was a small but popular mom-and-pop eatery located on the city's East Side. Luminaries from all over the country dropped by to sample Bob's tender, fall off the bone barbecue, smothered in his sweet, delectable, secret sauce. It was the envy of all other barbecue joints nationwide. It was this very same sauce that allowed the eatery to win award after award for its tasty barbecue. It was this very same sauce that brought Dante back, time after time.

Bob's was a friendly establishment, meaning it was in friendly territory, staffed by friendly people, most of whom the Reigns family had helped in some form or fashion along the way. It also meant that a heavy security detail was not necessary.

Dante entered into the small, smoky establishment and ventured to his left, where he took up his usual seat in the corner. His bodyguard, Greg took a seat in the corner, while another one of his bodyguards, Pete, went to secure the orders for the food. Pat and Melvin, two more members of his personal protective detail, ventured to the right, and took up a seating position across the room so that they could keep an eye on the front entrance. Ron, the fifth and final member

of Dante's detail, stayed outside and watched the vehicles.
Car bombs had a way of finding their way underneath unoccupied vehicles sometimes.

Dante lifted his hand and peered at the diamond and platinum Piaget watch wrapped around his wrist. He was busy thinking about how she was always late when she breezed in.

Angela spied Dante in his usual corner seat and headed for the table.

"Sorry, I'm late," she told him. She offered a friendly smile to Greg, who relocated himself to the table next to theirs.

"Don't worry, I'm used to it," Dante told her with a smile.

Angela plopped down in the chair directly across from Dante. She leaned to the side and sat a large Dooney and Burke handbag on the floor next to her. Pete brought them their food and drinks, placed them on their table, and walked to the far side of the room. He stood directly between Dante and the door.

Dante lifted his hand and motioned toward the white Styrofoam plates. "I hope you don't mind, I took the liberty of ordering for you."

"Thank you," Angela smiled. "I see that you still know what I like."

"Of course, how could I ever forget?"

Angela adjusted herself in her seat. "So, what's the deal, Dante?" She lifted a piece of smoked sausage and bit into it. "And give it to me straight, no bullshit."

"Always, so very ladylike," Dante smiled. "It's your timidity that has always attracted me."

Angela tilted her head and scowled, "Ha, ha, very funny. Look, time is money, and in my case, a lot of money. What's the assignment?"

"Marry me."

"Ha, ha, super funny. You're a regular comedian today." Angela lifted her styrofoam cup and sipped at her lemonade.

265

"Give me the job description and I'll give you my price."

Dante waved his hand and Greg stood. He dug inside of his dark gray jacket pocket and removed a small, black, felt box. He handed the box to Dante.

Dante sat the ring box on the table and then pushed it across the table to Angela.

"Open it," he told her.

"Dante, I don't have time for this." Angela lifted her petite hand and glanced at her wristwatch. "You want me to pose as your wife, that's fine. Just give me the parameters of the mission so I'll know what to wear, what to do, who to be, what voice to use, and everything else. I don't have time to play twenty questions or the guessing game."

"Dammit, Angela, if you'd just be quiet for a minute and listen, you'd understand that I want to marry you!"

"Marry me? You mean, marry me as in a wedding, a real wedding? One with tuxedos, sappy, pink bridesmaid dresses, and little, snot-nosed kids throwing flowers all over my shoes? Is that what you're asking?"

Dante nodded.

Angela Paxton broke out into an uncontrollable stream of laughter. "Get serious. You've got to be shitting me, Dante."

She rose from the table and bent down to grab her purse. Dante grabbed her hand.

"Angela, look, I'm serious. I...I made a mistake."

Angela rose and stared Dante in the eye. "You're goddamned right you made a mistake. Dante, how dare you! How dare you bring me here and propose to me! How dare you propose to me period! You had your chance Dante, remember?"

"Angela, I was a boy then!" Dante rose. "I was a childish, little boy with no idea of commitment. But now, now I'm a man, Angela. And I know what I want. I know what I need. There's nobody for me, Angela, nobody. Just you."

Angela exhaled loudly and shook her head. She sat back down at the table and stared at him.

"Dante, why now? What is all of this about?" Angela frowned at him. "Are you going to jail or something?"

Dante laughed. "No, I'm not going to jail. What this is about is tying up all loose ends. It's about completion. It's about realizing my mistakes and trying to make them right. Angela, you're the only woman for me."

Angela frowned. "And why is that, Dante?"

"Because you won't take any of my shit."

Angela and Dante laughed. Dante nodded his head toward the ring.

"Open it," he told her.

Angela lifted the black, felt box and opened it. Inside sat a flawless, ten-carat round diamond, nestled on a six-prong, platinum base. Angela gasped and her hands rushed to her face, covering her mouth.

"Oh my God!" She looked up at him. "Dante, this is beautiful!"

Dante removed the ring from the box, took her hand into his, and then placed the ring on her finger.

"I should have married you back then, Angela. I'm sorry. I'll never let you go again."

Tears came to Angela's eyes. She stood and walked around the table to where Dante was standing. He wrapped his arms around her and hugged her tightly.

"I love you, Angela. I love you more than anything in this world. I want you," he whispered softly.

She looked up at him and smiled, "Dante, do you really mean that? Can you really say that you feel that way?"

Dante nodded.

Angela held her ring up to the light and examined it, "Oh, my God. This means that I'm going to be related to Princess!"

Dante laughed.

"Dante, I will beat that bitch's ass if she gets out of line at my wedding."

Dante laughed and hugged her again.

Angela pulled away from Dante and looked around the smoke filled establishment. "Uh-um, why in the hell did you bring me here to propose to me? Why couldn't I get proposed to at a fancy French restaurant or something? And what ever happened to the get down on one knee thing? Oh, you're going to pay for this."

"Angela, this is where we first met, remember?" Dante lifted his arms into the air. "This is where it all began. What better place to come full circle…" he asked as he spun around. It was then, he saw them.

Dante shoved Angela to the floor and went for his gun, "Angela, stay down!"

The two suited gentlemen in line with the other patrons turned and opened fire. Pat was struck in the forehead above his right eye, while Melvin took his bullet in the ear. Dante fired his forty-caliber glock and struck the first suit in the chest. The impact from Dante's bullet caused him to fly back into the crowd. The second suit ducked behind a wall.

The guy wiping the tables pulled from his apron a large chrome Smith and Wesson automatic, and put a nine-millimeter round through the back of Pete's head. He turned to fire at Dante, but was caught in the chest by a forty-caliber round from Greg's handgun. Angela crawled to her Hermes handbag and pulled from it her micro Uzi sub machine gun pistol.

From the rear of the restaurant, another suited gentleman stood and fired a Mossberg pump shotgun toward Dante and Greg. A large chunk of the wooden table disintegrated. The suited gentleman stepped from behind the wall and fired at Greg, catching him in the shoulder. Dante fired back, striking the wall just in front of him.

From the area near the rest room, three suits appeared. Angela let her Uzi pistol loose. It burped rapidly, spitting nine-millimeter rounds across the wall and across their chest. They fell instantly.

"They're all over the place!" Greg shouted. "We've got to

get out of here!"

The shotgun came over the counter again, and Greg put a bullet through his forehead. Another suit quickly replaced the one who was firing the shotgun. This suit, however, held in his hand a Mac 10 submachine gun. He opened it up.

Bullets ripped across the wall just behind a ducking Dante and Greg, leaving a straight line of holes across the wall. The room was filled with smoke.

The suit hiding behind the wall stepped out and fired again, striking the table just next to Angela's head. Pieces of wood splintered off and struck her on her right cheek.

"Dammit!" she cried out. "These sonsofbitches are coming from everywhere. They're like roaches!"

The Mac 10 fired again, striking Greg in his shoulder, causing him to drop his gun and cry out. Angela sent a full barrage toward the suit with the sub machine gun. The suit slumped over the counter and his weapon fell from his hand.

The suit hiding behind the wall grabbed an old lady from off of the floor, and put the gun to her head. He started for the door using the old lady as a shield. Dante smiled.

Dante lifted his glock and pointed at the old lady, putting several shots in her. She fell, leaving the suit exposed. Dante smiled and then put a bullet through the suit's eye. He turned and grabbed Angela.

"Let's go!"

Angela pulled his arm. "Not the front door! Your driver's dead! We're going through the side door. My Porsche is parked on the side!"

Angela walked to the side door, and pointed her gun at it. She fired through the door, just in case someone was standing on the other side of it. She then shifted her aim and blew the locks off of the door. They raced to her car.

Greg climbed into the back of the 911, while Dante climbed into the passenger side. A suit stepped from around the rear of the building, and Dante stuck his gun out of the window and put a bullet through his heart. Angela hopped in

269

the driver's seat, revved up her Porsche, and pulled off.
Dante turned toward her, "Welcome to the family."
"Princess?" Angela asked while breathing heavily.
Dante nodded.
"Can I kill her before the wedding or do I have to wait until after the wedding?"
Dante laughed.
Angela hit the highway.

Chapter Thirty-Six

Grace's mouth fell open when Damian's Corniche turned into the driveway, and the home came within full view.

"Oh, my God." She turned toward Damian. "I thought you said that we were going to your parent's farmhouse?"

"This is it," he told her.

"This is what you call a farmhouse?" She shook her head. "No, Damian, a farmhouse is a little, quaint, whitewashed home with a front porch. This thing, this is bigger than the White House!"

Damian laughed.

The burgundy Corniche pulled to a stop just in front of the steps leading up to the massive wrap around porch. Damian exited, walked around the rear of the vehicle, and helped Grace out of the passenger side.

"Damian, look at those columns. This is a plantation!"

Again, Damian laughed. "Jonel, it's just a house, this is just a farm. And those people inside are just my family. Breathe, relax."

Grace gulped down air and again examined the gigantic Doric style columns that surrounded the massive plantation style home. The columns held up not only the raised first floor porch, but also the second floor veranda, which also wrapped around the mansion.

"You grew up here?" she asked him.

"You could say that," he told her. "The house belonged to my grandparents on my mother's side. They left it to my mother. I grew up in a place called The Dominion."

Grace shook her head and turned back toward the Rolls. "I can't do this."

Damian grabbed her, and turned her back around toward the mansion. "Yes, Jonel, you can. They are people, that's all, just people. Now, let's go."

Damian led Grace up the stairs and into the home. He was met first by Consuela, his parent's housekeeper. She hugged him.

"Señor Damian!" She planted a kiss on his cheek. "Hola, como esta?"

"Bien, gracias, y tu?"

She smiled and rubbed her lipstick off his cheek. "I'm fine." She turned toward Grace. "And who do we have here?"

Damian placed his arm around Grace's waist. "This is the love of my life, Jonel McNeal. Jonel, this is Consuela. She practically raised me."

Grace extended her hand. "Pleased to meet you."

Consuela shook Grace's hand.

"Igualmente." She turned to Damian, "Your parents are in the drawing room. Dajon is in the living room, Princess is in the den, and Dante is in the kitchen. As a matter of fact, if your brother has touched my cake, I'm going to beat his ass."

Consuela pinched Damian's cheek. "You boys are not too old for ass whippings."

Grace burst into laughter as Consuela walked off.

"Come on, Jonel. I want you to meet my brother, Dajon."

Damian led Grace across the marble floor of the two-story entry into the hardwood-floored living room. At first glance, Grace had to do a double take. Damian's brother Dajon was a dead ringer for Dante. The file on Dajon was thin. The Bureau had little interest in him, as he had little to do with his brothers and absolutely nothing to do with their

272

business. Dajon was the white sheep of the family.

He hugged his brotherm "It's good to see you, Damian."

Damian patted his brother's back. "Oh, it's great to see you Dajon. How's the wife and my niece and nephew?"

"They're great. They're all upstairs watching television."

"No way!" Damian turned to Grace. "Hey, I'll be right back. I've got to go and see Cheyenne and little Dajon."

Damian turned and walked out of the living room, only to bump into Dante in the hall.

"Hey, D, what's up?" Damian asked.

"Princess hit me at two o'clock this afternoon. I lost five bodyguards. Two dead, three wounded, Pete's dead."

Damian exhaled loudly, and his gaze fell to the floor, "Shit! Pete just had a baby, two weeks old," he shook his head.

"I know," Dante nodded. "I'll make sure that the family's taken care of. Trust fund for the kid, the whole nine."

"Her strategy is clear," Damian told him.

"She figures that if she takes me out first then all of your muscle is gone."

"Where is she now?"

"She's in the den."

"I'm going to run upstairs and see the kids and Mom and Dad."

"I'll see you when you come back downstairs," Dante nodded.

Dajon turned toward Grace. "How long have you known my brother?"

"A few months."

Dajon nodded and turned back toward the mantelpiece. The fire from the fireplace crackled loudly, amplifying the silence during the gaps in their conversation.

"What is it that you do for a living?" Dajon asked.

"I'm a manager at a local bank."

"Where are you from?"

"Well, I've lived a little bit of everywhere. My parents worked for the state department."

"Ahh," Dajon laughed. "A foreign service brat."

Grace smiled. "You could say that."

"Sounds like you come from a pretty good family," Dajon brushed his hand across his medium gray, oxford trousers.

"They were alright," Grace told him.

Dajon turned and walked to where Grace was standing and stopped just in front of her. He stared her directly in the eyes.

"I love my brothers, but they are monsters. They destroy lives, they destroy futures, and they destroy families. They destroy everything they touch. They are dream stealers. Run away from them. Run as fast and as far away from my family as you can."

Grace Moore's mouth fell open.

Dajon turned and walked to a large, highly polished, cherry wood, Steinway baby grand piano, and began to flawlessly perform an elegant, classical composition from Chopin.

"Save yourself, Jonel," he told her without looking up from the piano, "Save your soul."

Dante strode into the kitchen where, to his surprise, his sister Princess stood at the center island. She saw him coming and smiled.

Princess Reigns walked across the polished, stone floors, to the wine refrigerator, and removed a chilled bottle of Moet Chandon. She held the bottle up toward her brother.

Dante nodded, "I prefer apple juice or even a nice, cold glass of orange juice, but Moet will suffice."

Princess opened a nearby drawer and removed a champagne opener. She walked back to the center island where Dante was standing and handed him the bottle and the opener.

"Are we celebrating my funeral or yours?" Dante asked

her.

Princess laughed. She lifted her tiny, well-manicured hands to her head and adjusted her black Chanel hat. She then rubbed her hands against her black Chanel pantsuit to dry them. The condensation from the cool champagne bottle had moistened them.

"We're celebrating Marcus'," she informed him.

"What?"

Princess exhaled and opened the glass door to a nearby cabinet, from which she removed two champagne flutes.

"Killing Marcus now gets everything out of the way. It saves us all a lot of opening moves."

Dante popped the cork off of the champagne bottle. "What are you talking about?" he asked her.

"Killing my husband, it's very logical," Princess placed the two champagne flutes on the island's countertop just in front of Dante. "You made him die in an accident. I'm a grieving widow, too distraught to fight you for control. You hurt me by taking away someone I care about."

Dante poured champagne into the crystal flutes, filling them almost to the top. He sat the bottle down on the counter next to the glasses. "Princess, Damian would never..."

She waved him off.

"Oh baloney. Don't waste your time, Dante, and I don't mean explaining," Princess lifted the crystal flutes and handed one to Dante. "Don't waste family time and resources trying to do something that's already done."

"What?"

"Marcus is dead. I killed him an hour ago." Princess lifted her glass to her lips and sipped daintily.

Dante smiled.

"What, did you think that I would give you the pleasure?" Princess sat her glass down on the counter and walked into the adjoining breakfast area, where she grabbed her small black Chanel purse that was sitting on the breakfast table.

"He couldn't fuck worth a damn anyway."

Dante threw his head back in laughter. "How, may I ask?"

Princess removed a small, gold cigarette case from her purse, and from it, removed a long, slim, white cigarette. She lit it and blew smoke into the air seductively.

"I did it myself. I fucked him one last time and then I blew his brains out. He understood that it was only business."

Princess walked back into the kitchen, lifted her champagne from the countertop, and smiled at her younger brother.

"I explained to him that I wouldn't have time to attend a funeral, make arrangements, and play the grieving widow to his family. In the next few months, I only want to go to two funerals, yours and Damian's."

Dante laughed heartily for several moments and then sipped from his champagne. "It's hard for me not to love you, Princess."

Princess took another drag off her cigarette and blew a long trail of smoke into Dante's face. She knew that he couldn't stand cigarette smoke. "So, has he turned her yet?"

Dante knew that his sister was extremely intelligent and that she knew how to run the family business. She knew what they were up to as soon as they decided to do something. They could all read each other's minds.

"Yes, she's compromised."

"Bravo, an FBI agent in love and in the family. Priceless." Princess lifted her champagne glass to her brother. "I commend you."

Dante lifted his glass into the air. "It was Damian's idea."

"Bullshit."

"Really."

Princess laughed. "Sometimes I think he actually does know what the hell he's doing."

"He does. We've grown extremely wealthy since Damian

took over."

"We've also grown extremely weak. What's all the money in the world if someone can just roll in and take it?"

"What's the use of having a thousand soldiers on the payroll? It just draws unwanted attention."

"Dante, Damian doesn't have the balls to run things like they need to be run!" Princess forcefully stubbed out her cigarette. "We should have no competition anywhere in the south."

Dante exhaled loudly and yawned. "Damian doesn't need to have any balls."

"What?"

"I have them. He's the brains, but I'm the dick."

Princess laughed immensely. She placed her arm around her brother's waist, and drew him closer. She kissed him on his cheek. "Dante, it's hard for me not to love you."

Dante took a long swallow of champagne, and then sat the glass on the counter. "I'll tell you what; I have a deal for you."

Princess lifted an eyebrow. "What's that?"

"We make peace."

Princess frowned. Dante lifted his hands and made a calming motion.

"Just hear me out. You get the army. You get the contacts, the distribution network, plus the food chains to clean your money. You're semi-independent. You have total autonomy as far as decision making, but when we need you, you'll have to protect the family, provide the muscle, and fight its wars. The only thing the family wants is a thirty-percent rake off of the top. Well, Damian will probably want closer to fifty."

Princess' eyes flew wide, and she wrapped her arms around her brother and kissed him. "Oh Dante! Why didn't you tell me this before!"

"Because, it's just something that I've been thinking about. I haven't run it by Damian."

"You think he will approve?"

"He'll have some questions."

"Like?"

"Like what's to keep you from smashing us and taking over everything once we've given you the army and we're defenseless?"

Princess shook her head. "I won't..."

"I know." Dante raised his hands to silence her. "We'll keep a small cadre of soldiers, plus we'll have Adrian, Niccolo, Maceo, Dorian, Prince, and their people, plus myself. We'll be alright."

"But I wouldn't make a move like that anyway." Princess placed both her hands on Dante's. "I just want to protect the family, that's all. Let me make us strong."

Dante nodded slowly. "I think I can get him to go along. Damian doesn't want a war. No one does." Dante looked up and stared into his sister's eyes. "But here's the deal. You're on your own. No heat comes to me and Damian. As far as the business, we're out of that end. If the feds swoop down on you, you're on your own. We won't rescue you. Same thing if you go to war and get smashed."

"Oh Dante, I told you, I've grown past that. It'll be strictly business. No power plays, no futile wars, just business. This is all I ever wanted, just to protect the family, to make it strong."

"Here's the catch. We're pulling out slowly, so here's what we'll do. We'll cease the pullout, and we'll slowly hand over control of operations to you. It'll take time to clean things up and separate the books, but you'll eventually have the whole ship."

"Oh Dante, thank you! Thank you!" Princess extended her arms and wrapped them around her brother. She hugged him tightly. Then a thought hit her. She let go of Dante, leaned back, and stared at him.

"What will *you* do?" she asked him. "I mean, if Damian is whitewashed, where will your services fit in? Have you thought that through?"

"A little, I'll still handle trouble shooting. And I'll be the liaison between your operation and his. But mainly I'm just going to take it easy."

Dante lifted his glass of champagne from the counter and sipped.

"Works for me. You and I together again, it'll be just like old times." Princess placed her hand on top of his. "Dante, forget Texas. You and I together, we can take over the entire country."

"I was thinking more along the lines of settling down, raising a family. Spending time with Cheyenne and Little Dajon today has really reminded me of what I'm missing."

Dante shook his head, and stared off into space. "Maybe I'll buy a boat, sail, travel, who knows."

Princess tilted her head to the side "Dante, you're only twenty-six years old."

"Yeah, well, I feel like I'm a hundred and six," Dante exhaled. "Sometimes I feel tired."

"Of what?"

"Of it all."

Princess kissed two of her fingers and then touched them gently against Dante's cheek. "Who's the lucky lady?" she asked softly.

"Angela."

"Angela!" Princess recoiled. "That evil, sadistic, satanic, conniving, prissy little tramp?"

"That's the one."

"A woman after my own heart. You couldn't have done better if I'd picked one for you," Princess smiled. "You two will be great together. Congratulations."

"Thanks, hey Princey…"

Princess Reigns stared at her brother in shock. He hadn't called her that name in a long time. The fact that he did so now stirred something deep inside of her. Something that she hadn't felt in a long time. Something that she thought she could no longer feel.

"What, D?" she asked softly.

"Sorry about Marcus."

Princess cleared away the lump forming inside her throat and waved her brother's apology off. "It's nothing, I was tired of him."

"You loved him?"

Princess smiled sadly. "Dante, can either of us really feel that emotion...anymore?"

"Do you think it's too late to try?"

Princess knew what Dante was asking.

"I cared about Marcus. He was my husband." Princess leaned forward and kissed Dante on his cheek. She took her thumb and wiped her lipstick off of his face. "Have children with Angela, lots of them. The smell of baby powder takes it all away. The soft touch of a new life washes it away. Maybe, just maybe..."

Princess sat her glass down on the counter, turned, and strutted out of the kitchen. Her Manolo Blahnik heels clicked as she crossed the marble foyer and headed into the living room. Chanel No. 5 wafted in the air long after she was gone.

Dante sat his glass down next to his sister's, turned his palms up to the ceiling, and examined them.

Chapter Thirty-Seven

Damian sipped slowly from his glass of Penfolds Grange as he peered over the second floor balcony of his estate toward the blue-green lake at the edge of his backyard. The lake was beautiful, peaceful, and serene. The setting sun's red-orange glow reflected brilliantly off the tranquil waters, creating a breathtaking portrait. Damian loved the view.

"Did you make her the offer?" Damian asked.

"I did," Dante answered. He sipped at his glass of tangy lemonade and stared at the family of ducks making their way across the red-orange reflection.

"Did she buy it?"

"She did."

"So, I guess that gives us the time we need to recruit." Damian shifted his gaze from the lake to his brother, who was standing next to him. "I want this to be the last war, Dante."

Dante sipped from his glass and nodded. He understood the meaning of Damian's order. Still, he had other plans.

"It will be," Dante told his brother.

"When are you going to make the accident?"

"I don't think that will be necessary," Dante said solemnly.

"I'm listening."

"We make the offer real."

"Yeah right. We give her control of a drug empire and an army? There will be bodies from LA to New York."

"Not necessarily."

Damian exhaled and sat his wine down on the concrete balustrade. He stood up straight and turned toward his brother. "Explain."

Dante sipped and kept his gaze on the lake. "She won't go to war. She will expand, but without a major war. She'll knock off the small guys, gobble up their territories, and consolidate. She'll grow all throughout the country, but that's not a bad thing." Dante shifted his gaze from the lake toward his brother, "Everyone will fear her. We'll use that fear to our advantage. We'll rake in fifty percent off of the top. We're free of the business, and in less time that it would take us to dump it. We'll be free of the headaches, the day-to-day responsibilities, and the risk, but at the same time we keep the strength."

"At what cost?"

"The food chain, I told her we'd give her eighty percent of the restaurants and keep twenty percent of them. We can re-build the food chain from the remaining twenty percent. It's beautiful."

"I don't know about this."

"Look, you told me to handle it. I'm handling it. There will be no war; we are disassociated with the business, but we keep our strength through Princess. Plus, we get fifty-percent of the profits even after she's expanded throughout the country." Dante sipped. "The figures are incredible."

Damian lifted his glass from the banister and peered out over the lake. He sighed loudly. "Approved. Put it into effect immediately. I want to see the numbers on my desk today!"

"Done."

Grace walked across the stained wood porch and seated herself on the comfortable, white furniture. She noticed a pitcher of lemonade sitting on the glass patio table and poured herself a drink.

Elizabeth Holmes stood and removed the thick, gardening gloves she was wearing on her hands. She rubbed her sweaty hands against her large, yellow and white checkered sundress to dry them and then pushed her large straw hat further back on her head. She smiled at Grace.

"How's the most famous agent in the Bureau?" Elizabeth asked.

Grace waved her off. "Oh please, Liz, don't start that."

"Well, you may as well get used to it. You're a legend now," Elizabeth told her as she approached. "The way you stood up to Tom and Nathan, they'll be talking about you for years."

Elizabeth Holmes chuckled as she seated herself across from Grace. She reached onto the small glass tray, grabbed the glass pitcher, and poured herself a tall glass of lemonade.

Grace cupped her hand and placed it over her forehead. "Oh Liz, I want to forget that meeting, I want to forget this whole damn assignment."

"Well, pull out, Grace. You can always pull yourself out if things are getting to be too much for you."

Grace raked her hand through her hair, sending it back over her shoulder.

"No," she shook her head. "It's not getting too rough. It's just getting...I don't know."

"What's the matter, Grace?"

Grace Moore shook her head, lifted her glass of lemonade to her lips, and gulped.

Elizabeth reached across the glass patio table and grabbed Grace's other hand and held it.

"What's the matter?" she asked again. "Grace, I'm on your side. I always have been, and I always will be."

"Liz, I can't find anything. I've been to warehouse after warehouse. I've been all over his planes, his yachts, his

283

homes, his cabins, his ranches, everywhere. I've done everything, tried everything. He's...he's..."

Elizabeth released Grace's hand and leaned back in her seat. Her lips contorted, and she shook her head.

"You don't believe me?" Grace asked her.

"Grace, we've had this conversation before."

"Seven agents can't be wrong!"

"Six of them are dead!" Elizabeth stood. "Dead, Grace, they're dead."

"Dante..."

"Won't do shit without Damian's approval!" Elizabeth interrupted. She shook her head and stared at Grace. "Are you still sleeping with Damian?"

"Liz, what kind of question is that?"

"It's a valid question. Your judgment, Grace, it goes directly to your judgment. Are you?"

Grace turned away from Elizabeth and stared into the garden. It was a question she wanted no part of.

"Your garden is lovely," Grace told her. "How do you manage to keep it growing this time of year?"

"You can get anything to do what you want all you have to do is give it lots of attention, lots of tender love and care."

Grace turned her head quickly back toward Elizabeth. She didn't know if Elizabeth was referring to the garden to her or to both. She felt exposed, accused, and helpless.

"Liz, have you ever been married?"

"Grace, you know that I was married. My husband was a very distinguished politician. Why do you ask?"

Grace looked away. Her eyes focused in on the bricks forming the walkway into the garden.

"I've never been," Grace answered. "Have you ever wanted to be married?"

"You mean remarried?" Elizabeth sat down at the table again.

Grace shook her head. "No, I mean, did you want to be married?"

"Yes, I suppose. When I was growing up, marriage was something a young lady looked forward to." Liz sipped at her lemonade. "I suppose things are different now."

"Not really." Grace lifted her hand and ran her fingers through her hair. "I want to get married."

"Wonderful! Get married; have children; raise a family. The good thing about today is that a woman can have it all." Elizabeth reached across the table and placed her hand on top of Grace's. "When this assignment's over, Washington will give you your choice of assignments."

Grace nodded. She continued to stare into the garden.

Elizabeth sipped from her glass and gave Grace a scandalous smile. "So, who's the lucky guy?"

Grace turned and looked Elizabeth in the eye. "Damian asked me to marry him."

"And what did you say?"

"I said yes."

Elizabeth released Grace's hand. She lifted her finger to her chin and shifted her gaze to the garden.

"I don't know the legal ramifications, you know, as far as your being able to testify. I'll have to ask the Assistant United States Attorney about that. But, Grace, you have to stop sleeping with him. If it comes out, we'll deny it. But his accusations will have credibility if the judge finds out that you acted as his fiancée. All of the evidence will be tainted, all of our work will have been for nothing."

"Liz, I'm going to marry him."

"Grace, I know the evidence will be inadmissible if you go through with a bogus wedding with him."

"Liz, will you pull your head out of your ass. I'm not talking about a bogus wedding!"

Elizabeth Holmes recoiled. She now understood what her fellow agent was saying. She now understood Grace's previous line of questioning.

"Grace, have you lost your mind! You can't marry Damian Reigns!"

"Why can't I?"

"Because, you're an FBI agent! For Christ sakes, Grace, snap out of it! He thinks you are Jonel McNeal, and if he ever finds out otherwise, he will kill you! And that's just for starters. Number two he's the head of a notoriously violent, cop-killing, criminal enterprise!"

"We haven't been able to prove that, and I don't think we ever will be. And do you know why, because it's bullshit! We're all down here because Nathan's precious little BAP got her feelings hurt!"

"Grace, you're in too deep. You're too close. You can't see the forest for the trees." Elizabeth placed her hand over her forehead and shook her head from side to side. "I should have seen this coming. I should have pulled you out a long time ago. This operation is over!"

"I know it is." Grace stood and reached for her purse.

"Grace, wait." Elizabeth stood. "Where are you going?"

"Home, to my fiancé."

"Wrong, you're going home to Jonel McNeal's fiancé. What are you going to do, live the rest of your life as someone else?"

"If I have to."

"He's a killer, Grace. And he's going to Terra Haute, where he's going to die for killing those agents."

Grace Moore walked around the table until she came face to face with Elizabeth. They stood inches apart. She leaned forward and whispered into Elizabeth's face.

"You stay away from my husband. If you or Nathan or anyone else, comes near him..."

"You're going to do what?" Elizabeth smiled. "You're going to kill federal agents like he does?"

"Stay away from him!" Grace told her through clenched teeth.

"Nathan is going to nail your ass to the wall for this one. You'll be investigating missing sled dogs in Juneau, Alaska."

"Nathan can investigate missing sled dogs in Alaska,

because I'm through being his avenging angel. He can find someone else to help him avenge his sweet little princess' broken heart."

Grace turned and headed for the door.

"Grace! Grace!" Elizabeth called to her. "Grace, you don't know what you're doing!"

"Yes I do. You call Nathan, and you tell that son of a bitch that I quit!"

Chapter Thirty-Eight

Damian wrapped his arm around Grace and pulled her close.

"What's up, Jo?" he asked her. "You haven't been the same since you came back from visiting your aunt. Did you two get into it or something?"

"Something like that."

"She doesn't approve of your getting married?"

"Not exactly."

Damian leaned over and kissed her. "Don't worry, boo, after the wedding, she'll forget about all her reservations. Speaking of reservations, we were able to book San Fernando Cathedral."

"Wow, how did you manage that?"

"Baseball games!" Damian announced with a loud burst of laughter. "Sponsor enough little league baseball games and the diocese loves you. The road to sainthood, lies in the church's little league."

Grace laughed. She plopped her bare feet up onto Damian's massive, green, leather sectional and turned her attention back toward the one hundred and twenty inch large screen television.

Damian leaned over and bit her on top of her foot.

"Ouch!" Grace grabbed her foot and sat up. "Boy, are you crazy?"

"Jonel, forget about the television. I'm trying to talk to you."

"I'm sorry, I'm a little distracted," Grace extended her legs, placing them on Damian's lap. "Neimans called, my dress is ready."

"That's good! What's Kathy talking about?"

"I haven't spoken to her since yesterday. Damian, she sure is expensive for a wedding planner."

"She's the best. And for our wedding, I want the best of everything."

"You're going to give me the whole fairy tale, aren't you?" Grace lifted her hand to Damian's face and caressed his cheek gently. "I'm getting a story book wedding, a castle, and a handsome prince."

"A super handsome prince!" Damian told her.

"A super handsome prince," Grace agreed.

"A super duper, triple-whipple, handsome prince!"

"Well..."

"What? You're hesitating?" Damian lunged at Grace's stomach and began tickling her. "Say it! Super duper, tripple-whipple, handsome prince!"

"Stop it! Stop it!" Grace attempted to fight off his hands while laughing uncontrollably.

They never heard them walk in.

Grace looked up from their playful wrestling match and saw herself surrounded. She gasped.

Damian saw the expression on Grace's face. He thought it was his sister and her people. It was worse.

"Nathan!" Damian stood. "How dare you come into my home! How dare you! You've gone too far now, way too far! Do you understand me?"

Nathan Hess and the other twelve suits in the room stood around the sectional, forming a loose circle. Nathan's penetrating scowl never left Grace's face.

Damian saw who Nathan was focusing in on. "Leave her out of this, Nathan."

Grace lowered her head to her hands and sat at the edge of the couch with her face covered.

"I can't leave her out of it. She's the reason we're here."

"Nathan, she has nothing to do with any of this." Damian kicked at the leg of his stone and glass coffee table. "God dammit, Nathan, do you have a warrant?"

Nathan snapped his fingers without taking his eyes off of Grace Moore. Another agent produced a warrant, and handed it to Damian. Damian snatched the document and began to read it.

"This is ridiculous, it makes no sense," Damian told them. "This is a Federal Court Order to Enter and Rescue or Retrieve a Federal Bureau of Investigation Agent by the name of... Grace Moore..." Damian's voice trailed off as he turned toward Grace.

"You want to tell him, or should I?"

"Jonel, what is he talking..."

"Her name is Grace Moore dammit!" Nathan yelled, interrupting Damian. "Federal Agent Grace Moore!"

Grace's body trembled. She kept her head down and her face hidden. She felt naked, uncovered, exposed. She felt cold. Grace wished that she could be anywhere but there, at that moment.

Damian grabbed his stomach and sat down.

"You're an FBI agent?" he asked her. It was a whisper.

They could hear Grace crying and sniffling although her face remained in her hands.

"She *was* an FBI agent," Nathan corrected. "She quit. She says that she's going to marry you. Apparently, she's so convinced of your innocence that she's willing to give up her job and risk going to prison."

"Jonel... say something," Damian told her.

Grace Moore began crying heavily.

Damian looked up at Nathan. "You...you sent her after me..." He turned back toward Grace. "You slept with me. My God, you slept with me. Say something, dammit!"

Grace looked up. Her eyes were a deep red and her face was wet from her tears.

"I...I'm sorry."

"You're sorry? I took you to my family's home. You met my parents. You said that you loved me," Damian whispered. "I...you...you made me fall in love with you."

Damian turned toward Nathan. "Who are you people? What kind of FBI is this? What kind of sick people are you?"

Nathan Hess lifted his hands to calm Damian down. "This wasn't exactly planned. This was not exactly a pristine operation, and I take full responsibility for that. In fact, that's why we are here."

Thomas Peoples stepped from behind Nathan. "Mr. Reigns, my name is Assistant Director Thomas Peoples. Here to my right is United States Attorney Steven Bartlett, Assistant General Warren Williams, and Special Agent Elizabeth Holmes. To my left are Special Agents Vincent Gordon and Jonathon Price, Inspectors General Tom Banks, and Hiram Ward, and of course, you already know Special Agent in Charge, Nathaniel Hess. Mr. Reigns, we are here to bring an end to this mess."

Damian looked at the Untied States Attorney, "The Department of Justice is sending FBI agents to sleep with people?"

The agents cringed. Steve Bartlett looked at his boss; the Deputy Attorney General pointed.

"Mr. Reigns, that gentleman, Inspector General Tom Banks, is from the Office of the Inspector General. He is here today because the United States of America does not support, condone, and or initiate the type of activities that took place during this operation. I have spoken personally with the Attorney General of the United States. He is gravely concerned. He found the situation deplorable, inexcusable, and reprehensible. On behalf of the United States of America, we extend to you our sincerest regret at the actions and tactics employed by the Federal Bureau of

291

Investigations."

Nathan Hess maneuvered to the front. "Now, where are our fucking agents?"

"Nathan!" Thomas Peoples shouted at the top of his voice. "That is enough! We've heard enough from you."

Steve Bartlett cleared his throat. "Uh, Mr. Reigns, I've interviewed several dozen people, prominent people within the community, people whose veracity and credibility are beyond reproach, including Agent Hess' daughter, Stacia. I've come to the conclusion that the United States Government has wasted a tremendous amount of time and resources targeting you. All federal operations against you are at this time terminated. This does not mean that in the future, with a significant level of probable cause, you will not be re-targeted for investigation."

"That's all you Washington Bureaucrats want to do, cover your asses from bad press and expensive law suits!" Nathan shouted. "Well, you know what, I want my fucking agents! They aren't running for political office or trying to get appointed to the federal bench! They just want to be respected for doing their jobs, and a decent burial by their families!"

"That is enough!" Tom Peoples shouted. "Nathan, you are excused. Leave the room."

Nathan turned and stormed out of Damian's family room.

"That's it?" Damian asked. "You people are incredible. We sent an agent at you, you fell in love, don't sue us?"

Damian turned toward Grace. "I gave you my heart. I loved you. I loved everything about you. I used to wake up in the morning, lie in bed, and watch you sleep. There were times when I wanted to drop to my knees and thank God for you. I felt like you were the final piece that filled the void in my life, the emptiness in my heart. How could you?" he questioned.

Grace began crying heavily again. "Damian, I'm sorry.

I'm so sorry. I never meant to hurt you."

"You never meant to hurt me? You came here to hurt me. You came into my life to destroy me," he nodded slightly. "You could have done your job. But did you have to be so good at it? Did you have to make me love you?"

"I loved you too! You're not the only one who's hurting, Damian! I quit my job for you! I love you!"

"How?"

"Everything I felt was real! Everything we shared was real!" Grace reached forward and her hands gently caressed Damian's face. "I love you. You...you made my life complete. You chased away my loneliness, my emptiness. You were my knight, my savior, my beautiful, black prince."

"And the lies?" Damian asked. "What about the lies?"

"They were few," Grace answered. "My name, my job, but not my feelings, not my heart."

Damian placed his hands on hers and lowered them to his lips, where he began kissing them. "Trust...what other secrets are going to pop up?"

Tears streamed from Grace Moore's face. She shook her head. "There are no more."

Grace turned her head away from him and closed her eyes. "People break their marriage vows, but in time, they learn to trust one another again. If the love is real, then it will be strong enough to get a person through anything."

Damian released Grace's hand and lifted his hand to her face. He wiped away her tears.

"Is our love true, Grace?" he asked her. "Was your love for me real? Is this another FBI ploy?"

Grace shook her head, "No, Damian. This is no ploy. And my love for you was very real. It is real."

"What do you want from me, Grace?"

"I want you to love me. I want you to let me love you...forever."

Damian stood, put his massive hands inside of his English-cut trousers, and walked to the massive, floor-to-ceiling, celestial window. He stared out at the lake.

"Grace."

"Yes?"

"Where are we going to put the symphony? Near the gazebo by the lake or under a tent near the cabana?"

Steve Bartlett clapped his hands. "Looks like we're going to have a wedding, folks!"

Damian turned and smiled at them. "Of course, and you're all invited."

Grace covered her face and broke down into tears and laughter.

Chapter Thirty-Nine

"**A**nd I looked into her eyes and I said, 'trust... what other secrets are going to pop up?'" Damian laughed.

Dante joined in the laughter, "And the winner for the best male actor in a police drama is...Damian Reigns, for his role as a heartbroken, love struck fiancé!"

Dante began clapping and roaring to simulate a large crowd. Damian placed his hand on his stomach and began bowing.

"Thank you, thank you!" he patted the air with his hands, as if motioning to silence a large crowd. "I want to accept this award on behalf of all the little people who made this possible. Stacia Hess, and her idiot father, Nathan Hess, U.S. Attorney Steve Bartlett, Assistant FBI Director Tom Peoples, Inspector Tom Banks, Deputy Attorney General Warren Williams, and all the others."

Dante lifted his glass of apple cider to his lips and sipped. "Do you think Nathan will ever figure out that Stacia is on our payroll?"

Damian smiled. "Not in a million years. Dante, you are beyond brilliant. Your clairvoyance is uncanny," Damian lifted his glass.

"I knew that she would come in handy one day." Dante lifted his glass and touched it against his brother's, "To Stacia Hess, and her FBI husband and father."

"To Stacia Hess," Damian drank.

"Hey guys," Grace said to them as she walked through the door. "What are you two celebrating?"

"Dante was just giving me a congratulations toast."

Grace put her arms around Damian and kissed him. "Oh really?" She turned to Dante. "I thought you'd be upset with me."

"Dante, upset?" Damian wrapped his arms around Grace and kissed her. "Dante doesn't know what upset is. In fact, he's invited us to spend the night here at his penthouse."

"Oh really? That's nice," Grace turned and walked to the wall of glass, where she peered out over the city. "The view is lovely here."

"Good, I'm glad that you like it. You can take in the view, relax in Dante's jacuzzi, go downstairs and enjoy the spa. They have a magical Massage therapist."

"Oh really?" Grace smiled. "What's her name?"

"Ingrid," Dante answered, "But, they also have Miguel."

"Hmm, Miguel. Sounds like he has nice, strong, Spanish hands." she winked at Dante.

"I have to go to the office," Damian told her. "I'll be back late. Oh, and Grace..."

"What, Hon?"

"Don't make me whip Miguel."

Grace let out a seductive laugh.

Damian grabbed his briefcase and left the apartment.

Dante awoke to find his bladder full and his throat dry. He yawned, stretched, threw back his beige and gray silk covers, and sat up in his bed. He rubbed his face, wiped his eyes, and tried to focus in on his alarm clock. It was five A.M.

Dante shook his head and reached for his water glass, only to find it empty.

"Fuck!"

He hated nights like these. Dante rose from his king size pillow topped bed and stumbled into his massive marble and glass bathroom. He went straight for his commode.

When Dante finished relieving himself, he stumbled back into his bedroom, grabbed his water glass, and headed for the kitchen. That was when he heard the whispering. His first thought was to dash back into the bedroom, grab his ten-millimeter handgun from underneath his pillow, and empty a clip into the intruder or intruders. His second thought was to kill his bodyguards who were supposed to be in the hallway if they were still alive. Then he remembered, he had overnight guests. Only one of them would have any reason to whisper. However, only one of them would not want to be heard. He turned and went back for his glock.

"Yes," Grace whispered into her tiny cell phone. Her hand partially covered her mouth as she spoke into the receiver. "He's here, he's in the bedroom, sleeping."

Grace closed the massive door to the Sub Zero refrigerator only to find Dante standing on the other side of it. His glock was pointed at her head.

She whimpered.

Dante held out his hand. "Give me the phone, bitch," he told her through clenched teeth.

Shaking, she handed it to him.

Dante lifted the telephone to his ear.

"Hello?"

"Yes, Grace?" The voice on the other end of the connection asked. It was the voice of an elderly woman.

"Who is this?" he asked Grace after he lowered the phone.

"My grandmother!" Grace told him angrily. She broke down into tears.

Dante lowered his weapon and handed her the telephone. Grace snatched it.

"Nana, I'll call you back tomorrow," Grace told her grandmother. "Yeah, everything's okay. I'll call you tomorrow. Love you."

"What's that about?" Dante asked.

"It was my grandmother!" Grace told him again. "I was telling her about the wedding!"

"At five in the morning? Why were you whispering?" Dante nodded his head toward the refrigerator.

"Because it's six in New York, where my grandmother lives. I'm whispering because I didn't want to wake Damian up! And I'm in your damn refrigerator because I'm hungry, dammit!" Grace sniffled, and wiped the tears off of her face. "I'm hungry," she repeated softly.

Grace turned and walked to the center island, where she found herself on a stool. She raked her hand through her hair and then wiped her face again. She looked up at an expressionless Dante.

"I know that we all know what I do for a living, but I'm not here investigating your brother. I'm his fiancée. I love him."

Dante's face remained expressionless, blank. The red light from the microwave oven reflected off Dante's burgundy silk pajamas, making them appear as though they were glowing. The light reflected off of his pecan brown skin, giving it a reddish tint. His redness, surrounded by the darkness of the kitchen made him look evil.

Grace remembered the briefing in Washington. Dante is Satan, Satan is Dante. The fact that she was alone with him in a dark kitchen, and he was holding a handgun, scared her even more. She shivered.

"Dante, it's over. The investigation is over. Your brother is clean, he's clear, he's innocent. I'm here as his fiancée." Grace's eyes fell to the pistols he held in his hand. "Why did you point the gun at me?"

Dante stepped forward until he was standing only inches away from Grace. He leaned forward slightly so that his mouth could be near her ear.

"Let me explain something to you, little Miss FBI Agent," he whispered, "I understand that your little investigation is over. And it's good that it is, because you were just wasting

298

your time. If, I repeat, if I was doing anything..."

Dante's hand grabbed Grace's pajamas at the crotch and he yanked at them, "No FBI cunt would ever be able to catch me."

Grace gasped. She knocked Dante's hand away and stumbled backward off of the stool.

His laugh was hollow, evil, and soulless.

"If I ever think that you are trying to hurt my brother or my family, you'll be on a milk carton," Dante lifted his glock into the air and shook it. "Understand me?"

Grace nodded.

"I will kill you, Grace. No matter where the FBI sends you. No matter what alias you use. No matter how many surgeons alter that pretty little face of yours or how many agents they have watching you. If it takes me ten years, fifteen years, or thirty years, I will find you and kill you."

Dante opened the refrigerator door, pulled out a pitcher of water, and drank from it. When finished, he replaced the pitcher, closed the door, and belched. He then turned and headed down the dark hallway toward his bedroom.

"Oh yeah," he called back to her. "Welcome to the family."

Grace could hear his laughter fading as he walked away. She seated herself on the stool again, folded her arms, and stared into the darkness shivering.

Chapter Forty

Grace pulled her legs close to her and rested her chin on her knees. Her eyes were red and irritated, her hair disheveled, and her skin ashy.

After arriving back at Damian's lakefront estate earlier that morning, she had done little other than brush her teeth and shower. Her clothes were a wrinkled, baggy mess, her face was unmade, and her hair uncombed. She was too tired to do anything about her appearance. She was too tired to even care about her appearance. She had slept very little at Dante's.

Grace wanted to go to sleep, and although her body was tired, she couldn't. Instead she found herself in front of the television, watching the twelve o'clock news.

Damian strolled into the room with a tiny cell phone glued to his ear. He walked to his sectional where Grace was sitting, and kissed her on the cheek.

"Hey babe," he greeted her. He quickly turned away and began talking into the cell phone again.

Grace lifted her hand to her hair and ran her fingers through it. She hadn't told Damian about her late night conversation with Dante. She had decided against it. There was nothing he could or would do about it anyway. It happened. She had to admit to herself that her actions had not exactly endeared her to their trust. Dante would eventually learn to trust her, she told herself. She would prove herself worthy of his trust. She would be a great sister-in-law to him, a great wife to his brother, and a great mother to his nieces and nephews. That thought cheered Grace up. She lowered her legs to the floor, leaned back, and placed her hands on her stomach.

"Yeah, I have the television on right now," Damian said to the party at the other end of his telephone conversation. He tapped Grace on her shoulder, "Sweetie, could you turn the television up?"

Grace lifted the remote control from the coffee table and pressed the up arrow on the volume control. The news anchor's voice came alive.

"We'll have more on that story later, Walt." The news anchorman gathered his papers, turned away from his co-anchor, and stared directly into the camera. "New housing starts have been driving the economy as a result of ultra-low interest rates. Could this be the case of too much of a good thing? For the answer we'll take you to our top field correspondent, Andrea Hughes. Andrea."

Onto the television screen popped a large, well dressed, African American woman in her mid thirties. She held a large microphone up to her mouth and was standing in front of a large factory.

"Thank you Dick, I'm Andrea Hughes for Channel 12 News, and we are standing in front of the Portland Cement Company where I have with me Vice President of Operations for the Portland Cement Company, Mr. Hiram Beasley." She turned toward an older, graying, white male with a button down dress shirt, gold rimmed glasses, and a brand new, baby-blue colored hard hat on top of his head. Andrea stuck her microphone near his mouth. "Mr. Beasley, how severe is this year's concrete shortage?"

Mr. Beasley cleared his throat and leaned slightly forward as he spoke into the microphone. "Well, there is definitely going to be a shortage. We've ramped up production, but mild weather and low interest rates have greatly increased the number of new housing starts. Also, the Federal Highway Construction Bill is providing funds to the state for highway construction and improvement, and the sheer number of projects out there are contributing to the shortage."

"Will some projects have to be delayed?" Andrea asked him.

"I think that there will be a slow down in new housing starts, but I don't foresee any substantial delays in major construction projects."

"Can you put a time on the delay? Say...a home that usually takes four weeks to build, how long will it now take?"

"Well, I really don't want to put a number on it. It certainly will vary from region to region."

Andrea smiled at him, "One last question, Mr. Beasley. Is this the worst shortage ever?"

"Well, worst is a relative term. We've had shortages before and we've always managed to get through them," Mr. Beasley smiled for the camera.

"Is this the worst?" Andrea asked him again.

"I would have to say that this shortfall will be a lot more substantial than the others."

"Thank you, Mr. Beasley." Andrea turned back toward the camera. "That's all we have from here. We'll keep you up-to-date on the cement shortage and other related news. I'm Andrea Hughes for Chanel 12 News. Back to you, Dick."

"Relative my ass!" Damian shouted into the telephone.

Grace jumped. She had never heard Damian lose his temper like that before. She listened in to his side of the telephone conversation.

"Look, Kevin, I need cement. I need a hundred tons of it. I need thousands of tons of it. I use more metric tons of cement per year than most small countries. What you're telling me is that I'm going to lose in excess of a billion dollars in revenue because I'll be unable to take on new contracts and because of delay-induced cost overruns on the contracts we are already under obligations to fulfill. That, my friend, is unacceptable."

Grace sat up on the couch. Tons of cement? Damian had shown her a warehouse filled to the brim with cement. She could still picture the light golden-yellow bags with the black lettering. "Hecho en Mexico," they read "Made in Mexico." The Mexican Cement Company, MCC.

"Look, I don't give a shit what the Portland Cement Company says, you tell them that I want priority. If I don't get priority, I'll take my hundreds of millions of dollars and fat ten-year supplier contracts elsewhere! I'm quite sure Acme Cement would love another chance at the bid!" Damian shouted. He paused and listened.

"I know Acme is facing the same problem, but I'm sure they would give me first dibs. I have projects to finish, dammit! I'll tell you what, since you're so sympathetic and understanding of their problems, understand this one, you find me some damn cement or you find yourself another god damned job!"

Damian flipped the telephone closed and dropped it on top of the stone and glass sofa table. He turned and stormed out of the room.

Grace waited until she heard the front door slam and then lifted the telephone. She stared at the numbers on the keypad for several moments before finding the strength and resignation to begin dialing.

"Bureau," a stern female voice told her.

Grace rose, walked to the window, and stared out at the lake.

"Bureau," the voice repeated forcefully.

Grace cleared her throat. "Yes, this is 00021878-01, please put me through to Information and Research."

"Please hold."

"I & R," a male voice told her seconds later.

"Yeah, Tommy, this is Grace. How are you?"

"I'm fine, sweetie, how are you?" Agent Tommy Carls asked her in a light, lisping, soft voice. "Girl, you're the talk of the Bureau. What is going on in Texas?"

"I'll explain later, Tommy, but right now I need a favor."

"Uh, you women. I need this, I need that. You think just because you have titties the world is yours. Golly, I wish I had those thingies."

Grace laughed. Tommy was saving money for a sex change; this was a constant staple of Bureau jokes. "Look, Tom, I need you to check on a Mexican company. It's called MCC, or the Mexican Cement Company. I need you to dig deep and I need for you to dig fast."

"And what, may I ask, am I looking for?"

"I don't know, Tommy, I don't know," Grace told him. "I need for you to check something else for me also."

"And what is that?" Tommy asked.

"Can a dog sniff through cement?"

"Well, I wouldn't think so, unless he's Wonder Dog or Scoobie Doo or Hong Kong Phooey or somebody. But either way, Ms. Tommy here is information, not forensics. You need to talk to Willie, honey child."

"Can you put me through?"

"Am I invited to the wedding?"

"Of course you are." Grace laughed. "I wouldn't have a wedding without you."

"Oh, Grace, what a lovely thing to say," Tommy told her. "Can I be a bridesmaid?"

Grace laughed hysterically. "I don't think so."

"Oh, well, never a bridesmaid, and always a bride. I'll just have to put my pink dress back in of the closet."

"Tommy..."

"What?"

"You need to put more than that dress back in the closet."

"Oh no you didn't! You little hussy!"

Grace laughed. She felt good again. "Tommy, I miss you."

"I miss you too. Ms. Tommy will dig up everything she can find on that company. I gotta go! Hold on, I'll connect you to forensics."

"Lab!" a masculine voice answered.

"Willie, this is Grace."

"Oh, hi, Grace. Are you okay?"

"Sure, I'm fine," she told him. "Hey Willie, I got a question."

"Shoot."

"Can a drug dog sniff through a double wrapped bag of cement and smell cocaine?"

"We're talking powdered cement, right?"

"Of course."

"Well, let's see," Willie sighed. "If the bag is double or triple wrapped, and the cocaine is double or triple wrapped and is in the middle of the bag surrounded by powdered cement, it is quite possible a narcotics canine could miss it. I'll have to break down the chemical compounds of cement and see what it consists of at an elemental level, and then see if any of those elements or combination of those elements has any effect on a canine's olfactory senses. Hell, I'll just grab a dog, some coke, some plastic, and a couple of bags of cement. You wanna test?"

"Yeah Willie, do a test. Send the results to the San Antonio field office. My eyes only."

"Gotcha."

"How's Bertha and the kids?"

"They're great. Little Will is getting big. You know he's the pitcher for his little league team now."

"No kidding! Wow, a chip off the old block, huh?"

"Yeah, I guess you could say that. I had quite an arm back in high school."

"I remember, you've only told everyone a thousand times."

Grace and Willie shared a laugh.

"How soon do you need the test?" Willie asked her.

"Yesterday."

"Done."

"See ya."

"Bye."

Grace disconnected the call and placed the telephone back on top of the sofa table. Her mind played back the previous conversations with Damian, the ones concerning his construction projects in particular. She distinctly remembered him telling her that the cement in the warehouse came from Mexico. She very clearly remembered the markings on the bags. Yet she distinctly remembered him arguing with an employee just moments ago about doing business with a domestic cement company.

Maybe it was nothing, she told herself. Maybe he used so much cement that he augments what he gets from Mexico with what he gets from the United States.

Grace Moore was about to become Grace Moore Reigns. Yet inside her, she was still Agent Grace Moore, federal agent. She desperately hoped that she would be able to reconcile the two. One of those personalities meant that she had the trust of her husband and that she had to trust her husband. The other meant that she had the trust of her country, her fellow agents, and the people of the United States of America. She had to trust them—she had to trust in her training, her instructors, and her instincts. More than anything, she had to trust herself.

Grace leaned forward and placed her hands on her stomach. It was bubbling, brewing, stirring. She felt nauseated.

She looked at her transmitter ring, and held it up to the light. It was her safety net, her lifeline, and her link to her fellow agents. She held up her other hand and examined her engagement ring. It was her future, her link to her future husband, and the family they were going to build together.

Grace removed her FBI transmitter ring and sat it down

gently on top of the coffee table. She rose from the massive, green, leather sectional and walked to the bedroom, where she tied her hair into a ponytail. Grace took off her baggy, wrinkled clothing and put on her black, knit jogging suit, her dark colored tennis shoes, and her black gun holster which held her black, ten-millimeter, Sig Sauer handgun.

When finished dressing, Grace lay back on the massive king-size bed and waited patiently for the sun to set. Once night had fallen, she rose, walked outside the house, and climbed in her car, where she drove off into the darkness.

Chapter Forty-One

Grace removed her black backpack and sat it on the ground just in front of her. She unzipped the lid of the backpack and pulled out a pair of black goggles with red lenses. She lifted the goggles to her face and held them over her eyes. She could now see the red laser beams that criss-crossed the interior perimeter of the Reigns Holding Corporation's Industrial Complex. Grace lifted her backpack from the ground and followed the laser beam along the fence until she reached the first electronic reflector box.

The electronic reflector box received the signal carried by the laser and also sent out a laser beam with an encoded signal to another box which did the same. If anyone passed through the laser and the signal was interrupted, the reflector box would send a signal to the computer controlling the complex's alarm system, informing it that security had been breached. The computer would then sound the alarm and alert the on-duty security, the local sheriff's department, and the Reigns household. Grace needed to pass through the area patrolled by the laser without interrupting the signal and triggering the alarm. The Bureau knew how to do just such a thing.

Grace sat her backpack on the ground and pulled from it a large, clear, glass device with several tiny mirrors, glass prisms, and pieces of gold electronic circuitry inside. She lifted the box carefully, maneuvered it into position near the black reflector box, and then deftly snapped the clear, glass box over it. Nothing happened.

"Damn, it worked," she whispered to herself.

Grace followed the beam to the other end of the fence where she repeated the procedure. Once finished, she lifted her backpack and began to climb the fence. That was when she came across the first security guard.

Grace released the fence and quickly dropped to one knee.

"Hey, what are you doing here?" the security guard yelled. He went for his gun.

Grace reached for her leg holster and pulled out a large, bulky, semi-automatic tranquilizer gun. She quickly aimed, squeezed the trigger, and watched as the dart flew into the security guard's chest.

The security guard gasped, dropped his weapon, and reached for his chest. He collapsed instantly.

Grace pulled from her small backpack a tiny hand held remote control, and pressed the appropriate buttons. The clear, glass, electronic devices on each side of the fence came alive and performed their job brilliantly. They reflected the beams from the emitting part of the devices back into the receiving part. She had created for herself a gap in the invisible laser alarm system.

Grace scaled the wrought iron fence and ran through the compound using her goggles to dodge the remaining lasers. Upon reaching the appropriate window, she again reached into her backpack. She removed a diamond-coated glasscutter and placed it on a window. A few twists of the handle and she was able to remove a large round chunk of glass from the window. Grace set the piece of glass down gently, collected her glasscutter, and pulled another small device from her backpack.

The FBI's Science and Technology Department was the

Bureau's best kept secret, employing some of the best scientists and engineers on the planet. They were called the Little Blue Elves by their fellow agents. Their inventions had saved countless numbers of lives. Grace was thankful for the Little Blue Elves and all of their magical little devices tonight. She pulled out a little electronic device she had never used before, hoping that it worked as advertised.

Grace slid the device through the hole in the window, and placed it on top of the window's magnetic sensor. Her little toy would generate an electromagnetic current that would fool the magnetic sensor on the window and allow her to open it without triggering the alarm. That was the idea anyway. She unlatched the window, counted to five, exhaled, and lifted the window. Nothing happened.

Grace let out a sigh of relief and climbed through the window. She was inside one of the complex's floor manager's offices. Grace tiptoed through the office until she got to the door. She opened the door slowly and pulled from her tactical belt mini-binoculars. She removed her red goggles, placed them inside her backpack, and then lifted the mini-binoculars to her eyes. She peered around the warehouse.

There was one security guard in the warehouse and two motion sensors nearby. She knew that other motion sensors existed, but she would take care of them as she came to them. She first had to neutralize the two nearby.

Grace lowered her binoculars and removed a pen-shaped device from her tactical belt. She lifted the device, pointed it at the first motion detector, and pressed a button on the side of the device. The pen laser fried the motion detector's electronics, and the plastic case, which surrounded it. Grace repeated the procedure on the second detector. After examining them with the binoculars again, she put away the pen and the binoculars and crept into the warehouse.

Grace made her way around the elevated control box where the security guard was watching the Late Show. She crept across the floor of the warehouse until she made her way to the section that housed the tons of incoming cement from Mexico. The yellowish-gold bags were there, thousands of them.

Grace walked up to a stack of bags piled neatly on a pallet and rubbed her hand gently across them. "Please God," she prayed, "let them be filled with cement."

"Hey, how did you get in here!" A voice called from behind.

Grace removed her knit watchman's cap, and undid her ponytail. She shook her head and allowed her hair to flow freely.

Seeing that it was a woman, the security guard removed his hand from his gun as he came closer. Grace turned quickly and round housed the security guard with a hard punch to his face. He stumbled. Grace followed up with a karate chop to his throat and then a jump-kick to his chest. The guard flew back into a pallet full of cement bags while holding his throat. Grace reached for her leg holster, pulled out her tranquilizer gun, and pumped a dart into his chest.

"Hey!" The guard who was watching television now stood on the balcony just outside of the control box. He went for his handgun.

Grace dropped to one knee, lifted her arm, and rested the tranquilizer gun on her forearm. She fired twice. One of the darts caught the security guard in the throat. He grabbed his throat, pulled out the dart, and then fell over the railing onto the warehouse floor.

"Fuck!" Grace rose. The situation was getting out of hand. Her bosses would fire her and probably even arrest her for the warrentless search and for illegally borrowing the equipment she had taken from the supply room. By breaking into Damian's company's warehouse, taking out three security guards, and illegally conducting a search Grace was really asking for trouble. But she was here now, and it was too late to think about those things.

Grace holstered her tranquilizer gun and pulled a large

311

army issue knife from her tactical belt. She walked to the pallet of cement bags again, and jabbed her knife inside, penetrating the bag easily.

Grace sliced open the layers of thick paper and plastic which formed the bag and peeled them back. Gray dust rose into the air and gray powder sat in the bag.

Grace smiled. Her smile quickly turned into laughter as she stood there and stared at the gray powder. She bet that no one on this planet had ever been as happy as she was at the sight of cement. Grace laughed hysterically for several moments with relief. She laughed so hard that she began to think herself crazy.

Cement! What a beautiful thing! What a wonderful thing! Cement, marriage, and family. How much would it cost to have a gray, cement-colored wedding dress, she wondered. Or even better, a gray, ten-tiered wedding cake.

Grace Moore laughed and celebrated. Her life was back, her happiness was back. Grace placed her hand in the bag, clawed a hand full of cement, and tossed it into the air. She spun around as the dust floated through the air. They could have their guests throw cement dust, instead of rice!

Grace laughed, clawed another hand full of cement, and tossed it into the air. She went for a third, but stopped at the sight of a white circle of powder in the midst of the gray. Grace's heart froze.

She leaned forward, placing both of her hands in the bag, and cleared away the white and gray powder until she came to a solid white brick of cocaine wrapped in several layers of paper and plastic. Her knife had penetrated the top edge of the brick and had chipped off pieces of the brick, mixing it with the cement.

Grace placed her hands underneath the brick and carefully lifted it from the bag of concrete. A second brown wrapped brick remained inside. She placed her brick on top of another undisturbed bag of cement.

Grace bent down and pulled from her black bag a small

tube filled with red liquid. She unscrewed the cap from the tube, sat it on top of the undisturbed bag of cement, and scooped some of the white substance from the brick and placed it in the tube of red liquid. She replaced the top of the tube and shook it violently.

Tears streamed down her face as she watched the liquid change from bright red to medium blue. Grace threw her head back and opened her mouth to let out a silent scream. She slowly fell to her knees, and her body began to shake as tears poured from her eyes.

He had lied to her. He had used her. He had killed her fellow agents and made love to her. She had made love to him. Grace Moore lurched forward and began to vomit.

She sat on the floor of the warehouse and cried for nearly an hour before she finally rose and stumbled toward the door of the warehouse. Alarm or no alarm, Grace pulled her weapon from its holster, fired at the lock, and kicked the door open.

Before leaving, she looked back into the warehouse. She looked at the vomit on the floor, the wet spot where she had left a puddle of saliva and tears and the kilo of cocaine where she lost her hopes and dreams. She looked up at the name on the rear wall of the warehouse and thought about the person to whom she had lost her heart, the person to whom she had lost her soul. Grace Moore turned and stumbled off into the night.

Chapter Forty-Two

Dante stormed into the warehouse with the fury of a level five hurricane. He spied his brother across the room, standing next to an open bag of cement. He headed toward him.

"Glad you could finally join us," Damian told him.

"How bad is it?" Dante asked.

"We are compromised," Damian told him. "Nothing was stolen, but the guards were taken out...by a woman."

Dante and Damian exchanged glances.

"The Mrs. didn't come home last night," Damian told his brother. "This morning, the workers arrived to find the bags like this." Damian waved his hand toward the opened bag of cement and the opened kilo of cocaine.

Dante exhaled. "The alarm system?"

Damian shook his head.

"Did you check WANDA?"

Kevin Reigns cleared his throat. "What's that?" he asked.

"Warehouse Automation and Distribution Algorithmic," Dante told him with a smile. "She's the computer program that runs the place."

Dante clapped his hands loudly and shouted. "WANDA!"

The speakers popped and crackled as the computer came alive.

"Yes, Mr. Reigns?" a feminine computerized voice asked.

Kevin smiled. "Dante, you do love your toys."

"WANDA, what happened last night?" Dante asked.

"There was an unauthorized entry, Mr. Reigns."

"Was it one of the workers?"

"Negative."

"Who was it?" Dante shouted.

"Female. Weight: one hundred twenty five pounds. Height: five feet, nine inches."

Kevin leaned forward and whispered into Dante's ear, "How does she know all of that?"

Dante smiled. "WANDA, how do you know this?"

"Pressure sensors, profile scanning, video surveillance, and woman's intuition, Mr. Reigns."

Dante laughed.

Damian became angry. "Tell your fucking computer that I don't have time for any jokes."

"WANDA, why was the alarm not tripped?" Dante asked.

"It was, Mr. Reigns."

Dante turned toward Damian, "She cut the phone lines."

Damian nodded.

"WANDA, why was the security officer not alerted?" Dante asked,

"Security was alerted, Mr. Reigns."

"WANDA, how did she penetrate?"

"The intruder disabled the perimeter beams, crossed through grids 112, 652, 1192, 1732, 2272, entered through the west office window, and disabled two motion sensors."

"Were you hurt?" Dante asked.

"Motion sensors need replacing, perimeter beams are still not functioning properly, the left grid sensor is failing, the light in the gentlemen's room is out, the camera for docking station 8 is out, the camera for docking station 32 is out, the lifting device for dock number 53 is down..."

"WANDA, terminate warehouse systems, check!" Dante shouted. The system was still not perfect. "WANDA, do you have video from last night's penetration?"

"*Yes, Mr. Reigns.*"

"Please ready the video and set up monitor six in the sky control box."

"*Yes, Mr. Reigns. Digital video is ready for replay on monitor six.*"

"Thank you WANDA. That will be all."

"*Will there be anything else, sir?*"

"No," Dante shouted. He would have to have the programmers go over the software again. He turned toward his brother. "I checked the computer before I left home. She was here last night."

"How do you know?" Damian asked.

"The transmitter I had the jewelers implant in her engagement ring," Dante answered. "I had the computer backtrack her movements. This is one of the locations the satellite pinpointed her at. Guess where else she visited?"

"I'm listening," Damian told him.

"The San Antonio Field Office."

"Where is she now?" Damian asked.

"I'm going to go upstairs and check the video from last night," Dante told him. "When I'm through, I'll link up with the computer at the house, and have the satellite pinpoint her location."

Damian nodded. "When you're through with that, call Niccolo and give him her location. We can't chance her walking around knowing this." He turned toward Kevin. "Get every truck we have rolling. Hire outside companies and get this shit out of here. I want this warehouse emptied, and I want it done as soon as possible. And get our friends on the line for me. We have to stop all incoming shipments of cement for right now. Get cracking."

Dante turned and headed for the stairs to the skybox. Kevin headed for one of the main floor offices with a telephone. Damian exhaled, lifted his hand to his head, and began massaging his temple. He didn't see them walk in.

316

Grace walked in leading a massive army of FBI, DEA, ATF, Customs Agents, and National guardsmen. She walked right up to Damian and just stood in front of him.

Damian looked up to see his fiancée standing before him, dressed in full black FBI tactical gear. She removed her black Kevlar helmet, and dropped it to the ground. Her HK Mp-5 was slung around her shoulder, and her black, ten-millimeter, Sig Sauer handgun was strapped to her leg. She stared at him in silence.

Damian looked Grace in the eyes. He too remained silent.

A tear escaped from Grace Moore's right eye and rolled down her cheek. "Say something," she told him.

He said nothing.

"You lied to me," she whispered. "You used me."

"Grace, I..."

"You killed those people, Damian," she began crying heavily. "You visit your grandmother's grave every Sunday, and you kill from Monday through Saturday. You..."

"Grace, I kill no one," he told her.

"You kill everyday!" she shouted. "Every time your trucks full of poison leave this place, you kill! And you know what? You're the worst kind of killer, Damian. You kill families, you kill hopes, you kill dreams, you kill souls."

"Everyone has a choice, Grace. I don't make anyone do anything that they don't want to do."

"Yes you do, you self-righteous, blind son of a bitch!" Grace lifted her hand and pointed out the window. "Those kids out there see you riding around in your Ferraris, your Bentleys, sponsoring baseball teams and football teams, and they want to be like you. And you make it easy for them to take the easy way out."

"I do good things for the community, Grace."

"You're a destroyer, Damian. That token shit that you throw out there is just window dressing to hide the monster that you are inside."

317

Deadly Reigns, Teri Woods Publishing

"Grace, I..."

She slapped him.

Grace's hands flew to her face and she began bawling. Elizabeth put her arm around Grace and tried to lead her away. Grace resisted.

"No, Elizabeth, I have to do this. If I don't he'll forever have control of me. I have to take back my life, Liz, I have to take back my soul." Grace turned back toward Damian. "You're right, Damian, everyone has choices. Why did you choose to be evil? You...you're a knight, Damian—the best of the best. The best education, money, charm, good looks, everything. Why did you have to use it for evil? You betrayed your community, you betrayed everyone who ever believed in you."

"Grace..."

"You have the right to remain silent. Anything you say can and will be used against you in a court of law," Grace turned Damian around and placed handcuffs on his wrists.

"I love you Grace," he whispered.

Her tears ran down rapidly and she shivered, "You have the right to an attorney. If you cannot afford an attorney, one will be provided for you. Do you understand these rights as I have read them to you?"

Damian nodded.

Dante stepped from around the control booth in the skybox and pointed his ten-millimeter glock at Grace Moore. He had warned her fair and square. Now, he had to make a believer out of her.

Dante squeezed the trigger twice, sending two rounds her way. The agents scattered and ducked and drew their weapons. Grace Moore did not.

The first round struck Grace high in her right shoulder blade. The second round hit her directly on the left side of her chest, sending her flying backward. Beneath her black tactical raid gear, Grace wore a class IV ballistic vest to protect her from small caliber bullets. Dante, however, used

318

uranium tipped, ten-millimeter, armor piercing bullets. The rounds penetrated Grace's kevlar vest like a butcher knife through a cotton sheet. Grace lay on the floor of the warehouse bleeding profusely beneath all of her useless armor. Dante smiled, snuck back inside the skybox, and seated himself at the computer desk.

"WANDA," he called.

"*Yes, Mr. Reigns?*" the computer asked, coming alive.

"WANDA, transfer yourself to warehouse number six. Take over operations there. Everything is already set up."

"*Yes, Mr. Reigns.*"

"WANDA, before you transfer all of your software, execute one last command here. Initiate warehouse destruction sequence."

"*Yes, Mr. Reigns. You will have to verify.*"

Dante placed his hand on a liquid crystal display screen next to the computer so that WANDA could verify his identity using his fingerprints.

"*Codeword, please,*" the computer asked.

"Dante's Inferno!" Dante laughed as he stood.

"*Self-destruct will initiate in t-minus twenty seconds. Warehouse will self-destruct in nineteen seconds...*"

Elizabeth looked up at the loudspeakers.

A vaporous liquid began pouring from the sprinkler system.

Damian smiled at Nathan. "In ten seconds, this place is going to blow up. If I were you, I'd get out of here."

Nathan pointed to two hulking agents. "You two grab Agent Moore, and get the hell out of here! Evacuate the building! Everybody out!"

Nathan grabbed Damian by the arm, and ran for the door with the other agents.

Dante opened the escape hatch on the floor of the control box and climbed down a metal ladder. The ladder took him to a tunnel beneath the warehouse, where he removed a thick, yellow car cover from a canary yellow Ferrari Modena Spider.

Dante got inside the vehicle just as the first explosion rocked the ground above him. He smiled.

Unless the United States Attorney had a helicopter that could collect and analyze smoke, the evidence had just disappeared.

Dante pulled out a large Fuete Hemmingay cigar and lit it. Normally, he despised the things, but this was cause for celebration. He had just successfully avoided a life sentence and popped another federal agent and got away with it. Life was grand.

Dante smiled as he revved up the engine in his brand new, never used, Italian sports car. It paid to be prepared. Life honored the prepared. He broke into a wicked laugh as he flew out of the tunnel and turned onto a small farm to Market Road, heading back toward the city. He would meet Angela for lunch, get laid, and create an alibi all at once. Life was certainly sweet.

Chapter Forty-Three

"To Grace," Henry Abrahams said, lifting his glass.

The others in the room lifted their glasses as well. Grace, lying in her hospital bed, lifted a can of apple juice.

"The wonder woman who ended the Reigns distribution network," Henry Abrahams told the others.

The agents and attorneys drank from their glasses.

"Too bad the evidence was destroyed," United States Attorney Steve Bartlett told them. "It broke my heart to have to release that son of a bitch this morning."

Henry Abrahams patted Steve Bartlett on his back. "We'll get him eventually, Steve. He'll slip up again somewhere and we'll get him."

Deputy Director Abrahams turned toward Grace. "And you, young lady, you get plenty of rest. When you are ready, report back to work and name your assignment. Any job, any place."

"Thank you, sir," Grace smiled.

"No, thank you, Special Agent Grace Moore," Director Abrahams tapped Grace's newly awarded Special Agent badge which he had pinned to her sheet near her chest. "You're going to be a super special agent, Ms. Moore."

"Henry," Elizabeth interrupted, "she already is."

Everyone in the hospital room broke out into laughter.

"You're quite right, Liz, quite right." Director Abrahams rose and headed for the door. He was followed by everyone but Elizabeth. "Stupendous job, Agent Moore. Stupendous!"

Deputy Director Abrahams left the room, taking his entourage with him.

Elizabeth placed her hand on top of Grace's hand and smiled. "Well, you did it. Congratulations, Special Agent Moore."

Grace smiled and closed her eyes. "I like the sound of that. Say it again, Liz."

"Special Agent Grace Moore," Elizabeth repeated with a smile.

Grace laughed. Elizabeth joined in her laughter. The telephone rang.

Grace lifted the receiver and placed it to her ear. "Hello?"

"Hello, Grace."

Elizabeth watched Grace's expression change from happiness to horror.

"My brother was released from custody this morning, lack of evidence. I just thought you'd like to know. In case you wanted to drop by and visit us or something," Dante laughed. "Hey, Grace, you remember my promise to you, don't you? The promise I made you in the kitchen at my penthouse that night? Yeah, Grace, you remember. I said that if you ever crossed us, I would kill you. I'm going to kill you Grace. I don't know when, I don't know where, I don't even know how, but I'm going to kill you. You know what's good about that, Grace? You don't know either. Every time the wind blows and the leaves tumble across the ground, you'll be looking over your shoulder for me. Every time you open your front door, you'll think of me. Every time you open your garage door, your closet door, your fucking refrigerator door, you'll think of me. One day, I'll be there."

Grace whimpered.

"They can't protect you from me. No one can. No matter

how many agents you have around you, no matter how many times they relocate you, no matter how many times they change your identity, I can get you Grace. And you know I want you. You have something inside you that I want."

Grace whimpered, and this time her hands flew to her stomach.

"When you're dead, Grace, the state of Texas will award custody to my brother. The nurses tell me that it's a boy, Grace, a baby boy. I think he'll look like my brother, but I think he'll be like me, Grace. He'll be like me because of our special bond. We have a blood bond, Grace. We have a bond of the soul. Tell your mother in New York that I said hello. I'll still take the kid by to see her after you're dead."

"You're not getting my baby," Grace mumbled incoherently. She began sobbing. "You're not getting my baby."

Elizabeth grabbed the telephone.

"Hello? Hello? Who is this?"

The line went dead.

"You're not getting my baby!" Grace shouted. "You're not getting my baby!"

A nurse ran into the room and grabbed Grace. She turned toward Elizabeth. "What happened?"

Elizabeth shrugged her shoulders. "I don't know."

"You're not getting my baby!" Grace shouted hysterically. She was crying uncontrollably. "You're not getting my baby!"

A doctor and two additional nurses ran into the room. They grabbed Grace.

"Get me something to calm her down!" The doctor shouted to one of the nurses.

Grace pushed them away. "No! No! No drugs! He'll kill me if I go to sleep! He'll kill me!" Grace looked at her friend. "Liz, get them out of here! Get them out of here!"

Elizabeth placed her hand on the doctor's back and nodded. "I'll take care of her. Please, let me talk to her."

The doctor nodded and released Grace's arms. She had

calmed down. The doctor turned and guided the nurses out of the room.

Elizabeth closed the door behind them and then turned toward Grace.

"What is it, Grace?" she asked.

"Do you have your gun, Liz?" Grace asked her.

Elizabeth nodded. "Yes, why?"

Grace held out her hand. "Give it to me, Liz."

"Grace..."

"God dammit, Liz, give it to me!"

Elizabeth walked to Grace's hospital bed, opened her purse, and handed Grace her black Sig Sauer handgun.

"He was here, Liz," Grace told her as she took the gun. "He was here. He talked to the nurses. He knows, Liz, he knows."

"Knows what?"

"He knows that I'm carrying his brother's child," Grace began crying heavily again. She placed the gun beneath the covers, and raised her motorized hospital bed up higher.

Dante flipped closed the folding cell phone that he held in his hand and removed the green surgical mask that covered the lower half of his face. He placed the telephone inside his trousers and removed the green surgical coat which he wore over his dress shirt. The temptation to dispose of the surgical garments was strong, but he was a professional, and he knew better. He would have to carry them with him until they could be incinerated. FBI forensics was incredible. They could take a loose strand of hair and build a murder case upon it.

The sun was bright today and it reached down to warm his pecan colored skin. It felt good, a wonderful and welcome contrast to the brisk wind blowing across the south Texas Plains.

Dante reached down to his belt loop and unclipped the ID badge that was fastened to it. The person whom he had borrowed it from would no longer need it. They wouldn't find the good doctor's body for quite some time, he was sure of that. The smell would eventually lead them to him, of course. There were just so many nooks and crannies that you could stuff things into in a hospital of that size.

Laughter came to Dante as he disarmed the alarm system on his brand new Aston Martin Vanquish. He could imagine the blood draining into the various pockets within the good doctor's contorted body, even now. This is one he would definitely have to share with the boys.

Dante opened the driver's side door of the Aston and slid inside. He leaned forward and pressed the large, red button on the Aston's center console, firing up the engine. *Planning*, he told himself. He would have to plan every single step out to the minutest detail. Everything would have to be executed with the utmost discretion. The FBI were certainly not fools. But then again, neither was he.

Diallo, he thought. Diallo Reigns. What a perfect name for their brand new bundle of joy. Their successor, their heir, Little Dajon would need someone to help him run the family enterprises, and he and Dante would need strong nephews, nieces, sons, and daughters to keep them safe in their old age. He had seen it happen before. Men get old, and the sons of their enemies seek them out and avenge decades old infractions. No, it would not happen in this case. Little Dajon, Diallo, and one day, Little Dante, would make sure that it did not.

Dante eased his Aston out of the parking lot into the semi-busy intersection. He would go to Princeton, like his uncle, Dante though. Harvard just wasn't what it used to be. Yes, little Diallo would go to Princeton.

Grace sat in her hospital bed, staring out the window into the streetlights below. In her hand she held her friend's ten-millimeter handgun, while her other hand rested gently on top of her belly.

"You're not going to get my baby," she mumbled. "You're not going to get him." Her tears continued to fall.

The End

Teri Woods Publishing
an Entertainment Investment Group

ORDER FORM

TERI WOODS PUBLISHING
P.O. BOX 20069
NEW YORK, NY 10001
(212) 252-8445
www.teriwoodspublishing.com

DEADLY REIGNS	$14.95
Shipping /Handling (Via U.S. Priority Mail)	3.85
TOTAL	$18.80

PURCHASER INFORMATION

Name: _____

Reg. #: _____
(Applies if incarcerated)

Address:_____

_____

City: _____ State: ___

Zip Code: _____

HOW MANY BOOKS? _____

For orders being shipped directly to prisons, TWP deducts 25% of the sale price of the book. Costs are as follows:

DEADLY REIGNS:	$ 11.21
Shipping and Handling	$ 3.85
TOTAL :	$15.06

Coming Soon...

Double Dose

Masturbating in front of the toilet in his jail cell, he was on the verge of climaxing. With a miniature zip lock bag in one hand and his penis in the other, he managed to capture every drop of semen as he sealed the bag. He placed the bag on the desktop and grabbed a shaving razor. He cut a small portion of his pubic hair and placed it in a separate zip lock bag the same size as the other. Making sure his penis was clear of all his semen, he zipped himself up, washed, and dried his hands with a Polo towel. He picked up an envelope already addressed and placed both zip lock bags inside it along with a letter he'd written earlier.

He thought to himself that one of his pen pals, which was a homosexual, had to be a sick-minded motherfucker. He imagined for a split second exactly what the faggot did with his semen and cringed. As long as his pen pals kept sending money, he didn't mind making a freak happy. Long distance happiness! He'd done this many times before, especially for this particular pen pal, and it didn't bother him at all.

He sat on the bottom rack of steel bunk beds and smiled. Soon it would be the end of pen paling with perverted men and lonely, desperate women. He'd done the crime and the time. All eight years of it!

---Two Months Later---

Two racks on top of one other, a toilet, sink and a steel desk, with three layers of shelves piled on top of one another were cramped into one tiny cell. Two inmates occupied each cell in the facility. The cellies were also issued foot lockers for their personal belongings, which was useless if an inmate had a lot of property.

Tyrell Stants lay sprawled across the bottom rack assigned to him with his arms folded behind his head and his legs crossed. His cell-mate, known as Money Wise, sat at the desk fumbling with the radio dial trying to get a clear station.

Money Wise was a lifer convicted of two counts of aggravated murder and had been incarcerated for eleven years now. He was also Tyrell's best friend. Money Wise stood five feet ten inches and was built like a Mack truck, as a result of many years of lifting weights. His light skinned complexion and shiny bald head gave him a handsome, but devious look.

Satisfied with the clarity of the radio Money Wise turned toward Tyrell.

"This is the cut," he said referring to the song now playing on the radio.

"No doubt," Tyrell responded shaking his feet to the tune.

They both were waiting for the institutional count to clear.

"Pretty soon you'll be listening to this in your car," Money Wise commented.

Tyrell slightly smiled thinking of the few days he had left before he'd leave the prison on parole. It was a long eight years for a rape charge that was more exaggerated than anything. He still couldn't believe he had gotten caught up in a bunch of bullshit with a bitch. Especially since, he was the one going out of his way trying to be responsible. The girl said she was pregnant and so he did the right thing, he let her move in. But, she lost their baby in her sixth month. It didn't matter though, Tyrell loved her and they continued to make a life together until he came home and caught his homie in his bed, banging his woman. In a blind rage, he beat them badly, first his friend, then her. He threw them out of his house into the street, both were naked. Two days later he was arrested on one count of rape and two counts of assault. He plea bargained with the courts and received a four to fifteen year sentence for one count of rape.

So there he was, eight years later, still in his prime. At age twenty-seven he was conditioned to the utmost in mind, body, and soul. He had plans and was ready for the streets once again. Tyrell stood six feet one inch, weighing one hundred and ninety-five pounds. Cut up like a wooden dummy, with a dark-brown complexion that was smooth as melted chocolate. His slanted brown eyes were a mystery to most women and the way he looked at a person would cause anyone to look away. It were as if he were able to read their thoughts with a single glance. He'd been growing his hair for five years now, and hid the true length by wetting it thoroughly, and packing it with pomade. If the actual length was exposed it would mean a mandatory hair cut, due to the institutions three inch regulations. Tyrell's hair hung an inch past his shoulders.

"Yeah, but first I have to get a car," Tyrell responded to Money Wise's comment.

"The way you speak of your plans, it don't sound like it's gonna take you long," Money Wise countered.

"Ain't no puzzle, I still got to take it slow. The slow way is the for sure way," Tyrell volunteered.

"I still don't know what makes you think all those women are going to hand over their hard earned money so easily, but more power to you if they do," Money Wise cracked just as the correctional officer slid several pieces of mail under the cell door.

He picked the mail and handed it all over to Tyrell after taking a quick glance seeing that none was for him.

"If you don't know by now that I'm raw with my pen game, you will never know," Tyrell said as he pointed to a stamp marked $150 dollars on the back of the envelope.

This was done to let the inmates know a money order was sent with the letter. He was sure he'd find a few more money stamps in his pile of mail.

Money Wise shook his head and smiled. "You're right about that. You do have a gift, my brother. Is that from the freak?"

The 'freak' was a private nickname between the two of them. His real name was Barry Winslow. He was one of the many pen pals that had been taking care of Tyrell for the past few years. Money Wise witnessed Tyrell receive several food boxes, clothes boxes, jewelry, and no less than a hundred dollars every two or three days from various pen pals.

Tyrell and his homosexual pen pal, Barry, never met personally. They corresponded through letters, phone conversations, and exchanged pictures. Barry often pleaded with Tyrell to let him visit him, which would bring him all the way from Culver City, California to Ohio. But, Tyrell always denied Barry of this particular wish saying he didn't want to meet so informally. Barry reluctantly accepted the rejections, because he didn't want Tyrell to feel pressured in any kind of way. Barry's worse nightmare was Tyrell getting out of prison and not being with him. The truth really was that Tyrell didn't want the other inmates to see him in the visiting room with a homosexual. But, if push came to shove, for the money Tyrell would kiss him on the lips in front of almighty God! It was the freaks and perverts that kept him living like a king while imprisoned. To hell with what anyone thought about his life.

"To elaborate on the comment about how I'll convince these fine women to depart with their monies," Tyrell began as Money Wise sat attentive, "Love is a bad motherfucker, especially if you

331

use it to your advantage. Ninety-five percent of the women in the world live off love and will do anything to keep that love alive. With me that love is one-sided. I have no love for any female. They may think it's there, because I tell them everything they want to hear."

Tyrell sat up on his rack and slid his feet into his house shoes all while continuing to speak what he truly felt about women in the world.

"The only thing a broad can do for me is give me some money. It's twelve women to every one man out there and I'm leaving prison in a few days to get my share of them. I got that blow, that glow, and I'm good to go in the bed you know! I'm on a different level of the game. They don't have to sell any pussy for me to get paid. All she needs is a damn good job, and some money. When I'm finished, muhfucka be lucky to have a toilet to piss in. No holds barred Money Wise, I'll take a broad eighteen to eighty, blind, cripple, or crazy. If they open they door for me, they bank account gonna be empty!"

Tyrell's facial expression was trance-like as he concluded his sermon meaning every word. Money Wise himself was lost in Tyrell's seriousness.

"Damn, yous a shrewd dude. But, I feel you."

The count bell rung to signal it had been cleared followed by another bell to signal dinner. Tyrell wouldn't be going to the mess hall. He had a locker box under his rack full of food. As Money Wise left the cell Tyrell picked up the stack of mail and began to read.

IN STORES NOW...

True to the Game
B-More Careful
The Adventures of Ghetto Sam
Dutch I
Dutch II
Triangle of Sins
Tell Me Your Name and
Deadly Reigns